Also by ⌐

Standalones:
The Evil Beneath
Girl on a Train
Dark Place to Hide
No Longer Safe

The Dr Samantha Willerby Series:
Inside the Whispers
Lost in the Lake

Writing as Alison Waines
The Self-Esteem Journal
Making Relationships Work

Chapter 1

Rachel

I knew something was wrong the moment I slipped the key into the lock.

A light was visible through the keyhole. I teased the door open a fraction and stopped dead. The fluorescent strip light wasn't the source, instead there was a dim glow at the far end of the cellar. I edged the door open another couple of inches with my foot, holding it firm against the self-closing spring. The beam was coming from behind the empty stainless-steel kegs stacked on the floor under the trap door. Was there a cleaner here with a mop? The landlord fixing a leak? It couldn't be. The landlord was in Marbella and the pub had been shut for nearly two weeks for refurbishments. No one had keys but me. There was only one explanation. An intruder must have got in and was snooping around with a torch.

I stood frozen on the top step, torn about what to do. If I backed out now I'd attract attention – the door always made a juddering sound when it closed. If I called the police from where I stood, I might be overheard. I had my eyes fixed on the light the whole time, hardly daring to blink, waiting for the beam to bob around to see which direction the burglar was moving in. Except the light didn't move.

A man groaned, then came a scuffle, then a woman whimpering. 'No. Let me go…get your filthy hands off me!'

Beth.

I didn't need to hear anymore. I knew my daughter's voice anywhere and could tell instantly what was going on. In that split second, my mind was on one thing and one thing alone.

1

I hurried down the remaining steps, not caring if I made a noise. I found Beth half-naked, shivering, her hair roughed up in a black tangle as a man I'd never seen before leant over her, his trousers down, gripping her struggling torso from behind.

'No…no…stop!' she yelled.

I rushed towards the pair of them, no words forming in my mouth, instead letting out a primaeval scream that must have sounded like a tortured horse. Something terrible was happening to my daughter and I had to save her. Rescue her from the brute who was forcing himself on her, his hands on her bare back, shoving her over a wooden chair. I charged at the figure as he straightened up. Bastard. My reaction came from a place of outrage, of maternal protection, from a gushing surge of rage and horror. I was doing what any mother would have done without a second's thought.

I'm strong. I carry kegs and crates down to the pub cellar every day and when I'm on a mission, there's no stopping me.

I threw myself at him, lashed out with my tight fists. His face was caught in an expression of dumb surprise and he was off balance, his legs trapped by the trousers caught around his ankles. He toppled backwards and there was a loud crack as his head struck against the protruding tap on a full cask of pale ale. Then he went down.

I thought I was saving Beth. I thought I was doing the right thing. I stormed in to save my daughter from being raped. Only I got it all wrong. Badly wrong. And now a man I've never met is lying dead a few inches from my feet.

Chapter 2

Rachel

I've rerun that scene in my mind so many times since and I still don't think I overreacted. It was only later that I realised the source of the light I could see was a lamp. The pretty table lamp from my sitting room to be exact, with a silk shade the shop assistant had described as 'eau de nil'. Who on earth brings a lamp down into the grubby cellar of a pub?

If I'd asked myself that question at the time, events could have taken an entirely different turn.

All I saw were clothes strewn on the floor and my daughter facedown over a kitchen chair…and a stranger's bare behind, his shirt tail flapping around, holding her down as she writhed and cried out. I mean…what was I supposed to think? What was I supposed to do?

I'm not a bad person and during the period that followed, I didn't even do a bad thing – well, not at the outset. I responded in what I thought was the only possible way under the circumstances. Beth was shouting *No…no…stop!*, but if I'd taken the time to look at her, I'd have realised she was yelling at *me*, telling *me* to stop. But all my focus was on him, this crazy, vile maniac who was attacking her. I didn't hesitate. Not for a moment. I flew at him and knocked him off his feet. I shunted him with all my might.

I keep seeing the look on his face, winded and aghast like he'd been hit by a truck before he caught his head on the tap. And that was that. He crumpled instantly to the floor.

'Mum! What the hell have you done?' Beth screamed, tugging off the ropes that had been tied around her wrists. I'd been expecting to see utter relief on her face, but instead she looked horrified. After freeing her hands, she pulled down the blouse that had been ruckled up around her neck and ran over to the half-dressed man lying on the flagstones.

My hand went to my mouth. 'Oh, God...'

He hadn't moved since he fell and his eyes were slightly open, his mouth sagging and his tongue hanging out. She crouched down beside him, scooped his head and shoulders into her arms and smoothed away strands of hair from his eyes as though she cared for him.

'Carl...speak to me, Carl? Please...' She stroked his cheek, gave it a gentle tap.

'You *know* him?' I gawped at the shape on the floor and back to Beth, confused. 'I thought he was...raping you...' I whispered.

'He's...not moving...oh my God,' she said.

I bent down alongside her and took his wrist. Having worked in a pub most of my adult life, I know the basics of first aid. I'm used to seeing customers merrily propped on a stool one minute, slumped on the floor the next. But I've never once been unable to find a pulse. I shifted my fingers over the veins running into his hand, then tried his neck, waiting to feel his blood pumping back at me, sending out a signal that he was still with us. Only it never came.

Ten minutes have gone by since then. I pumped up and down on his chest and tried mouth-to-mouth resuscitation, but he hasn't moved an inch. His eyes remained open a fraction, his gaze never faltering and before long a glaze like raw egg-white formed over the corneas, so I gently pressed them shut. It was too late to call an ambulance.

Beth is sitting on the chair making herself small, snivelling quietly with tears rolling down her face. She's pulled on her jeans but hasn't got as far as putting on her sandals. I went upstairs to the bar and found a woollen blanket to wrap around her shoulders and brought another to cover the body on the floor, making sure it hid his face.

'Who's Carl?' I asked, standing over him.

'Peter introduced him to me at a party a few months ago,' she said, as if I should know.

Peter is Beth's fiancé, a well-respected producer in the film business. They'd met in London when Beth was a runner for a TV company last year. They're getting married in April – in five weeks and three days' time to be precise.

'I don't understand,' I said. 'What were you two doing down here?'

'It was a kind of game,' she said. 'We were acting out a scene from a film.'

I dropped my head in my hands.

Beth wants to be an actress. She finished drama school nearly two years ago and has had numerous auditions, but no call-backs. Following her brief period in London with the TV company she's now come back home and is biding her time as a quiz show researcher. She's waiting to get noticed, hoping for her big break, but her dream is slipping further and further away from her.

'I borrowed your spare keys,' she said, pointing to a bunch on the table next to the lamp that she'd also borrowed. 'We were improvising a scene from *Basic Instinct*.'

I let out a despairing breath. That was meant to explain everything, was it? It was make-believe. How was I to know they were playing roles from a movie? It all looked pretty real to me.

'I take it this wasn't the first time, then?'

'No…' she replied sheepishly.

Until now, Beth has been in a gormless trance driven by shock. All of a sudden, she gets to her feet.

'We should call the police,' she says. She reaches for her phone lying beside her slingbacks on the floor.

I move towards her. 'Wait…' I glance at the bundle beside us and realise the only sign that this terrible thing has happened is Carl's body. There's no blood, not a drop, on the flagstones.

I think quickly.

There will be fingerprints, of course, and DNA. The cask tap will need cleaning, but if the police don't know to look down here, it can easily be wiped away.

I take the phone, put it down on the table and gently hold both her wrists, like I'm about to lead her in a dance.

'Who knows you're here?' I ask.

'Er...no one,' she frowns, 'as far as I know.'

As if this appalling nightmare is only just dawning on her, she starts quivering. She pulls away from me and paces around, her sobbing escalating into hysterical shrieks.

'Shush! Be quiet. For goodness sake sit down. We need to sort this out.'

She sinks down gingerly.

I point at the shape under the blanket and back to Beth. 'Is this...an affair...a fling...or what?' My voice comes out sounding harsher than I want it to.

Her eyes are unfocused, her hands trembling as she leans forward, hugging her knees. 'It was a secret,' she moans. 'He's married.'

'How did he get here?'

'He walked...'

'From where?'

'The train station. His wife thinks he's still at the theatre. That's why he's in Winchester.'

'And you?'

'I walked over from home, as usual.' The King's Tavern is only ten minutes on foot from our house.

'Did you meet anyone coming over here? Did anyone see you?'

She narrows her eyes. 'I don't think so.'

She glances at her phone again. 'We must ring 999,' she says, reaching for it.

'Let's stop and think about this first.' I peel open her hand and let the phone rest inert in my palm. 'You realise what will happen if we ring the police, don't you?' I say. 'All this will be splashed across the front pages of the papers.'

She erupts into another spate of howling.

'Beth! Keep it down,' I hiss at her.

She glares at me and, in that instant, some recognition that she needs to pull herself together settles on her and she sniffs loudly and looks up.

'Why were you here anyway, Mum? The pub's all closed up. No one's supposed to be here this late.'

'Marvin rang me from his holiday to ask me to re-set the heating.'

She straightens up. 'We could say someone broke in and it was self-defence. I could pretend I don't know him.'

'Except you just said Peter introduced you.'

She blinks, looks away, then back at me again. 'I'll say I didn't recognise him, then.'

I shake my head. 'There's nothing to suggest a break in. There are no broken windows. Besides, he's half-dressed and drenched in after-shave. Hardly the disguise of a burglar.'

'We could pull his clothes back on, smash a window at the back or something…make it look like he got in…'

'But why would he break into an empty pub that's part way through being refurbished?' I scan round at the stacked up bar stools, tins of paint, paint trays and rollers, bundles of dust sheets. 'It's a tip in here. There's nothing to pinch.'

'He wouldn't know that though, would he?'

I let out a sigh. 'Who is this Carl, exactly?'

'He's a businessman. Carl Jacobson. He's involved with films.'

'Did he take advantage of you? Did he use his position to promise you things?'

'No way!' she huffs. 'It was consensual, believe me. I was the one who made it happen the first time. We were just trying stuff out. He said I was talented.'

I bet he did…

I watch her 'faking a burglary' idea shrivel to nothing in the light of her description of him. 'You're right,' she says. 'Why would someone like Carl break in? It doesn't make sense. We'll have to tell the police the truth,' she says. 'You came in to sort out the heating and you misread the situation…you overreacted…'

My mouth falls open. '*Excuse me*…overreacted?! Beth…do you…can you..?'

Words fail me.

I take a breath. 'If we come clean about this, you know what will happen, don't you? There will be an enormous scandal. Are you prepared to lose Peter just like that?' I snap my fingers.

'Oh, God…' She frantically chews her thumb nail, her mind twisting about trying to see what other options we could possibly have.

'I've just killed someone, you realise that, don't you?'

I glance down at the blanket and shake my head, unable to believe what I've just done.

'But they *must* see it was a mistake…an accident…'

She gets up and slips on her sandals this time, ready to get moving. Beth is tall and willowy and still has the look of a teenager. She fixes her green eyes on mine waiting for a better solution. They're stunning eyes, easily surprised and full of affection and allure, but no doubt I'm biased.

'What if they don't?'

'But they will, of course they will, when we explain everything.'

Now isn't the time to go into the real reason I can't own up to this. We can't tell the police anything about it. Full stop.

'Even so, you'd be ruthlessly cast aside by the rich and proper Roper family. Are you ready to give up your marriage, your future – the security it would bring you, the arms Peter could twist to get your feet finally on that red carpet? It would all be over.'

Using the threat of losing her career is the strongest leverage I can think of to get her to hold off.

My stomach is bubbling. 'God, Beth, what were you thinking?' I plough my fingers into my hair.

'It was just a bit of fun. Carl is…was…' She licks her lips but doesn't seem able to put what she has to say into words, or at least not into words she's prepared to share with me.

'Peter loves you. He adores you. *He's* the one who's going to help you get started on your career. He's already given you introductions – he's serious about it. He knows the right people and could guide you.' I clasp my hand over hers. 'We can't let this ruin all that. Do you understand?'

She opens her eyes wide and gets to her feet. 'But...' she stares incredulously at the body, 'what are we... supposed to do?'

Without warning, she starts wheezing and doubles over, her breathing fast, snatching at the dusty air.

'Where's your inhaler?'

Clutching her chest, she points to her bag hanging over the edge of the chair. I grab it and hand it to her. Her asthma is mild and most of the time she has no symptoms, but she's rarely without her medication. She shakes the inhaler and takes a dose, then leans forward, her hands on her knees.

I stroke her back, getting her to sit. 'You're going to be fine. That's it...nice and slow...'

She nods, gradually recovering, her breathing easing.

'I'm alright...' she says, squeezing my hand sharply twice. It's been our signal since she was tiny that she's going to be okay.

I let out a breath and think for a moment. 'We have to carry on as normal,' I say. 'We must pretend this didn't happen and your marriage to Peter will go ahead as planned.'

She blows out a rush of air. 'Really? But what about...?' She blinks fast and points to the body.

I bite my lip. 'Leave it to me,' I say.

Chapter 3

Rachel

I have no idea what to do next.

I may have sounded gung-ho and self-assured, but to be honest I'm bluffing. I only know I can't think straight with a corpse so still and larger than life right next to us. I need to get him out of the way so I can work out some kind of plan. Besides, the decorators are starting work in the toilets tomorrow morning and all their paint gear is lying only a few feet away. We have to get Carl out.

Thankfully, the CCTV cameras at the back of the pub are either faulty or missing, due to be replaced as part of the refurbishments, so no electronic eyes will be watching us. What we need to do next, without any fuss, is go home and collect the car.

I instruct Beth to put her jacket and gloves on and grab a rag that's been left drying over a bucket. I'd taken one glove off briefly when I checked Carl's pulse, but instinct had told me to put it back on again. While Beth slips her arms into her jacket in a daze, I'm wiping down the chair, the small table, the tap of the cask.

'Did you or Carl touch anything else?'

'The door,' she says, turning round, 'the lamp…'

I wipe the door handle on both sides, the door itself, the plug socket for the lamp and the main light switch, too. Then I complete a circuit of the place, rubbing down everything they could have touched, before stuffing the rag in my pocket.

'Okay, let's go.'

'We're leaving him?' she says aghast.

'Only until we've got Marvin's car. We're coming straight back.'

It feels desperately precarious leaving him there like that, but we won't get far with him without a vehicle. Thankfully, Marvin, the pub landlord, left the car keys in my 'capable' hands, together with overseeing the refurbishments while he's away.

Beth looks like she's sleepwalking as I guide her out of the back door and lock it behind us. I take an odd route home, avoiding the streets where friends live. It's probably a futile gesture; as a barmaid in a popular pub, it's rare for me to walk through the city without being recognised. Our saving grace is it's raining again, so I slip my umbrella out of my bag and we huddle underneath it, keeping our heads down all the way back.

Beth goes straight to the passenger door of Marvin's Skoda, but I beckon towards the house, first. Something has occurred to me.

She sits at the bottom of the stairs with her head in her hands, while I open the laptop and check the City Council website for a list of CCTV cameras. I'm thinking ahead. We can't afford to be picked up on a camera somewhere.

There are over three hundred council-run cameras in the area, so with a map of Winchester beside the laptop, I sketch a route between our house and the pub, avoiding every single one of them. It doesn't account for any private cameras, of course, but I'm hoping these will be aimed at conservatories, porches and garages, not at the roads.

Only then do we return to the pub. I pull up close to the back exit which, I hope, will be out of sight due to the row of sturdy cypress trees along the edge of the beer garden and I lead the way to the cellar door.

Beth stiffens once I've unlocked it. She's deathly white and hangs back at the top of the steps. I take her wrist, firmly.

'I can't do this on my own,' I tell her. I give her shoulders a squeeze; half-hug, half-bolstering to get her moving again, then flip on the light. 'Keep your gloves on.'

She creeps down after me and waits limp and silent beside the body.

'You take his feet,' I instruct and bend down to lift his head and shoulders. The only way I can do it is if I imagine he's a heavy sack of potatoes. He's too heavy for us and instead of carrying the body, we drag and hump it up the steps into the main bar.

'We're going to need something to hide him,' I tell her, thinking aloud, seeing only torn dust sheets and flimsy strips of cardboard around the place.

Beth speaks for the first time. 'The rug...' she mutters.

Minutes later, we drag him outside and straight into the boot of the car. His body is more manageable now that he's rolled up in the threadbare oriental rug from the fireplace. It's still raining hard and I'm not sure if that's a good or bad thing, but perhaps it means fewer people will be about.

In order to get him in, the back seats have to be folded down and, once the bulky load is laid flat, his feet are clearly sticking out of the end. I pinch a dust sheet from the lounge area to cover them and we add boxes of crisps beside his head and an upturned bucket halfway along to make the bundle more of a hotchpotch.

I go back to the cellar to grab the lamp, too. It's not going back where Beth found it. It's going to go straight in a bin somewhere. I don't want it anywhere near me. I'd never be able to switch it on again, without seeing the vision that greeted me tonight.

Beth is mute the entire time, doing what I ask of her without question. She seems to have accepted my argument that if the facts of the situation come out, her marriage to Peter would be over and, with it, the chance of getting a foot in the door of her beloved career. It appears sufficient to persuade her to go along with me.

When we are certain the body is disguised as much as possible, I drive us to the south of the city to the late-night supermarket for a handful of random provisions. I fold the receipt carefully and tuck it into my purse. It will give us a reasonable explanation for using Marvin's car that night, if anyone asks.

We have only three more days before Marvin comes back. As his trusted 'number two', he's expecting me to pick him up at the airport on Sunday.

On the return to our house on Barnes Road, Beth spots a skip outside a community centre, so I pull up at the kerb and wedge the lamp down the side of it, under planks of wood and next to a broken toilet bowl.

'Once we're parked just get out of the car and walk straight up the path,' I tell Beth, as I draw up outside the house. 'Don't look inside the car, don't do anything. I'll bring in the shopping.'

Beyond this point, I still don't have a plan – not yet. So, I decide to speak to the one person who would understand, as soon as it gets light.

When I wake before dawn, it's still raining as though it's never stopped. I've spent the night in and out of patchy troubled sleep, all the while feeling like a black sickness is swallowing me up.

I leave Beth a note by her phone, in case she flies into a panic at finding me gone when she wakes. I tell her to stay where she is and not speak to anyone. Beth is barely able to last an hour without making contact with one of her huge circle of friends, so it's a tall order. I suggest she bakes a cake. Baking is one of the few jobs around the house she'll do without kicking up much fuss and it will keep her occupied. I throw on my anorak and hurry towards St Andrew's Church.

I speak to Russell every day, even though he's been dead for ten months. He died of pancreatic cancer two days before my thirty-eighth birthday last year. We'd been together for thirteen years. Usually, I chat in person at his grave, where I sit cross-legged on the grass or on a nearby bench under a cedar of Lebanon.

Beth only knew him as a tenant in the same house, renting a room like we did. She misses him, but not like I do. She never regarded him as a parental figure, more as a kind of good-humoured uncle and he, in turn, never tried to be her dad. He always understood we were 'Rachel and Beth united'. It means the grief is largely mine and because I don't want to fill our home with misery, I go to the churchyard alone to give a private voice to my loss.

Russell's grave lies between that of someone called Margo Rand, who made it to seventy-one, and a man called Raphael

Dubois, who passed away at the age of thirty-three. At first, I liked to think Raphael was an angel sent to his side to keep watch over Russell until Father Roland told me Mr Dubois was a night-club owner who died of alcohol poisoning.

Before I tell him about the dreadful thing I've done, I scan full circle to check there's no one about who's going to overhear me. I needn't worry. It's barely light and I'm the only one here. I stand at the foot of his grave in the damp grass. I always imagine it's the foot of his bed and he's lying quietly, having woken from a short nap. Judging by the way the stones have aged, the earliest graves are situated at the front and I'm behind the church in the more recent patch, the headstones dating from around 1960.

I let him know I'm here, but I can't seem to get any further. I'm thinking about Beth and whether it was a mistake to leave her on her own with Carl's dead body flat out in the car outside the house. She might do something rash in a bid to 'try to help'.

The horror of what we've done – *I've* done – momentarily takes my breath away. Failing to report a crime is one thing, concealing it another. What was I thinking? What *am* I thinking? I wonder if it's not too late to come clean, but deep down I know it's not an option. We've already gone too far.

Renewed vigour in the rain makes me get on with it and I blurt out my dilemma to Russell's speckled headstone, letting the wind carry my words into the trees.

'We're in a terrible mess, Russell. I thought if I slept on it an idea would come to me by morning, but it hasn't. I don't know what to do with the body.'

Russell joined us when Beth was ten years old. I could no longer make ends meet with my income from the pub and had to persuade Beth to give up her bedroom for the tiny box room. I remember her being unaccountably gracious about it. I was so proud of her.

Russell was the first person to reply to my ad in the local paper and I liked him straight away. A mellow smile never left his face during that first visit, but more significantly, he brought along a bunch of fresh daffodils. He stood on the doorstep hiding them behind his back when I answered the door, as though we were on a date. I'll never forget that gesture.

It seems such a long time ago.

'Send me a sign, darling – anything, so that I can sort out this dreadful mistake.'

I take a walk along the edge of the grass under the sycamore trees and bring memories of Russell to the centre of my mind.

Shortly after he died, I found gifts he'd bought tucked away in little hiding places around the house. There were earrings and necklaces and collections of my favourite lingerie, all items I'd pointed out to him during dreamy, fantasy moments while we'd been window shopping. He'd bought them all, wrapped each and every one ready for future anniversaries, each purchase extending the bottomless coffers granted by one of his magic credit cards.

The gift destined for my birthday was a silver locket hidden in a drawer in his bedside cabinet, a box wrapped in pink tissue paper with a tag saying, 'To my darling Rachel' with a wonky heart drawn around the words. He always used tissue paper to wrap his gifts. There are wads of it still left in the cupboards he used and whenever I hear the distinctive crackle of it, it makes me well up.

I come to a stop at the point where a patch of crocuses have claimed the grass and wait, in the hope that Russell will have engineered some kind of message in the material world for me to see.

A bird drifts high in the smouldering sky over the clock tower, a lorry putters from the high street, but all else is still and there's nothing drawing my attention in any direction. I listen for words to come into my head, an instruction of some kind, but I know it's stupid.

A figure all in black with a white collar comes out of the main entrance to the church and pours water from a vase down the nearest drain. Father Roland, the parish priest, raises his hand as he sees me. He addresses me by my first name, these days, as I come to the church so often. Not for services – that would be stretching things too far – but to tidy the graves and do a spot of gardening in the few hours a week I have when I'm not working at the pub. It makes me feel like I'm looking after Russell and helps to distract me from the gigantic hole he's left in my life.

I like plants anyway and might well have been a florist, owned a garden centre or a vineyard in the south of France if getting pregnant at fifteen hadn't flung me down the road of motherhood. Beth doesn't know how lucky she is with her training in drama school behind her and a marriage to a highly respectable man lined up. That bloody drama training was expensive. I saved long and hard to put her through that.

Father Roland disappears and, in the distance, the high street is starting to come to life and I know this is pointless. I'm hoping a spark of inspiration is going to hit me, when it's clear Russell can't help me with this one. I'm on my own and I need to get back to Beth. I turn and whisper a hasty goodbye to the headstone and head for the rear gate.

On the way, I pass the most recent interments, where flowers still languish in their plastic wrappers. At the end of the row, there's a fresh mound of loose soil where the latest burial has taken place. As a child, I remember asking my mother why there was always too much earth to fit back into the hole and she reminded me that it was because there was now a big box down there, taking up space.

Someone has left white lilies on this final mound, but the stems are too long for the glass jar, so it has tipped over, draining away all of the water. As a result, the flowers are limp and starting to curl. Small things like this make me tearful, so I take the empty jar to the standing tap along the path and fill it.

As soon as I nestle it into the crumbling earth, I know what we have to do.

Chapter 4

Beth

June – nine months earlier

'Is he here yet?' he asks me.

Gerry started as a floor runner here a week after me and we always watch each other's backs. There's so much to learn and so many ways to make mistakes. And runners get blamed for *everything*.

'Yes, he's with Gloria, having a quick chat before she sends him up,' I tell him.

I check my notepad – the one that's glued under my arm at all times. I'd be stuffed without it. It tells me Peter Roper, a film producer, is being interviewed this morning for a documentary about dance in films. I'm meant to get him a coffee before he goes in. That's not top of my list, however – I've got eleven more tasks to fit in first.

I run for the stairs. I need to clear room seventeen on level three. There's just been a post-production meeting up there and papers have been left strewn everywhere. I must empty the bins, collect Millie's dry cleaning, put sandwiches together for the casting crew in room five, not forgetting Donald's chair, which needs to be fixed before 1 p.m. He has a weird way of sitting on it, twisting it to one side all the time. It's the second chair he's managed to ruin in the six months I've been here.

Working at the TV company is meant to be a stepping stone; just temporary. It's not the normal route for an actor, but enough people in the know suggested it's worth a try and I've got to the point where I'm low on options. Twelve months out of drama college and not one sniff of a part. The plan was to earn some cash while finding myself in the right place at the right time to get my 'big break'.

I know it's a long shot, but I certainly have more chance of being 'spotted' here, than if I'm lying on my bed all day, learning lines for auditions. Craig, from college, was a runner for only three weeks before he bagged the lead in a national ad. The casting guy took one look at him as he handed out the coffees and said, 'Can you stand over there and look like a gladiator?' and Craig was in.

I don't want to reflect on the fact that nothing remotely lucky like that has happened to me and I've only got two months left for something earth-shattering to turn up. London is too expensive and by August I'm going to have to move back in with Mum and rethink everything.

My phone bleeps with an instant message. It's Gloria. She wants me to meet our guest at the lift in five minutes to 'keep him entertained':

Sorry, going to be longer than we thought. A hold up in the studio. Problems with the camera track and Margaret's been taken ill. Might be a while.

Shit! Margaret is the interviewer. We could be in for a long coffee break. I hope Mr Roper is in a good mood.

I scoop a scattering of Kit-Kat and Twix wrappers into the bin, then swap it for the bin in the room next door. I haven't time to take the rubbish to the canteen.

Five minutes later and a coffee pot stands steaming beside two cups and saucers on a tray and there's milk in a jug. There's cream, too, in case he prefers it. A neat circle of ginger creams and bourbons decorates the plate.

I scurry along the walkway to the lift as it glides up the outside of the building. It always reminds me of the bubble inside a spirit-level. Like most of this amazing structure, it's made with aluminium and glass so that the whole thing is see-through.

Everyone can see everyone else 'reflecting an ethos of truth and transparency', according to the publicity brochure.

In the basement there's the cinema and recording studio and in the three storeys above ground are open plan and cellular offices, editing and telecine suites and the DVD library. I've never been right to the top – that's for executives only.

The doors to the lift swish open and the man I've been waiting for steps out. He already has a smile on his face and instantly reaches out his hand, as though I'm someone important.

'Hi, I'm Peter,' he says. 'I'm all yours until they fix something downstairs.'

'Yeah – a minor technical hitch, I'm sure,' I say with confidence. 'Follow me, I've got the coffee on.'

According to the notes Gloria gave me, Mr Roper is thirty-five, single and straight, is into boats and remote islands – and spends his life with celebrities in film and showbiz. As a former ballet dancer, he certainly appears fit and has a glowing tan.

We stride across the walkway and I notice him looking down through the glass floor to the landings below.

'You can't afford to be afraid of heights working here,' I tell him as a friendly icebreaker.

I hold the door open for him and invite him to sit while I pour the coffee. He helps himself to cream and a bourbon. 'Oh, my favourite…' he says, like a kid in a sweetshop. My efforts to go that extra mile were worth it.

He asks me how long I've been at the company and what it is I do, exactly.

'I'm mainly involved with post-production on documentaries, but I'm also designing questionnaires for social media. We're analysing the TV viewing patterns of 16–24 year olds. There's no average day here, so it's stimulating.'

He looks interested so I carry on. 'I'm trained as an actress, really,' I tell him, sipping my coffee. I doubt I'll get the chance for another cup until I finish today. 'They're good here. They give me time off to go to auditions. I wouldn't have taken the job, otherwise.'

'How are the auditions going?'

I press a crease out of my pencil skirt. 'Not great, to be honest.'

'I saw about seventy wannabees read for a film, last month,' he says, 'and if I've learnt one thing, it's that you have to have an edge. Something none of the other try-hards have got. You have to second-guess the casting director, too; look deeper, dig beneath the surface of the parts you're playing and surprise them.' He looks up. 'What's your edge, Beth?'

As he says my name a spark shoots down the back of my neck.

'Oh…I move well,' I say, 'and I'm happy with the way I look. That's rare, these days, I think. Everyone wants to look like either Kim Kardashian or Keira Knightley.'

He gives an approving nod. 'What else?'

'I'm a self-confessed drama queen. I love dressing up and I'm a bit of a chameleon, good at fitting in. I pick things up quickly, remember my lines. I can do a feisty action-girl as well as a meek kitchen maid. And everything in between. My mum says I spend my life in fantasies, making up who I want to be each day. She says I do a really mean American accent and I'm fearless on stage.' I stand up and do a twirl in front of him. 'I've got a great autograph, too. That's my edge.'

It comes out sounding cringingly twee, but better than muttering something self-deprecating. You have to put yourself out there in this business. There's no room for shrinking violets.

He laughs as I sit down again. 'Well…at least you've thought about it. So, why *this* job?'

'Oh, mainly to meet the right people. I'm good at networking, at encouraging people to share ideas. I know how to put people at ease and make things run smoothly. Plus, I'm very keen to learn, I'm open, adaptable and I bring my own concepts to the table. I'm game for anything, really!' I laugh, tossing back my hair. I've had to spout it off so many times, it comes out sounding more rehearsed than I intended.

Oh, well. I notice him looking at the way my hair falls on my shoulders.

'So if I was to ask you what questions *you'd* ask me at the interview today, that wouldn't faze you?'

'Er…it would help if I had some advance warning, but I'd give it a go. Yes.'

'Fire away, then.'

'Sorry?'

'Ask me the kind of questions you'd throw at me for the documentary. You know what it's about, I take it?'

'Of course.'

He's toying with me, but I'm not about to be beaten.

I sit upright and clear my throat. 'So, Mr Roper, I assume you went to the Dance on Camera Festival in New York, in February?'

His eyebrows go up, looking impressed. 'I did, yes. And call me Peter.'

'Okay…' I glance down at my hands getting my brain into gear. This isn't easy and he knows it. 'So, Peter, how do you see choreographic storytelling being developed on screen in the UK?'

'Mighty fine question,' he says.

We start batting ideas back and forth. He's easy to talk to. He's not trying to trip me up or act all superior. I'm in my element, completely losing track of time until my phone buzzes with another message from Gloria:

Sorry for delay. Margaret has gone home. Taxi gone out to pick up Laurie Felderstone. Can you tell Mr Roper? Keep him occupied for another twenty mins, please.'

I pass on the information.

'Do you want the grand tour?' I say, getting to my feet. 'It's a shame to be stuck in one room.'

'Sure.' He follows me out. 'You were good. I dare say I won't get such insightful questions in the interview itself,' he says, as we reach the lift. 'I was rather enjoying myself.'

I can't tell whether he's being serious or buttering me up, so I pretend I'm thinking about where we should go next.

I decide to take a risk and press level four as we step into the lift. No one's going to stop me on the top floor if I've got a VIP by my side.

We follow the corridor past executive offices until we reach the boardroom. The sliding bar on the door says it's vacant, so I breeze inside as though I know it like the back of my hand. The room opens out onto a sweeping roof terrace overlooking the landscaped courtyard below.

Peter follows me outside and leans over the glass partition, looking down onto the fan palms, olive trees and raised beds below. The drone of city life together with perfume from lavender and jasmine seems incongruous.

He exhales loudly. 'You've transported me to Bali,' he says.

'A bit short on sand, though…and the hammocks are all taken,' I say.

He looks serious for a moment. 'Okay. Here's a question for you.' He pulls out his phone. 'I need a photo to go with a magazine interview I'm doing tomorrow. Is this a good one, do you think?'

He shows me a black and white photo of himself wearing a tweed suit. He's seated with his elbow resting on a table, a finger pressed into his cheek. It looks posed and stiff.

I take the phone. 'No, not that one – you look too much like the lord of the manor.'

'Starchy, you mean?'

I smile letting my tongue linger between my teeth. 'Yep, a little bit.'

I flick through several others. I realise I'm flirting with him and I don't want this to end.

'What about this one?' I say. 'You look more relaxed in this. Or this. Suave and self-assured with the potential for playfulness, perhaps.'

He throws his head back and laughs, his eyes glistening with coy embarrassment. 'Okay, that's enough. You're making fun of me.' He crooks his finger at the phone.

I get an instant message from Gloria on mine at that point, asking me to bring Peter to the recording studio.

'They're ready for you,' I tell him.

'That's a shame.'

There's a potent silence as I walk ahead of him back to the lift. I sense his eyes tracing every line of my body as I move.

'Are you this forward in every respect?' he asks, as he holds out his hand for the mobile I'm still holding.

I wait a beat. 'You'd have to find out,' I say, stepping inside.

Chapter 5

Rachel

Thursday, March 9

Beth is frantic and angry when I get back. She has, however, managed to follow my suggestion and is halfway through baking a Victoria sandwich.

'How could you *do* that?' she wails. 'How could you leave me with…with…?' She flings a floury hand towards the car parked beyond the front wall. Her hands are shaking and she's managed to get cake mix in her hair and eyebrows.

'I'm sorry,' I tell her. 'I needed to think. I needed to sort out what we should do.'

'And what's the verdict?' she snaps. 'What the hell *is* our next move?'

Ever since she was little, Beth's been melodramatic. It makes everything about her intoxicating, larger than life. She channels it best when she's acting. I saw it first when she played Mary in a nativity scene at infant school. Her unexpected interpretation involved dancing across the stage to take hold of the baby Jesus and spinning him around in her arms. The audience burst into spontaneous applause. It's as though a light went on in her tiny body and she glowed with effervescence.

That's when she most comes alive – when she's on stage. Acting is the only thing that really interests her and she aches to be picked for a part in the public eye; a film, TV series, drama, a West-End show.

'Where did you go?' she says, picking nervously at dried egg on the side of the hob.

'To see Russell.'

'Oh...' Her eyes drop.

She's not sure whether to admonish me for wasting time or to ask if I'm okay. She gives me an awkward hug without using her hands.

Russell's death is the first big thing that's happened in our lives that Beth and I don't share in the same way. Even so, Beth has been incredibly sensitive since it happened; preparing light meals, doing extra jobs around the house, answering the phone when she can see I'm not up to it, folding up all Russell's clothes when I mentioned clearing his wardrobe.

'Did it help?' she says finally.

'Judy Welsh, the elderly widow, died last week.'

'Why are you telling me that?'

'I'll explain later. Get your wellington boots, a thick parka and a pair of old gloves ready for tonight. We're going out when everyone else is fast sleep.'

Taking the same zigzag route as before, I draw the car into the parking area behind the church reserved for the parish priest, tucked away from the road.

It's windy when we get out of the car and Beth is chanting, 'This is mad...this is crazy...' under her breath, as she pulls her hat down to her eyebrows. I've given her clear instructions about what we're going to do, all she has to do is play her part. She should be capable of that. I nudge her to be quiet and she stops.

First, we take the spades from the boot and hurry inside the rear gate. It's a cloudy night with no moon poking through to throw a spotlight on our transgressions. I have a small torch, but I know the dips and folds of the terrain well enough from my frequent visits and don't need much light to see my way ahead. I skirt the benches and a group of low hanging trees with Beth right behind me.

When we get to the correct spot, I whisper a sombre apology to the dead soul whose grave we are about to disturb. I discreetly found out her name from Sarah, the sour-faced woman who does the altar flowers at St Andrews. Judy died at the age of ninety-four – 'beloved grandma to Lauren and Joan', her headstone will say. I knew her, vaguely. She came into the pub with her family for Sunday lunch, now and again. In the past few hours I've told myself, repeatedly, that as a parent and grandparent, she would understand.

Beth stares in utter disgust as the despicable thing we're about to do hits her. She covers her mouth and races back to the car. I go straight after her and slide into the driver's seat, sitting calmly beside her with the lights off, waiting for her to speak.

'I can't do this…' she mumbles.

Okay. Now I have to lay it on thicker than ever.

'Beth, we *need* this marriage to Peter.'

That didn't come out right.

'Need it? What do you mean?'

It's time to tell her about our finances. It's my last hope of steering her towards a plausible reason for blatantly flouting the law, without telling her the truth.

'Russell, bless him…he left us in a lot of debt.'

She turns to look at me, but it's too dark to see her expression.

'He wasn't dishonourable,' I go on, 'it's not like he threw money away on gambling or anything like that, he just borrowed money from me, always intending to pay it back – but the astronomical bills he spent on my credit cards never got paid off.'

I don't go into how many sleepless nights I've struggled through since Russell departed this world. I lent him nearly everything I had to get a new business in vapour cigarettes off the ground, on the understanding that he was due to inherit a huge sum from his ailing aunt Nora.

But, in the end, it was all down to bad timing.

Nora was in a hospice and had only months to live, he'd said, and everything was due to be paid off just as soon as she passed away. It wouldn't be long, he'd said. Only the cancer took hold of him when his back was turned – and he died first.

We'd never married – he'd been married before and didn't want to do it again – so I never got a penny when Nora slipped away in her sleep, just before Christmas.

'Oh…' Beth says vacantly. 'But we're going to be okay, aren't we…'? She says it as a statement rather than a question. She still doesn't grasp the implications. Money for her is still a well, sunk somewhere out of sight that never runs dry.

'Once the pub reopens, I'm going to have to squeeze in more hours behind the bar,' I tell her. I'd already been doing double shifts, but I'd have to do more. I place my hand on her knee. 'And we won't be able to hang on in Winchester for much longer.'

She shakes her head in disbelief. 'No way! I had to leave London because I couldn't afford it and now you're saying we have to leave *here*?'

I look at her gravely. 'I thought you left London to be with me,' I say.

She looks down. 'I did…yes…as well.'

I turn to the window so she can't see how crushed I am.

'What about the car?' she says.

Beth passed her test before Russell died and we'd talked about getting a small run-around we could share.

I slowly shake my head.

'You're kidding me!' she says.

'You'll have to fit more hours in, too. We're really going to have to cut back.' Beth isn't qualified for anything other than acting and whenever I've mentioned the possibility of adding another job to the temporary one she got with the quiz show when she left London, she's invariably thrown a strop.

She jerks her knee away. 'But, I *have* to find auditions, Mum, you know that. I have to keep in the loop and go for anything that comes up. I can't be washing dishes or serving at tables in the few hours I've got free.'

'That's why we have to do this.'

I wait to let what I've said sink in. I hope it's enough, because I really don't want to have to divulge the truth.

Without a word, she opens the car door and gets out. We go back and work quickly, scooping the mound of soil piled over Judy's coffin into a fresh heap alongside it. It's recently dug earth, so is easy to shift, but there is a lot of it and it seems to go on forever.

We're both fit. Beth is at the stage where she wants to look 'perfect' and, like all her friends, is fixated on keeping her stomach washboard flat and creating curves to highlight all her muscles. If she's not at the gym every day, she's swimming. Her natural body shape is more Lara Croft than Amazonian woman, but she's strong and she throws herself into the shovelling with gusto.

When my spade hits wood, a wave of nausea almost gets the better of me. On the drive over, I told Beth to expect feelings of revulsion at our actions and when she snatches a breath, I react quickly. I can see from her terrified eyes that she's about to scream, drawing all and sundry to the graveside no doubt, so I slap my hand over her mouth. 'Come on. I know it's hard. It's okay. We can do this. We have to.'

I can't allow myself to admit that we're taking the biggest risk of our lives. What we're doing is nothing short of madness and, if we get caught, we have absolutely no leg to stand on. I'm banking on the fact that it's a dismal moonless night and we are two unidentifiable figures out of sight.

In the next moment, we hit a snag. I haven't accounted for how heavy the coffin is and how completely embedded it is into the ground. Old Judy Welsh has made her new home here, dug her heels in and isn't budging an inch. In my mind, I'd foolishly hoped we could get Carl's body *underneath* the coffin and re-pack everything as it was, but that isn't going to be possible.

Instead, we hurry back to the car boot and carry his body inside the rolled-up rug to the graveside. We tip the coffin to one side as best we can and squash him in alongside it, together with the rug and dust sheet.

I loathe myself for every inch of soil I shift, and I'm appalled by the thought that I'm traumatising my daughter in this way, but I can see no other option. She seems to have accepted the reasons I've given her. I can only hope she never has to know the truth.

What a blessing, what a miracle, that Peter came along when he did and for him to fall completely in love with Beth. It means she has an escape from our mountain of debt, as well as securing her best chance of making it as an actress.

Since that first nativity play, acting is all she's ever wanted to do. It's typical of my daughter that she chose such a cut-throat career. She's always been headstrong and done things the hard way, never taken the obvious, straightforward route. So, her dream is my dream – and I want nothing more than to see her gain her rightful place in the limelight.

When I first met Peter Roper and grasped he was twelve years older than my daughter, I wondered if Beth's impetuous energy was what he was most drawn to. Or perhaps it was simply her looks. She has the kind of face you only ever see in portraits of fine ladies by Gainsborough. The ones with exquisitely pale, flawless skin and a natural sheen, like smooth marble.

It goes against all my feminist values about independence to accept the fact, but there is no denying that their marriage could solve many problems in one go. And sometimes needs must.

We fill in the hole, leaving the mound as before and make sure we've left no obvious boot prints. To any onlooker, nothing has changed. Nothing added, nothing taken away. Then we hurry back to the car and drive home, leaving it a few streets away from the house. We'll give it a good clean in the morning.

We have little to hide now, just muddy boots and spades. Nothing unusual. I'd been seen plenty of times at the church getting soil on my hands – just not at this hour of the night. The timing is the only bit we need to worry about.

We've barely exchanged a word since we got on with the job, but once we're back inside the house, Beth can't stop.

'Oh my God, I can't believe we just did that! Totally unbelievable! Do you think anyone saw us? Did you see that coffin? When we tried to get it over on its side, I thought it was going to split open and that old woman was going to fall out. Shit…I thought…'

I make her sit on the sofa and look for signs she's going to have another asthma attack. Her chest rises fast, but smoothly, and I brush the hair away from her sticky forehead. It's still imprinted with the cable pattern of the knitted hat she was wearing.

'It's okay. It's done now – everything is over with. All we need are watertight alibis.'

She draws back. 'Why? The police won't come to us, will they? Why would they?'

'We must cover every eventuality, that's all. Carl is only "missing" for now, but I won't sleep unless I know we can fight our corner if the worst happens.'

In truth, fool-proof alibis aren't *all* we need. We also have to hope that Carl hasn't mentioned his little dalliance with Beth to anyone and that he wasn't spotted on his way to the pub, on Wednesday night.

I cup her chin gently so she's looking at me. 'We need to be really clear about where we were these last two nights and stick to it.' I lighten my tone. 'You should be good at this, it's going to be like acting. We're going to pretend we're playing parts in a film. We're going to be really calm and unperturbed.' It sounds good in theory, only right this minute, she looks anything but calm and unperturbed.

Beth plays around with different roles most days to such an extent that it's hard to know who she really is at times. She's slippery, changeable and always relishes the idea of pretending to be someone else. Only now, just when we need a solid performance from her, she's flummoxed.

'We've done something despicable,' she whispers.

'I know. But I hope you know why.'

Only, of course, I know she has no idea at all.

Chapter 6

Beth

June – nine months earlier

I'd barely thought of Peter Roper until I took coffee in to Tom, in the editing suite. He was putting together a voiceover script for the 'Dance on Screen' footage.

While Tom found a space on his cluttered desk for the mug, I looked over his shoulder. Peter was right. The questions he was asked in his interview weren't half as astute as mine. I smiled as I caught a few of his responses, remembering the way he'd been with me; at ease, charismatic, teasing. On camera, he's straight-laced and intense and I feel privileged I saw a more intimate side to him.

While I was folding tea-towels in the kitchen, I overheard Gloria ask her PA, Trevor, to contact Mr Roper to ask about the copyright holder for one of his photographs. I made a point of walking past Gloria's desk and spotted a full-screen image of him on her computer. I felt the same shiver down the back of my neck as I had when he'd said my name, that day. It was the photo I'd chosen from his phone – the one I'd insisted he use for the magazine interview.

After lunch, Trevor put a call through to me on my mobile. I'm on the move so much, I don't really have a desk and just then I was on my way to the television studio. The presenter was about to do a piece about a disbanded boy-band and her zip had broken.

'That guy from the documentary wants a word with you,' he said. 'Just putting him through.'

I stopped at the next seating area and put down the sewing box I was carrying.

'Hello, Beth Kendall speaking.'

'It's "that guy from the documentary",' came Peter's smooth aristocratic voice, with a chuckle. 'Peter Roper, remember him?'

'Hard to forget,' I said, unable to keep the teasing edge out of my voice.

'I'm heading off to New York tomorrow, but I wondered if there's any chance you might be free for dinner tonight?'

I nearly dropped the phone. 'Dinner?'

Me?

'I know it's short notice. It's…I'm sorry.'

'Actually, that would be lovely. I finish here at six.'

'I'll send a cab for you, if you like?'

'No…it's fine. Where shall we meet?'

'Say, eight o'clock at the ground-floor bar at the National Theatre? We'll go on from there.' There was a beat of hesitation. 'Do you like fish? Something a bit exotic?'

'Absolutely. I fell in love with spicy shrimp soup and monkfish curry in Thailand.'

'Excellent.'

That was it. The call ended.

Y-e-s!

I punched the air with both hands, not caring who could see me through the glass panels from every angle, like the hall of mirrors at a funfair.

He's a hot-shot in the film industry and he wants to see ME…

The question was, who should I phone first to tell about it. Then I froze. I glanced down at my baby-pink wrap top and white trousers – smart enough for the office, but not going to cut it for a posh meal out. I had nothing with me to change into. Peter Roper was clearly loaded and sophisticated. I couldn't turn up wearing this!

I reached down for the sewing kit. I was heading for the studio anyway, so I'd check the green room. There was a slim chance there might be something I could borrow for the night, but I wasn't hopeful. Programmes are mostly filmed off-site by independent makers, so there's only one studio and no wardrobe department as such. It would be a long shot.

'I've never had dinner on a boat before,' I tell him as he leads the way down the gangplank. A faint breeze warmed by the persistent sun softly brushes my bare arms.

'Not even in Thailand?'

'I've eaten overlooking the water and had food on the go on ships and boats, but not a proper sit down meal, like this.'

I can see straightaway this isn't any old boat. It's a sleek white luxury yacht and we appear to be the only guests onboard.

A waiter, wearing a bow tie and with a white napkin draped over his arm, guides us through to the bar area, then asks what we'd like to drink.

I take my glass of Bollinger and head straight through the sliding glass door onto the deck to take in the views across the Thames. Out here, the sky feels like it has doubled in size. It's a luminous cornflower blue and below, a thousand crystals are scattered across the surface of the water.

'We have about an hour of daylight left,' Peter tells me, coming up beside me against the railing. 'They'll let us go as far as Putney Bridge, then we'll head back this way for sunset…'

He turns around, his back to the water, stroking the stem of his glass. The engine rumbles and we start moving.

'I have a question for you. Would you like to watch the sunset at Big Ben or Tower Bridge?'

'Seriously? I can honestly say no one has ever asked me that before.'

He's more attractive than I remembered. He waits for my reply and I go for Tower Bridge.

'That would have been my choice,' he says. 'By the way, you look stunning in that dress.' I've felt his eyes glued to me virtually every moment since I found him earlier in the theatre bar.

As I'd feared, there was nothing I could use in the wardrobe at work, so in a panic about the whole 'what to wear' conundrum, I'd phoned my old friend from junior school, Tina.

'Well, you have no choice, Bee. You can't go to Top Shop if he's that important. You need to get yourself over to Bond Street or Knightsbridge.'

'That's what I was thinking. And a cocktail dress? Gown? LBD or what?'

'Where's he taking you?'

'No idea, but I reckon it'll be expensive.'

'Go the whole hog. I would.' Tina is someone who'd think nothing of spending two hundred pounds on a pair of exquisite shoes – but then she's just been offered a part in *Hollyoaks*, so her monthly income will have quadrupled.

In the end, I used my credit card to buy a long gown from Harvey Nicholls with a plunging cross-over bodice, made of emerald green silk. Mum is always going on about making the most of my 'simmering green eyes'.

I managed to get to a charity shop before they shut and bought a pair of strappy sandals, then charged over to the NT to change in the Ladies'. Luckily I had what I needed to refresh my face in my make-up bag.

We glide past the Houses of Parliament towards Lambeth Bridge, feathers of white foam fanning out behind us. The breeze tugs at my hair and Peter gently brushes back a strand as it catches on my eyelashes and I feel that tingle again.

He asks me about my upbringing and I risk telling him the truth – that I never knew my father and Mum found herself pregnant when she was underage. I realise as I say it, that it's a test on my part and I'm relieved when I read concern in his eyes, rather than disapproval.

'Forgive me if this seems rude,' he says, 'but you appear very refined.'

'For someone from a single parent family who didn't go to public school, you mean?'

He wrinkles his nose. 'No. For anyone. Sorry, it didn't come out the way I wanted.' He stops to think. 'What I mean is, you sit like a dancer, with a straight back and long neck, your nails are immaculate…you got out of the taxi like a gazelle, like royalty…'

'I'm an actress, don't forget,' I say, turning to look at him over my shoulder in a deliberately seductive pose.

I don't tell him that 'playing' demure and ultra-feminine come very easily to me, which is odd considering I'm no innocent wallflower.

'Seriously though, my grandmother was from Chile and I've always had this thing about rhythm and moving well.'

'You dance?' He looks taken aback.

'Sort of. Latin-American. Anything from salsa and rumba to cha-cha-cha. I love to swing and sway – it's in my blood.'

The waiter hovers behind us. 'Ah, it's time to eat,' Peter says. 'If you're cold, we can go inside.'

'No, it's perfect.'

The waiter leads us to the table at the back of the boat. It looks like it's made of marble.

The first course is soup, then the main course arrives.

'How cool is this?' I exclaim. 'It's exactly what I had in Chiang Mai.'

So…he'd been listening carefully during our brief chat this afternoon. A good sign.

'I'm glad I got it right.'

I ask Peter whether it was hard to give up dancing to work behind the scenes.

'Age got the better of me, as I knew it would. I could no longer perform at the highest level. But after so long in the business, I knew all the right people and where to find them, so it was an obvious transition to make films involving dance.'

We reach Putney Bridge and the yacht turns round and heads back to the city. Dessert is light and lemony, then we take our drinks and stand as the river curves and the light fades. With the faintest orange flares of remaining sunlight singeing the sky, the boat pulls into the bank near Tower Bridge.

'This is unbelievable…' I say, as we look back inland and watch the sun giving away its final flames for the day.

'Not bad,' he says, leaning close to me.

I know this must be nothing compared to the kinds of awesome experiences he must have had in his life, but I'm touched he's indulging me.

'I'll let you into a secret, the boat belongs to an acquaintance of mine. In fact…he might be a good person for you to meet sometime…that's if we…you know…' He twists his hands into an ambiguous shape in the air. I hide a smile. He does quite a bit of wriggling, I've noticed. For someone who seems to be a consummate man of the world, he's remarkably modest.

'What does this acquaintance do?' I ask.

'He's a big name in films – commercial blockbusters. You might have heard of him: Carl Jacobson.'

I draw back, stunned. 'You know him?'

He nods nonchalantly. For someone in my position, *anyone* in movies is worth meeting, but Carl Jacobson is right up there on my wish-list. 'Well, yes…an introduction, one day, would be incredible,' I say.

'He's a decent guy. Known him for years.'

He nods at the waiter, claps his hands together decisively and I feel a shiver of dread. It looks like everything is going to come to an end and I'm not ready to go. I want to take in more of his creamy, educated voice, the musky, sexy smell of him and to revel in being the focus of his attention. I want to hear more about what he does, the life he lives.

I've had lots of boyfriends, but I've never felt this way with anyone before; hovering on a precipice between perilous and invincible, all wrapped up in a kind of heady yearning for more.

'Where do you live?' he asks.

'Chiswick.'

I don't tell him it's the same tip of a bedsit I've lived in since my student days. Nor do I say I can't even afford *that* anymore and I'm thinking of moving back to Mum's.

He clears his throat. 'I have an apartment in Chelsea. It's not far. Do you…would you like to nip over there for a night cap, if it's not too forward of me to ask?'

I run my finger around the rim of my glass.

'I like *forward*,' I say with a smile. 'I'm quite good at forward. It means people know where they stand, and they can stop wondering if they've misinterpreted a situation.'

'That's very refreshing,' he says, blinking fast, as though he hasn't heard anyone be so bold before.

I don't notice a great deal about Peter's apartment, because as soon as we're inside, he swoops me by the hand straight into his bedroom.

There's a subdued glow seeping from a lamp in the corner that must have come on automatically, once it got dark. Peter breaks away from me to draw the floor-length curtains, but instead of returning to my side, he sits on the bed.

He was all gung-ho a moment ago and now he's looking pensive.

'Sorry,' he says. 'I don't want to rush and spoil everything.'

'You're going away…' I say, sidling over and reaching down to touch his shoulder.

He looks forlorn. 'Yep. New York for three weeks.' He pats the space beside him and I sit.

He turns to me with measured deliberation. 'Beth, from the moment I saw you – when I stepped out of the lift and found you waiting for me – I haven't been able to stop thinking about you.' He trails his finger along my bare arm.

I'm bubbling inside, tingling all over.

He carries on. 'You're probably seeing someone…and I'm far too old, but…life is short and I thought it might be worth a shot.'

I swallow hard, taking in what he's saying.

'Are you…seeing someone?' he asks.

I look up. 'I would have said by now, if I was.'

There's a thin film of sweat glistening in his palm. He's really serious about this.

'And am I too old? Are you…humouring me?'

Are you kidding me?

I shake my head, fixing my eyes on his. 'No way.'

It's a lot to take in. We're poles apart in terms of upbringing, standing and social status, as well as our ages. I'm basically one step from being on the dole and he probably thinks nothing of spending a thousand pounds on a meal. Then I think of Russell: how one minute he was fine, then the next, he was rapidly going downhill, until one day he wasn't there anymore.

Peter sees me thinking hard and gets up.

'If it's all too much, I'll get you home straight away. It's been a wonderful evening.' He kisses my hand. 'Just perfect as it is.'

I look up at him. 'No,' I whisper. 'Sometimes you have to go for things if they feel right.'

'And does it? Feel right? You being here, like this, with me?'

For a split second I think about the implications: successful movie mogul seduces aspiring young actress. The press would have a field day. Was this just a casting-couch cliché? Did I actually like him or was I only interested in what he could offer me?

'Be honest,' he says.

My heart is battering inside of my ribcage like a wild creature desperate to be let loose. I breathe in the outline of his lips, the tight line of his jaw and want nothing more than to fold myself into him.

I don't need any more time to decide. 'Yes. It does feel right.'

I know it with every bone of my body.

He pulls me to my feet and embraces me, wrapping me firmly in his arms and holding me against him for a long time. I can feel his heart thudding against my throat, his breath husky and eager beside my ear.

'I've been wanting to do that all night,' he says, then tips up my chin. I close my eyes and as he brushes his lips over mine, I feel the most delicate of touches that melts the point at which my mouth ends and his begins.

'And I've been wanting to do that all night, too,' he adds.

I'm startled by his self-restrained approach. There is something distinguished and utterly respectful about every move he makes.

I stop him as he starts to unzip my dress and for a moment he must think I've changed my mind. Without letting my eyes leave his, I take hold of his hands and carefully press them away. Then, following an overwhelming urge to take the lead, I undo his tie and one by one, I begin unbuttoning his shirt.

So – moments later, it's *he* who is half-naked standing before me while I remain fully clothed.

And it's *me* who gives that tender, but no-nonsense nudge, that sends him falling back on to the bed. From that moment on my feelings for him escalate on a par with a blaze ripping through an oil refinery.

In the weeks that follow, we're lifted up and carried away on a passionate and sensual voyage of discovery and I never want to come back.

Chapter 7

Rachel

Saturday, March 11

The plan is to carry on as though everything is normal. But we're both falling short.

I've been obsessively cleaning like a mad woman and Beth's avoiding me. We were inseparable when she was growing up and she's never blocked me out before. She's never had a secretive or reclusive phase, not even when Russell and I got together, and I'm not sure how to handle it.

Now is *the* most urgent time for us to be talking to each other, but she's been spending hours at the leisure centre. She comes back each time looking wrecked and hides in her room.

'Going up and down the pool is the only thing that keeps me sane,' she told me yesterday, the only words we exchanged over breakfast.

Beth's eyes are puffy and sore. She wears sunglasses even though the sky carries nothing but overlapping clouds in shades of grey. She even wears them around the house. Our roles are strangely reversed. After she moved back home in August, I was the one moping around in slow motion, grieving for Russell, and she was getting on with her life.

This morning she's supposed to be putting together quiz questions on pop music, but she's disappeared again and her swimsuit is no longer on the radiator.

I head to the King's Tavern to check all the refurbishments are going to plan. The wrong carpets have arrived for the back room and one of the drains is blocked, but there's nothing I can't sort out.

Since the accident, Beth and I have managed to have only one proper discussion: to get our stories straight. Our little script starts on Wednesday night, when we'll claim she came over to the pub to meet me on her way back from taking a walk and we came home together. Then we used Marvin's car to do a quick shop at the supermarket.

I'll tell the truth and say that during the period when he was away, we used the car for a handful of shopping trips and to take gardening tools up to St Andrews to do my usual grave tending. That should take care of any soil strewn in the back.

Then the truth goes blurry again. The story for Thursday night is we didn't go anywhere. We've agreed to say we watched *Basic Instinct* on DVD from about 8 p.m., because neither of us is likely to forget that title, and then we went to bed. Beth already has the film in her vast collection, so that's easy.

'We need to be very careful when we refer to Carl,' I told her. 'You need to say Peter mentioned him in passing and that you'd heard he came over to the Theatre now and then. You met him at a party, just the once. That's it. Simple.'

As it happens, there is one aspect in this awful mess that will work in Beth's favour. She swears there was no online connection between them and no trail that could possibly link the two of them. Carl was obviously a past master at sneaking around and had insisted that Beth *never* got in touch with him. In turn, he made contact solely from public telephones in hotels and stations. Perhaps his wife was a consummate snoop and had made life difficult for him in the past.

Yesterday, we cleaned Marvin's car inside and out, in full view of all the tradesmen at the pub. I made a point of joking around with the hosepipe in front of them, just so everyone would recall how relaxed we were. I also remembered to change the timer on the heating controls, the job I never got to do on Wednesday night.

'You two sisters, then?' Rolf, one of the builders, threw out during the banter.

He isn't the first to suggest Beth and I look alike. Having her so young has shrunk the typical age difference between mother and daughter and I've lost weight since Russell died. We both have sleek dark hair, mine is shorter than Beth's and usually parted in the middle, but I occasionally part it the same way as hers.

Beth overheard and made a pukey sound. 'That's gross! You can't see the wrinkles and double chin from there,' she jibed, then gave me a look to check whether she was overstepping the mark. I glared at her, sprayed water in her direction and she squealed. That was the only time in the last few days that she's been her usual self.

Electricians and decorators have been back and forth to the cellar since the incident, but there's nothing to see. No one has noticed there's a dust sheet missing, or the rug, for that matter. There was no blood, so there's no tell-tale stain on the flagstones like in a Hitchcock film, no discarded shoe or dropped receipt that's been overlooked. The internal security camera was taken down last week so the ceilings can be painted, so there's no CCTV footage.

I'm confident I've covered every potential loophole.

I had hoped Beth would have settled into her role of 'smooth operator' by now, but she's been more nervous and jittery than ever.

It's not the first time I've been worried about her. Since drama college, she's had to learn to ride one disappointing setback after another. Beth is twenty-three and hasn't managed to find an agent or get a single callback. In short, she's been turned down for every professional part she's auditioned for.

Peter has already been twisting arms to get Beth in front of the right people. As his wife, he'll be able to showcase her to his heart's content and do it now, while she still has that 'little-girl-lost' look he's apparently remarked upon.

My fear is that without Peter's help, her career as an actress will be dead in the water.

Of course, I'd never want her to marry for ulterior motives and I'd hate to think I was encouraging her to take such an important step if she wasn't seriously head over heels in love with him. I'm not that kind of mother. But Beth has shown all the signs that Peter is 'the one' and I've had no reason to doubt her. Until now, that is.

Beth can be so dizzy at times. Often serious and refined, she frequently reverts to the fresh-faced dreamer she truly is underneath.

What was she thinking getting caught up with this Carl guy?

As the last builders' lorry leaves the car-park, I lock up the pub and head back home. So that I don't alter any aspect of my routine, I stop by Russell's grave on the way.

My stomach lurches as I stand so close to where we dumped Carl's body. I try to block it out, but I'm fumbling over my opening words to Russell. I can't find anything to say. My eyes keep wandering over to the mound covering Judy Welsh's coffin, several rows along. The wind carries the smell of wood-smoke towards me from nearby cottages and my heart flutters. Were we seen on Thursday night?

A couple of windows are visible from where I'm standing, but as soon as I take two or three steps to my right – towards the fresher graves – the view is blocked by an evergreen magnolia. I press my hand over my chest in relief.

I find a bench further away so I can no longer see Judy's grave, and sit down.

Would Russell forgive me for what I've done? Would he understand?

I sit in silence, not daring to ask the questions.

He didn't know about my past, about Southampton…the real reasons for reacting the way I did in the cellar.

'I'm going to have to speak to Peter about the wedding costs,' I mutter, eventually. 'We should have sorted this out by now, but he's been so hard to get hold of. I can't afford anything like the sort of show his family are expecting. They're dreadfully posh. Peter dropped Beth back home in a Jaguar convertible when she spent the weekend with him, last month. You'd have loved it. He lets her use his flat in Chelsea, while he's away on business.

Oh, dear…families with that kind of money are going to expect something special for their son's wedding, aren't they?'

What looked, last night, like snow on the ground I now see is blossom buffeted from the overhanging branches of cherry trees.

I suck in a slow breath.

Things are not always what they seem.

I rattle on. 'We still need to get the flowers, the wedding car, the cake…and there's the bridesmaids' outfits and…'

If he'd been beside me, Russell would have stopped what he was doing and listened to me with all his attention, then patted my hand and said everything was going to be all right. 'People are generally decent,' he would always say.

When it became clear that Russell had left me in dire straits, financially, my close friends insisted I ought to be angry with him.

'He left you in the lurch, Rachel,' they said. 'He let you down.'

Still, I've always stood up for him. 'He meant to pay me back,' I told them. 'It was all done in good faith. He didn't *steal* from me.'

I knew it was true. Nevertheless, Beth and I had been left in an untenable position. We were on the verge of going under.

Chapter 8

Rachel

When I return to the house, Beth is crooning in front of the mirror by the front door with a hairbrush in her hand. A sad echoey song by Beyoncé is playing on the old hi-fi system in the corner. She's wearing a long blonde wig and a skin-tight purple dress.

'I'm trying to cheer myself up,' she says mournfully.

Her phone screen is lit up on the chair arm beside her, then goes out.

'Who've you been talking to?' I ask casually, unable to take my eyes off it.

'Just Sienna. She's replacing an understudy in *The Jersey Boys* at the Piccadilly Theatre. Don't worry,' she says, her hands on her hips, glaring at me. 'I didn't say anything.'

She turns off the music and flops onto the sofa.

The sitting room is the first room you come to in our run-down terraced house beyond the tiny square porch. At some stage, interior walls have been knocked down, so everything is open-plan on the ground floor, with stairs before the kitchen leading directly from the sitting room up to our bedrooms.

A selection of Beth's clothes are strewn everywhere, making the place resemble a shop changing room.

In spite of the incense stick burning by the bottom of the stairs, a cloying smell of damp manages to cut through. I've been trying not to notice the blotches of mildew that are bleeding through the wallpaper.

I peel off my coat and switch on the oven, then slip a pie I made from yesterday's leftovers into the oven.

'What's going to happen when people start looking for him?' she asks, out of the blue. She has a habit of idly twirling a strand of hair around her finger, then tugging it across her mouth. She doesn't even know she's doing it.

I sink down beside her. 'People will ask questions. You must be ready for that. Before long, someone will report him missing. His wife, probably. They'll want to know where he was and who saw him last.'

'His wife must be going mental.'

I fold my arms. There's a grating pain in my chest. 'Who knew you two were…seeing each other?'

She answers without hesitation. 'No one.'

'Are you sure?'

'It was a secret, Mum – I'm supposed to be getting married, remember.'

'Do you know his wife?'

She toys with the fringe of the throw that covers torn patches in the sofa cushions. 'She's called Amelia and is into horses. I met her briefly when I was introduced to Carl.'

'Any children?'

'Two boys, I think.'

I swallow hard. I know what it's like to lose someone, but I can't imagine what it would be like to have your husband or father never come home and disappear forever. At least I got to say goodbye to Russell. I had eight months of preparation while he was ill, whereas Beth and I are going to be putting Amelia and the boys through torture.

But I can't let myself dwell on that.

'Where do they live?'

'Carl has a flat in London, but the family home is near Arundel, I think. They own a farm as well. They're into race horses and yachts.' She sniffs and I realise she's crying. I pull a tissue from a cardboard box beside the fireplace and hand it to her. She blows her nose.

'I thought you loved Peter,' I say softly.

'I do.'

'So – how could..?'

A strand of hair is in her mouth again. She's going to have to grow out of that quickly, once she's married to Peter.

She looks pensive. 'I was shocked at myself if I'm honest. But it just happened. I gave in to lust on the spur of the moment.'

'But, it wasn't just once, was it? You saw him again. How many times?'

She has the decency to look ashamed. 'Three…or four. It was like being two people,' she says, not looking at me. 'With Carl, it was like escaping reality. It was daring and secret, like I was in a magical bubble.'

'Even though you were engaged to Peter?'

She wrinkles her nose. 'Yeah…I know. Now, it's all over, I'm disgusted with myself.' She lifts her gaze to meet mine. 'But you can love people in different ways, can't you?' she says with authority.

'So why Carl?' I'm not sure if it's a good idea to talk about him, although I'm inclined to think on balance that if we discuss him freely in private, it might stop her from being tempted to turn to one of her friends. 'You sure he didn't exploit you?'

'No way! I'd never get into that. He was really good-looking and kind of dangerous and intoxicating. I should have had more willpower, only Peter's been abroad so much.'

Is this how young people treat their relationships these days? Going behind their lovers' backs the instant they're absent? I hate to think that my own daughter has behaved in this way, but now isn't the time for a morality lesson.

'So you haven't changed your mind about Peter?'

'Oh, no,' she says immediately. 'Peter's brilliant. He's perfect.' She dabs her lashes carefully so as not to smudge her mascara. 'I shouldn't have let things go so far with Carl. We got carried away.'

She gets to her feet. 'I can't believe we haven't told the police. And that poor woman…did we really have to mess up her grave and..?' She grinds to a halt.

'Yes, I'm afraid we did. I told you why. I wouldn't have suggested we do something like this lightly, you know that. It's a dreadful, appalling thing we've done, but we had to hide what happened. It'll be fine if we keep our heads. We just have to act normally and carry on exactly the same.'

'You said there's no money.'

'That's right. There isn't.'

She keeps her eyes away from mine. 'What about my wedding dress?'

'I've already set aside an amount for that – that's one thing you don't need to worry about, as long as it's the same one you showed me – the one that was in the sale.'

'Yeah, it is. I've had fittings and everything.' She snatches a breath. 'Oh, God, my big day isn't going to be really embarrassing, is it? Second-hand shoes, hand-me-down bridesmaids' dresses and a veil made from our old net curtains?'

She glances over at the tattered grey nylon at the front window that needed replacing months ago.

Exaggeration is second nature to Beth.

'Of course not. I'll try to get every single thing you want, but listen, I can't pay for any more dance classes, no more clothes or make-up. Once your gym membership runs out, that's that. No trips out for either of us and we'll have to exist on the basics in terms of food and socialising. You're going to have to tighten your belt until you marry Peter.'

Beth has never been good with money in spite of my encouragement to save. She still thinks that if she pleads long and hard enough she'll always get what she wants. She's got a lot of growing up to do, although having said that, Russell was far worse. I'd have done something about that if only I'd known.

'Okay,' she says, blowing out a long breath. 'I'll try.'

I reach out to hold her hand. She lets it go in a matter of seconds.

'It will be worth it in the end,' I say.

She unzips the dress she's wearing and tugs it off over her tiny hips, revealing a racy black bra and matching knickers.

For a moment, I'm in awe of the fact that she's been able to make the journey from schoolgirl to young woman on her own terms. That was something I never had and can never look back on with any sense of emancipation. In my case, I was a kid making daisy chains one minute and rinsing nappies the next. It certainly wasn't what I would have chosen.

She gathers up a handful of clothes. I watch her, a smile creeping onto my lips. I see my mother in the way she moves. They share the same natural sense of rhythm, as though she can hear music playing inside her head the whole time. She's never clumsy, there are no rough edges about her.

She dallies at the foot of the stairs and I know there's something she wants to say.

'Listen, don't bite my head off, but I've just remembered something.'

My breath catches on the inhale. I wait.

'When I was on the way to meet Carl at the pub that night,' she grits her teeth, 'I spoke to someone…'

Chapter 9

Beth

August – seven months earlier

I'm not sure when that enchanted moment was, but at some point during that first night together in June, I was smitten. Instantly, my life was split into two: the period before being with Peter when I was a frivolous, naïve non-entity, and this new existence where I had suddenly blossomed into a diva. Simply with his eyes, Peter had turned me into a sophisticated and elegant prima donna worthy of the limelight.

He treated me like I'd already proved myself, already made my mark and was his equal. In one night I had taken that imperceptible step across an invisible threshold into a life that was bubbling with possibilities.

Now we're a couple. I can't believe his ardour is aimed at me; a lowly wannabe like thousands of others who thought she'd be forever stuck at the lowest rung of the ladder. Not that being with Peter is all about success and status. It's so much more than that. Every time I think of him, I feel uplifted. I breathe and move like the world is spinning faster.

There's something enthralling about him; his cornflower-blue irises that seem to have a light shining behind them, his soulful refined voice. He stands like a Greek marble statue, the prominent curves of his muscles still taut from years of dancing, giving him the torso of a man easily ten years younger.

He's not all dignified and proper, either. When he's had a bit to drink he can be fiercely irreverent about people, a wicked mimicker. We laugh all the time.

On our third date we went to see 'Twelfth Night' at The Globe. I wore a simple red silk dress. He complained in the interval that he hadn't taken in one word of the play.

'I'm too distracted,' he said, 'I've got this incredible vision of beauty sitting next to me and my hands are tied. I can feel the heat from her thigh radiating against mine and if I touch her, I won't be able to stop. I'm in torment.'

Once we were alone, I slowly peeled away the straps of my dress and let it fall for him. I'll never forget the way his lips slowly parted in wonder. It was like Howard Carter coming across the tomb of Tutankhamun. I loved the way his eyes licked ardently across my naked curves at first, then his fingers joined in and finally his tongue.

I Googled him after that date, curious to see how he was depicted in the media, but mainly to see who his previous girlfriends had been. Under 'personal life' in his Wikipedia entry, only two women were mentioned. A well-known Italian film star, Aurora Belluci, and a dancer from the English National Ballet – both of whom looked impossibly glamorous.

The search told me two things; Peter didn't appear to have casual flings, preferring instead long-term relationships, and the last liaison, with the dancer, had ended over a year ago.

Another section, on his career, described how he'd been lined up for various starring roles, only to have other dancers step in at the last minute. Poor Peter – he'd had a tough time.

My short-term contract as a runner came to an end and I cleared all my gear out of the flat in Chiswick. Chelsea was easy enough to get to, so I found the temporary quiz job I could do from home and stayed in Peter's flat when I had auditions.

During those first few months, I couldn't get enough of him. I craved our next meeting as soon as the last one had come to an end, hanging on his every text and phone call. He was important, in demand, on tour with dance groups and the kingpin in various dance-film deals – and I had to wait my turn.

'I've never felt like this before,' he said, during one of his video calls from New York. For someone who must have had girls falling over themselves to be on his arm, I took that as a massive compliment. Old-fashioned love-letters started landing on the doormat from Chicago, Paris, Rome, then double bouquets of roses. Everything about him was bold and unfettered.

Fearing that Mum would think I'd stooped to sexual favours with an 'older man' in return for promises of fame, I hadn't mentioned him straightaway, but with so many items arriving at the door, I gave in. I told her everything – well, not quite, but I gave her the general gist. She scooped me up in her arms.

'How wonderful, I'm so delighted for you. Peter sounds amazing.' It was the first time since Russell had died that I'd seen tears form in her eyes that weren't from grief.

She asked how we'd met and as my words tumbled out, a look of concern progressively pulled her smile out of shape. I pre-empted her warnings before she could spoil my news.

'Peter has influence in the film business and might be able to nudge me in the right direction,' I pointed out, 'but *I'm* the one who's going to have to do all the work. I know that. I'm under no illusions that suddenly I'm going to be swept off to Hollywood just because I'm with him.'

I remember the look in her eye then. A sense of victory, like Peter was the answer to everything.

On the odd occasion when he was back in London, I arranged get-togethers so that everyone I knew could meet him. My friends adored him. They thought he was engaging and generous and, the best bit, they were unanimous in exclaiming how obvious it was that he was in love with me.

The speed and intensity of my own feelings towards Peter left me in no doubt that he was 'Mr Right'. I'd had crushes and fancied boys before, but the relationships were exploratory and tentative – like pale rehearsals for the real thing. What I had with Peter was big, special.

When we got engaged, I was the happiest I'd ever been in my life and Mum was ecstatic. We knew everything was about to change forever.

Chapter 10

Rachel

I drag Beth to the sofa and make her sit. She drops the clothes, but is still holding the hairbrush microphone.

'Who did you speak to?' I snap, my eyes scrutinising her face, 'on the way to meet Carl?'

'I gave money to a homeless guy lying in a doorway on Melcham Street.'

Beth is a sucker for lost causes. Her tender spirit is one of the things I love most about her, but I worry that people will take advantage of it. 'Had you seen him before? Does he know who you are?'

'I've done it before. And yes, he…kind of recognised me.'

'Does he know your name?'

'No, I don't think so.'

'Well…I don't think that will be an issue.' I feel the tension slip away from my shoulders.

She nips a strand of hair between her lips and stares at her feet. I know that look.

'That's not all, though, is it?' I say, the anxiety creeping back.

She reaches for a magazine and starts doodling with a biro on the cover. 'No. I forgot. I bumped into Angie.'

My heart is thudding. 'Where?'

'In Henshaw Street – she was wheeling her bike.'

'What did you say to her?'

'I asked about her new job, that's all. I didn't say where I was going.'

I stop and mull over whether this is likely to be a problem. 'Is that everything?'

She nods, then wrinkles her nose and looks down.

'What?' I say, gripping her shoulders.

There's more?

She chews the end of the pen. She's done this ever since she was little and it drives me mad. I'm forever pulling a biro out of my bag and finding the end has been mauled into two distinct rings of teeth marks. That's another thing she's going to have to put a stop to when she marries Peter.

'Angie asked about my jacket. She kind of implied I was dolled up.'

I realise our original plan to claim that Beth went for a walk that evening will need revising. 'And what did—?'

At that moment, the doorbell breaks through with a loud jangle, making us both jump.

We freeze and stare at each other. I can see her chest rise and fall rapidly as if she's been running for a bus.

This is how it's going to be from now on.

I swallow. 'Just be normal,' I whisper.

'Who is it?'

'How do I know?'

I open the door to find Angie, the old school friend Beth has just mentioned, on the doorstep.

'Hi,' I say, oozing fake delight before I can stop myself.

'Is it a bad time?' she asks, her eyebrows raised.

'No…' I say quickly. We mustn't give away any signs that anything's wrong. I glance behind me. 'Beth isn't properly dressed, that's all.'

I swing the door wide to let her in and turn to Beth, who is peering over my shoulder.

'Oh, it's you,' Beth says, anxiously tapping her chin with her fingers.

Come on girl, get a grip.

'I said I'd pop in…remember?' says Angie. She looks at the two of us in turn cautiously, in the way people do when they think they've interrupted an argument.

'Oh yes, when we…' Beth halts, presumably not wishing to mention the evening when our world turned upside down.

Beth catches my eye anxiously as if begging me to say something. A scorching smell is heading our way from the kitchen and my gaze drifts to the carriage clock Russell bought me a couple of years ago. I need to get the pie out of the oven, but I don't want to leave Beth to stumble her way through this encounter on her own.

'Beth said she met you the other day, when she was on her way to see her grandad,' I say breezily, nodding at my daughter. 'Fancy a tea or some juice?' I add, as I push Beth's CDs to the edge of the sofa to give Angie room to sit down.

'No, thanks, I can't stop.' She turns to Beth. 'I just wanted to wish you luck for your audition. Monday, isn't it?'

Beth is looking nervously at Angie, nervously at everything, I realise.

'Yeah. Thanks,' she says, barely more than a whisper.

With the upheaval of the last few days neither of us has mentioned the part she's going for at Elstree – the role of a pregnant woman in *Holby City*.

'Will you get to meet the cast?' Angie asks, her eyes wide. I now recall Beth once saying that Angie's favourite subject at school was 'celebrity gossip'.

Beth's cheeks are red, her forehead clammy, even though she's wearing virtually nothing. 'I doubt it. It'll just be a couple of people I've never heard of behind a desk in a tiny room.'

A pang of sympathy goes out to my daughter, having to gear herself up for a sparkling performance at a time like this. Her auditions have been gruelling at the best of times.

'Anyway, look, I'm really sorry,' Beth says, 'but I need to go through my lines again.'

Angie shuffles towards the porch. 'Oh, yeah, of course. I hope you get it.'

Only when Beth shuts the front door do I breathe again.

'Shit...' she says, aiming the magazine she's still holding at a cushion and knocking over an empty mug on a side table, instead. 'Hell, it's so cramped in here.'

'You did really well,' I say.

It's not exactly true, but I want to give her encouragement. I leave her, not wanting our supper to be shrivelled to a crisp.

'So, I caught the bus over to Grandad's on Wednesday evening, is that the story, now?' She's leaning against the doorframe, one foot on top of the other, still in her underwear and totally unselfconscious about her body. She looks like a water-nymph, poised and delicate.

'It helps explain why you were wearing decent clothes.'

'But why would I be going over there so late?'

'That's easy. Put it down to his dementia.' I open the oven door and waft away the smoke, then stand still, thinking. 'Let's say he lost something and you went over to find it for him.'

'Lost what?'

She opens the back door to get a flow of fresh air.

'I don't know...er...how about the key to the greenhouse?'

'At nine o'clock at night?'

I burn my finger through the hole I keep forgetting about in the oven-gloves. 'Well, *you* think of something, then...' I say sharper than I mean to.

The scorched pie splits as I get it out of the dish. It looks like it's exploded.

'I don't want any,' she tells me. 'I'm not hungry.'

I want to yell: *YOU were the one who got us into this mess*! But I manage to hurry outside, feigning a coughing fit from the smoke, to smother my words.

I need to remember I've had more practice at covering up a devastating secret than she has.

Chapter 11

Rachel

January, two months earlier

I warm to Peter the moment he walks into the green room.

'Rachel…what an absolute pleasure, at last.'

He clasps both his hands around mine and looks deeply into my eyes, as though he's been waiting for this moment for weeks.

It sends my rehearsed phrases: *So delighted to meet you…Beth has told me so much about you* – clean out of my head.

I grin like a Cheshire cat, instead.

'I can't believe Beth has kept me from you for so long,' he adds.

There's a large crowd backstage after the performance; family and friends of the principal dancers and conductor, as well as other well-wishers flitting about. Peter ignores them all to focus on the two of us.

'So, what did you think?' he asks, looking from me to Beth and back again. 'Be honest, I know it's not everyone's cup of tea.'

We've just witnessed a collection of new ballet commissions, ending with an established classic, *The Rite of Spring* – seen from the best seats in the house, thanks to Peter.

Beth reaches out to kiss his cheek and he pulls her close with an impassioned embrace.

'I loved it,' she says. She's wearing a knee-length sky blue dress with matching longline jacket that she found in a second-hand shop. It's probably more suitable for a wedding, but Peter doesn't seem to mind. He's looking at her like he's never seen anyone so dazzling before. 'The Stravinsky was incredible,' she concludes, making angles with her hands, 'so raw and primitive.'

'And you, Rachel?' He keeps his arm around Beth, but waits for my response.

'Bewitching…it's so brutal…very dynamic.' I give a light-hearted laugh.

'Oh, you can come more often,' he says, with a chuckle, extending his other arm to include me.

'Beth said you helped with the choreography…'

'Yeah…' he says, with no shred of arrogance. 'Fabulous job when you're working with such amazing talent.'

Peter is as delightful and affable as Beth said he was.

He apologises as he's tugged away by a man hovering with a clipboard. Beth hands me a glass of champagne from the tray that is doing the rounds.

Peter used to be a dancer with the Imperial Dance Group, a spin-off from the Rambert Dance Company and he has an unusual grace, holding his chin high and his shoulders back when he moves, totally at ease with himself.

I watch him as he greets the people who have funded the project, giving each his full attention, pressing his hand against his chest and giving a half bow, accepting praise in a dignified, humble way.

He's twelve years older than Beth and shows no sign of gathering any weight around his waist. Beth says he does yoga and takes great care of his health. One thing, at least, that they have in common.

The door opens and Peter throws his arms around the conductor. 'Craig, I was blown away. Congratulations!'

He gets swept up into a group and I take a sip of my drink.

'They're bonding,' laughs Beth, knowingly. 'I'm glad it was such a good audience. Sold out apparently.'

Later, once the accolades have died down, Peter leads us out of the stage door and along to a small restaurant behind the opera house.

He's booked a table for three and there's already another bottle of champagne on ice standing in the centre. Peter draws back my chair first, a nice touch, then Beth's. He's the consummate host, explaining the Indonesian dishes on the menu and pouring water for us, once the waiter has gone.

It occurs to me that this is nothing extraordinary in his routine. Everything about him; his accent, etiquette, his small classic cufflinks and pristine knot in his tie betray a lifetime of privilege. Nevertheless, Beth says he's careful to be understated about his wealth. She had to look up his family on Google to discover that his parents own a country estate in Kent. When she asked more about them, he reluctantly told her they spend most of their time at a villa in the mountains of Vermont.

I can't believe Beth's actually going to marry him!

I'm too excited to eat and I pick at the starter, a small beetroot salad, when it arrives. It's the first time I've seen the two of them together and I'm curious about the dynamic between them. Beth told me she loves the way Peter isn't ego driven and takes a genuine interest in her. It seems he remembers exactly what she's involved with, recalls the full details of an audition or the part she's learning – a great listener.

She leans over and whispers something in his ear, then turns away and laughs. Lust saturates the aura around her – everything about her is sensual. Her alluring green eyes seem to draw Peter into a place of serenity and composure.

I feel a bittersweet stab in my stomach – the pride of knowing she's my own flesh and blood, mixed with, I have to admit it, jealousy. Beth's skin is soft, plump and tight at the same time. Mine will never be like that again, the juice has been sucked dry over time, it already has the look of a lizard about it.

She's coy with him, casting cute, teasing comments over her shoulder and he seems bowled over by her. Perhaps Peter has waited years for someone like Beth to come along. In turn, nothing about Peter is trying to impress her or demonstrate superiority. He doesn't name drop or seem to have anything to prove.

As we wait for the main course, I'm keen to know what, exactly, it is in Beth that has put a spell on him. She gets up to go to the bathroom and his eyes follow her every move, like he's watching a rare butterfly. Beth is the only person I know who glides across a room, rather than walks, adding a little hip-swing. How she manages it in those ridiculous shoes, I have no idea. I tried them on this afternoon while she was out and they're like sky-scrapers. I couldn't stand up in them, never mind sashay sexily across a crowded restaurant.

I want to stand up and punch the air. She's well and truly landed on her feet with Peter – he seems the epitome of a first-class gentleman. I couldn't wish for anything more for my only child. I only hope she recognises how lucky she is and hangs on to him.

Chapter 12

Beth

Monday, March 13

My phone beeps as I'm getting out of the shower at the pool. It's Peter again. Another racy message. He's staying at his flat, ready to jet off to New York again, next week. He wants us to do a video call, but I just can't face it. Face *him*. What I've done is written all over my face. Two massive sins – cheating on him and covering up a death. If he knew only *one* of them, he'd run a mile.

I pat myself dry and slip into my jogging gear. I remember when we were on the boat and Peter's deep bass voice vibrated through the wooden bench beneath me when he spoke. I want nothing more than to watch the way his right eyebrow tilts when he's about to make a funny quip. The way his teeth are impossibly white, all even and flawless. I'd love to have him fold his arms around me, but I don't trust myself not to break down and spill everything.

I haven't dared tell Mum my job at the quiz show has finished early. I can't break it to her so soon after she made it clear how skint we are.

I catch myself in the mirror as I go. I haven't slept and big fat slugs have taken up residence under my eyes. My hair is brittle and my skin's the colour of dirty water. I look like I've spent hours in make-up preparing for a scene in a vampire movie. I pull up the hood of my top and make a run for it, before anyone speaks to me.

My audition was a shambles. I didn't even make it into the room. After everything that's happened, I felt like shit the morning I caught the train and when they called my name, I was in the

Ladies' puking up – and that was that. There were so many people going for the part, they refused to find me a later slot. All that way for nothing.

I can't tell Mum about that either. I don't want her thinking I'm going flaky on her. I'm just pretending it went well, then in a few days I'll make out I got another rejection. Truth is, I'm finding this 'act normal' lark so bloody difficult. She seems to be forging ahead like nothing's happened and all I can think of is the moment she flew at Carl and shoved him against the barrels. I keep hearing that horrible crunching sound as his head hit the tap. It happened so fast.

I can't bear to dwell on those images, so I force myself to go back to when I first met Carl. To the time when he was larger than life, oozing seduction and making me tingle all over.

I wasn't strictly honest with Mum when I said Peter introduced me to him. That happened about an hour *after* our actual encounter at the high-profile party to celebrate the opening of the Hepworth Theatre.

It had been a tedious affair at the start. I'd had a stonking hangover from a brilliant after-show party in the West End the night before and wanted nothing more than to lie down in a darkened room. Peter, however, said it would be worth my while.

Having said that, he'd left me standing around in the ballroom while he swanned off to have 'important chats' with 'high-flying executives'. Most of the elite were huddled into established groups and whilst I made several attempts at conversation, as soon as it was obvious I wasn't anyone significant, people made excuses to walk away.

While Peter conversed with an elderly man smoking a cigar by the grand piano, I went outside onto the broad terrace overlooking the lawns, with my third glass of champagne. Ridiculous, with a hangover, but it seemed to stave off the symptoms.

There was a handful of people out here, but I sauntered towards the one individual who was alone, at the far side. He had his back to me, leaning out over the stone balustrade. A champagne glass was standing perilously at his elbow on the stone ledge. He turned when I joined him.

He looked younger than Peter, with wavy blonde hair and unsettling pale-blue eyes.

'You haven't been ordered to drag me back inside, have you?' he said with a playful grimace.

I laughed. 'Are you hiding out here?'

'Definitely. Had a dodgy curry last night and I need fresh air.'

We both turned at the distant ting of a spoon against glass. The hum inside dropped to a hush.

'Ladies and gentlemen…' a voice called out. 'It's my pleasure to introduce…'

'Oh, for crying out loud – Frank Tennerman is about to make a speech,' said my companion, with a growl.

I'd heard about Mr Tennerman and his dreary, long-winded addresses, from Peter.

'He'll drivel on for ages,' he groaned. 'I need to escape.' He took his glass and began strolling purposefully towards the steps.

'Mind if I come?' I asked, hurrying to catch up with him.

'Who are *you* hiding from?' he asked.

'Everyone,' I said.

We scurried away like two kids bunking off school.

'I'm Beth, by the way,' I said.

He held back a prickly branch at the bottom of the steps. 'Best if you don't know who I am,' he said, mysteriously. I took his reticence to mean he was a chauffeur or one of the catering staff, who should have been behind the scenes at someone's beck and call.

He took a right at the edge of the forecourt and strode through an arched iron gate into a rose garden.

The place was refreshingly deserted.

He stood impassively, staring into my face, probably a little too close.

'Now what shall we do?' he asked, lifting one eyebrow.

I was reluctant to drag my eyes away from him. His soft jawline, those unnerving wild eyes. There was something brooding about him; intense and enigmatic.

In one corner of the rose garden was an open-sided gazebo and in the other, a small white summer house. It had large windows and was clearly visible from the fountain in the centre.

'This way,' I said and headed straight for the summer house.

I could hear his footsteps right behind me: a rat following the Pied Piper. I made my decision there and then. I'd flirt with this boyish rogue for a while, simply to pass the time. I'd seen his wedding ring. It would be a one-off. No one would know. What harm could it do?

Once inside, he closed the door and turned to me. He didn't smile, nor did he look away, but simply set his eyes on mine and wouldn't let them go.

'This is very naughty,' he whispered. 'Do you often hide in summer houses with strange men?'

'Whenever the mood takes me,' I told him, nonchalantly. I held my glass steady for a split second, level with my cleavage, then slowly raised it to my lips and took a sip.

In that moment, our juvenile caper had turned into something else.

He stood as though he was transfixed by me, as if he'd never seen anyone like me before. With a string of recent failed auditions behind me, it gave me a warm glow. I should have apologised and left straight away, but I was caught up in the thrill of it, like it was an extreme dare.

Before I knew it, I reached out and found myself touching his shirt. I stared at my hand pressed against his warm chest as if it belonged to someone else. I hadn't meant to do it. We were supposed to be just chatting.

He took my hand and led me to a spot in the shadows, beside the door. Apart from being exceedingly attractive, there was an edge to him, like a smouldering firework that I couldn't resist. Starting at my bottom lip, he ran his thumb down my body, trailing it between my breasts all the way to the inside of my thighs. The pressure was assured, but sensitive, like he was unzipping my soul. It made me melt.

'What if someone comes in?' I whispered, snatching a breath.

'We'll tell them we're playing I Spy,' he muttered, without hesitation.

I knew in my head it was wrong, but somehow it didn't feel real. I was fizzing with excitement and taken aback all in one. I'd had sex in a few unorthodox places; on sacks of grain in a windmill and at midnight in a private swimming pool, but never when there was such a high risk of being discovered. Our actions were audacious, to say the least.

I don't know why I went along with it. Probably too much champagne, but that's no excuse. I got carried away. I felt turned on and risqué, and to be honest, a tiny bit neglected by Peter, who'd been away until last week and was now spending all his time smooching with A-listers, without me.

In spite of the constrained circumstances, there was no mad scramble, nor was it over in a flash. My illicit lover took his time – he was attentive and gentle. That came as a surprise.

'Much as I'd love to spend all afternoon in here with you, I'd better get back,' he said, afterwards, buttoning up his shirt. 'My wife is here, somewhere.'

'Me, too,' I said, smoothing down my dress. 'My fiancé will be wondering where I've got to.'

As we reluctantly ambled back through the gardens, it occurred to me that I still didn't know his name.

Chapter 13

Beth

I tear myself away from the memory and slide my key into the front door. The place is silent. Mum's not working until tonight, but she must have popped out. I'm relieved I've got the place to myself.

I pour myself a glass of juice and find myself daydreaming again.

I recall how, after our diabolical naughtiness, we'd furtively reintegrated ourselves into the party. I took a seat by a tall window and chatted to a middle-aged woman about the pitfalls of stilettos on gravel. Shortly afterwards Peter found me and took me over to meet someone.

And there he was – standing beside his wife.

'This is Carl Jacobson,' he said.

Carl Jacobson! Shit!

I shook his hand, barely daring to meet his eye.

On our way here, Peter had said that of all the people here worth ingratiating myself with, Carl Jacobson was top dog. He was one of the key investors film agencies were turning to and he'd actively promoted a young actress who'd just landed a major role in a film alongside Casey Affleck.

'Carl was an undergrad at Oxford when I spent a summer there doing a short course on ballet in film,' Peter said. 'He's sometimes over in your neck of the woods, Beth, at the theatre in Winchester.'

'Really?' I said, feeling a tingle in my breasts, as if he was still touching me.

Amelia looked older than Carl, but attractive, with a polished tan and long flowing blonde hair. I found her stare unnerving, as if she knew exactly what we'd been up to.

'I was led astray,' Carl interjected, letting his gaze catch mine for the briefest of moments. 'Peter was a terrible influence.'

Peter laughed. 'We met originally in a pub, that's true. I'd just finished a run in a West End dance production – only I wasn't the one knocking back the Pimm's.' He cleared his throat in mock disapproval.

Carl held up his hands. 'It's true. I was a dreadful student.' He was natural and betrayed no awkwardness. I was convinced no one knew a thing.

A figure stole up behind Amelia and draped her arm around her neck in a sisterly fashion.

'This is Nancy,' said Amelia, holding her arms out by way of presentation. 'Our boys' godmother and my confidante…do people use that word, anymore?'

Nancy gave us a smug smile. 'I think it's *soulmate* nowadays, darling,' she said. She was holding a cigarette in an old-fashioned holder and looked close to forty, but judging by the amount of flesh on show in her low-cut dress, she was in total denial about it.

'Aren't we getting music?' Nancy asked, peeling off the thin shawl around her shoulders, which seemed slightly overzealous given it was mid-winter and the best we were getting was sunny intervals. 'Do I need to make a stir?' she added, batting her eyelids.

Amelia puckered her lips. 'You're good at making a stir, dear, why don't you go and see?'

Nancy slunk off and I caught Peter watching her bum as it wiggled its way into the distance. I glanced up at Carl to see if his eyes had followed her too, but he was looking sideways at me. I dropped my gaze instantly and turned to look at Peter.

I never meant it to be the start of anything. It should have been a one-off, a moment of madness, but in the months to come I slipped up and we met a few more times in secret.

'Why didn't you tell me sooner who you were?' I chastised, as we met for the second time, at a hotel near Green Park.

'I didn't want you to react differently to me because of my position. I wanted to see who you really were.'

When we met those subsequent times, it wasn't just about sex. He asked me about my ambitions and the parts I wanted to play.

'You've got the look directors are keen on these days,' he told me, 'fierce and fragile – it's a winning combination. A woman-child who wants to win, but who'll inevitably get hurt.'

During our subsequent encounters, I learnt that he was a generous lover who paid great attention to turning me on. I'd had boyfriends before who'd fumbled and grabbed, carried away by their own gratification, but this man was different. He had a way of teasing and tempting me that drove me delirious. He seemed instinctively in tune with my body and unique desires. It made me feel special, even though I assumed from his knowledge of the female anatomy that I must be one of many lovers – on a very long list.

There was nothing serious about what we were doing and we both agreed to call it a day as soon as I walked down the aisle. The odd thing was that none of it seemed to spoil what I had with Peter. He was still the one I'd chosen. Being with Peter was like coming home; I felt safe, secure and wrapped up in love when I was with him.

I'm idly pondering on this when there's a ring at the door.

As I open it, my throat seizes up. It's a uniformed policeman. I'm not ready for this. Where's Mum?

I stand staring at him, terrified he's about to arrest me.

'Is Mrs Rachel Kendall here?' the officer asks.

'Er…no,' I croak, my mouth dry as dust. He asks who I am and I reluctantly give my name.

My mind goes blank and I can't remember any of the lies I'm supposed to tell, all the lines I'm supposed to have learnt for this grotesque performance Mum has set up for us.

'We're visiting the area about a crime that's taken place…'

A buzzing sound fills my ears and my frantic brain makes up its own version of the rest of his sentence… *and we know all about what happened in the cellar…you were seen in the graveyard…and you're going to spend the rest of your days in prison…*

'…so we're just checking to see if you know anything about it,' he concludes.

I barely register his actual words. Instead, my mind flips over itself latching onto the fact that Mum and I never agreed on the reason I went over to Grandad's the night Carl was killed. He's going to ask me about that, I know he is.

His words come at me again. '…checking the local neighbourhood…so did you see anything?'

'Sorry?'

'The break in…at the corner shop,' he says deliberately, as if I've got learning difficulties.

'Oh, right,' I say. 'A break in? Is that all?' He must be wondering what kind of person I am, because all I can do is pat my chest and let out a stupid laugh.

'It was Friday night,' he says, 'at about seven in the evening. The owner was assaulted.'

'Oh…' My overarching thought is that Friday night is the one night I don't need to worry about. 'Mum and I were here at seven o'clock. Mrs Granger, next door, can vouch for us, she came in to collect a parcel.' It sounds far too detailed and precise, I realise, as soon as it's out of my mouth. Besides, I'm reeling it off like he's asked a different question altogether.

It's his turn to laugh. 'I'm not here to find out exactly where you were, just to find out if you saw anything at the Stop'n'Shop?'

'Oh. Right. No. I'm afraid I didn't see anything. I don't know anything about it.'

I could kick myself. So stupid.

Mum is back ten minutes later.

'A policeman was here,' I tell her before she can get through the door. 'I was shit scared.'

'What did he want? What did you tell him?' She hurries inside.

'Nothing. There was a break in at Stop'n'Shop, apparently, on Friday. He wanted to know if we saw anything.'

'What did he ask exactly?'

I recount the conversation.

'I can't believe you told him where we were, as if he was asking for an alibi!' she snaps.

'My mind was on something else. I wasn't expecting it…I panicked.'

'I can't always be with you,' she says, sounding like a schoolteacher. 'You're going to have to be strong and handle this when you're on your own.'

'I'm not useless, you know. In any case, we wouldn't be in this mess if you hadn't barged into the cellar!' I yell.

I see her hands tighten into fists. 'I think I need to remind you where this all started, my girl. *You* were the one dallying with a married man. *You* were the one playing silly sex games when you're about to marry someone else. Don't you *dare* blame me.'

'They weren't silly,' I mutter.

She ignores me. 'We've got to carry on as if none of this happened. We must forget everything about your sordid little affair and what followed. It's as simple as that.'

I storm off upstairs after that. I know she's doing this for me. I know she wants me to follow my dreams and make it as an actress, but I'm all over the place and she doesn't seem to understand how hard this is.

I can't tell anyone. That's the worst bit. I'm going through hell, having nightmares and seeing repulsive images in my head – Carl's eyes turning milky, and his heavy, lumpy body when we dropped him into the earth. I'd never seen a dead body before. At least Mum's had practice with Russell. Then there was the musty smell of the rug we wrapped him in. I can't seem to shift that out of my nostrils, either. I just want to run and tell people how awful it was: Maria, Tina…Peter. I want to scream it from the deepest hollows of my lungs. As time goes on, I can't be certain I'm going to be able to keep my mouth shut.

Chapter 14

Rachel

'I can't believe you invited Peter here without asking me!'

'I thought you'd be over the moon, sweetheart, given how little you've seen of each other lately,' I retorted. I hadn't expected Beth's face to fall.

'How can I be chatty and light-hearted when this horrible mess is the only thing I can think about,' she snapped.

'I thought it would be just what you needed…to refocus on your future.'

She glared at me. 'You seem so…unaffected…'

'Believe me, that's not true. I'm struggling in my own way.' I don't want her to know how many hours I've prowled around the house at night, how many times I've had to rush to the loo because my digestive system wants to explode; the palpitations, the sweating whenever I see a police car. But if I buckle under, we'll be in real trouble. I have to be strong, to hold everything together for our own safety.

'It's just the timing's terrible,' she muttered.

I didn't mention that the real reason for inviting Peter for lunch is to have a long-overdue conversation about the wedding finances before my bank account is bled dry.

Beth's face is deathly white when she answers the door. I stand to one side, behind her.

'Wow, I'd forgotten how similar you look, like peas in a pod!' Peter says as he offers me a hug instead of a formal handshake.

'Thanks for coming all this way,' I tell him, as I invite him into the sitting room.

The first thing I notice is how expensive he smells. Not just his aftershave, but a 'just showered' kind of fragrance that's slightly peppery. I feel the fabric of his suit against my chin, spot the high shine on his handmade shoes and I can't avoid feeling utterly relieved that Beth will have this level of luxury for herself soon. Only then can I stop fretting about being so hopelessly ill-equipped to give her a good start in life. There's no two ways about it – Peter, with all his wealth and good standing behind him is going to get us out of a mess.

We can't afford to take him out to eat, so I've prepared one of my speciality dishes, hoping he likes coq-au-vin made with budget ingredients. I'm lucky there's a bottle of wine left over from Russell's wake to put on the table.

He's brought a bunch of velvety red roses for Beth and a bottle of Cognac for me.

I invite him to sit at our only table – the one we dragged through from the kitchen, an hour ago. He takes off his jacket, hooking it carefully over the back of the chair. Beth is in a hurry to pour us all a glass of wine before he's even got settled and I sit with the two of them as I wait for the oven timer to ping.

Peter is obviously delighted to see Beth, but he's gracious enough to ask lots of questions that only I can answer; about the house, my job, the cooking.

His next comment is about my skirt. 'Lovely colour – really suits you.'

'Oh, it's an old one of Beth's that she never wears,' I tell him.

'Would you call that shade turquoise, teal, or petrol, do you think?'

I smile. It's good to have a banal conversation about shades of blue after the brittle exchanges Beth and I have been having lately.

Peter's sensitive, hooded eyes are never still. They find their way into every corner of the room, making me feel self-conscious about how lowly this place looks with its cracked tiles around the fireplace and threadbare carpets. More to the point, his eyes track every fold and curve of Beth's body.

He and Beth continue the discussion about the colour of my skirt while I dish up the main course. Since Russell's death, I've lost nearly a stone in weight, so that many of my dressy garments hang like sacks on me – hence turning to Beth's wardrobe. I was tempted to put up my hair for Peter's visit, only realising in time that it might seem like I was trying to emulate her.

He's diplomatic about our cramped home, making me feel like he's touched to have been invited. He pretends not to notice that we keep banging our ankles under the table, because it's so small. He says all the right things about the meal, too. Beth leans against him, nuzzling into his neck and takes his hand under the tablecloth, but she isn't her usual carefree self. She seems to me like she's trying too hard.

As I watch the two of them eat, I wonder how compatible they are. It's not the first time I've tried to figure out what they might have in common, apart from a love of keeping fit. It's only been nine months since they met, and everything happened inordinately fast between them. Furthermore, they've had extended periods apart. How can they really know each other?

Beth needs to mix with lots of people and has strong attachments to key friends. Will Peter want to whisk her away from them and have her all to himself? As I wipe my mouth with my napkin, I wonder if I should be concerned.

When I bring through the lemon-meringue pie for dessert, he asks about Beth's latest audition.

'Oh, I had an email this morning,' she says, 'I didn't get a callback. They said they wanted someone who was more "effortless".' She sends her eyes to the ceiling, then glances across at me. 'That's probably why I'm a bit quiet.'

I don't react, even though I know nothing about this. A wave of dizziness hits me when I realise that, before long, I'll never be the first person to hear her news.

After lunch, Peter suggests we take a walk. He seems to know his way around and leads us past Winchester College and along the river towards the top of the high street.

'I need to ask you both something,' he says, stopping on the bridge beside the old mill.

He looks serious. 'Since we booked the registry office, I've had a chat with my mother. This is a bit tricky, but…' He runs his tongue under his top teeth. 'I'm thinking of changing the venue. How would you feel about that?'

I jump in before Beth can respond, seeing only escalating pound signs before my eyes. 'Wouldn't it be too late to book somewhere else at this stage?'

'Well…' he smiles, putting his arms around both of us. 'I've actually had a chat with someone this morning, just in case you were happy to go ahead.'

I clear my throat and bite the bullet. 'I'm just a bit concerned about the costs of everything,' I tell him.

There, I've said it.

'Oh, don't worry about that.' He flaps his hand. 'We'll take care of all the wedding costs at our end. Everything. I should have said sooner, I'm sorry.'

'Oh…right…' I feel tremendous embarrassment that I'm not in a position to argue with him, nevertheless a huge weight tumbles off my shoulders.

'Send me all the wedding payments to date, okay? Every last penny.' His eyes rest on mine and I have no doubt he means what he says.

He points ahead of us. 'Let's take a look at the place I've got in mind, shall we? Follow me.'

It doesn't take me long to realise we're heading straight for St Andrew's Church. Beth must have mentioned my connection there at some stage. As I'm a member of the church and mother of the bride, they would be entitled to marry there.

Beth stiffens as we approach, then hovers at the gate, is if we're about to enter a field full of bulls.

'Here?' she mutters. I see her swallowing hard.

'Don't you think it looks perfect?' Peter says with a chuckle.

Beth puts her hand over her mouth. 'I can't…I'm really sorry.' She gives me an imploring stare, then backs away. 'Actually, I don't feel too well.' She clutches her stomach and hurries out of sight.

We find her outside the florists a few doors down, chewing her thumbnail. I go to put my arm around her, but Peter gets there first and pulls her away from me. For an instant I feel put out. I'm not used to someone else being the first port of call for her and it stings. It's something else I'm going to have to get used to, though, because after April 15th, she'll be gone for good.

I trail my fingers across the arm of her jacket. Not long ago, it occurred to me in a flash of horror that she might even move to America, given Peter's connections there, although I haven't mentioned it to Beth for fear of putting the idea into her head.

'You don't like it?' he asks her gently, lifting Beth's chin with his finger. 'It's my fault. We haven't really discussed it properly, have we?'

Beth looks dazed, as if he's speaking in another language.

'It's not that,' Beth tells him, a deep frown taking over her face. 'Isn't there another church? It's just…'

I step in. 'This one might be difficult…' I say, 'for me, that is.' I take a moment. 'Russell was buried here.'

'My goodness, I had no idea,' Peter says, turning to face me.

I drop my head. 'No…it's…don't worry,' I say.

'I knew you lost your partner, of course, but…no…I'm so dreadfully sorry…we'll leave things as they were.'

'Unless we can find another church at short notice?' says Beth.

'I'll look into it,' he says, patting my arm. 'I do apologise.'

Beth squeezes my finger in gratitude.

I link arms with her on one side, just as Peter does on the other. We each walk either side of the greatest treasure in our lives, returning to the house for coffee, before he has to catch his train back to London. As I'm pouring from the cafetiere, Peter's phone chirps.

'That's odd,' he says, reading the message. 'It's the wife of a friend of mine.' He addresses Beth. 'You've met them: Amelia and Carl.' Beth's hand visibly shakes as she reaches for the jug of cream. She puts it down hastily.

'What's happened?' I say in a bland tone usually reserved for conveying polite interest.

'Amelia's had to call in the police. Carl's gone missing. She's not heard from him in over a week.'

Chapter 15

Beth

I've been bracing myself all along for this moment. I knew that following Carl's disappearance, the police would be brought in with their metaphorical searchlights blazing. They'd start probing Carl's final movements: who he was with, where he was going – and Mum and I would need to be on our guard for potential scrutiny. Just in case.

We're meant to be ready for this.

Once I've walked Peter back to the station, Mum makes me sit down beside her.

'The police won't come to speak to us, will they?' I ask her for the umpteenth time.

'I can't think of any reason why they should, but the more we expect them, the more prepared we'll be.'

Mum's trying to sound cool and collected, but it's all a front. I can hear the catch in her voice.

'It's a long time to notice your husband isn't around,' she adds, looking puzzled. 'The accident was over a week ago.'

Mum seems to have settled on calling the whole situation 'the accident', as though what took place was an unfortunate event we had no control over. As though it could have happened to anyone. I know what she's doing, she's trying to take the sting out of it, but it doesn't fool me.

Mum takes me through our stories once more, but I'm not really concentrating. What's worrying me is that Peter appears to know Carl and Amelia a lot better than I thought he did. I thought they were only acquaintances. The last thing I want to do, though, is draw this to Mum's attention.

'I'm going to my room,' I tell her, and slip away before she can object.

It was difficult seeing Peter for lunch. I wanted to tell him the whole story. I wanted him to wrap me up in his arms and tell me everything was going to be all right. But, of course, I couldn't mention a word of it.

Moreover, seeing him again made me feel overwhelmingly ashamed. What Carl and I got up to in the last two months was terribly wrong. It was barefaced cheating, but Carl had a weird hold over me right from that first meeting. For sure, he was a playboy, but there was something dark and dangerous about him that I couldn't resist.

With the news from Amelia, I'm flung right back into the vivid flashbacks. If only she knew. Carl's body laying lifeless on the cellar floor. Having to move him. That was bad enough, but it didn't end there; creeping around the graveyard in the dead of night with spades. Totally sick! All so I can marry Peter.

With the pub still closed, Mum's been at home a lot, fidgeting all the time, picking things up and putting them down again. She keeps asking how I'm coping and I'm finding it claustrophobic. It's all we seem to talk about and it's doing my head in.

I change out of my posh dress and comb out my hair. Having spent most of the morning before Peter arrived at the gym, I'm at a loss as to what to do. I'm waiting for the worst to happen.

I can't stand it any longer.

With no job anymore, I'm going to escape for a bit and take a bus over to see my grandfather.

Mum is flitting around with a duster when I leave.

'Apart from checking how he is,' she says, 'it will give you a genuine visit you can tell the police about.'

Even Mum's comment about Grandad is really about Carl.

The bus trundles through open countryside between villages. I try to switch off and lose myself in the wispy branches on either side, coming to life now it's Spring, but all I can think is that this is the journey I'm supposed to have taken on the night Carl was killed.

I pull myself back to the present and focus for a moment on where Peter and I might go for our honeymoon. We haven't talked about it yet. I don't know whether his idea of a dream getaway would be Iceland or India or whether he'd prefer a world cruise. Does he ski? I have no idea. Would he like to see a Formula One race or watch a performance of Cirque du Soleil, while we're away? I haven't a clue. All in all, it's becoming clearer to me that we've barely scratched the surface in our discussions.

Seconds later, Peter phones me from the train. He wants to know Mum's favourite flowers, so he can send her a bouquet to thank her for lunch. He's so giving and thoughtful. I do love him. I can't believe I've betrayed him so badly.

Before I know it, he's talking about Carl again. 'He's gone missing before,' he tells me, 'so it may not be too serious. Sometimes he disappears on the yacht for an impromptu break. Amelia said on one occasion he didn't even tell her, he just took off because he didn't want to be contacted. She's got used to his free-spirited attitude, but I can't say I approve.'

This news should buy us time and make me feel better, but it doesn't. Sooner or later, it will become clear that Carl *isn't* swanning around topping up his tan in the Bahamas. There's no way he's coming back from the place he's gone to.

'I hope he gets his act together before the wedding,' Peter adds. 'He's my best man.'

Best man!

'I didn't know that…' The words slip out. I didn't mean to say them out loud.

Why didn't I know they were such good friends? Carl must have played it down, but then he would, wouldn't he? He wouldn't have wanted to bring my fiancé into the equation left, right and centre.

He's speaking again. 'I've been doing a ring-round on my journey home and I've found us another church. It's on the opposite side of the city: St James's. Know it?'

I can't picture it from the name, but I conjure up an old chapel with melodic bells ringing out, splashes of bright colours cast across the floor through the stained glass and a smell of lavender furniture polish.

'I'm sure it will be perfect,' I tell him.

Shame we didn't get to choose it together, but at least his mother will be happy.

I'm so busy daydreaming about our special day, I almost miss my stop and charge down the aisle of the bus just in time. Out here, in the middle of nowhere, there are big gaps between stops and I don't want to have to walk back for miles.

Grandad is leaning over the water butt in his front garden, fiddling with the downpipe when I arrive. In the last few years, Mum has called him 'Adrian'. It's since he started getting Mum and his long-dead wife, Vera, mixed up. It got to the point where he would only answer when she used the same name that Vera used for him. Mum only calls him 'Dad' these days, if she's angry or upset with him.

I never knew my own dad. Mum fell for a 'lovely boy' – that's always the way she describes him – when she was only fifteen, but he took off when she got pregnant, so that part is blank on my birth certificate. There are no photographs of him and she's never even told me his name. Maybe I chose an older man like Peter because there's always been a hole in my life where my father should have been.

It's so sad to watch Grandad losing his marbles. Mum said he didn't recognise her when she came over last time, but he waves and smiles when he sees me trot up the path.

'Hello you,' he says. 'Cuppa?'

I bring the bag I've been hiding behind my back into view. 'Ta-da…left-over lemon meringue pie.'

He makes a satisfied chewing sound, *yum-yum-yum*, like a child.

I save time by boiling the kettle myself. Simple tasks like making drinks and getting dressed take him ages. He stops to think halfway through, then loses his way, then starts another job without finishing the first one. Nevertheless, having exchanged a few sensible sentences with him already, today seems like it's a 'good' day for him.

'Way-way said your young man was coming over for lunch,' he says, as we sit in a thin band of sunshine in his lean-to, using teaspoons to eat the pie. He always calls Mum Way-way; apparently, she couldn't say Rachel when she was little and her attempt at it stuck. It makes me think that Peter and I don't have nicknames for each other.

'I can't wait for you to meet him, Grandad. You'll like him. He's so warm and bright to be with. I'm so looking forward to starting our new life together.'

'You're a lucky girl. Way-way said he's going to put you on the stage.'

'Well,' I laugh, 'he knows the right people, so hopefully I can get my foot in the door and finally start acting. But I want to blossom as an actress in my own right, not just because Peter is behind me.'

'Of course.'

'I'm not marrying him because of his position, you know. That's just going to be a bonus.'

He finishes his mouthful, grinning. 'Your mum is so excited about your big day.'

I smile back. I know only too well. Giving her the job of 'wedding-planner' was the best thing for her in the circumstances.

'She was in hell when that man of hers passed away…what was his name?' he asks.

'Russell.'

'That's the one.' He nods to himself. 'It was a beautiful gift you gave her – agreeing to marry your young man.'

I nod. 'I knew she'd like Peter.'

'It's all she talks about,' he says. 'I've seen such a difference in her – totally uplifted since you set a date.'

It's true, although Grandad doesn't know the half of it. After Russell passed away, I used to hear Mum crying in bed every night.

It was about time she turned a corner. I'd hoped that by telling her we were going to tie the knot, it would brighten up her world and it worked a treat. If Mum hadn't been in such a bad way, I think I might have waited until Peter and I had been together for far longer.

'Better than traipsing over to that graveyard every day,' he says. 'I don't think it's good for her, standing in the rain talking to dead people. This marriage is all about new beginnings.'

He's making a lot of sense today, as if there's nothing wrong with him. These days are rare. Usually, there's something that needs sorting out. Last time, an unaccountable mound of soaking-wet towels had been dumped in the bath and he'd spilt fabric softener all over the kitchen floor. Mum and I keep a few of our things, old clothes mainly, in a chest of drawers in the box room, so we can do spur-of-the-moment jobs without getting our outfits dirty.

He asks me about plays and films I've seen and if I've got any auditions coming up.

'I've got two soon from a list Peter sent me, but to be honest, I'm finding it hard to concentrate on learning my lines at the moment with…' I stop myself just in time.

'Yep…because of the wedding,' he says, with a knowing smile.

I draw a breath and compose myself. Since Carl's death, my mind has been full of holes. I nearly slipped up. I must be more careful. Once Peter and I get married, it'll be easier. I'll be away from here and can immerse myself in my new life. I just need to hang on in the meantime and hold my nerve.

'Your mother didn't think I knew about it, but I did,' he adds.

I wait, wondering whether I've missed something or if his mind has reached a junction inside his head and has veered off.

He taps his nose, conspiratorially. 'I didn't know everything, but I knew enough.'

'Knew what, Grandad?'

'It was in the news.'

A shiver coils its way up the back of my neck. 'What are you talking about?'

'When the bad thing happened…in Southampton.'

I pat his hand. His brain must have got stuck at a signal box and his train of thought has taken a branch line towards Timbuktoo.

When I get back Mum is folding ironing. We never iron in our house. She must have been desperate to occupy herself.

'How was he?'

'He's fine, mostly. He's excited about the wedding. He went a bit vague before I left.'

'Going on about Vera, no doubt?'

'No. It was something else. He mentioned a "bad thing in Southampton".'

She stops what she's doing and stands completely still. 'What did he say exactly?'

'That was it. There was something bad in Southampton, he said, but then he lost the plot and I didn't understand anything after that.'

'Maybe it's not such a good idea for you to be going over to see him on your own, Beth.'

'Why? He's doing really well – it's just now and again he gets confused.'

'I don't want you getting upset.'

'I'm not a kid, Mum, it's fine.'

I go up to my room and out of habit log onto social media. I haven't felt like sharing my usual tweets and posts since 'the accident' and I glance at the messages that have been piling up. Hundreds of them, by now.

They all seem so inane after what's happened, and I can't bring myself to respond to any of them. Instead, I find myself looking up Amelia's name to see if there's anything I need to know, but as her page is loading, I come straight out of it. I've seen enough TV detective dramas to know I mustn't leave a trail. It's just the kind of stupid mistake the police could jump on, if we were ever suspected of being involved.

I lie on the bed clutching my phone.

Carl and I were careful, weren't we? It was *always* him who contacted me and never the other way around. He made a point of using different phones – payphones on the street or at the Underground, never his work phone or personal line. No messages or emails either. It was the rule he insisted on to avoid detection. At least Mum doesn't have to worry about that.

She insists we're in the clear, but my stomach keeps getting flooded with waves of nausea. What if someone found out about Carl and me? What if he let something slip by accident? I just hope he hasn't left anything lying around that might lead prying eyes to connect the two of us together.

All of a sudden, my heart bolts into overdrive. Now I'm putting it under scrutiny, I realise in horror that I'm wrong about never calling Carl's number.

There was just that once.

Chapter 16

Rachel

I'm caught between a rock and a hard place. I want to encourage Beth to see her friends and speak to Peter, so it looks like nothing's wrong, but I'm worried about her state of mind. In a moment of weakness, might she let our terrible secret out of the bag?

I used to be concerned that she was always on social media – sharing, posting, chatting – wherever she might be. I was afraid she'd never learn how to be on her own, to enjoy her own company and relax into who she is, always turning outside herself for stimulus. In the past week, however, she's cut herself off from everyone as far as I can tell. I have to confess, I'm relieved. It means one less thing to worry about. On the other hand, she doesn't appear to be knuckling down to any work either, just pacing about looking miserable.

And now Adrian has made himself off-limits for another reason entirely! Why on earth is he bringing up all that old stuff now? From now on, I'll need to be there when Beth goes to see him. I can't allow him to give away any further details about what happened in Southampton all those years ago.

The pub reopens today, and I start work tomorrow, which is a terrific relief. Marvin's pleased with all the refurbishments – the paintwork is 'fennel grey', a popular heritage colour for shabby-chic bars these days, and there's a new logo on all our publicity. We're rebranding ourselves as a gastropub, but we've still got the cask ale, old timber beams and open fireplace to preserve the traditional tavern feel. It's got a snug feel to it now, with crates of antique books stacked in the alcoves and candles on the tables. Even ancient maps in frames on the walls, like an old sitting room.

There's a fresh oriental rug in front of the fire replacing the one we took to wrap around Carl. The place is transformed – I love it – and all trace of him has gone.

My fellow barmaids, Gilly and Paula, have been in touch about the rotas and the sooner I throw myself into pulling pints, wiping down tables and discussing football results and TV soaps with punters, the better. Things really can go back to how they should be.

Kate, my closest friend, calls as I'm about to start vacuuming my bedroom.

'How are the wedding plans going?' she asks. I can hear her chewing. She's one of those incredibly slim women who always seems to be eating something.

'Oh, great news – Peter is paying for everything, so that's a huge weight off my mind.' Kate is privy to all my deepest secrets, barring one or two.

'Did the lunch go well? Still think he's the bees-knees for Beth?'

I move downstairs out of Beth's earshot. 'He's wonderful. He really is. He's clearly besotted with Beth and seems clean-cut and honourable, somehow. He doesn't try to lead or take control, but there's something almost regal about him that invites you to put him centre stage.'

'Cripes – sounds a bit daunting, if you ask me.' There's a rustle in the background; she's either munching her way through a packet of cheese and onion crisps or chunks of peanut brittle. I make a bet with myself that it's the latter.

'Not at all. He's really easy to be with. Ever so thoughtful and dripping with charisma.'

There's an odd silence and I wonder if she thinks I'm a little too keen on him.

I ask Kate about her new job. She and her husband have just taken over a farm shop outside Winchester, selling organic vegetables and everything you need in a salad.

'It's seven days a week at the moment as we're covering the Hampshire farmers' markets every weekend.' I picture her speaking to me from the front seat of their new delivery van, dressed in her trademark khaki dungarees.

'You'll do brilliantly. You always work so hard.'

Kate and I met at a Halloween party, years ago. Someone stole her bag and I gave her the taxi fare home. A day or so later, a stunning orchid arrived on my doorstep, with *Thank you* written in sequins and her phone number on the card. Since then, we've always been each other's chief cheerleaders.

'I've forgotten what it's like to sleep in beyond 6am,' she says, 'and I'm stuffing my face with snacks all the time to keep me going.'

'Peanut brittle,' I say, pointedly.

'Oh, blast! Am I that predictable?' She dissolves into laughter. 'Seriously, though, we're hiring people to help out soon and I wondered if Beth might like to have a go at one of the market stalls. She's so good with people and you've been talking lately about getting extra work.'

'Oh…nice idea, thanks…but Beth is a bit tied up with the wedding now. And getting her to focus on anything other than bridal magazines as well as auditions is impossible!'

I hate lying to Kate, but I can't risk Beth being around lots of people right now. Not until she's on an even keel.

'Is she excited about her hen do? What have you got planned?'

Hen do…

I'm caught completely off guard. 'Oh…I think it will be a pretty small affair.' I'd forgotten all about it. 'Probably just a pub do.'

'I thought Beth was going to do something wild. Last time I saw her, she was talking about a Bollywood dance spectacular or a Flamenco night.'

'Really? I doubt it. I think she's going for something more low-key. Besides, we're on a budget. I can't expect Peter to pay for the hen night – he's paying for everything else.'

'Even if he doesn't, Beth can do better than a night in a pub, can't she?' She lets out a groan. 'She's not going all strait-laced and boring now she's marrying into nobility, is she?'

'Peter's not nobility! Beth is…she's just…' I can't find the words. As I hesitate, I hear Beth's footsteps as she pads in her bare feet from her bedroom across to the airing cupboard. It's such a familiar, comforting sound and a spike of guilt jabs against my breastbone. Am I expecting too much of Beth? She's only twenty-three. What am I putting her through?

'Rachel? You there?'

I know if I speak again my voice will break, but I'm saved by someone ringing the doorbell.

'I'll call you straight back,' I tell her.

It's Father Roland from St Andrew's. He looks solemn, rolling his hands around each other, his shoulders hunched.

All the muscles in my face freeze. 'Come in,' I say, standing back. 'Is everything all right?'

'I've got some bad news, I'm afraid. I wanted to see you first before you came to the church.'

'What's happened?'

'It's about the grave,' he says.

A rush of heat floods my face from the neck up. I've invited him to sit, but he remains on his feet. I sit instead, my knees suddenly incapable of keeping me steady.

'The grave has been disturbed,' he says. 'It's hooligans. They've vandalised it.'

I can't breathe. 'The grave…'

All I can see is Judy Welsh's coffin and the uninvited guest who is now keeping her company down there.

'Yes…Russell's grave,' he says.

'Oh, Russell…' A surge of relief makes me want to blow out a heavy breath, but I drop my head and cover my mouth to hide it. 'What have they done?'

'There's graffiti on the headstone and the turf has been dug up…only a little. Thugs with nothing better to do, I'm afraid. The police said the graveyard at St Lawrence's has also been targeted.'

I close my eyes, finding no words.

He bends over towards me, resting his hand on my shoulder. 'Russell…himself…hasn't been disturbed.' I feel his breath in my hair. 'I'm so sorry, my dear. It might be best if you don't come to the church for a day or two, until we put everything straight.'

'Oh…okay…'

'Is there anything I can do?' He says, standing upright, his palms together. 'Apart from sort it out and pray, of course.'

'Thank you. No…I…'

He nods and makes a move towards the door.

'Was it just…was Russell's grave the only one?' I say, following him.

'Er, no. Two or three have been randomly attacked, by the looks of it.'

'Which ones?'

'Don't you worry about that, Rachel. In a day or two, no one will be able to tell there's been any problem.'

After he's gone, I hesitate about calling Kate back until I see that, for once, it's reasonable for me to be agitated and upset. Nevertheless, I keep my call short. What I really want to do is dash over to St Andrew's to see if Judy Welsh's grave has been disturbed. Father Roland will surely have reported it to the police, so they will certainly be sniffing around. It's the one place I don't want them to be.

Kate wants to come with me to the church, but I lie and tell her I can't face it, right now. In truth, I need to go on my own, once I've primed myself in case there's any fallout.

Beth comes down the stairs and sees the look of anguish on my face.

'What's happened? Who was at the door?' she says, dropping the trainers she's carrying.

'It's nothing, only Kate,' I say, waving away her concerns. Another lie. 'Asking about your hen night and we haven't got anything arranged properly, have we?'

'I don't want one,' she says flatly.

'Of course, you do. You have to have one.'

'Why?'

'Because we already said we would and we mustn't do anything out of character.'

'All right, then. I'll just hire a room and have a karaoke or something.'

'Okay. That'll be fine. We need to fix a venue and send out invitations.'

Beth slumps into the chair by the fireplace. Sending out invitations looks like the last thing in the world she wants to do. I go over to join her and kneel at her feet, resting my hands on her knees. As soon as I touch her, she starts to cry.

'I'm sorry, Mum. I'm not very good at this.'

'It's okay. I'm so sorry you're having to go through it.'

'I'm supposed to be getting married in a few weeks and I feel like shit.'

She's been wearing the same jogging bottoms and hooded top for days, which is so unlike her. Usually she's parading around in vintage or 'statement' outfits that she changes every five minutes.

An image of her at the age of three wearing a lime-green Tinkerbell outfit comes to mind. She used to rehearse little songs and dances to perform at Christmas and birthday parties, dressing up as cowgirls, fairies, Cherokee Indians. That sparky young thing seems a long way away, right now.

'I know you thought I was in danger, but we should never have done what we did.' She picks her nails and doesn't look up. 'I know you thought you were protecting me, but I was in shock afterwards and wish I'd never gone along with burying Carl.'

'I couldn't come up with anything better. We needed a place where no one would find him. All I could think was that no one would go looking for a body in a graveyard.'

'You seemed so...ruthless. So, overbearing. It was like there was no other choice.'

I bite my tongue. She doesn't know why I reacted so fast. She has no idea about what it triggered in me.

Not for the first time I consider what this tortuous episode has done to her mental health. In any other circumstances, if she wasn't eating, not sleeping and spending hours in isolation, I'd suggest she see a counsellor straightaway. Beth's a talker and finding a safe place to express her feelings would be the obvious step when she's in such a bad way. But not in this case. Not when any counsellor would invite her to tell the truth. In our situation, the truth is not up for grabs. It's the one path we have to avoid. For Beth and for our future. And for me.

'Have you thought about writing down how you feel, somewhere private and safe?' I propose, instead.

'Not really.'

'It's an idea, as long as it's totally secure – not online or a notebook under your pillow!'

She lets out a weak laugh.

'I kept a journal after Russell died, you know? It was like a special place I could let off steam and be totally myself. I burnt it a few months ago.'

'I didn't know,' she says, looking taken aback. 'You could have talked to me instead.'

'I didn't want to burden you. I didn't want my sadness to be the first thing you found every time you came home. You've been trying to prep for auditions. You've needed inspiration and encouragement, not being forced to sit with me being miserable. I didn't want to bring you down.'

'That's life, though, isn't it?' she says, stroking my hair. 'You can't just pretend it's rosy all the time.'

At times her sensitivity chokes me.

A vision of the two of us curling up on the sofa to watch a mushy film together comes to mind; cosy in our dressing gowns, dipping our fingers into a bowl of popcorn nestling between us.

We haven't done that for a long time.

***

While Beth goes to the pool for a long swim, I slip out to the church to witness the damage for myself, wearing a headscarf and sunglasses.

Breezing along the path by the back gate, I glance surreptitiously at the graves. A group of people surrounded by buckets and wearing rubber gloves are scrubbing away at Russell's headstone. It makes me want to weep that a bunch of idiots have done this to him. Another grave in the row in front, and one alongside it, have also been sprayed with white paint. I can't read the words. I don't want to know what's been written.

I shift my gaze a few feet.

Judy's grave is untouched as far as I can tell.

I turn and hurry home, but I'm not reassured. Just a random attack? What if the vandals come back and do a better job of things next time?

Chapter 17

Beth

I don't want to be here. Standing around in the chilly conservatory of a huge house trying to look composed and interesting. I've got goosebumps on my arms as though a troop of biting ants is crawling all over me.

I can't believe I let Mum push me into this, but she said it would take too much explaining if I didn't come.

'This could be your last chance to see Peter before he goes to America,' she told me. 'It would look terribly odd if you didn't jump at the opportunity. He's obviously gone to a lot of trouble to make sure the right people will be there: important people for your career.'

The party is being held in the posh end of Wimbledon to celebrate a British film that did well last month at the Oscars. All kinds of important film people are here; actors, producers, casting directors, names I've actually seen on the screen. I'm meant to be bubbling with enthusiasm and fawning over everyone, but I just want to curl up and hide in a cupboard under the stairs.

My re-heeled stilettos clack on the white tiled floor, making a sound like someone is using a typewriter behind me the whole time. I keep being shuffled from one gathering to the next, trying to keep up my plastic smile. The worst part is that Peter insisted I wear the same backless dress I wore when I first met Carl. It even *smells* of Carl. I want to rip it off and make a run for it.

Peter looks in his element drifting from group to group, making witty comments and offering congratulations. Everyone seems to love him; smiling, touching his arm, his shoulder. They all want a piece of him. Soon I'll have him all to myself.

As figures mill around, the constant twirling of champagne flutes, wafting parlour palms and array of Ming vases make me feel dizzy. This is what it must feel like to be royalty, always having to be gracious and polite no matter how you feel inside. Everything reminds me of the day I first met Carl and there's a nauseous coating at the back of my throat the whole time, as though I keep expecting him to walk in.

Peter's doing his utmost to introduce me to people, his hand tenderly on my back. I'm all too aware this is a great way to let people in the know 'discover' me, if only I could relax.

'Parties are a great way to showcase you,' Peter told me some time ago. 'Producers often have a particular "look" in mind for a film and that can often be the overriding factor, even though there may be more talented actresses around.'

I'm sure he didn't mean it, but it felt like a subtle way of reminding me I've got a long way to go before I even make it into the celebrity 'D list'.

He went on. 'Right now, the "waif-child" look is exactly what many of them are looking for.'

I'm sick of hearing that stupid description.

Peter reaches past me to tap the elbow of a man laughing at his own joke.

'Jeremy, how are you? You must meet my fiancé, Beth Kendall, she's fending off offers by the truck load.'

Jeremy has got a thick grey moustache turning orange at the edges and his skin is craggy. Ravaged by too much alcohol, I deduce, and the effects of smoking cigars.

Jeremy does me the courtesy of half turning towards me and looking me up and down in a cursory fashion. 'Fending off which offers, exactly?'

I draw a breath, but for once I have no idea how I'm going to reply. Thankfully, Peter steps in.

'Just about everything. She's able to pick and choose…so we're waiting for the right part to launch you, aren't we?' He gives my waist a pat. I feel like a poodle at a dog show as faces turn and eyes appraise me.

Normally, I'd say something outspoken at a time like this to show people what I'm made of, but my head is full of images from the night we buried Carl. There's no room for anything else.

'Jeremy used to work at Paramount. He's back in the UK launching a new production company.'

'But I'm always on the lookout for new talent, my boy. We're in pre-production on a mood piece right now with a European ambiance to it. Do you speak Italian, my dear?'

'Er…not really,' I tell him.

Argh! I should have replied using the teeny bit of Italian I actually *do* know. I should have said I'm a fast learner.

'Ah…shame.'

I can't believe I'm being so meek and pathetic. What's happening to me?

'I'll bear you in mind for the future,' Jeremy adds in a throwaway tone that doesn't ring true. 'Email me your details,' he says over his shoulder. He's obviously not sufficiently interested to pull himself away from his little clique. 'Better still, get Peter to do it. I get so much rubbish in my inbox, I'd probably delete it unless I recognised the name.' With that he turns his back on me.

'Don't worry,' Peter tells me, leading me away. 'They're all too big for their boots when they're doing well. When his next film flops, he'll come grovelling back to me.'

Peter waves at someone on the far side of the room and tells me he'll be back in a moment. I drift towards the conservatory desperate for some air and on the way I pass the group we've just left, their backs to me, but sufficiently close to overhear one of them speaking.

'She seemed a bit gormless, if you ask me,' I pick up.

'… and the problem with this woman-child trend is that it has a shelf-life,' someone says, 'in a couple of years she'll lose those carved cheek bones and no one will look at her.'

'I don't like that pale, sunken look anyway…'

As if that isn't exasperating enough, I get to the patio and freeze. I recognise her from that first party when I met Carl.

It's Amelia. Beside her is Nancy, her friend, who was introduced to us, last time.

Amelia has tired chalky circles under her eyes and she looks distressed, her arms punching angular movements like she's fighting her way out of an invisible bag.

I turn to retrace my steps, but Peter is right behind me, urging me forward.

'Good idea,' he says, linking my arm, 'it's stuffy inside.'

Within seconds, he's seen Amelia and is heading over. It'll look odd if I don't go with him.

He reaches out and gives her a hug. 'Any news?'

'Nothing,' she says, air-kissing the space alongside his ear. 'I was just telling Nancy, the police won't do anything because he's gone AWOL before.'

'And he doesn't have a history of depression,' adds Nancy, knowingly. Her hair is a shade too dark for strawberry blonde, edging it into the orange category, which clashes with today's salmon-coloured jumpsuit. On the plus side, the outfit matches her flushed cheeks.

'What about his bank accounts?' Peter asks.

'He hasn't accessed any of them,' says Amelia. 'That's what worries me...when he swans off somewhere it's never cheap. He hasn't booked any flights or made any new travel arrangements.'

'And he's not answering anyone's calls or emails,' Nancy chips in, tapping ash from the cigarette in its holder, onto the floor. Her cloying perfume is making me feel peaky.

Nancy turns to me. 'Did you know Carl?' she asks, innocently, blowing smoke out of the side of her mouth while glancing down at my dress. She hasn't moved an inch, yet seems to be right in my face.

I'm starting to feel giddy.

'Oh, no. Well...' I glance at Peter, 'I've met him, but...just... you know...'

God, I'm so hopeless at this. I've always been brilliant at bluffing. I got an A+ for improvisation at college and was always fooling Mum and Russell whenever we played card games. Since 'the accident' I've completely lost the knack of thinking on my feet.

'He had important meetings he should have been at by now,' says Peter. 'It's not like him.'

I gulp down a sip of champagne to avoid having to say anything.

Nancy grips Amelia's arm. 'He's not having an affair, is he?'

'Nancy, please!' snaps Amelia, spilling her drink as she recoils.

Nancy totters in her heels. 'Well, it would be preferable to…you know…and let's face it, he's not exactly a novice in that department.'

'He hasn't strayed for a long time,' Amelia says defiantly, running a finger around the rim of her glass.

'Maybe that's the answer, then. He's overdue.' Nancy throws back the rest of her glass in one inelegant swig.

'What about his phone? Can't the police trace it and find out where he is?' Peter asks.

All of a sudden, the ground is giving way.

His phone. I'd forgotten about that. *Where is it?*

It was in his jacket when we were in the cellar…I think…or was it in his trousers? What happened to it after that? Is it going to lead the police right to his body in the graveyard?

'We're waiting to hear from them,' says Amelia.

'We've been going through his phone records,' Nancy adds. 'I'm sure there'll be something…'

I feel as though my heels are sinking and I stagger backwards, certain my stomach is about to hurl its contents out any second. Lifting my arm by way of apology, I rush inside, desperately searching for the door marked 'cloakroom'.

I lock myself in and drop down on the toilet lid, my head in my hands. I want nothing more than to hide here until I can slip away home.

After all the times Carl told me not to contact him, there was just one slip-up. One time when I called him on his mobile. How could I have been so stupid!

It was two days before the night we last met, to confirm I'd be able to get the keys to the cellar. Amelia will find that number, *my* number, on his phone records. She won't know it's me, but the police will be able to trace it.

After a while, I can hear tapping at the door.

'Beth, what's going on…?' It's Peter. 'Are you okay? Can you come out?'

After checking the mirror to make sure I look human, I ease open the outer door.

'What's the matter?' he says.

'Sorry to rush off like that. I'm not feeling well…'

He strokes my back. 'What's wrong, exactly?'

'I feel sick…just been under the weather for a few days.'

He stalls, looking wary, then leans in close. 'You're not pregnant, are you?' His whisper comes as a brittle hiss in my ear.

I pull away. 'No…'

He shakes his head. 'Because that would be a total disaster.'

I don't like his tone and he seems unnecessarily rough as he tugs me away from the cloakroom door.

I tell him I have to go home. I'm in no fit state to 'meet and greet' with anyone, like this. All I want is to go straight to my room, climb into bed and shut out this entire farce.

His voice softens. 'This is for *you*, Beth,' he says, sending out his arm in a dancer's flourish. 'To give you a chance to meet the right people and *showcase* you.'

He kisses my cheek, softly. *Showcase.* I'm starting to hate that word. It makes me feel like I'm trapped inside a glass box being peered at. 'You could be the perfect leading role for someone in this room, but you have to make the effort. You need to let people see who you are. The clue is in the title – it's *show*business.'

'I know. I'm really sorry. Any other time and…'

'Okay. I'll put you in a taxi and I'll stay and work the room without you, as best I can. Will you be all right getting home on your own?' He seems back to his usual loving self.

I nod. 'That would be the best thing.' I say, holding his arm.

He's punching numbers into his phone, ringing for a cab.

'I must have picked up a bug or something.' I rub my stomach, grateful I've got something to blame.

Chapter 18

Rachel

Beth bursts in through the front door as I'm mending the zip on my work trousers.

'Where's his phone?' she yells, without any greeting.

'Beth! Steady on…' I've got a needle in my hand and pins sticking out everywhere. 'What if someone had been here with me? You need to be more careful.'

She's back sooner than I expected. Her hands jab at her hips. 'I'm sick of all this sneaking around, not being able to say anything.' She's shaking, her hair dishevelled. All is not well.

'Are you okay? Where's Peter?'

She kicks off her stilettos and drops onto the sofa. 'He's still at the party. I couldn't stomach any more of it.'

'What happened?'

'She was there…Amelia, at the sodding party! I couldn't believe it.' She brings her knees up to her chin, clasping her arms around them. 'She and this other woman were talking about where Carl might be and asking about his phone…and I couldn't remember what happened to it.'

'His phone? It's okay – I switched it off when we were in the cellar. Then I threw it in the river. It's untraceable.'

'When?'

'Earlier this week, on the way home from talking to Russell at the church.'

She lets out a gusty breath. 'Why didn't you tell me? I've been petrified.' She stretches back, flopping both arms out to the side.

'What else were they saying?' I ask.

'I don't know…that him taking off without using his bank account was odd…that he might be having an affair.'

'You didn't…give anything away, did you?'

'NO!' She yells at me, storming off.

I am working at the pub that evening, so we have an early meal. Beth rustles up something simple, but neither of us are hungry. Since the accident she's been on one long detox, at first cutting out wheat, then dairy, then sugars. There's not much left she can eat. I know what she's doing – she's trying to cleanse her system. It's a futile attempt to purge herself of the dreadful thing we did.

I watch her push peas and baby carrots around her plate, aware that she's getting thinner by the week. I could see the bones of her hips poking through her dressing gown this morning.

'How's the quiz work going?'

'All right,' she says vaguely.

'When's your next audition?'

'Next week.' She gets up even though her plate is barely touched. 'I'll have the rest later,' she tells me and takes it into the kitchen. I know she won't. Most of her meals for the past week have ended up in the bin.

'When does Peter leave for the States?' I ask. I manage to finish my vegetables, at least, but like her, I can't stomach the lasagne.

'Tuesday,' she mutters. 'I'm glad. I've been so shallow. Such a bitch.'

'Beth…' I stand up, reaching out to give her a hug, but she backs off.

'Aside from what we did afterwards, I can't believe I did that to Peter. What kind of person am I?'

'I have to say, having met Peter, I'm rather surprised you felt the need to be with someone else. He's such a lovely man.'

'He deserves someone far better than me.'

'Well…you made a mistake, that's all. Show me any woman who hasn't been tempted to stray at some stage in their relationship. Apparently, it isn't uncommon just before getting married – a kind of final fling before long-term commitment.' *Although personally, if you really love someone, I can't see why.* 'You're certainly paying a price for it. If you're remorseful, it's a sign you won't do it again. It's a *good* sign, darling.'

On the way home from my shift, I get an unexpected call from Peter.

'I'm sorry to bother you, but I'm trying to reach Beth. She's not answering her phone and I wanted to check she's okay…after the party.'

'Oh, I'm sorry. She's been off her food and quiet, but she's fine. I can't see why she wouldn't answer her phone.'

'I'm a bit worried about her, to be honest. She's usually the life and soul of the party, but she doesn't seem to have been herself at all lately. Like she's shutting herself down. Is something worrying her? Is it the wedding?'

'Goodness, no… she's thrilled to bits about getting married to you.' It comes out sounding stilted.

'Is she ill? Has she said anything?'

I think swiftly on my feet. 'Maybe it's these auditions. She keeps getting one rejection after another. Everyone seems to be doing so much better than she is.'

'I wish she'd talk to me. I've sent messages and emails, but she's not responding.'

'Don't worry, I'll have a word with her. I'm certain it's a misunderstanding. She adores you, you can be sure of that.'

When I get back, I go upstairs to find her. I can hear her, in her room, talking to someone. I'm hoping she's made contact with Peter, after all.

I don't want to eavesdrop, but I linger a moment, just to set my mind at rest. Then I hear the words 'lover…killed…can't carry on…'

What the f—

She's on her phone *confessing* to someone!

I burst in and find Beth standing in front of her full-length mirror.

'Who..?' I'm expecting to see her mobile in her hand, but there is only a loose batch of papers.

'Beth…who are you talking to?'

She tuts loudly. 'Mum…I'm trying to rehearse my lines…'

'But, you were talking about…it sounded like…'

'It's a dystopian thriller…I'm going for the part of Nerola, the woman who finds her father has killed her brother in World War II…I told you about it.'

I sink down onto the bed; fully aware she's waiting for me to leave. 'I'm sorry…it sounded a bit too close to the bone.'

She stops staring at me and leans against her dressing table, making all the jars on it wobble back and forth. 'I know,' she says, with a weary sigh. 'I thought that when I read the synopsis. I'm not sure I can do it.'

There's an arid silence between us.

'Listen, Peter rang me,' I tell her.

'You? When?'

'Just now. He's trying to reach you, Beth…he says he's been trying to get in touch and you're not answering. What's going on?'

'I can't face him. I feel so terrible about the whole thing.' She flings the papers on the bed. 'If he's the slightest bit nice to me, I'm scared I'll break down and tell him everything.'

I launch to my feet. 'You *have* to speak to him, be your usual self – just don't let your guard down.'

'But I've been so awful behind his back. Sneaking around with Carl was a terrible mistake. I'm such a lousy human being.'

'People shouldn't be defined by the worst things they've done,' I tell her.

'Yeah, but even if you discount the fact that I covered up a murder, I'm still a cheat.' She lets out a hollow laugh. 'I feel so crap. If I speak to him he's going to wonder what the hell's the matter with me.'

'He's already asking that. He's starting to think it might be the wedding that's the problem.' I grab her skinny wrist. It feels like loose bones wrapped in clingfilm. 'You've got to draw on all your acting skills and turn this into a star performance, like we said. Think of it as a part you're playing in a big Hollywood blockbuster.'

She drops her head. 'I'm trying, I really am.'

'Ring Peter…I can stay with you in the room, if you like.'

'No, it's okay. I'll give him a call tomorrow.'

I leave her to carry on rehearsing and go down to the kitchen to make us both cocoa, but I can't relax. She's so close to the edge and jumpy, I can imagine her spilling out what happened all too easily – to Peter, to one of her friends. Either way, it would be a disaster. Every day, I'm half expecting to find her resolve has crumbled and the police are at our door.

I can't let that happen.

Chapter 19

Beth

I'm sitting near the window in my bedroom, huddled inside my dressing gown, drying my hair. Peter will be in New York by now. I'm hoping the time difference will mean it's easier to avoid speaking to him.

Mum has done a U-turn. Until yesterday, she'd been hassling me to speak to him and smooth everything over, but then, suddenly, she said she 'understood' that speaking to him could be difficult right now. She's promised to stop pestering me about it.

'Why don't you give me your phone?' she said, yesterday evening, 'then I can check who's calling and I can be right by your side if you actually want to speak to him.'

I told her that was a bit extreme.

'Okay, but don't speak to him on your own, you hear me?'

'Fine. I don't want to, anyway.'

I keep coming back to the call I made that links Carl to me. The one I haven't told Mum about. Surely, the police won't have the resources to follow up that one tiny piece of information. It was only one call, after all. A short one. As a high-powered businessman, he must have taken hundreds of calls from different numbers.

My phone lights up on the bed with another message I won't be answering. All my friends are going mental, wondering what's wrong with me. I've barely spoken to any of them. I put a general post up on Facebook to say I'm mega busy with auditions and the wedding and not to worry if I don't get in touch.

I messaged Maria and Tina personally to say pretty much the same. Maria came back saying something about me being 'so in love' and Tina said he hoped I wasn't going to forget everyone now that I was stepping up the social ladder.

Laura and Giles, my mates from drama college, are both working on films at the moment, so I don't need to worry about them, but if I speak to any of my closest friends, they'll know instantly there's something badly wrong and they'll wheedle the truth out of me in about twenty seconds flat.

I have to suck it up to protect Mum, more than anything. If it was just about me, I think I would have given in by now.

Mum still visits Russell, but it's less often. She's doing double shifts at the pub and when she comes home, she immerses herself in wedding plans.

By now, we've sent out the invitations for the hen night and I'm trying to be super enthusiastic, because I know it means so much to her. We're holding it at Mum's pub. Unbelievable! The scene of the crime – but it's the cheapest option.

Mum says it looks like a totally different place after the makeover. She says I need to pretend 'the accident' happened somewhere else. I've got a few weeks to pull myself together before then, but right now, I'm dreading a party in my honour. Any other time and I'd be totally wired. Normally I can't get enough of being the centre of attention, but not now. I'll have to tank myself up with drink to get through it and just hope I don't let anything out of the bag.

Mum's also ticked the wedding car off her list this week, together with the reception flowers, the catering and the photographer. We still need to sort out the music, the flowers for the church and arrange the seating for the reception.

I've just had another dress fitting and the seamstress is going to have to bring it in at the waist, yet again. I should be over the moon I'm so thin, but I feel lacklustre most of the time. Mum is coming shopping with me on Saturday to get shoes and a tiara. This event should be any girl's dream, but I can't drum up genuine gusto for any of it.

Mum continues to watch my every move. I've started writing down how I feel in a diary, like Mum suggested, but it's not the same as talking the whole thing through with someone. I actually punched in Maria's number yesterday but managed to cut the line before she answered. I've got to be so careful all the time, I can't afford one tiny blunder.

I'm just about to go to bed when Mum calls me from the bathroom.

'It's Peter,' she whispers, holding out her phone to me.

'Again?'

She flattens the phone against her chest. 'He wants to speak to you. What shall I tell him?'

I acquiesce and take the phone. Mum hangs at my shoulder, waiting.

'Hi, Peter…I know…I'm sorry. Yeah…been focussing on my audition.'

She smiles at me, nodding with encouragement.

He tells me about his hotel room, how close he is to the Guggenheim and how he came across a crew filming a remake of *The Ipcress File* in Central Park, yesterday.

'I wish you were with me…I miss you like crazy,' he says.

I try to be normal with him, but I can tell my voice sounds strained and my chit-chat is half-hearted. He says he loves me and I pretend there's a blip on the line to avoid responding.

I give Mum a knowing stare. I can't help myself, I have to ask about Amelia.

'Thanks for asking. She's worried sick, actually. It's nearly two weeks now and the police are taking it more seriously, but they're coming up against dead-ends. She's been obsessively going through Carl's paperwork looking for clues to his whereabouts.'

I hand the phone back to Mum shortly after.

'You did really well,' she says. 'That should keep him quiet for a day or two.'

My next audition is a disaster. I knew it would be. I did surprisingly well at the piece I'd prepared – the one I was rehearsing when Mum barged in on me, about a character who's lost her brother during the war. In fact, it was easy, all I had to do was think of Carl and Peter and the mess I'm in and I was in floods of tears. They looked impressed, but only until they asked how I might respond if I'd discovered the brother was alive. I couldn't stop crying. They tried to do an upbeat improvisation with me but I was a wreck. I think they'd got the message by then that I was a one-trick pony and sent me packing.

The only person I can talk to is Grandad, so when Mum is out, I catch the bus over there again. He says it brightens his day, so it's worth it for both of us.

We play cards and I put an evening meal together for him. I wash up, then do a batch of laundry and ironing while I'm there. It feels safe being with him because he doesn't ask tricky questions and often he forgets what I've said and asks them again, anyway.

He has periods of time when he forgets about the wedding altogether and it's a relief not to have to pretend to be all full-on about it. During this visit, he seems more confused than ever. He keeps taking his slippers off and leaving them in front of the fire, then putting them back on again as if he's been searching for them.

I'm almost tempted to spill the beans and tell him that Way-way killed a man and we buried him in the graveyard, but I manage to keep myself in check. It's not fair on him, even though he wouldn't remember a thing after about twenty minutes.

On the bus home, I think about Peter. I love how the sculpted muscles move in his jaw when he speaks, how trim and fit he is from dancing, his expressive hands, his husky voice.

The more I think about sneaking around with Carl, the more I wonder what the hell I was playing at. How could I ever have gone behind Peter's back? What drove me to follow Carl to the summer house in the first place? Total madness. He seemed to strip away all my defences.

Peter's so perfect. When we're together we talk all the time, share our private thoughts and have a real laugh about the odd things people say and do. We cross-examine each other after every film we see; he likes heart-rending biopics, I prefer French and Scandinavian domestic noir.

I just wish the wedding wasn't so soon. I need time to sort myself out properly. I'm still in shock after what happened. Even now, I can't believe it.

I start to wonder about how things will be after we're married, what life will be like five years down the line. I'll be safe by then and all this will be behind me. Then I muse over the dad I never knew.

When I was with Grandad earlier, I asked if he could remember anything about him, but he seemed to get mixed up and started talking about a pub.

'Is that where Way-way met my dad?' I asked, 'in a pub?'

Mum has always said my dad went to her school in Southampton. Pollard's secondary school near the station.

'You must never go near it,' he said.

'Why? Which pub, Grandad?'

'Such a bad thing…but we all kept our mouths shut.'

After that, he appeared to lose interest and wanted to watch the football on television, so I left it there.

Strange, though. I can't help thinking there's something about my history that Mum has kept from me.

Chapter 20

Rachel

I've just returned home from an appointment at the florists when Beth comes charging in.

'They're digging up the cemetery,' she yells at me. 'They know something.'

She's hyperventilating, then stoops forward, her hands on the arm of the sofa, as her gasping develops into a full-blown asthma attack. She's trying to suck in huge gulps of air, her eyes bulging, darting blindly around her.

'Beth, where's your puffer?' I rush to her bag and she nods frantically, reaching out her hand.

I press the blue inhaler into her palm and she pumps a dose into her mouth. I ease her into a seat, stroking her back. 'It's okay…easy…slow down…'

She's wearing a tatty baseball cap and tracksuit. It's so unlike her. She never had a tomboy phase. From an early age everything about her has been feminine. Lately, however, it's as if glamour is a concept she's never encountered. I barely recognise her.

She lets me stroke her, cosset her and for a moment I feel a pang of nostalgia; this is how it used to be between us.

Once the attack has subsided, she gives my finger two squeezes, our secret sign – and a sharp sting creeps behind my eyes.

'What's happened, exactly?' I say softly.

'There are people in the churchyard near…where we…and they're digging up the earth. They're looking for him.'

'The police…?'

'Yes…' She hesitates. 'I…I think so.'

'Well…was there a police car, and blue and white tape cordoning off the area, any officers in uniform?'

'Er...I'm not sure. There were definitely men in yellow bibs with spades and a mechanical digger with caterpillar tracks.' She shivers. 'I took one look and ran back here to tell you.' Beth gets to her feet. 'We must go and check. They're going to find him.'

'You're not going anywhere,' I tell her, putting out my arm, so she has no option but to fall back onto the sofa.

I hadn't told her about the vandals defacing Russell's grave, last week. I didn't want another tremor under her feet unsettling her, but now she needs to know. 'It's not about Carl,' I tell her, holding her hand. 'It'll be about Russell's grave. A bunch of thugs sprayed graffiti over it and they've been fixing it up.'

She looks dazed as though she's just woken up.

'That would account for any police,' I add. My voice fizzles out. As I'm speaking, I'm taking in what she actually said.

Mechanical digger...caterpillar tracks...

Why are they *digging* five days after the graves were defaced?

'I'll pop over and check just in case,' I say, trying not to look agitated.

Beth stares straight ahead, waiting for her breathing to slow back to normal.

I grab the coat I've just left on a hook by the door and snatch my keys from the ledge. I'm about to leave, then stop myself. I can't leave Beth here in this state. It's not just the asthma attack, it's her state of mind. She's shaking like a leaf. If I leave her alone it wouldn't surprise me if she does something stupid – runs to tell someone else or even turns herself in to the police.

'Okay, let's walk back together,' I say, 'but you mustn't react or say a word to anyone. Just stay close to me, nice and calm, okay?'

She nods.

I hold her jacket open for her, like I did when she was little and she slides her arms into it. It's moments like this I wish I could capture and hold on to forever. 'Make sure you've got your inhaler.'

I bundle her out of the door and we head over to St Andrew's Church, taking such rapid strides, we're almost breaking into a jog.

We pass the main building and take the footpath around the back. I force her to slow down like we're just talking a stroll.

'See…' she hisses into my shoulder, 'there are men in…'

'Yellow bibs. I know. It's not the police, it's health and safety. Don't worry.'

Without another word, I link Beth's arm and pull her away from the gate, back to the main high street.

'It's okay. They're digging for the next coffin, that's all,' I tell her as we walk purposefully away. 'They're not digging anybody up.'

Beth seems barely able to walk in a straight line. She looks pale and dead on her feet. Have my rash actions in the cellar turned my confident and courageous daughter into this flimsy, feeble young woman in one cruel blow?

Even though we have no budget for meals out, I suggest we stop at a café. 'When did you last have something to eat?' I ask gently.

'I had a few brazil nuts this morning...' It's now nearly three o'clock.

As we walk, a police car screams past us and we both whip round to see where it's going. We're like deer caught in headlights.

The car crosses the mini roundabout and takes a right out of town. We both breathe out in unison. Beth mutters under her breath and leans into me and I wrap my arm firmly around her.

We find a table in the French deli near the bridge and share a pot of tea and an omelette.

She's silent for a while, taking ages to chew her food. 'Why don't you ever tell me much about my dad?' she asks.

I stretch my eyes wide. 'There's not much to tell. He was young and still at school when we got together. He ran off when I got pregnant and I hardly ever saw him again. You know all this.'

'What did he look like? What was he interested in?'

Hairs on the back of my neck shoot up. 'Where's this coming from?'

'Just getting married…families, you know. I was looking at the list of people for lunch and apart from Grandad, there's no proper family on our side.'

'There's not much to tell. He was just an ordinary schoolboy; shaggy blonde hair, blue eyes. He played the violin.'

'You never told me that before.'

I shrug. 'That's about it.'

'But, what about his name? Don't I have the right to know? Have you never wanted to look him up and see if he might be interested in me?'

'He made it clear he didn't want anything to do with…us.'

'When?'

'When I got pregnant.'

'But that was years ago. He was a kid…probably scared to death when he knew you were in trouble. He'll be nearly forty now, he might have changed his mind.' She looks up at me. 'What's his name? Why won't you ever tell me?'

I *can't* tell her. It would be too much of a risk if she tries to take it further.

'He knows *my* name,' I say pointedly. 'He's never come knocking on my door.'

That sends her quiet for a while.

'How did you meet him again, was it at school or in a pub?'

'A pub?' A film of sweat breaks out on my palms and I almost drop the teapot.

'Who've you been talking to? Have you been to see Adrian again?'

She nips her lips together and looks down at her plate.

I sigh. 'It was at school. We only saw each other for a few months.'

'I thought you said you'd been going out together for nearly a year.'

I hesitate. 'No…you're right. It was probably more like a year. I'm tired…let's get back shall we?'

Beth is silent on the way home, but my head is buzzing. I must be more careful. I've got too many lies to keep track of.

Chapter 21

Rachel

I notice the letter in Beth's room when I pop in to see if she's borrowed my hair straighteners. I found it two days ago on the mat and left it on the kitchen table, so she'd see it when she came down for breakfast. I couldn't help spotting it had Peter's hotel details on the back. How romantic and old-fashioned. Two days later and it's on her dressing table – still unopened. How long is it going to stay there?

I've been liaising directly with Peter in my role as 'wedding planner' instead of getting Beth to check arrangements with him. She's spoken to him once or twice, but only when I've been there to supervise her, to make sure she 'sticks to the script', as it were. She's been polite, but reticent with him. It's better than blanking him altogether, but before long, he's bound to get seriously worried that she's got cold feet, if he hasn't already.

Beth's out collecting her finished wedding dress. I turn the envelope over. It has a UK post mark, so must have been posted before he left for New York. He'll be expecting some sort of reply any day.

Peter has become such a touchy subject, I barely dare mention his name anymore. I can almost hear the eggshells splintering beneath my feet as I walk around her.

In a split-second I make a decision, snatch the envelope and take it downstairs. Boiling a kettle, I use the steam to prise open one of the sides. It will look less obvious if it's been opened there, than if I peel open the flap. When I glue it back together, it will look like it got a bit squashed in the mail, that's all. I hesitate as I slip out the contents, ashamed that I'm prying into my daughter's private world. I'd never do such a thing if I didn't think it was justified – my thinking being that once I know what it says, I can help Beth put together an encouraging reply to smooth things over.

I hold the letter at arm's length as I read it, as though keeping it at a distance makes it less intrusive. As expected, it's a proper love-letter, bordering on erotic. He refers to shared special moments that have stayed in his mind, explains how he feels about my daughter.

My cheeks flare up with disgust and shame at this invasion of their privacy. With every word, I know what I'm doing is wrong; prying into the sensitive, intimate territory of Peter's feelings for her – but I have no option. Towards the end, he writes:

You've been so quiet and hard to reach, lately, I'm worried I've done something wrong or I've upset you in some way that you won't explain to me. I need to know this marriage is definitely what you want.

Then later:

If there's something getting in the way, Beth, I need to know about it now, then we can get it out into the open and resolve it together.

He asks her to reply and be totally honest about her feelings for him.

Oh, boy…

I fold the letter and slip it back in the envelope, alarm bells ringing in my ears. Whenever we speak about wedding details I brush off his concerns, reassuring him that Beth is a hundred per cent sure about tying the knot with him. I've been telling little white lies about how she can't stop talking about him and can't wait to be his wife. But there are only so many times I can do that before he's going to ask why Beth, herself, isn't following through with the same level of eagerness. There's no question about it, he knows something isn't right.

I spend the next ten minutes scrabbling around in drawers and cupboards searching for the stick of glue I need to seal the envelope again. Beth is due back any moment. Finally, I come across it in my sewing box and get the job done, but before I put the letter back where I found it, I make a note of the address in New York where he asks her to send a reply.

As I enter her room, I hear the front door slam shut and, in my rush to rest the letter against the mirror, I knock over a bottle of perfume. She's quick to climb the stairs and I'm backing out of her room when she reaches the landing.

'What are you doing?' she asks, her wedding dress in a cloth cover, over her arm.

'I…wondered if you still had my denim jacket,' I stammer. In the frenzy of the moment, I've forgotten the real reason for going in there.

'I put it back in your wardrobe yesterday. I told you.' She narrows her eyes and gives me a stare riddled with suspicion.

I swiftly throw my attention onto her dress.

'What's it like? Aren't you going to try it on for me?'

'No,' she says curtly, swans into her room and shuts the door in my face.

Beth seems to assume I'm breezing through this without a care in the world. If I let her see how appalled I am by what we've done, she'll crumble and collapse. I need to keep my chin up, stay grounded and sensible – even though it makes me look cold as ice.

Much later, I hear her go out again. I find myself creeping upstairs as if she's still in the house and go into my own room to sit on the bed. Now that Russell has passed away and Beth has claimed her old room back, she and I share the 'Jack and Jill' bathroom, an odd feature for small spaces that allows the two bedrooms to access the facilities from either side.

It took some getting used to when Russell first moved in; perfect for on-stage farces, but not so hilarious when you always have to remember to lock the opposite door when you're inside.

Beth and I have always been comfortable naked with each other, unabashed about using the bathroom together, but lately

I notice she's been locking my access door, preventing me from getting in.

More and more frequently, since the incident in the cellar, she's been storming off in a hissy fit about something or other, hiding herself away. It feels as though barriers are going up between us daily and there are barely any occasions when we can have a relaxed chat together like we used to.

I go into the bathroom and open her access door. I want to take a peek at the dress. It feels almost a lifetime ago since we first pored over the wedding magazines, giggling and exclaiming in awe, until she finally came across the one she wanted. If anything, it's that feeling I want to relive as much as to see the finished article.

I'm forced to ease the whole dress out of the cover in order to take in the full shape of it. It's perfect for Beth; no straps, so it makes the most of her smooth elegant neckline and it's figure hugging, all the way to the floor. It looks like it's been dipped in silver beads and sequins, all catching the light to make it sparkle. It takes my breath away.

Since the grief of Russell's untimely death stole my appetite last year, Beth and I have been sharing clothes more often. When her wedding came on the horizon, I made a concerted effort to trim down even further, determined to be a credit to Beth on her big day. A few months ago, I tried on her skinny jeans and we were both in hysterics when I couldn't get them over my thighs, but earlier this week I tried them on again when she was out and they fitted like gloves.

I stare at the stunning dress. I couldn't, could I?

I'm taking it off the padded silk hanger before I'm aware I've made the decision. My arms seem far away as they encounter the soft feel of the silk. It's as though I'm watching someone else. I strip off to my panties, then quickly and carefully step into it, breathing in to ease up the long zip at the back. The dress smells of the shop we visited; lavender with a background hint of rose from the essential oil diffuser they used. I squeeze my eyes shut, then turn to face the mirror.

I well up as I stare in disbelief at the vision before me. There are a few surreal seconds when my mind plays tricks, telling me it's Beth standing there, not me. No wonder people say we look alike. There's no denying I look unbelievable – staggeringly beautiful, like the cover of a wedding magazine.

Before long, my tears of wonder turn to tears of sadness. I've always shrugged off the fact that Russell never asked me to marry him, but lately it's become a considerable regret. We could have been a proper couple, man and wife, who took that final step to seal the knot. We could have made precious vows to each other in public. I could have walked down the aisle looking like this on our special day. A day we would have treasured forever. Beth doesn't realise how lucky she is.

Reluctantly, I peel off the dress with great care and put it back on the hanger. No one will ever know.

As I step over to the interconnecting door, I notice the letter is still there exactly where I left it, untouched, the perfume bottle still on its side. There's nothing else for it.

An hour later, as I drop an airmail envelope into the post box at the end of the road, the acidic taste in my mouth tells me that I have seriously stepped over the line.

Chapter 22

Beth

Mum's doing a great job of being a go-between with Peter. I don't have to speak to him at all, now.

It's such a relief not having to pretend everything's hunky dory with him. To be honest, I've put my phone down somewhere and can't find it, so that's a good excuse, too. I'm not using it much anyway. I'm just going from one day to the next keeping myself to myself at the gym, running through my lines for my next audition and trying to stay composed. The thought of landing a role in a production is the one thing that keeps me going.

I don't want to think about the wedding, but I must show willing and sound a bit excited about it. For Mum. Getting her involved seemed the only way to lift her out of her misery over Russell, so I have to stay peppy for her. I showed her the dress, although I didn't want to prance around in it. I had to try it on in the shop, so I know it fits, but I feel a total fraud at the idea of wearing it.

'Aren't you having any?' she says, as I lay a single plate with scrambled eggs on the table.

I rub my stomach. 'Don't fancy it,' I tell her, 'I'll have porridge oats, later.'

I'd prefer granola, but we're out of it and it's expensive, so therefore off limits. Oats will have to do.

In my mind, I leap to the future and picture having breakfast with Peter on a veranda somewhere in the sun. For some reason, I can envisage our lives further down the line and feel almost calm about it, but I can't think about the bit that comes before it, the stage we're in now. It's as though it's a different me I envisage in the future. The old me, awesome and intrepid, not this grey shadow I've shrunk into.

How I'm going to get the old me back is a mystery to me.

The worst part coming up is the wedding day itself. Each minute will be flooded with memories of betrayal and from that murky place within me I'm supposed to look pure and innocent and say my marriage vows, like I'm made of sweetness and light. The thought of it makes me want to throw up.

As Mum slices into her egg, I drift back to my fantasy veranda in the sun. Where will we live once we're married? In his apartment in Chelsea? In New York? With Peter away so much, we haven't talked about where we'll settle and, of course, with finding it impossible to face him right now, we're not discussing those kinds of big decisions, either.

'What about the letter?' Mum says, trying to sound casual. 'I couldn't help noticing it was from Peter.'

'I haven't read it. He knows I've got it.'

'Oh, Beth. It's been around for days. What's he going to think?'

She's exasperated with me, I know, but what can I do? I shut my eyes. I refuse to cry. I'm sick of crying. I'm sick of feeling so crap.

'Come here,' she says. She opens out her arms for me and I fall in. I sit on her lap and cuddle up to her and we stay like that, as one, as the clock ticks and the world carries on around us.

'How about I read the letter for you and if there's anything that's urgent, I'll tell you?'

'Yes. That would be…yes, please.' I bury my face in her fleece feeling eight years old, like the strong, powerful core of me has snapped in half and got washed away.

I fetch the letter and hand it to her. She tears it open straight away, but I walk away. I don't want to watch her eyes as she drinks in the words meant for me. Nevertheless, it's a weight off my mind.

I think then about my father. Mum's definitely hiding something about him. She seems to have forgotten what she's told me in the past, giving me new information when I press her that doesn't quite fit earlier versions. Who is he and why won't she let me find out more about him? I might have to pop over to Grandad's again soon to see if I can prise any more out of him.

A couple of hours later, as she's getting ready for the pub, Mum knocks on the door of my room. I'm lying on my bed battling with lines from a turgid script about a priest and a young woman who's been abused.

'I'm off now,' she says, with a big smile. 'Nothing to report in the letter, by the way. It's all fine, don't you worry. When I next speak to Peter, I'll tell him you're under the weather with flu or something.'

'Great. Thank you.'

Her smile fades and she hesitates in the doorway. 'You're not depressed are you, Beth? Do you need to see the GP?'

I shake my head violently. 'No way…I'm not seeing anyone. She'll want me to open up, ask what's been going on and…'

'No, of course.'

'I'm just coming to terms with the…you know…I'm not depressed. Just in shock. I need time, that's all.'

'Okay, if you're sure.'

As she's backing out, I ask a question. 'By the way, you haven't seen my mobile, have you? I can't find it anywhere.'

She puffs out her bottom lip and stops to think. 'No. You can borrow mine if you like.'

I shake my head. 'It's okay. I don't want to use it. I just wondered.'

'You know we can't afford a new one, sweetie, if you've lost it,' she tells me with a forlorn look.

I smile. 'I know.'

She matches my smile. 'We'll get through this together, don't you worry,' she says and closes the door.

Chapter 23

Rachel

Beth thinks she's lost her phone. She'll never think to look inside the shoebox under my bed.

It started as soon as I replied to the letter. I'd backed myself into a corner by then and there was no other way. I couldn't let her use it anymore.

When she went out on Thursday, I read everything between them I could find; on our shared laptop, her phone, the odd postcard he'd sent, from a pile in her sock drawer. I made myself look at Peter's amorous words, at Beth's equally raunchy replies. I had to fight my discomfort and scour the string of messages to see how she addresses him, how she signs off, and the kind of language they use. I had to discover the exact tone of their interactions. It wouldn't work, otherwise.

I found a batch of her college notes under her bed and rifled through them, so I could make a stab at copying her handwriting.

Then I replied to his letter, pretending to be her. I apologised for my scrawl, telling him I'd hurt my wrist, to cover any obvious differences.

I only meant it to be a one-off, to stall Peter for a short while, but it didn't end there. Not long after I dropped the letter into the post-box, a message popped up on Beth's phone:

To: Beth
From: Peter
Looking forward to getting a reply to my letter when you get a moment. Send times when we can video call asap. I'm only five hours behind you. Worried about you and love you to bits, P x

I replied in an attempt to put him off:

To: Peter
From: Beth
So sorry to make you worry. Your letter totally made my day and a reply is in the post. As to a video call, not feeling too well, just flu or something, but better to message as I'd scare you on screen looking this awful. Love you, really do, B x

Once I'd sent the message I had to delete it, otherwise Beth would have found out what I'd done. But then, of course, he messaged back!

To: Beth
From: Peter
Don't care what you look like…just want to see and speak to you. Let's fix a time. Get better soon. So wonderful to be properly in touch again. P x

Oh, what a mess I've made. I only did it to buy us some time. Now I've begun spinning a sticky web and I'm stuck right in the middle of it. How stupid am I?

To: Peter
From: Beth
Really can't do video at the moment…lost my voice and croaking like a toad but speak soon I promise. Your B x

I pressed send before I realised what I'd done. Why did I say I'd speak to him *soon*?! My little attempt to help things along has got totally out of hand. I've opened the floodgates and it's too late to force them shut again. Beth has put her foot down about contacting him, so now what can I do? How long before she's ready to speak to him again?

That isn't the only problem. Since Beth 'lost' her phone, messages have been coming in left, right and centre, from Peter, friends and drama contacts. People are concerned that she isn't getting back to them. It isn't fair on Beth.

The only way out was to stop him using this phone and start from scratch on a *new* phone that had no connection to Beth. It was too dangerous otherwise.

Before I got myself totally tied up in knots, I sent another message:

To: Peter
From: Beth
I'm getting a new phone, so just to let you know I won't be using this one anymore. I'll send new number v soon. Your B x

After that, I had to go out and use precious money from last week's overtime to buy a new pay-as-you-go phone. One that only I could use 'as Beth' to message Peter. Now I've started this, I must keep going. At least it means I'll be able to monitor and respond to any contact he makes and keep Peter happy.

I know it's for the best and I wouldn't be going to such lengths if I didn't believe Beth is wholeheartedly in love with him. Peter is so right for her. Her fling was just a silly irresponsible blip before she settles down.

Beth has shown no interest in speaking to anyone, so I'm keeping both phones under my bed for the time being, monitoring them every so often.

I'm also snooping on her email account in case anything comes through about auditions, since she appears to be stonewalling all means of communication.

Peter is sending emails to her, too. He talks about keeping the little bars of Dior soap for her that he gets fresh in his hotel suite every day, about an elderly woman along the corridor who is secretly keeping a poodle in her room.

Last night, he emailed photos from Central Park; a couple getting married on Bow Bridge, a famous tennis player practising on the courts. Beth could easily come across them if she uses the laptop. They refer to 'her' recent messages, so I have to put a stop to them:

To: Peter Roper
From: Beth Kendall
Subject: Loving you
Your emails are wonderful, but Mum often uses my laptop (now we only have the one since Russell's crashed) and I don't want her reading them! I hope you understand. Phone is better – much more private. Miss you loads, your B x

It's two days since I claimed the flu was making a call impossible and this morning, I knew what was coming. Sure enough, Peter wanted to set up the dreaded video call.

I tried to fend him off, saying I had to prepare for auditions, but he said if I was able to rehearse, I should be able to speak to him. I couldn't fob him off any longer.

I'd backed myself into a corner. He wouldn't take no for an answer. What else could I do?

We've set a time. I made sure Beth would be out, searching for a new strapless bra for the wedding. I gave her a list of groceries we don't really need, just to make sure she stays out longer.

I've got ten minutes to go and I'm terrified.

Chapter 24

Rachel

Using the straighteners, I smooth down my hair and part it on the side just like Beth does. My hair is shorter than hers, so I pin it back with her hairclips in a style she often uses.

I borrow her make-up and copy the eye-shadow technique she uses. Scrutinising a photo of Beth on the dressing table, I realise my eyebrows are too thick, so I madly pluck at them, then do my utmost to cover the bags under my eyes and the crows' feet at the edges.

My saving grace is going to be the light; I deliberately close one of the curtains in her room to keep it low and shadowy.

I have to 'be' Beth in the flesh. But what choice do I have? She can't lose her voice forever.

I sit before the video cam and practice speaking with a higher timbre to my voice. I know Beth better than anyone, but I don't know who she is when she's alone with Peter. In my written messages to him, I can replicate the terms she uses, but it's another matter altogether to convince him that it's really my daughter sitting right in front of his eyes.

Finally, I tweak the settings on the webcam, fiddling with the brightness, contrast, sharpness and backlight composition to make the picture obscure, without going overboard.

The clock finally clicks around to 5 p.m. It must be midday in New York and there's a bleeping ringtone to indicate an incoming call. I swallow in a loud gulp. This is it.

'Ah, it's *so* good to see you, darling,' he says. 'It feels like ages. How are you feeling?'

I clear my throat. 'Oh, a lot better. My voice is still ropey as you can hear.'

'You certainly don't sound quite right. It's a bit gravelly.'

I try to remember how Beth laughs and it comes to me just in time.

'Your hair looks different,' he says.

'Oh, just been for a swim that's all.'

If only Peter didn't have such an acute eye for detail. Surely, there's no way I can pull this off.

'So, what have you been up to?' he asks.

For this to work, I need to pretend I'm a little bit in love with him, but he's such a warm, open kind of person – how hard can it be?

'Oh, counting down the days to our incredibly special moment, mostly. Mum's started getting lots of acceptance cards back. I can't believe I'm going to be your wife. I can't wait.' Beth has a way of keeping her eyes closed a fraction longer than most people when she blinks and I do this now, as a way of bringing in a familiar mannerism.

You're doing that blinking thing, again,' he says.

I giggle, girlishly. 'No, I'm not.'

'God, it makes you look so seductive.'

'Sshh…you mustn't,' I scold. 'Mum's around.'

I've got to cut this short.

'You're not usually this coy,' he says.

'Stop it, Mum's pottering about. She might come in.'

With a sigh, he sits back and folds his arms, relenting. 'Incidentally, you're a bit dark,' he says. 'Can you brighten the picture? I can barely see you.'

'No…I can't…it's the video cam; it's been playing up. Sometimes it cuts out altogether.'

'Oh, better not fiddle with it, then.'

Even when his face is relaxed it's as though a smile is on the way. It's undeniably endearing.

'What else have you been doing?'

'Learning lines, dance classes…hanging out with Mum, making the most of the time we've got left. She's going to miss me terribly.'

He rides straight over that statement. My heart is in my mouth, terrified about what he's going to ask me next.

'Tell me more about the rest of the wedding preparations,' he says. 'Going okay?'

I let my shoulders drop. Now that I *can* tell him. I go on to reveal all the aspects of their big day that I know about inside out and that Beth herself should be gushing about. In turn, Peter tells me how boring his meetings are, but that they're making progress with some deal or other.

'You're wearing those earrings I bought you,' he says. 'Remember what I said when I gave them to you?'

Oh no. I knew this moment would come. Inwardly my heart sinks. How am I going to wriggle out of this?

'Why don't you remind me,' I say, seductively. 'I've seen you so little these last few months, I think I might need to hear those words again.' I twist my mouth in the coy way I've seen Beth do since she was about three.

'Well…it was something like "you're the most precious thing to me and I can't believe how strong my feelings are for you after such a short time".'

'Aw…' I say, my reaction genuine.

A rush of conflicting emotions descend on me all at once; joy that Beth is marrying such a terrific man, sadness that I'll never hear sentiments like this from Russell ever again, and shame because these words aren't meant for me. I try to stop a tear from bubbling over, but he spots it straight away.

'Beth, what's wrong?'

'It's just…so wonderful,' I blubber.

He whispers endearments after that and I tell him I love him – the words falling out of my mouth remarkably easily. Then he tells me he has to get back to the boardroom.

'Just one thing,' he says, 'you were asking about Amelia when we last spoke on the phone. Carl is still nowhere to be found. She's convinced his absence is sinister now though, because he missed their son's birthday and he'd never do that, apparently. She's also found something that makes her suspect an affair.'

'Found something? What?'

'She didn't say. She's used to turning a blind eye to his various dalliances, mainly because she's got everything she wants – her horses, the boat and all the rest, but she certainly has the feeling something was going on before he disappeared.'

'Listen, I have to go. Mum's calling,' I lie, glancing over towards the door.

'Oh, if she's there, can I have a quick word?'

'Er…' White noise gathers momentum in my ears.

Think!

'…she's in the bathroom…they've been trying to start the neighbour's car and she'll be covered in grease…but I'll get her to ring you.'

He blows me kisses to end the call and I reciprocate, then flop down onto the bed as soon as I disconnect him, exhausted.

My life is turning into an endless string of lies. One after another.

Seconds later, the front door slams and there's a mad rumbling as Beth's footsteps come thudding up the stairs. I grab the laptop, bolt out of the connecting door into the bathroom and flip out the hook-in earrings, secreting them in my hand. I don't have time to wrench out the hair-clips before she comes bursting in on me. She's out of breath, snatching air between loud wails.

'They've found him!'

Chapter 25

Rachel

Beth collides straight into me as I try not to look caught red-handed in the bathroom. I'm still wearing her frilly retro blouse.

She doesn't appear to notice. She's got bigger issues on her mind.

'It's all over, isn't it?' she whimpers, clinging to the edge of the basin. 'They know he was killed. They'll find DNA. Our DNA.'

It's policy at St Andrew's Church, apparently, to dig for the next burial patch very close to the last one. It's an issue of space. I wish I'd known. A few more inches to the right and they might never have found him.

Once they started making a new hole, the grave diggers noticed a bad smell. They thought they'd hit a drain and spent a couple of days scouring the plans of the sewer system. Then someone pointed out that the ground had been disturbed since the last burial and Judy Welsh's coffin was not as deep as it should have been.

That's when they came across him. It's now a murder hunt.

I reach out and take hold of her shoulders. I have to hold myself together, in spite of the pressing urge to break down. If things were different, I could see myself bolting along to the church to confess everything to Father Roland. But there's too much at stake and I have to stand firm or Beth will fall apart.

'We were careful. This doesn't mean the police will trace it back to us. We just have to keep our heads.'

Beth hasn't done a great job of doing that so far and I can't see it getting any better after this. Unearthing Carl's body really is a massive blow and I'm going to have to think very carefully about how we proceed.

'There's no reason for the police to come to us,' I tell her, bringing her through to my room and easing her down onto the bed. She's holding her asthma inhaler in her hand. 'Have you used this, already?'

She nods. 'I'm okay.'

'Let's get a few things straight just in case anyone does start asking questions.' I fold my arms. 'You touched him, but you hadn't actually had sex that night, right?'

She nods again.

'No proper sexual contact? No penetration? No condoms? No oral sex?'

'No…but what about the rug?'

'Okay. There's no reason for them to trace the rug to the King's Tavern, it could have come from anywhere. The CCTV wasn't working and there are no cameras at the church, so we're safe there. And the night you met Carl, you saw only that homeless guy on Melcham Street and Angie – and you told her you were going over to Adrian's?'

'Yes.' I can see no issues with that story. Adrian won't be a reliable alibi because of his dementia, but there's nothing to connect Beth and Carl in the first place, so it won't get as far as that.

Beth disappears and returns holding her jacket.

'Where are you going?'

'Just out. I need to clear my head.'

Beth comes back as I'm putting together a stir-fry in the kitchen. I nearly scurried after her when she rushed off, tempted to follow at a distance so I could intervene if she put a foot wrong, but I can't watch her twenty-four-seven.

To be honest, I didn't mention it, but I *am* worried about the rug we wrapped around Carl's body. Why didn't we drag it out from under him and burn it?

Except, I know why. We both wanted to get away from there as fast as we could. Furthermore, extricating the rug when it was so tightly bound around him could have caused all kinds of problems.

Beth is wearing a baggy ribbed jumper I've never seen before, with sleeves that cover her fingers. It makes her look like she's shrunk over the last few days. She flips on the TV without a word and puts her feet up on a pile of wedding magazines.

I've got about twenty minutes to wolf down my meal and change before heading out for my shift at the bar.

'I'm dishing up,' I call out to her. Wafts of ginger and hot sesame oil have seduced my stomach into feeling hungry, for a change.

'I'll have some later,' she says. It's her stock reply these days.

I take my plate upstairs, snatching forkfuls as I'm pulling on my trousers, when I see a police patrol car pull up outside.

I rush to the landing and shout down. 'Don't panic, but it looks like the police are here.' I hurry downstairs, half-dressed.

'What?' She drops the remote and it splinters open as it hits the carpet. 'We need to run through what we're supposed to say again,' she stammers. 'I'm not ready.' She's frantically trying to force the batteries back into the plastic compartment.

'There isn't time,' I say, buttoning up my blouse. 'It's okay. Calm down. It's good we haven't gone over and over our story. We mustn't say exactly the same thing or else it will look like we've rehearsed it.'

The doorbell chimes and I waltz past Beth to open it. Two officers are standing there who introduce themselves as PC Dean and PC Atkins. PC Dean confirms both our names and writes something down on the clipboard he's holding. He's left handed, I notice, and has that awkward way of holding a pen that left-handed people often have which makes him look like he's trying to write upside-down.

'May we come in?' asks the female officer, tilting her head on one side.

I stand back and they shuffle through the porch into the sitting room.

'You might have heard the news that a body has been found at St Andrew's Church,' says PC Dean. 'We understand from

Reverend Roland that you're a regular visitor to the graveyard, Mrs Kendall.'

'It's Ms. Yes, I am. My partner was buried there last year, and I often go to his grave to tidy up and leave flowers.' I wait for my breathing to calm down; they just want to ask if I saw anything.

The male officer nods. I'm poised to tell them I need to get to work, but he turns to Beth. 'When did you last see Mr Carl Jacobson?'

'Me?' She grips the collar of her baggy jumper. 'I haven't seen him, what I mean is I know who he is…'

I step in before Beth blunders into muddy territory she can't get herself out of.

'Who is Carl Jacobson?'

'He's been identified as the victim found at the church.'

I look deliberately at Beth with a questioning look. 'You know him..?'

'Yes. My fiancé introduced him to me at a party a few months ago…'

I chip in. 'Oh, I remember. But you haven't seen him since then, I don't think, have you?'

Beth shakes her head. 'That's right, I haven't.'

'When was this party?'

'Oh, er…it was December sometime. I can't remember the exact date, but I can find out.'

He nods. 'On Tuesday evening, March 7th, Mr Jacobson was seen at Winchester station.'

It was the day before Beth met him at the pub.

PC Dean folds back the top sheet on his clipboard. He's been doing the lion's share of the talking so far.

I start to chew my lip, then stop myself.

'This is a still frame from the CCTV footage at the station,' he goes on. 'Someone from the theatre recognised him. It shows a woman next to Mr Jacobson's shoulder.' He leans forward to reveal a black and white image. 'Is that you, Miss Kendall?'

'Er…is it? I don't remember.'

There's barely masked terror in her eyes as she looks over at me. I can't rescue her, she's on her own now. 'I…er, bumped into someone at the station. Yes, I did. I remember now. It must have been him. We both said sorry. I didn't recognise him at the time. I'd only met him once.'

'Where were you going?'

'Me?' She looks lost. 'Nowhere,' she says, sounding confused.

PC Atkins takes a step forward, but it's PC Dean who speaks. 'Well – had you come in on a train or were you catching one?'

'Oh, I see. No. I dropped into the station to…' She hesitates, the silence taking all the air out of the room and running on for what feels like ages. '…to, er…check the trains to Waterloo – I've had a number of auditions in London and I needed to know the times…'

I let out a breath, unaware that I've been holding it.

'And you didn't recognise him?'

'No.'

'Did you stop to chat to each other?'

'No. I don't know him.'

'You've not had any contact with Mr Jacobson…' PC Dean glances down at his notebook, 'since you met him at the party in December?'

'No,' she says, shaking her head.

They seem satisfied for now. He nods at PC Atkins and they wrap things up after that.

As soon as their footsteps have reached the front gate, I turn on her.

'Why the hell didn't you tell me you'd seen Carl the day before?'

'Because nothing happened…and we didn't need an alibi for then, did we?' Beth swings her weight to one hip with an exasperated sigh.

'But someone *saw* you together. Your name has been linked with his. What were you doing?'

'I knew which train Carl was catching from London that day and I wanted to be there…to meet him and give him a surprise,' she says with a pout. 'It was the one and only time I did it,' she adds, as if that makes it any better.

'What happened? Did you hug him? Kiss him, what?'

'Nothing. He wasn't too pleased, as it happens. He basically told me off, said it was a really bad idea to be seen in public together.'

'And you obviously *were* seen…by a work colleague of his, and managed to get yourselves caught on CCTV.' I'm furious by now. 'How ironic! My stage-struck daughter finally gets caught on the one camera we want her to avoid!'

She folds her arms aggressively. 'You're the one who killed him!'

I rock back as though she's struck me. 'How *dare* you make out this is my fault. I thought you were being raped! I was being a good mother. I was protecting you!'

Beth storms off into the kitchen. She flings open a cupboard and rips open a fresh packet of cream crackers.

I go after her. 'Don't open those yet, there's a packet of Ryvita's to finish.'

'They're soft,' she shouts, her mouth full.

'Someone's got to eat them – you can't just waste them.'

Beth's mantra is always 'want it now'. She has no sense of deferred gratification, of curbing indulgences in order to save money.

'By the way, just so you're prepared,' I say, 'Peter and I were discussing the wedding and he told me that Amelia now suspects Carl was having an affair.'

She shoots round. 'When did he say that?'

I avoid looking at her, keeping my eyes on the half-eaten cracker she's holding in her hand. 'Recently.'

'Why…what makes her think that?'

'She didn't tell Peter the reason.' She drops a cracker onto the worktop and turns away. 'And you're going to have to start looking happy about this wedding, my girl. It's got to the stage where everyone's asking what's wrong with you.'

She sighs heavily, her shoulders drooping, staring into the sink. 'You're so controlling all the time. *I have to do this, I have to do that.* So many rules, so many decisions you seem to make for me.'

I jerk my chin back in shock at her audacity. 'Oh, like making you go to an expensive drama college and bleeding me dry? Oh, no, wait a minute, that was *your* idea.' I put my finger to my lips in a mock thinking gesture. 'Like having an affair when most girls would be bowled over by the chance to marry someone like Peter? Oh, no, hang on, that was *your* choice.'

She keeps her back to me, her arms gripping the rim of the draining board.

'I feel claustrophobic here, trapped, I can't breathe anymore.' With that, she turns on her heels and storms out.

When I return home later that evening Beth's bedroom door is closed and all is quiet. My sense of respite is short-lived, however. As I get ready for bed, I notice a flannel and towel are missing from the bathroom. My chest pounding, I realise her toothbrush isn't there, either. I gently ease open the door to her room and that's when it hits me. She's gone.

Chapter 26

Beth

It's raining when I emerge from the tube station at Sloane Square. I need to save money, so I drag my trolley bag along the King's Road, but it's further than I remember and I didn't think to bring a brolly.

Peter's apartment is on the second floor and when I let myself in, the place is cold and smells of oranges past their best. I'm about to wheel my bag straight onto the carpet, but manage to think in time and leave it dripping in the hall. The first thing I see in the sitting room is a framed photo of the two of us, on the white marble mantelpiece.

It was taken minutes after we got engaged and there are other snaps behind it, without frames. I look at the stunning girl looking out at me; relaxed and sexy and can't believe it's me. Peter had taken me to Paris for the opening night of *Mon Ami, le Loup,* a play produced by a friend of his and we'd had champagne in the backstage bar afterwards.

I was feeling flamboyant after the performance, chatting to everyone I could find about how incredible the sets were and my opinion of the lighting, the costumes, the twist in the story at the end.

There was a battered upright piano in the corner and someone had lifted the lid and started playing 'Fly Me to the Moon'. I broke away from the group, spellbound by the music and joined in. It's one of Mum's favourites. I knew all the words. The gathering fell to a hush and from that moment on the room belonged to me. It was surreal. I felt like I was the one they'd all come to see, that night.

When the song ended, everyone cheered, then Peter took me to one side.

Before he could speak, I apologised. 'That was thoughtless,' I said. 'I didn't mean to steal the limelight.'

'You're amazing, you know that? No matter what you do, you will always steal the limelight.'

Then he asked me to marry him. Just like that.

The memory is a blur. It happened so fast that I don't even recall his exact words. All I recall is saying 'yes' without a second's thought, as I fanned my face with a programme left on a nearby chair.

It seems, now, as though it happened to someone else.

Peter's apartment is in Chelsea's Mansfield Square, overlooking a small park open to the public, dense with trees and bushes. He gave me the keys soon after we met, inviting me to stay over whenever I had an audition if he was away. I'd done so several times, but somehow this visit feels different – as though I've never been here on my own before.

I slide self-consciously onto the edge of the grey leather sofa, trying to imagine what it would be like to own a place like this, to be living a life where these luxurious furnishings and stylish fabrics are the norm. I notice for the first time the white window-shutters on the Juliet balconies. There's enough plush material in the curtains to make the sail of a ship.

I get up and brush past the figurine of a tall thin woman made of polished black wood, watching me, as she stands elegant and demure on a glass table. This is what the future will look like when I marry Peter. No second-hand clothes, no penny-pinching, no fish and chips eaten out of the wrapper.

I slipped out of the house last night and caught a late train before Mum came home from work. I had to get away. I needed to think and sort my head out, but I did leave a note.

She's in my face the whole time, grilling me about who I've spoken to and complaining that I should be more upbeat about the wedding. She doesn't seem to recognise the enormity of what we've done, forging ahead choosing ribbons and ordering canapés, as if she hasn't a care in the world.

I can't get my head around it.

Nor can I sit at home, jumping out my skin every time the doorbell jangles, bumping into astonished neighbours at the shops who've heard about the stray body found in the graveyard. Everyone will be speculating about it, wondering if there's a maniac on the loose.

I go to the kitchen and I'm about to boil the kettle when I spot a single empty wine glass on the worktop. Tucked under it is a note saying, *Wine in the fridge – help yourself, love P x*

There's a pen lying next to it and I pick it up and idly roll it around in my mouth, before I realise it's not a cheap biro, but an expensive fountain pen. Mum would have a fit. She keeps going on at me about my 'bad habits'. It's getting on my nerves. I put the pen down so I can't be tempted to chew it and open the fridge.

Sure enough, there's an unopened bottle of Chablis. My favourite.

I smile and reach in. It might just take the edge off. I turn full circle trying to recall where Peter keeps the corkscrew. I come across it not in a drawer, but in a terracotta jar beside the fruit bowl and it makes me wonder who will decide where things go in our kitchen, wherever that might be: London, Kent, Surrey, New York, L.A.?

Will we have a cleaner or will the place be grand enough for a housekeeper? I take a long swig of wine to quell my questions – so many of them we haven't properly addressed yet.

I refill my glass and take a tour, reacquainting myself with the rooms, getting halfway round before it occurs to me to take off my boots. The carpets throughout are a deep fluffy pile in 'ivory oyster' – slightly more grey, I see, in the areas where I've just trodden.

I unzip them and senselessly tip-toe into the hall to park them, then resume my inspection, checking out his bookshelves on the way back, noticing all his volumes are lined up according to height, graduating towards the edges.

I potter into his bedroom and the smell, slightly spicy and peppery, takes me straight back to a time we were here in bed together. I remember I ran my finger over a little bump he had on his neck.

'What's this?'

'Insect bite, I think,' he said. He raised his shoulders. 'Can you bear my imperfections?'

'You're gorgeous,' I told him and sank into his kiss, blown away by how incredibly lucky I felt to have met him.

It seems a lifetime ago.

I step forward and open his wardrobe. Everything is neat, his suits lined up in blocks of different colours; grey, navy, black. His drawers are the same; T-shirts, boxer shorts, pyjamas folded into well-ordered bands of white, grey, black. Where are the bright colours? I try to recall. Does he ever wear them?

It's trusting of him to give me free rein of his personal domain I reflect, as I return to the hall. I'm not sure I'd do the same for him. I wouldn't want him finding old letters in my bedroom, a diary or any of my ropey underwear.

I catch myself in a mirror – I'm such a state and I can't blame the rain for all of it. My hair is flat and limp and my lips look grey. I browse my way through his belongings in the bathroom, the kitchen, then return to the sitting room.

If I didn't know Peter, I'd conclude that this is the home of an innocent, solid, trustworthy man. There's nothing out of place, nothing untidy, but also nothing surprising or particularly interesting. I ponder then on how much I really know him after nine months, taking in his Mahler CDs, books on the rise and fall of the Third Reich, the international history of heraldry and radio-controlled gliders. His collection conjures up a world a million miles away from mine. A world I don't feel part of in the least.

Suddenly I feel like I'm in the wrong apartment; as if I've found my way into the home of a boring old uncle. Will there be a price to pay for this degree of privilege? Will I need to make myself into a different person to fit into this world?

I sit on the sofa and pull my stocking feet under me. Will I be allowed to sit like this when we're married? Will there be a whole string of new rules I'll have to learn, about how I must dress, how I must carry myself and appear before guests? Royal weddings spring to mind. Is this what commoners have to face when they marry a future monarch?

I think of Princess Diana and the twelve-year age difference between her and Prince Charles. Bulimia, depression and self-harm found their way into their relationship as a result of their incompatibility and the absence of lasting love between them.

In that moment a great wave of fear washes over me as I see myself losing all the freedom, spontaneity and choices I currently have. I feel as though Beth Kendall is going to be squashed in a closet somewhere and told to keep quiet, while a mechanical imposter takes over.

No. Peter wouldn't want that.

He loves me for who I am, not who I might become following an intense programme of shaping, elocution and deportment lessons.

On the spur of the moment, I want to hear his voice. I want to connect with him to reassure myself that everything is going to be all right between us. I reach into my bag for my phone before I remember it's gone AWOL, so I track down the landline, in the bookshelf beside the fireplace and call his mobile.

Seconds later, the voice I hear isn't his: *Sorry…the number you're calling is not available…please try again later…*

He must be out of range. It's happened before when he's been in the States. I decide to try his hotel, working out it should be around 6 p.m. in New York.

The receptionist tries to put me through, but there's no reply. He's either still in meetings or it's cocktail hour and he's in the bar. The twangy American accent asks if I'd like to leave a message, but I decline.

Just as well, I conclude, as I'm not feeling particularly bright and breezy. I'd only worry him, as if my cutting him off with barely a word hasn't done that already. Thank goodness Mum is able to act as a go-between. I'm sure she's been conjuring up all manner of excuses as to why I'm not able to speak to him.

Almost as soon as I put down the phone, it rings, making me jump. I'm on the verge of picking up until I see the number on the handset; it's Mum calling from home. She must have read my note. I let it ring and she doesn't leave a message.

The building seems noticeably quiet after that and I shiver. I return to the kitchen and flip on the heating, but even when the radiators have warmed up, it doesn't seem to eradicate the chill I feel. I'm left with a sense of distinct isolation in this space that's beautiful, but not mine.

I notice Peter's spare iPad on the bureau and log in. He's not the least bit bothered about sharing his passwords, so I punch it in and wait as it loads.

I haven't spoken to friends in almost three weeks and I'm starting to feel like I've been shipped off to a desert island. Mum says I'm the queen of over-sharing and I miss posting stupid poses on Instagram, online videos of experimental hair-dos or studded nail art and Tina's latest range of shopping bags.

I log in to all my social media accounts, lining up the tabs across the top of the screen, one after another, then start scrolling through recent posts to see what has passed me by. Maria's knock-out Jimmy Choos, Giles at a stag night, Laura's invitation to her birthday party, which has now passed, Tina's suggestive twerk-dance video. It's completely banal, but nevertheless it's the familiar and multi-coloured tapestry of my life. I miss the silly chat, the instant messages that make me feel I belong. Lately, I barely feel as if I even exist.

I flip on the TV and catch a playback episode of *Catastrophe*. As I finish my glass of wine, I make a decision: tomorrow I'm going to splash out on a new phone. Grandad slipped me a twenty-pound note when I last saw him and I couldn't bring myself to refuse. I must reconnect with everyone before the wedding or else I'll go stir-crazy. Mum says I should hold off because we're skint, but I can't wait until Peter bails me out. Surely, by now, I can trust myself not to blurt out the truth to anyone?

Chapter 27

Rachel

As soon as I wake, I remember that Beth isn't here. Her note was short and to the point: *Gone to London. Back whenever, B x.* At least she signed it with a kiss. It means she doesn't totally hate me.

As I mindlessly pull on yesterday's jeans, all I can think of is that she must have run to someone else by now. I should have known. She's too much of a people person to carry this almighty burden by herself. She's bound to have let someone in on her dark secret, perhaps told Maria, Tina, Laura or even Peter. I must prepare myself for the worst.

I boil the kettle for black coffee going through the motions, but I can't eat a thing. My stomach is acting as though I ate a dodgy curry last night, even though I only managed half a grapefruit. I've lost even more weight in the past few weeks. Gilly, at work, said I am looking like a lolly stick.

By 10 a.m., I breathe again. If Beth *has* confided in someone, the police haven't been told about it or they would have been on the doorstep again, by now.

I apply cherry lipstick and put on my cheery face ready for a shift at the pub that will see me through to late afternoon. After that, I'll go to talk to Russell again at his grave. I've been going less often since we defiled Judy Welsh's final resting place, and I miss that sense of connection with him more than ever.

I flick the net curtain aside in my bedroom to check whether it's stopped raining, then let it go. That's the second time I've seen a figure standing beside the garages at the far side. Hidden under an umbrella. I can't tell if it's a man or woman, but they seem smartly dressed in a long raincoat and dark trousers.

I wait a few seconds then slowly slide the curtain to one side again, but they're walking away.

At the top of the stairs, I grab the banister as a swirl of vertigo threatens to take me down faster than my legs will carry me. It comes with the thought that when Beth is married and gone for good, this is how the house will be; bleak and barren, with only me rattling around in it.

I'm opening a box of crisps behind the bar when I hear a familiar voice. Tina, one of Beth's friends, is leaning over calling to me.

'Hi, Rachel…I've just been to your house,' she says, 'Beth's not answering her phone. Has something happened?'

'Actually, she's lost it…and she's lying low for a bit.'

'She sent me a weird message last week – do you know what's going on?'

'She's fine, Tina. Honestly. She's been so busy sorting out the wedding and with work and auditions – she got a bit snowed under. That's all. Nothing to worry about.' I've been using the same casual spiel with everyone. It rolls off my tongue by now.

I hand her the pint of Guinness she's ordered. 'It's not like her to drop off the radar,' she continues. Another customer is huffing to my right, craning for my attention.

'Sorry…can't chat,' I say, pleased to have an excuse. 'The hen do is in a couple of weeks,' I add, edging away. 'You'll be coming? It's here at the pub.'

'Oh, definitely. Beth said she had something outrageous in mind, so I can't wait.'

With that, she turns to join a group of others at the stripped timber table with the wonky leg, by the window.

Something outrageous in mind. I don't like the sound of that. When did she tell Tina that, I wonder? We want a party that's totally under control, with absolutely *no* surprises.

Mid-afternoon brings the moment I've been dreading. The bar is quiet and I'm leaning back against the till with a damp bar towel in my hand, chatting to Gilly about ordering more sachets of tomato sauce, when Marvin asks me to change a barrel. I knew this time would come. I've managed to avoid having to go down to the cellar until now and I can think of no reason not to, this time.

I unlock the door and close my eyes, bracing myself before I go in. I've replayed this scene so many times, mostly at around three in the morning. In my mind I hear Beth crying out, hear Carl grunting, see him pressed up against her from behind. I know I would react in exactly the same way if it happened again.

The cellar seems smaller than I remember it. The spot where Carl fell looks entirely unremarkable and the tap that actually killed him has long gone, due to a routine change of barrels. I stare at the one in its place – identical to the inadvertent weapon that snatched away his life. In my nightmares, I see a pool of blood spreading in a thick splodge across the slabs and I'm clutching a cloth, but people keep getting in my way so I'm unable to bend down to wipe it clean. I picture them walking into it without noticing, then see their faces change as trails of bloody footsteps appear across the floor.

My hands shake as I fiddle with the tubes and switches, shifting from the old cask of ale to the new one. I'm about to go back upstairs when my phone clangs in my back pocket. It's Peter.

'Rachel speaking…' As soon as I say my name, I dip into a panic, confused for a second about whether I'm supposed to be Rachel or Beth. Then I remember which phone I'm holding and all is well.

'I'm just ringing to see how things are going,' he says, sounding tired. 'I don't know if you've being trying to reach me, but I've been out of range.'

'Oh, no, I haven't rung…all going to plan,' I tell him. 'The bridesmaid's dresses are ready, the seating is sorted for the reception and the menus printed.'

'That's wonderful. How about drinks?'

'Yeah, drinks are ordered and I've got together a playlist for the ceremony and the first dance. Beth said you both wanted 'Fly Me to the Moon', is that right? The DJ will take it from there, but we've asked for jazz favourites from your list and Beth has chosen a few, too.' She hasn't yet, but she will. 'We just need to finalise your personal vows. Can you send me an email with your thoughts on those?'

'Of course. I must get together with Beth.'

My heart sinks at the thought of another phone or video call where I have to step in as her imposter.

'I've transferred another amount into your account,' he continues, 'but please let me know if it doesn't cover everything.'

'That's very kind, Peter. Thank you.'

Inevitably, it isn't long before he's asking more about Beth. I don't want to tell him she's in London in case he rings his flat expecting to find her there.

'She's gone to the library, I think,' I tell him instead. 'Looking up background information for her next audition.'

'Oh, good. I'm sure it's only a matter of time before she lands a big one,' he says, without a great deal of conviction. 'She's seemed a lot better recently, so that's a relief.' There's a whooping sound of a New York siren in the background. 'I heard the news, by the way.'

'News?'

'A friend of Amelia's emailed me to say Carl's body was found.'

'Yes, it was all over the news here.' A film of sweat gathers in my palms. *Don't show anything in your voice.*

'I looked up the report online,' he goes on. 'Apparently, he was found in a cemetery in Winchester…'

'That's right…so gruesome…'

There's a sigh of disbelief. 'I recognised the photograph. If I'm not mistaken, it was the same church where I suggested Beth and I get married.'

'I know…that's right. How utterly bizarre…'

'I can't imagine what happened to him…obviously the police are looking into it, but why there?' He clicks his tongue.

'I heard he was in Winchester meeting people at the Theatre Royal,' I say, intent on taking the focus away from the church.

'Awful, awful business…' There's a catch in his voice. 'That's also why I'm ringing, actually. Carl was my best man…'

I'm glad Peter's not with me to see the colour drain from my face. 'Oh, my God. I didn't know…'

Why didn't Beth tell me?

There's an awkward gap while Peter struggles to speak. 'And… well…Amelia was invited to the reception, but…obviously…'

He stumbles through the words, his voice breaking.

'Right, of course, I'll sort that out.'

I'd completely missed the fact that the two of them were invited to the wedding. I'd need to make sure their place cards don't end up on a table.

I take a mini detour in my mind. What would it have been like for Beth having Carl at the wedding? Then instantly return to the present.

'How's Amelia?' I ask, in lieu of more pressing questions I want to ask, such as: *What was it Amelia found?* and *Should I be worried?*

'Oh, coping pretty badly, as you'd expect. She's always been, how can I put it – emotionally fragile. It doesn't take much to tip her over the edge. She's been hysterical, needing medication… sorry, I shouldn't be…'

'No. Honestly, it's fine.'

'She's definitely got it into her head that Carl was having an affair. She came across a gold pendant in a box in his desk a few days ago. She's convinced it wasn't for her. It appears she only likes diamonds and it's a pendant with an emerald in the centre. She's becoming obsessed with finding out who he was supposed to be seeing, but…I think she's just grabbing at anything…'

An emerald. My mind leaps to the vibrant colour of Beth's eyes. People constantly refer to them as emerald green. It's so obvious, I can't believe Peter hasn't made the connection.

He's speaking again. 'Carl was always getting jewellery engraved for friends – he gave me a watch with a message on the back for my 30th birthday. It wouldn't surprise me if he planned to get a few words added for Amelia – I'm sure it was meant for her – although she's adamant it's not her style.'

There's a pause.

'Well…I'm actually at work and I suppose—' I want to wind up the call, but he's speaking again.

'Amelia's always been hyperactive, but she's gone into overdrive. I think it's to avoid the grief, but she seems to be on a mission to find a jeweller's receipt or note or some indication about who it was for.'

I squeeze my eyes shut, praying the necklace wasn't meant for my daughter and that it has no trail that could lead back to her.

'Amelia's tearing the place apart, determined to find proof of an affair. She thinks if she can track down another woman, it could lead to his killer. A jealous husband or boyfriend, maybe, or an altercation gone wrong, if Carl was trying to end it.'

He stops for breath.

I grit my teeth, waiting for this ordeal to be over.

'Sorry I'm banging on about this, but I feel so useless over in the States and I can't get back to England – not just yet.'

'No, of course. He was your friend. You're upset. It's…terrible.'

'The police are on to all his paperwork now, as well as checking phone and bank records, his laptop…that sort of thing. I'm sure they'll find something. Shocking business. It must be someone who knew the area, surely, for him to end up in the graveyard, like that.'

Chapter 28

Beth

I woke early the next morning, glad to be miles away from the scene of the crime. I was about to help myself to bread from the freezer, then changed my mind and decided to head out for breakfast in a local café. Peter has a favourite haunt around the corner that does rich coffee that will blow away the cobwebs.

When I was at drama college and lived in Chiswick, I used to have breakfast out all the time. I ran up a bit of an overdraft, as it happens. So many meals out, trips to the cinema, parties, taxis home. Nothing extravagant; merely that London is expensive. Mum bailed me out a few times. Neither of us knew the money was going to run out.

Chelsea is more upmarket than Chiswick and when I see how little is in my purse, I toy with finding a cheap takeaway, before having a change of heart and sauntering into the French café on Hollywood Road. There are never any prices in the window – always a sign it's expensive. Inside, a woman with a glossy Harvey Nichols' bag is checking her lipstick in a small mirror and a couple of Japanese tourists are poring over a map on an iPad.

I settle at the table Peter and I often choose, by the window, and buy an Americano with cream, together with an almond croissant. For the first time in three weeks, I have an appetite and the pastry is warm and flaky. Each mouthful – which costs around fifty pence, I calculate – melts in my mouth. This is the world I'll soon be stepping into, I think to myself, running my fingertips over the pristine lace cloth on the table. After the wedding, it's going to be like walking on to a stage and playing the role of someone else for the rest of my life.

After getting no change back from my ten-pound note, I walk along to the main road looking for a phone shop. Before long, I have a new pay-as-you-go phone, ready to use, in my pocket.

I head onto the King's Road and am drawn to the displays in the windows; platform shoes, vintage dresses, jump suits, my passion for fashion resurging with every step. A bunch of guys digging the pavement stop in unison as I pass, their pickaxes held in the air, and I can't hide a smile. Nothing has changed, yet being so far away from the source of my worry has sent it spinning off into the far distance.

In this new frame of mind, I pull out my phone and make my first call.

'Hi, it's me...'

'Where the hell have you been, girl? We've all been worried sick. What's going on? Where are you?'

'I'm fine. I'm really sorry I went off line,' I tell her. 'Just got… bogged down with so much going on…but, listen, I'm in London right now and I wondered if you'd be free for lunch.'

'Ooh…you're lucky. I'm free from noon for an hour or so,' she says, 'can you get to Covent Garden?'

'Tell me when and where.'

We agree on a restaurant that covers three floors near the Seven Dials. It's spacious and airy and will give us chance to chat without feeling we need to free up a table.

Maria's been my best friend since my second year at drama college. She's wacky, forthright and a fabulous listener. And she's Spanish, with deliciously trilled 'r' and breathy 'h' sounds in her accent. She's also a terrific sword coach and we met when she took my class through a whistle-stop course on stage combat.

We both order a crab salad and I jump in with questions in the hope of staving off the inevitable barrage of inquiries that are sure to come my way.

She tells me anecdotes from her recent stint on 'Romeo and Juliet' at The Globe.

'And the big news is that Tony has got a recording contract with his band,' she gushes.

I manage to get through a full twenty minutes shining the spotlight on her, before she turns it on me.

She looks down for a moment. Her plate is empty, mine still barely touched. 'So, Beth, what is going on?'

I've always loved her directness, embedded in a fulsome warmth and lack of judgement.

'Just busy…you know…the wedding, auditions – crap auditions, as it happens…work…'

She keeps her eyes on me. 'It's so unlike you to be out of touch. Laura and Giles, we didn't know what to think.'

'It's no big deal, honestly.'

She's not convinced.

For a second I'm tempted to tell her everything.

'Look at you,' she says, 'You're skinny, girl, you look tired.' She reaches over and inspects a clump of my hair, 'you're out of condition – tell me what's going on.'

I knew it would be like this. That's why I haven't been able to speak to her. Usually, her persistence is exactly what I need to draw out what's bugging me. But not this time. Having her face me like this, with her concerned and searching brown eyes, makes me feel like I'm about to be thrown to the lions.

'It's complicated…'

'That's okay, Pequeño.' She always calls me 'little one', a cute mannerism I love about her. 'Start at the beginning and see how you go.'

She puts down her glass of water and takes my hand.

I have to tell her something.

'It's Mum.'

'What's she done?'

A couple on a nearby table break into laughter and I feel a shudder of misery.

'She was in a terrible state when Russell died last year. She wasn't coping; always putting on a brave face, but underneath she was a wreck.'

Maria nods thoughtfully. 'Yeah…I know all that.'

'Well…she still goes to his grave nearly every day and I'm sure it's not good for her. It's like she's not letting him go. She told me recently he left her in a lot of debt and I think that's part of her suffering; it's as if he betrayed her, cheated her.'

'That's tough, that's hard, when the man, he's gone, and she can't…' she searches for the word '…confront him about it.'

I nod. 'Mum's tried her best to hide her misery from me, but for months there was this heaviness and despondency in everything she did.' I fiddle with the leather bracelet around my wrist. 'That's until I told her about Peter. She was utterly blown away when she knew I'd met someone. Then when I said he'd proposed to me…whoa…it changed everything. It was like she suddenly came back to life again. She really likes him and she's been throwing herself into planning the big day; eating again, smiling again. It's as though she's found a reason to get up in the morning.'

'That's good,' she says, 'but what about you?'

I glance down. 'Marrying Peter…it feels like a big rush. I barely know him, yet soon we're going to be together for the rest of our lives.'

'You need more time?'

'I don't know. When we first got together I thought he was amazing…he's so sure of himself and powerful.'

'He's does seem a real catch, but I've only met him a couple of times.'

'He's been away a lot. But he's funny and sweet and warm… and…'

It feels like I'm trying to convince her.

'Getting married is a big step.'

'That's it. That's right. Mum asked me after he proposed if it was too soon to think of marriage. She asked how I could be so sure about him after only a few months and I said I just *knew* he was the one. But now…'

'Now your heart is changing?' she says, watching my face.

I love the way her translations into English make her words cut to the chase. I bite my lip, then shrug. 'I'm so mixed up. I haven't seen Peter properly for ages. I stayed in his apartment last night and I'm looking at his things, thinking "who is this guy?"'

She nods, looking serious, waiting for more.

'Mum's so involved in the preparations. It seems like that's what's keeping her going. Everything's steaming ahead. I'm getting swept along and it feels out of control.'

I come to a stop then, aware that every word I've said is true, even though I hadn't fully admitted it to myself until now. It's by no means all of the situation, but it's certainly part of it and the only part I'm able to tell her.

'The wedding is on April 15th, right?' she says.

I nod.

She takes her hand away from mine and counts on her fingers. 'Two and a half weeks. You've got time,' she says. 'Some couples get as far as the day itself before one of them has wet feet.'

'*Cold* feet,' I say, looking up at her, unable to hide a smile.

'Where's Peter now?' she asks, checking her watch. She has a class to get back to and our time is nearly over.

'In America until the end of next week, I think. Thing is, I'm not really talking to him. I feel so confused and churned up, I don't know what to say to him.'

She sits back, mulling it over.

'That's not good. You must try to take your mother out of the calculation.'

'She just wants me to be happy. I know that. She's well aware that Peter's got money and status and he could help me in my career…she wants all that for me and it's very tempting.'

'Like a ticket to success?'

I laugh. 'It sounds so sexist, but it's not like that. Mum seems to think he's going to "rescue" me, but I see us making an incredible partnership instead. A formidable team. Peter says I inspire him, make him feel like he can take risks and branch out. I make him creative, help him see possibilities, open his eyes and make him dream. It's not all one way.'

'Is it true love?'

'I think so...' I stop. 'I'm not sure.'

She shakes her head. 'Your doubt is there for a reason, Pequeño. It's too easy to make mistakes.'

'That's true. At the moment, there are too many gaps. I don't know what he wants for the future – if we want the same things. I don't even know where we're going to settle. We've talked generally about stuff, but we haven't made any proper plans. It's all too open-ended, even for me!'

I attempt to laugh, but it sounds hollow.

'Trust your heart. If you're not ready, he should respect you. If he truly loves you, he will give you space and time.' She looks up gingerly. 'Then you might need to speak plainly to your mother.'

It's the last bit I'm dreading the most. If I can't go ahead with the wedding, how the hell am I going to tell her?

I reach over, pull Maria's hand towards me and kiss it. 'Thank you.'

'This is for the rest of your life, Pequeño, you have to be certain. Don't let anyone push you into anything.'

As we hug outside on the pavement, I realise I've done well. I've got through this close encounter with my best friend without blurting out the whole story. I also know her advice is spot on and I can no longer avoid it – I'm going to have to speak to Peter as soon as I can.

Chapter 29

Rachel

'Where the hell have you been?' I ask, as Beth strolls in through the front door two days after waltzing off.

'I've been at Peter's place. I told you,' she says, parking her trolley bag at the foot of the stairs.

'I've been ringing his apartment. Why didn't you answer?'

'I've been out. Besides, I needed space to think, Mum. That's why I went.'

To get away from me, in other words.

I clear my throat. 'Have you spoken to anyone?'

She strips off her jacket but doesn't sit down. 'I saw Maria, but don't worry, we didn't talk about…*that*.'

'You sure?'

'Yes.'

Beth looks brighter I notice. There's colour in her cheeks for a change.

'I've been worried sick.' I take a step towards her and she slides into my arms. We fold around each other in a firm embrace and I breathe in the herbal smell of her hair.

'What have you been doing all this time?' I mutter into her neck.

'Saw a film, went for walks. I made a cake at Peter's this morning.' She dips into a plastic bag by her feet. 'lemon drizzle cake – your favourite.'

She hands me a plastic container.

'Sweetheart…' My throat clams shut, I can barely get the words out.

I put the cake on the table and beckon for her to come outside. The sun is out, making the colours sharp as if the world has become three-dimensional all of a sudden. There's no breeze for once, allowing the soothing rays to settle on my bare arms.

'I've been sweeping the patio,' I tell her, setting out the tattered deckchairs I'd propped against the shed. 'Orange juice?'

She nods and throws her scarf over the back of one of them. 'And a piece of cake,' she says, coyly, sticking her tongue between her teeth.

I come back with a tray holding our refreshments, sit down and stretch back, shutting my eyes against the sun's brightness. A faint smell of blossom floats over the fence from the neighbour's shrubs. I'm emerging from a dark tunnel having been trapped for months. Everything is going to be fine.

Beth reaches into her pocket and puts something on the table. It's a new phone.

I snatch a breath.

'I got it yesterday,' she explains, 'It's okay, it's just a cheap one.'

I try not to look uneasy. 'Have you called Peter?' I say, trying to keep the tremor out of my voice.

'Not yet, but I'm going to.'

'When we last spoke about the wedding, he said he was going to be out of range for…ages,' I say, gulping down the panic in my voice.

'Whatever…I'll try in a while, then,' she says, clearly disappointed.

The mouthful of cake I was about to have has no appeal anymore. I'm flattening down the edge into crumbs, toying with it, when I hear the doorbell. Beth is nearest the backdoor and gets up. She comes back with all of the new colour wiped from her cheeks.

'It's the police again,' she says, pitching her voice higher than normal in a bid to sound casual.

We both go inside. It's the same officers, but it's PC Atkins who takes the lead, this time. PC Dean stays by the front door, but PC Atkins sits down, which unnerves me. It implies she doesn't intend this visit to be brief.

She has pale eyelashes, almost white, and her hair is beach-blonde and tied back. Several wisps have escaped from under her hat and are floating against her forehead like feathers.

'There's nothing to be alarmed about. We're just conducting house-to-house enquiries. We're in the process of putting together a picture of Mr Jacobson's last movements and the final sightings of him,' she says.

I sit beside her while Beth sits on the pouf – the seat that's furthest away.

'To be honest, we're a bit confused.' PC Atkins glances down at her notebook and turns to address Beth. 'Miss Kendall, you said you bumped into Mr Jacobson at Winchester train station at around 6.30 p.m. on Tuesday, March 7th, but didn't recognise him, is that right?'

'Yes.'

'And you've had no other contact with him since you met him at a party in December?'

'That's right.'

She takes a laboured breath. 'No contact at all, before or after then?'

Shit…

'I don't think so…'

'Okay.' PC Atkins turns to a fresh page in her notepad. 'Can you tell us where you were between Wednesday evening, 8th March and Friday evening that same week?'

Why is she asking this? What has happened to bring them back to us?

I step in. 'Are you allowed to ask these kinds of questions? I mean, shouldn't we have a lawyer or something?' I try to make my voice sound breezy, as though this whole set-up strikes me as a time-wasting exercise.

Her head whips round to face me. 'You're free to ask us to leave,' she says, pointedly, 'but these are just standard questions as part of the house-to-house investigation.' She stares at me. 'Are you okay to continue?'

'Fine,' I say, nipping my lips together.

PC Atkins repeats her question. PC Dean is poised to take notes. 'I'm not sure,' says Beth. 'I'll need to check my online calendar.'

Good thinking, Beth – how many people know exactly where they were three weeks ago?

She disappears to fetch the laptop, while I avoid looking at the officers.

'Right,' says Beth, resting it on her knees. 'On the Wednesday evening I was here with Mum, having tea at about 6.30 p.m. and later, I went over to see my grandad in Abbot's Worthy. I met a friend, Angie Wilton, on the way, in Conway St.'

'What time was this?'

'I bumped into her…er, it would have been just before nine o'clock. Then I caught the bus to Abbot's Worthy.'

PC Atkins glances over to the officer by the door. 'That seems quite late to be setting out to pay your grandfather a visit. What made you go over at that time?'

My fingers, folded loosely in my lap, twitch. Beth and I never did agree a reason for her late visit to see Adrian.

I force myself to keep my hands still. I'm counting on Beth, praying she's thought this through.

'He'd…lost his watch,' she says, drawing out the words. 'My grandma gave it to him and he was distressed. He gets easily confused and upset about things and he'd rung to see if I could go over and find it.'

A shiver of panic scampers down my back. Only Adrian *didn't* ring up. If the police check our phone records they'll find out he never made any call.

Beth carries on, 'I found it, but it was late by then, so I stayed the night.'

'And the Thursday and Friday?'

'I came back here on Thursday morning, did some work – research at home for a quiz show, then after tea, Mum and I watched *Basic Instinct* from about eight-ish,' she points to the DVD in a stack beside the television. 'After that, we went to bed.'

PC Atkins draws a line in her notebook and Beth goes on to tell the truth about where she was on Friday. By then it was all over, although the police don't know that.

PC Dean is planted in front of the doorway like a bouncer. 'Can you give us a brief rundown of where you were, Ms Kendall?' he asks.

I feel Beth's eyes burning into my skin.

I explain that I popped in to the King's Tavern to change the heating on Wednesday evening, then used Marvin's car to get a few items at the supermarket. Thankfully that's not a lie and I still have the receipt, if they need to check. My DNA will be all over the pub, the cellar too, but there's nothing untoward about that, given that I work there.

I try to drop in as many alibis as I can for the forty-eight-hour window they're investigating, including the time Jeremy from next door came in to ask about our water bill on Thursday afternoon.

'He thought his statement was really high and wanted to compare it with mine,' I explain. 'Turned out he'd got a leak.'

It all sounds ordinary and spontaneous to my ears and I expect them to be on their way, but there's more.

PC Dean eyeballs Beth. 'We've checked Mr Jacobson's phone records and on Monday 6th March, three days before he went missing, a call was made from a mobile phone registered to you, Miss Kendall, lasting four minutes.'

*No, no that can't be right…*I have to draw on all my energy to stop myself getting to my feet.

PC Atkins is speaking again. 'Can you tell us why you made that call, Miss Kendall? You said you hadn't had any contact with Mr Jacobson.'

Beth gives me a wary stare as she opens her mouth.

'No wait a minute, officer,' I butt in, 'she lost her phone…'

PC Atkins sighs. 'When was that?'

Beth is shaking her head, looking agitated. 'No, that was later, Mum…I lost my phone last Saturday.'

Something shrinks inside me. We're making a complete hash of this.

Beth leans forward and clears her throat. 'I did ring him. You know what…I forgot. Of course, I did.' She throws her eyes up. 'I'd had something to drink and it slipped my mind.'

'Right,' says PC Dean, with a huff. 'So you *did* call Mr Jacobson.' He vigorously scribbles a few words in his little book. 'Can you tell me why you called Mr Jacobson that Monday night?'

'Peter, my fiancé, is friends with him and he'd said Mr Jacobson could be helpful to my career. That's why he introduced me at that party I mentioned. I was feeling miserable one night – I've had a run of crappy auditions and I'd had too much to drink…' she glances over to me looking guilty. 'I rang him to see if he might have some advice for me.'

'How did you know his number?'

'Peter had given me his card ages ago. I still had it in my purse. He was busy when I called and didn't say much. I asked him some dumb questions about acting and he fobbed me off with vague clichés. He was just being polite because he and Peter were friends. That's why I forgot. It wasn't worth remembering.'

'Have you had any other contact with Mr Jacobson?' PC Atkins asks, stabbing the tip of the pen on her page. 'Think very carefully.'

'No. I don't think so…honestly.'

She looks close to tears.

'I think we need to finish, there,' I say. 'My daughter clearly made a mistake…she forgot.'

PC Dean steps into the porch and PC Atkins gets up without a word. Only once I've opened the front door does she stop and turn to us. 'We may need to speak to you again,' she says sourly, as the other officer pulls down his jacket sleeves.

I calmly close the front door after them and turn to Beth.

'I'm sorry, I'm so sorry…' she says, rushing towards me.

She stops when she reaches me, unsure about whether a hug is going to be welcome. I fold my arms, blocking her, shaking my head. 'I don't believe this. You *rang* him!'

'It was just the once.'

I send my eyes to the ceiling, 'Just the once…' I grind my teeth. 'Why?' I know it wasn't for the reason she claimed earlier.

'To let him know I'd got the spare set of keys to the pub…to confirm Wednesday night.'

For fuck's sake…

I stare at my slippers. 'It's not looking good, Beth, it's not looking good at all.'

'There's something else,' she says, fiddling with her lip.

I lean back against the wall, my body limp, waiting for the next bombshell.

'After I'd told the officers about my alibis, I realised about the buses.'

'What buses? What do you mean?'

'I said I saw Angie just before 9 p.m. and she'll confirm that. But I can't have got a bus to Grandad's after that.' I stand open-mouthed as she delivers the final blow. 'The police will know I lied. The last bus to Abbots Worthy is at eight thirty.'

Chapter 30

Rachel

Saturday, April 8 – one week before the wedding

Nearly a week has passed since the visit from the police and we've not heard anything about the alibi that doesn't fit.

Beth and I are expecting the efficient PC Dean and prim PC Atkins to come back any day with questions about the bus service to Abbots Worthy. I've primed Beth to say that she and Angie must have got the time slightly out – by about half an hour – an easy mistake. That's the only way Beth could have caught the last bus over to Adrian's.

Peter sent me a text earlier in the week to say he had to catch an urgent flight out to Colorado Springs, an area of the US where the signal is notoriously poor. It meant he would be out of contact for a few days. A blissful breathing space, while it lasted.

Beth's new phone – the one Peter doesn't have the number for – is sitting innocently on the arm of the sofa. He'll be back in range by now. I both welcome and dread the time when Beth speaks to him again. On the one hand, I want her to reach out to Peter, to seal their intentions to be man and wife. But I also know their experiences of the last two weeks aren't going to match up.

In Beth's world, she's had no contact with him and in Peter's, he's had her letter, exchanged instant messages and spoken to her twice, catching up and sharing loving sweet-nothings.

What a shambles.

Knowing Beth was going to call Peter, I staged the discovery of her original phone, claiming I found it under the drawers beside her bed when I was vacuuming her room. There are stacks of calls she's missed and I don't want her to lose out on anything important. I've deleted everything between Peter and I.

'But, I checked there,' she said, defiantly.

A few hours before her hen night is due to begin, she joins me in the kitchen, saying she's finally spoken to him.

'How was it?' I ask, innocuously, as I'm dragging wet laundry out of the washing machine. The spin isn't working properly.

'Fine. A bit weird, actually.' She sticks out her bottom lip. 'He didn't seem particularly surprised to hear from me or grill me about not being in touch. Not at all, in fact. I thought he'd expect an explanation.'

'He must have been very busy with work, Beth. He told me he's been all over the place; New York, Los Angeles, Colorado… and don't forget, I've been filling him in on how you've been.'

'Yeah…I suppose…' She looks pensive. 'Odd though, he was talking about an instant message I sent him a few days ago, but I didn't send any.'

'Oh, I've had that happen before,' I tell her breezily. 'Sometimes old messages come through ages after they were sent or get repeated, for some reason.' I bundle past her with the laundry basket.

She makes a little 'hmmm' sound, but thankfully, with the party hours away she doesn't have long to reflect on it.

She goes to her room, puts the latest CD by Miley Cyrus on loud and begins her ritual of trying on clothes to find the best outfit.

I get the closest to feeling relaxed that I've been for weeks. My daughter is communicating with Peter, managing to hold her nerve and she's taking the next step towards her wedding. I'm about to open a bottle of Prosecco so I can take up a glass to her, when there's a loud rumbling and she comes charging down the stairs.

'It was Peter on the phone again. Nancy's just been in touch with him.'

'Who's Nancy?'

'She's a snooty friend of Amelia's…a real busy-body. She's putting all kinds of ideas into Peter's head!'

I push the unopened bottle of cheap fizz to one side and get her to sit down.

'There were photos from that party in December, when Peter introduced me to Carl,' she says. 'They were posted on Facebook at the time and no one paid much attention. But Amelia has been manically going through *everything* to do with Carl in the last few months and she's been checking the pictures again. She reckons she's found a shot that shows Carl and I in the background, looking suspiciously like we're sharing a "moment" – and she's told Nancy.'

'And Nancy has told Peter,' I add. 'That's kind of her.'

She nods, blowing hair out of her face, looking hot and bothered.

'What did you say to Peter?'

'Oh, well, I denied it, of course. I said Amelia's just looking for a reason for his death and she's going to be clutching at anything and claiming it's suspicious. But she probably knows by now that I called Carl that Monday night.'

'But you made it clear that was completely innocent.'

'Yeah, but it's planted a seed, hasn't it? And now Peter's asking lots of questions.'

She pulls her bare feet up onto the wooden chair and buries her face in her hands.

'It's falling apart, Mum…' She starts weeping.

'No, it's not.' I put my hands on her shoulders. 'There is no evidence that you had anything but a vague professional interest in him. Nothing at all, you hear me.'

She doesn't look up.

I glance at the clock. My stomach's bubbling. 'We've got a big party in less than two hours and you're going to have to bring the performance of your life out of the bag.' I bob down beside her. 'You'll be fine, sweetheart. You'll be with all your friends, you can get up and do some singing and dancing and be the centre of attention. You'll be fabulous.'

She lifts her tearstained face, looking anything but.

'Come on, show me what you're going to wear.'

She's shaking her head the whole time. 'I don't feel like it,' she grunts, and sidles off upstairs.

I take a shower and flick through the hangers in my wardrobe searching for something that will fit me. Everything looks too big. I try on my best cocktail dress, which used to be a snug fit, but there are floppy wings at the side where my hips used to be.

Beth's wardrobe will be a better bet and I approach her room through the bathroom. That's when I realise the music has stopped. I press my ear to the door and can hear her sobbing.

I tap on the door, not waiting for a reply, and go in. I sit beside her on the bed. She flings herself back on to the pillow with a loud groan.

'It's doing my head in...all these lies...all this sodding secrecy.'

'You need to stop this right now,' I tell her, an edge in my voice. 'You're not the only one affected here. It isn't just your secret that you can do whatever you like with. I could go...*would go* to prison for what we did.'

She blocks me out with her arm over her eyes, but she's stopped crying.

I get up to go.

'You're not wearing *that*, are you?' she adds, without rearing up.

I'm still in the dress that hangs off me.

'No. I wanted...I wondered...'

She laughs. 'Help yourself,' she says and swings the wardrobe door open with her foot. 'I'm wearing the silver one.'

It's the pleated Grecian gown we call the 'Oscar' dress. She looks stunning in it.

'Nice,' I say, picking out a pair of black silk culottes and a red frilly blouse. Her clothes are much more glamorous than mine and they'll fit.

'I was a little bit in love with Carl, you know,' she whispers.

I stop in my tracks, holding the hangers against my chest. It's something I hadn't accounted for – her grief.

'I'm sorry. About everything,' I say, then as an after-thought. 'And Peter? Are you still in love with him?'

She sits up. 'Oh, yeah,' she says, dismissively, her eyes not reaching mine.

Before I leave, I make a sweep of the room. I don't know what I'm looking for, but I'm uneasy. 'You're not going to do anything rash tonight, are you?'

She huffs out a loud sigh. 'No, Mum.'

As I leave her, my mind is still not set at rest. Beth loves a party. She wants to be the person who makes it memorable. The one who gets noticed. Is she planning on giving some kind of dramatic performance tonight, without telling me?

I shake my head.

What can I do?

Chapter 31

Beth

Mum is standing beside the bar telling everyone I've got pre-wedding nerves, but people are also whispering that I may be pregnant. I don't care what they think at this point. Anything to get them off my back.

I met Tina in the car-park earlier and threw myself at her. I felt like I'd returned after months missing on a perilous voyage. We linked arms and headed towards the source of the music, but I drew to a complete standstill once we reached the entrance.

I couldn't go inside. I completely froze. I pretended my stiletto had got stuck in the metal grille and stood back to let other people through, then I made out I'd left something in the taxi and aimlessly tottered across the tarmac.

Mum came out at that point, hurried after me and took my arm.

'It's totally different inside,' she insisted, speaking right into my ear. 'It looks different, smells different, feels different. Just focus on all the new décor and party frills and you'll be fine.' With that, she dragged me over the threshold.

Mum has certainly done a great job of making the pub look primed for a celebration. Gold balloons, banners with the words *Bride to Be*, cupcakes iced with hearts, white roses, scatter-sequins on every table in the shape of stars.

She's right. It barely looks like the same place.

Behind me is the cork board from our kitchen, with the label, *Keepsake Kiss.* There are squares for each party-goer to plant their lipstick pout. Three pink prints are already there, each signed underneath.

On a table in the corner, there's a patchwork of numbered photos of me at different stages in my life, from toddler onwards. The caption, *How old was the bride?* is pinned to the top of the panel and there are coloured pens in jars beside answer sheets.

Mum's thought of everything.

Once I'm inside, I'm greeted with squeals of 'Here she is!' followed by several rounds of embraces, swamping me with clammy bare arms and a clash of floral perfumes. Most of them are admonishing me for being out of touch.

'Where've you *been*?'

'What the hell happened to you?'

'Why didn't you return my calls?'

Tina asks what I want to drink and as soon as she heads for the bar, Laura emerges from a group to my right, presenting me with a glass brimming over with champagne bubbles. Within the first five minutes, I've gulped down both offerings. A buzz of electricity shunts around my body and I feel, at last, like I'm shedding the tight skin of dread and remorse that has kept me rigid for weeks. One thing is certain, tonight I'm going to steal the show.

It's the first outing for my silk 'Oscar' dress. It was meant for a big night in the spotlight, crossing low over the front and back in soft silver pleats, then floating to the floor like a marble column. I look like a Greek goddess. Russell bought it for my twenty-first, for me to wear at a special film function, no doubt on Mum's credit card from what she's told me.

'Doors will open up once you've secured a part alongside the big names,' he'd said. 'Or maybe save it for when you're nominated for a role in a Hollywood movie!'

Nice idea. Problem is, I'd have to land a part, *any* part first, and 'the accident' has set me back months. My confidence is shot, I've been distracted and emotionally all over the place, when it's come to showing audition panels what I'm made of. All since Carl hit his head in the cellar.

Not anymore.

I've decided that tonight is going to be *my* time. It's my party and I'm going to shine. I'm going to have a few more drinks and wow everyone with one hell of a performance. There must be over a hundred people here already and I'm going to give them a stonking surprise. Reveal something I want everyone to hear. *That* will shut them all up!

'So, how does it feel to wave goodbye to your single life and become Mrs Roper, next Saturday?' It's Pamela, a neighbour Mum invited. She's managing to carry four wine glasses at once.

'Oh, I'm not changing my name,' I tell her, abruptly. 'I'm going to be Beth Kendall forever. Celebrities never change their name when they get married.' Pamela stares at me, her mouth open, as though she must have missed something. 'It's what you do when you're famous,' I tell her, walking away. I know I sound like a bitch, but I don't care. Tonight, I'm going to show them. I'm sick of feeling like a loser.

The DJ finally puts on *La Bamba*, one of the songs I asked for, and I take to the dance floor to show off my best moves; twirls, shimmies, spins and nifty footwork, all the while swinging my hips.

Everyone's eyes pan round towards me, and groups clear the floor to watch. I'm in my element.

An hour and several drinks later and I'm holding the mike at the karaoke, singing my heart out to 'Wrecking Ball' and wowing everyone again. I get a massive blast of applause and take my bows.

It's all going swimmingly until Laura asks why I've just sung a song about a couple splitting up.

'It's about giving all your love and getting wrecked in return,' she says, sounding almost as drunk as I am. 'It's about calling it off and not going through with it…'

'I just like the song,' I retort, shaking my head and staggering off the stage for a breath of fresh air.

As I'm coming back inside, Peter calls and stupidly, I answer. Things start going off the rails after that.

He accuses me of being 'different'. He says in the last few weeks I've been odd with him, asking questions I should know the answers to and confusing him. He says I've been blowing hot and cold – all over him one minute and distant the next.

I'm worse than tipsy and his voice comes and goes. I don't want to listen to any of it, but I catch a few scraps: 'badly wrong' and 'not the same'. Then he asks if there's someone else.

'Abslootly not… don't be silly,' I say, slurring my words.

As I'm speaking, a terrible thought occurs to me.

Carl always called me from random public places. He never rang from his own phone, and either he had an amazing memory or he must have written my number down somewhere. He *must* have done.

My call with Peter fizzles out after a string of silences and I find myself at the bar, accepting more drinks. I want everything to go away. I want to return to feeling as I had done just five minutes ago. The star of the show. But my mind is racing away. Where did Carl keep a record of my number? Would he have thought ahead and kept it somewhere Amelia would never look? With every sip I take, I'm doing my best to wash the problem away.

Before long, Mum is intercepting my drinks.

'That's enough, Beth. You're wasted. Don't make a fool of yourself on your special night.'

'Let me enjoy myself for once,' I throw back at her, with a glare that says *don't touch me*.

She takes me on one side, growling into my ear. 'I know the damage you can do, Beth. Pull yourself together.'

I snatch my arm away from her and stumble back to the karaoke and once I've got the microphone, I order the DJ to stop the music.

'Okay, everyone, listen up,' I say, my voice bellowing across the hush. 'I've got something to tell yo'all…I've got a little announcement…'

The crowd erupts into a loud 'Whoooo!'

Before I can speak again, Mum has stormed onto the platform and wrenched the microphone away from me.

'What are you doing?' she yells at me.

'Leave me alone. I want to tell everyone.'

She's got a firm grip on my arm and is dragging me across the dance floor. 'You stupid girl, don't ruin this one chance of happiness,' she hisses.

She's wearing shoes with lower heels than mine and single-handedly hauls me out of the room and along the corridor towards the toilets.

'I can't believe you're doing this,' I say, feeling dizzy at the sudden movement. She props me against the wall in the Ladies' and checks the place is empty.

'No more stuff on stage,' she says. 'In fact, this is the end of the evening for you, my girl. I'm calling a cab to take you home.'

'You can't do that! This is *my* party! I want to dance...' I feel woozy and flop against the hand-dryer, using it to hold me up.

'Look at you. You're a mess. An announcement? What's that about? I can't trust you.'

Suddenly everything I've been forced to bottle up in the last month surges to a raging tornado inside my head.

'This is all *your* fault! You had to come in and spoil everything that night, didn't you?'

She's affronted. 'I came to change the central heating. You know that.'

'You just barged right in and...and...you were a total maniac. You flew at him. You didn't wait for me to explain—'

'Keep your voice down,' she spits in my face, her hands gripping my wrists.

'I'm sick of you following me around, checking up on me...'

She toys between grappling with me and reasoning with me.

'I only want what's best for you...you know that.'

I wriggle free. 'We should own up,' I say, keeping her at arm's length as if I'm fending off an aggressive dog. 'We should tell the police everything. We should—'

'*Shut up!*'

She thrusts her hand over my mouth, smothering my words, crushing me against the wall, but I manage to duck out of her reach.

'What we did was an atrocity…you hear me…an ATROCITY!' I yell the word with all my might.

There's a resounding smack and I realise from the sharp sting on my cheek that she's hit me. We both stagger back as if someone has fired a shot at the pair of us. She's never done that before. She shrinks back, her hands over her mouth.

'No! My God. Beth, I'm so sorry…'

Her face is white and within seconds she's dissolved into sobs, trying to touch me, trying to reach out to me through her tears.

'I didn't mean to…my baby…I'm *so* sorry…I'd never hurt you…what have I done?'

I stay back, between the sink and the hand-dryer, my arms raised, but she's weakened now with remorse, wanting only to placate me.

'What are you really protecting?' I scream at her. 'My future or yours?'

I hear footsteps coming towards us and make a split decision. I kick off both my sandals and scoop them up, then grab the clutch bag I've left behind the taps and make a run for it.

Chapter 32

Rachel

I can't believe it. I can't believe I actually hit her. My own daughter. What have I become?

It's all I can think about as I stride back from St Andrews, having spent half an hour spouting emotional ramblings to the stone that's standing upright again on Russell's grave.

This time, I don't feel the weightless caress of his hand against my coat sleeve or any wispy breath sending me his words of comfort. There is none of that. I don't deserve his understanding and compassion and he knows it.

The morning is one of those dazzling starts to the day that signals the unfolding of spring. Aubrietia, like clusters of amethysts, is tumbling down stone walls – the multiple tones of pansies, magnolia and tulips vying for attention. There's beauty at every turn, but none of it reaches me.

I found out from Maria that the 'big announcement' Beth was all set to make last night was nothing to do with what we did to Carl. It was something else altogether. Apparently, she's got her first callback for a part in a dystopian film and she wanted to tell everyone on her special night. Her first callback – and I ruined that precious moment for her.

Maria was one of the thoughtful guests who stayed behind to help clear up. She knew something had happened between Beth and I, but was tactful enough not to ask. She did say, however, that Beth especially wanted the audition news to be a surprise for me, to go some way towards showing her gratitude for putting on such a great party. I found that hard to stomach.

Beth's been out all night. I can only assume she's gone to one of two places; either back to Peter's flat in Chelsea or to Adrian's in

Abbots Worthy. It was probably too late to catch a train to London by the time she left the party, so it's probably the latter, by taxi.

I can't face breakfast when I get back. The house feels hollow and is silent, but I creep into her room anyway, to check she isn't hiding from me. No sign of her. Her new phone is back in its packaging on her dressing table, so I least I know there's no point in calling that one.

I pour myself a strong black coffee and wonder whether it's too early to ring my father. Undoubtedly, Beth will have a hangover and speaking to Adrian isn't likely to get me anywhere. Beth might even have primed him not to answer my calls.

When she doesn't answer my texts, I ring her phone over and over and finally she picks up with a snarl, mid-morning. She claims she's only answered so I'd know she isn't lying in a ditch somewhere and cuts it short, refusing to engage with me.

The doorbell rings before I have time to dwell on it. It's PC Atkins asking me to come to the station.

'What's it about?' I grab the doorframe.

'It's in connection with the murder of Mr Carl Jacobson,' she says.

My throat tightens, producing a hoarse whisper. 'Why? What's happened?' I feel like I'm falling, plunging downwards through the doormat, through the earth into an abyss beneath.

She won't tell me any more than that. The police ran an appeal for information on TV yesterday. Perhaps someone has come forward.

I follow her, feeling dazed, and climb into the back seat glad for once that Beth is out of the picture.

At the police station, I'm taken to an interview room where a more senior officer, DI Longcroft, and another officer whose name I don't catch, want to ask some questions about the refurbishments at the pub.

'I understand that Marvin Henson, the landlord of the King's Tavern, left you in charge of the renovations while he was away?'

'That's right,' I tell them. I can barely breathe, all the air seems to be squashed out of me.

DI Longcroft confirms the dates.

'Can you describe the nature of the work that was undertaken?'

'Er…the place was more or less stripped.' My voice comes out husky and shaky. 'The old radiators replaced, new toilets put in, re-plastering, re-wiring of the electrics, new window frames round the back, painting and decorating, new carpets.'

I'm waiting for them to ask about the cellar. They've found something. I know it.

'And all the old furniture, fixtures and fittings – they were all taken away?'

'Yeah.'

'Where to, exactly?'

I stare at him. 'Where to?'

'Yes. All the old chairs, picture frames, light fittings, lampshades..?'

'There was a skip at the back. It went back and forth to the dump until the work was finished.'

The casks of ale in the cellar. The flagstones in the cellar. The cellar. When is one of them going to mention it?

Then the other detective asks how many workmen came and went from the pub during the weeks it was shut, about how secure the back was and who might have had access to the skip.

'There must have been over twenty workmen who actually visited the site,' I tell him. 'Then we had cleaners in at the end. The car-park was left open all the time and the skip was to one side, so everyone had access. Any member of the public could have walked in, I suppose…'

Next DI Longcroft produces an A4-sized colour photograph. 'Do you recognise this, Ms Kendall?'

It's the dark red rug we rolled Carl up in before we buried him. The rug that used to be in front of the fireplace at the pub, but which would have been thrown out, if we hadn't put it to an alternative use.

I blink as if I'm facing bright headlights. 'I think it used to be at the pub.' I take a look from a different angle, pretending to take in the zigzag pattern. 'Yes, I think it is.'

'We found traces of candle wax, cigarette burns, splinters from logs and chewing gum,' he says.

I swallow hard. 'Sounds about right. Where was it?'

Neither of them answer the question.

As he puts the photo away, I try to think back to when the rug was last hoovered. It would have been weeks ago. They will no doubt check for recent specks of dead skin, boot prints, saliva, sweat from fingerprints, especially on the back as it was rolled up, but thousands of traces of DNA would be present. Beth and I wore gloves the whole time we handled both the rug and Carl's body, but we could have left hair. Although given that I worked there, would that really be a problem?

'During the time you were supervising the work at the pub did you come across anything unusual? Any windows left open or broken, doors unlocked, anyone hanging around who shouldn't have been there?'

I stare at Longcroft's shoes. 'I don't…think so,' I say hesitantly, as though I'm lost in thought.

'We'll need the names of all the companies you used. And a list of individual workmen, if you've got it?'

I nod. 'Some of the guys are locals we've used before,' I tell him.

'We'll also need the work schedule so we can see who was at Wyburn Road on which days,' says the other detective.

I tell them I'll do my best and within minutes it's all over and I'm being led back to the foyer. I can breathe again.

They must think someone working at the pub killed Carl, or at least the killer murdered him elsewhere and pinched the old rug from the skip out the back to wrap him in.

The officers didn't mention the cellar, but the forensic team must have searched the pub from top to bottom, given that the rug came from there.

I feel like punching the air. We're in the clear. I'm merely helping the police with their enquiries.

Chapter 33

Beth

There was no way I could go back home after what had happened. With my cheek still stinging, I spent my last pennies on a taxi to Abbots Worthy and turned up on Grandad's doorstep.

He'd been asleep in front of the television and didn't seem to register how late it was or question my incongruous fancy silver frock. He was just delighted I'd come over to see him. He seems to think we must have arranged it and keeps claiming he was expecting me.

I made up the camp bed in the box room and we had breakfast together this morning, as though everything was hunky-dory. Thankfully, I could change out of my posh dress and slip into a couple of items from the bundle of tatty clothes we keep for cleaning, upstairs.

Despite feeling a bit worse for wear after last night, I've been doing laundry for him and tidying out the shed. A proper little helper. Grandad made me cups of tea and read the Sunday paper, dropping it down below his eye-line to watch me from time to time, with a smile on his face. At least someone was delighted by my impromptu behaviour.

Mum got last night all wrong, but it was too late to put things straight. I fended off calls and messages from about twenty people asking why I'd disappeared so suddenly. Most were along the lines of:

Yr mum said you weren't feeling well – r u ok? Message me.

I went along with it, claiming a migraine had wiped me out. More lies and cover-ups.

I managed to find a decent pair of jeans in the 'spares' drawer and took Grandad out to lunch at his local pub. On the way back, I picked handfuls of wild bluebells from the endless flourishes that have sprung up along the verge leading to his cottage.

'I wish Vera was here to share your special day,' he said.

I took hold of his hand.

'You are just like her, you know?' he went on. 'So full of spirit. You wake people up, Beth. You come into the room and you have this shimmer of magic around you that makes people want to be with you.'

I squeezed his hand, biting my lip to stop a tear from brimming over. I didn't know what event he was remembering to make him say this, but it was one of the most beautiful things he'd ever said about me.

'I wish I'd known Vera,' I said. 'I can't remember her.'

'She took it to her grave, you know?'

'Took what, Grandad?'

'The secret. She took the secret to her grave.'

I took hold of his arm and tugged him to a stop. 'What secret? What are you talking about?'

I'd been too rough with him and he looked perturbed. His hand trembled as he brought it to his mouth.

'Sorry, Grandad. What secret did Vera take to her grave?' I stroked his cheek.

He blinked and shook his head. 'It's gone,' he said, walking on.

He opened his gate and just before he reached the front step he turned to me.

'They were here again…' he said.

'Who was here?'

'They've been a few times…just watching.'

He dropped his keys on the ledge inside the front door and strode off into the kitchen to boil the kettle.

I caught up with him, blocking his way to make him face me. '*Who* has been watching, Grandad?'

He blinked, then his face scrunched up in confusion. 'Who's watching?' he said, 'Watching television?' His eyes lit up and he left the kettle he was poised to fill and went into the sitting room to switch on the TV. In a matter of seconds, I'd lost him again.

I didn't know what he was talking about, but could only assume it was another set of wires in his head that didn't link up to reality.

I finished clearing the shed during the afternoon, chucking out packets of seeds that were past their use-by date, emptying watering cans full of stagnant water, tipping rotting bulbs onto the compost. It was good to keep busy. Grandad tried to give me a wad of cash for my trouble, but I refused, then later on I found it stuffed inside the pocket of my spare dressing gown, so I hung on to it.

Not once did he mention the wedding, or the fact that it's due to take place in six days' time.

Chapter 34

Rachel

Surprise, surprise – Beth isn't answering her phone anymore and now I've got a string of missed calls from Peter while I've been at work. He says he called Beth during the party and she was decidedly 'off' with him. Now she's avoiding his calls.

Of course, he wants to know what's going on. I ring back and invent every excuse I can think of to explain her behaviours; illness, wedding nerves, audition blues, but they all sound feeble and none of them hold any water with him at this stage. He must be sick and tired of not being able to get a straight answer from her about anything. Six days to go before the wedding and everything is up in the air.

I've seriously considered haring over to Adrian's, bundling Beth into a taxi and locking her in her room. Then, at least I might be able to talk some sense into her. More pressing matters, however, have kept me at the pub. I've been rifling through the paperwork for the refurbishment, making a list of everyone who came and went during the weeks it was closed. I felt rather smug about how many names were on it when I finally emailed it through to DI Longcroft. That should keep him busy.

On my way home, I'm surprised to get a call from Beth.

'I want to come clean about Carl,' comes her voice, choking with emotion.

I stop in my tracks. 'Where are you?' I sink down onto a nearby wall, feeling queasy.

'Still at Grandad's,' she sniffs. 'I can't marry Peter like this. We're asking him to marry a criminal!'

The world spins. 'Don't be silly, of course we're not. Peter knows that's not who you are. It was one mistake, one slip up, an accident.'

'But, how can I possibly be the same with him? This is huge. How can I not mention what we did?'

'It's still a shock, right now. It'll get easier. You just have to be resolute and keep your head. Every family has secrets.'

'It's not right. With every breath I'm stepping further away from him. He and I should be confiding in each other, but instead I'm hiding things from him, covering up.'

Her breathing comes through the phone like a pressure cooker about to blow.

I need to be careful. She's on the verge of giving everything away because it's the 'right thing to do'. All the same, I have to nip this in the bud.

'In which case, you can say goodbye to your future. It's not just about Peter. You'll be locked up for concealing a crime and I'll be charged with murder. Is that what you want?'

'It's all right for you, ordering me around. This is about the rest of my life.'

'That is *exactly* what I'm worried about!'

'And what about the affair? I can't carry on with Peter like before with that hanging over us, as well.'

'Well, you should have thought about that before you started messing around with a married man!'

'I've *got* to own up. You just don't get it, do you?'

I blink hard. 'If you say one single word about your affair, it's going to link straight to Carl's death and the outcome will be exactly the same.' I hammer out each word to her as though she's a young child. 'You can't. Say. Anything!'

At which point, she cuts me off.

At 8 p.m. I get another call I've been dreading.

'My parents are coming over from New York in a day or so,' Peter tells me. 'They're coming to England especially for the big day – and…well, I can't drag them all that way, only to find that Beth doesn't show up at the church.'

'She'll be there. I know she will.'

I admit that Beth has still not come home, but stress that I'm expecting her to turn up any minute.

He sounds understandably cheerless.

'I need to hear that from her. I think I've spoken to you more times that I have to Beth in the last few weeks,' he says with a lacklustre chuckle. His words are truer than he could ever know. 'Is anything bothering her? Something I don't know about?'

'Not that I know of,' I say, weakly.

'I'm prepared to give her whatever time she needs, if she'll just explain herself to me. I mean, what's the point in tying the knot if we can't even talk to each other?' I can't bear the grating exasperation in his voice.

'She probably doesn't want to burden you.' I throw my eyes up to the ceiling, patently aware of how insincere my argument is.

'If she thinks that, then she really doesn't know me at all.'

'Please give her another chance,' I say.

I can't believe I'm begging someone to marry my beautiful daughter.

'She seems all over the place. Are you sure there's nothing wrong with her? She won't give me a straight answer about the wedding or even about how she feels about me, anymore. She says she didn't say certain things, she can't remember half of the conversations we've had in the last few weeks.'

I drop my head in my hand. This is my fault. I stammer a response about not noticing anything odd about her behaviour.

'She seems so different. When we first got together, she told me she loved the idea of scuba diving in the Red Sea, then only last week she's telling me she's never thought about it. I don't know where I am with her. She couldn't even remember my mother's name from just a few days ago. It's as though she's had some kind of blackout or breakdown or something. I don't feel I know her at all.'

I close my eyes.

I'm entirely to blame. I've made things far worse for all of us with my ridiculous idea of pretending to be Beth. It has created a layer of inconsistency between them, as well as giving him false encouragement. I cringe as I remember I even said the words, 'I can't live without you' in a recent text. What was I thinking? No wonder Peter is confused.

'You say she's staying at her grandfather's in a village called Abbots Worthy?'

'Yes,' I say, hesitantly.

'In that case, I think the only thing left for me to do is to come over from London tomorrow and have it out with her in person.'

'I'm not sure that would be a good idea.'

There's a hiatus and a thud, as though he's no longer holding the phone.

'Sorry…another call from Amelia is coming in. Third time today…sorry, what did you say?'

'I don't think there's much point in coming all the way to Winchester, just now.'

He sighs. 'Beth's been on and off with me for weeks. I need to know what's going on. If I can only sit down with her, just the two of us, somewhere she can't avoid me – perhaps then at least I'll know for certain, one way or the other.'

No! Beth will break, I'm sure she will. She'll tell him everything.

For one crazy moment I consider whether I could get away with wearing a thick white veil and walking down the aisle myself, but instantly, I let the ridiculous idea go.

In the meantime, Peter has made his mind up.

'I'm really sorry to insist, but I'm going to come to see her tomorrow. Otherwise, I think we're going to have to call the whole thing off.'

Chapter 35

Beth

I'm in the middle of baking a ginger cake when Grandad's doorbell rings.

I answer it, but turn away as she steps inside.

'I'm not coming back,' I call out, before she says a word, flinging the oven gloves over my shoulder.

She follows me along the hall.

'She's not coming back,' echoes Grandad from the sitting room, as if he knows what's going on.

I stand in the doorway as Mum goes into the room and gives him a peremptory hug that also acts as a way of pushing him back into his chair. Then she points to the kitchen and ushers me towards it.

She pulls out a seat for me, but I remain standing, leaning against the fridge-freezer. She sits on the wobbly wooden chair herself.

'Beth,' she says, rolling her hands around together, as though they're covered in thick moisturising cream. 'I'm *so* sorry. I can't tell you. I didn't sleep a wink, last night. I'm horrified at what I did. I...'

My hand goes to my cheek, involuntarily. 'What's done is done,' I say philosophically. I don't want to let her off the hook just like that.

'Well done for your callback, by the way. Maria told me.'

I nod, but don't say anything.

'Your bridesmaids are pestering me. They want to know about rehearsals for next Saturday.'

'There aren't any rehearsals,' I tell her in a flat tone. 'They should know that.'

'But, I thought…' She stops.

I fold my arms. 'I don't know you at all,' I say. 'I feel like you're the enemy.'

'Can't you see, I'm doing this for *you*. You'll thank me in time to come.' She reaches her arms towards me, but I don't move.

'No, I won't, I'll hate you.'

She looks down. 'I can't believe it's come to this.'

'I'm not coming back…' I'm about to add 'tonight' but decide to let the statement hang open-ended instead. Let her make of it what she wants.

She traps her thoughts behind a frown and shakes her head. It feels powerful to make her worry, to punish her for what she's done.

Mum's face seems to shut down, then her chin quivers a little and her mouth puckers into a snarl.

'You have no idea, do you?' she says. 'The sort of suffering I've gone through for you. I had you when I was fifteen… *fifteen years old*, do you know what that's like?'

She gets to her feet and glares at me. I back into the corner between the oven and the cupboard by the back door. I've learnt only too well in the last month what she's capable of in a fit of rage.

'My childhood was ripped away from me,' she declares, throwing up her hand. 'I had to leave school before I was ready and you became the centre of everything. I *never* had the chance to go to college, *never* lived the carefree life I wanted to. I had to get out and earn. Vera and Adrian had nothing. They couldn't help me. She was devastated when she lost the twins, then my sister, Leyla, was stillborn. Then my mother died herself when I was twenty. *Twenty.* That's three years younger than you are now.' She reaches out and grips my arm, her nails digging into my wrist. 'I'm still waiting to have an adolescence!'

A question is on my lips, one that I've never dared ask before.

'Why did you keep me, then?' I snap, flaring up with equal fury. 'If I was going to be such a burden to you? The father wasn't interested, so why didn't you have a termination?'

She grinds her teeth and glowers at me, like she's about to boil over.

'My mother lost three young children,' she yells. 'Can you imagine her simply standing by to watch me deliberately wipe out another tiny life?'

'Why did you tell her, then?'

'Vera wasn't stupid,' she says, with a half-laugh. 'There are telltale signs a good mother will always notice, you know. I was sick in the mornings, off my food, needing to go up a bra-size...' She glances down as if she's not sure whether to say what she wants to add next. 'You know what? I was in denial at first and I acted as if I wasn't pregnant; flinging myself around in the gym at school, pushing myself to the limit on the sports field, drinking too much behind my parents' backs, smoking the odd joint now and again. Anything, to make it go away.'

She's never told me this before.

I recoil as though she's punched me. In fact, I'd rather she had, because her words hurt me far deeper than a blow ever could.

'To make *me* go away...' I say, my voice breaking. 'You didn't want me...'

'No. Not at first...' she says. She stops and looks away, refusing to grant me the words I need to hear.

I blink away a tear. She must know how much I could do with her reassurance, to hear her confirm her love for me – that unwanted baby – right now.

She shakes her head. 'I can't do any more for you. I can't get you where you want to be. But Peter can. This terrific man you've treated abominably! Who thinks the world of you and wants to help you reach your dreams.'

When I don't respond, she takes a step closer and flings her arms down by her side. The raging avalanche isn't over.

'I cannot believe how ungrateful you are. Peter has been understanding and incredibly patient every time you've cruelly ignored him. Anyone else would have walked away, but he's hung on in there while you've turned your back on him, refusing to take his calls, casting him aside.'

I can't hide my dismay. 'But you know why I've had to blank him.'

'Because you have no composure or self-control. Because you can't trust yourself to keep ONE simple secret.' She tosses her hand in the air and turns away in despair.

'Two secrets,' I correct her, then wish I hadn't.

She laughs. 'The affair with Carl is frankly indefensible. I'm *disgusted* at your behaviour.' She spits out the words. 'You should be pulling out all the stops to make it up to Peter, not tossing him aside like this.'

I sigh. She doesn't see how complicated it is. My feelings for Carl, my shame and guilt about cheating on Peter, my impulse to come clean, but knowing it would lead straight to suspicion about Carl's death. I'm still trying to make sense of it all.

'I don't know how to be with Peter,' I scream at her. 'I'm so confused.' I turn away, clutching my head, grabbing handfuls of my hair.

'Well, it's crunch time. He's coming to Winchester tomorrow to have one final showdown with you. So, you'd better get your act together, girl, because otherwise you're going to blow the chance of a lifetime.'

I draw back as she storms past me, out into the hall. She stops and turns around.

'So…are you coming back with me, or what?'

I stand my ground, not moving an inch other than to shake my head. 'No.'

'Peter will be here in a matter of hours. You've got until then to make an appearance. Otherwise, I can guarantee you that the wedding is OFF.' She hooks her hands into her hips. 'And bang goes your ticket to any hope of a life in the limelight. Or any sniff of luxury. You'll spend the rest of your life, mopping up spills and wiping the floor, like me.'

She steps forward wagging her finger at me. 'And if you let that happen, if you let this one golden opportunity slip through your fingers, then I don't think I'll be able to bring myself to look at or speak to you ever again.' Spittle flies into the air and her knuckles are bony-white, as she forces herself to keep her clenched fists by her side.

'I'm not coming back home,' I say. 'I need space. I need to think and get my head round everything.'

'If you let this lucky break go, *don't you dare* come to me for money,' she snorts, 'because there isn't any! You'll be on your own. Then you'll see what life is really like!' Her eyes are smouldering, her entire body trembling and she's pitched forward like a cannon about to fire. I've never seen her like this before.

With that, she flings open the front door, storms out and slams it closed with a reverberating crash.

After she's gone, I slip quietly into the sitting room to see what impact all Mum's yelling has had on Grandad. He's sitting frozen in his chair, his arms stiff against his side, staring ahead like he's expecting an army inspection.

A wash of fury curdles in my stomach for the way Mum has frightened him.

'It's okay, Grandad. Nothing bad has happened. It's just Mum getting angry…about somebody. But she's gone now.'

'Is it Way-way? Is it Vera?' His eyes dart around him, agitated and muddled.

'It's all right. She's gone. Everything's fine.' I pat his hand. 'Shall I get you a cup of tea?'

He nods and clings on to my fingers, a look of anguish on his face.

'I'll put the kettle on,' I say, cheerfully. I slowly pull away and he lets me go.

When I get to the kitchen, I flop into a chair and drop my head into my hands.

I don't know which way my decision is going to go about Peter yet, but whatever I do, I'm not sure Mum and I can ever come back from this.

After a cup of tea, Grandad seems to have forgotten the outburst – a hidden blessing of dementia. He seems chirpy and insists on watching a re-run of *Cash in the Attic*, so I look for yet another job to take my mind off things.

His bedroom is tidy, he's naturally that way, although often items are put away neatly – just in the wrong place. Last time I had a tidy up, I found half a tuna sandwich in his sock drawer and I'm not in the mood to start picking through any recent surprises there might be in his cupboards.

As I swing the door to, I spot the metal stick leaning beside the long curtains on the landing, the one Grandad uses to open the loft hatch. Inspired by the show he's watching, I peel down the folding ladders and climb up to see what treasures might be tucked away up there.

There's a bulb above my head that lights up piles of boxes, most neatly stacked, but the path once carved between them has filled up over the years with stray items; a rolled up sleeping bag, tennis rackets, books, an old vacuum cleaner. The boxes are labelled and in a single scan around, I skim over the key stages of Grandad's life: *wedding, new house, Rachel – early years, Rachel and Beth*.

There's a box beneath ours with the label torn off, so I kneel down and slide it out to take a peek. Inside are several smaller flat boxes, the kind that men's shirts are sold in. They carry the names of Mum's dead siblings, the children she referred to earlier; Robert, who died of leukaemia, aged three, and his twin Olga, who died at five. I remember Mum telling me Olga had a virus which led to cardiomyopathy – a problem with her heart.

Buried amongst handfuls of photographs are birth certificates, death certificates, medical records, funeral notices and orders of service.

In one photo taken outside Buckingham Palace, Olga is looking cute, holding onto her hat in the breeze, next to Mum who looks about ten. I've not seen this snap before. Olga has my Mum's almond-shaped eyes. No one could have known then that she didn't have long to live. So tragic.

Others are of Mum as a child; one on a campsite beside Grandad's battered old Ford Cortina, another on the dockside in Southampton. There's a later one with me aged around three, with Mum and Vera, who's wearing one of her jazzy poncho tops the Chilean's call chamantos. It was taken a year before Vera died.

Leyla was the baby who was stillborn nearly twenty years ago and complications then led to Vera's death. I sit back on my heels. It's strange that I had all this family and never knew them. I don't even remember Vera.

Underneath that photo is a large brown envelope.

I can hear the television through the floorboards. Grandad's hearing isn't so good these days, so it's constantly loud. He won't even know I'm up here. The envelope is blank on the front – surely it would say 'private' or be sealed if it was anything important.

I lift the flap and slip out the contents. Inside are clippings from several newspapers about a teenage girl, Tracy Limehouse, killed outside a pub in Southampton in 1992. The year before I was born. She was run over by a car.

Why did Grandad keep this? Why is it with photographs of Vera? What does it mean?

Chapter 36

Beth

I left Grandad stocked up with more tea and a chunky slice of the stickiest ginger cake I've ever made, grabbed an old jacket and took the next bus into Winchester. From there I caught the train to Southampton Central, using the cash Grandad had left in my dressing gown.

After the sickening confrontation with Mum, I was glad of a new distraction. I needed more time to think about whether marrying Peter was really the best thing – not for *her*, but for me.

I kept hearing the words she'd spat at me, hateful words about how she'd never wanted me during her pregnancy and how much she'd missed out on because I'd come into the world. I've cried so much lately that I didn't seem to have any tears left. I've swung from feeling numb and empty to being overcome with surges of rage for her. How can she not understand what this has been like for me?

I should have said there and then that we should definitely at least postpone the wedding, but I'm sure both she and Peter would have seen that as me backing out altogether. A coward's way of calling it off for good.

In the last few weeks something has definitely shifted between Peter and I. I can't put my finger on it and I'm not sure where it leaves me, but it certainly means I've got to hold fire and review everything.

I feel so much more grown up since the terrible thing happened. I look back at my time with Peter and it feels like make-believe, as though I was just a naïve teenager soaking up the attention. I keep coming back to the fact that if things had been right between Peter and I, I would never have allowed myself to be led astray by Carl.

One thing I also need to do is to separate out how I feel about Peter, as a person, from what he seems to be offering me. It's so tempting to be taken in by the allure of stardom and wealth. If I choose to marry him, I wouldn't have to worry about money anymore and that would lift such a massive weight off my shoulders. But it's also about living day in and day out with this one man. Mum thinks he's the best thing that's ever happened to me, but she doesn't know one or two things.

Peter and I had a brief discussion about children before the hen party and it totally threw me. It started with a bit of a clash about my auditions. He rang when I was at the market, stocking up on cheap fruit.

'Shame about your last one,' he'd said. 'I had a word with the casting director beforehand and she liked your photos. What went wrong?'

I tutted, manoeuvring my way around shoppers to get away from the main drag. 'I'm working so hard, I don't know what more I can do.'

Peter's voice stiffened into the lecturing tone I'd heard once or twice before.

'The problem is, it looks like you are. Working too hard, I mean. That's what she told me afterwards.'

'You spoke to her?'

'I wanted to get her feedback. You've got to let it come more naturally, more organically. It needs to flow, you need to own the part – you can't afford to *play* the parts any more. Do you understand?'

'I think so.'

'Don't forget you never film in the right order. You must have a character in your bones, so that one minute you can play a scene from the end and the next, you can play that same character at the opening.'

I half-laughed at his patronising tone. 'I know that. It was one of the first things they taught us at college.'

'Well, you're going to have to do something special soon or it's going to be too late.'

'Too late?' Within the space of two seconds I'd shifted from feeling put out to downright nauseous. *He's going to give up on me.* 'Is there a deadline, then?' I said, bluntly.

He was calling from a rehearsal studio on Broadway. I could hear people applauding in the background. 'You're aware of my history and how much I value dedication and focus. You know I expect you to give your all to getting your acting career off the ground. That can't be new to you, surely. It's not going to be easy. You've got to prove yourself, even with my help, you're not simply going to walk into a role that happens to fit you like a glove.'

'I *know* that.'

His next sentence came at me with a bang. 'But whatever the situation, I take it that we'll be starting a family before long.'

'A family?' My voice shot up an octave. 'I thought you wanted me to be an actress! I thought you were going to pull out all the stops to help me.'

'I am, but I'm not going to do it forever.'

I stared at the brick wall ahead of me with my mouth open. 'I can't take time out to have a child. I'm not ready to have children.'

'If you were a dancer it would be different, you'd have to take a career break, but as an actor, you can come straight back to it.'

'Only if I'm established, if I've got a platform to come back to.'

'You'd only need twelve months off, if that. In fact, you could be filming until you're about four or five months' pregnant. Then you could have a nanny and get straight back to it.'

My eyes blinked hard in amazement. 'You've got it all worked out, haven't you?'

I couldn't take any more after that and flung the phone into my bag. Later, he sent a text apologising for 'being a bully', but he didn't retract what he'd said.

The train is held at signals just outside Eastleigh and I have more time to kill. Whatever happens, I can't see myself going back to live under the same roof as Mum after this. I'll have to collect my gear and perhaps stay at Grandad's until I work out what to do. Maybe, by that time, I'll have landed the part in the TV series that I've got the callback for and I can set myself up – *without* Peter's help.

I've been so worried about Mum's state of mind that I've allowed her obsession with the wedding plans to steamroll over my fluctuating emotions. As a result, I've completely lost touch with how I really feel about Peter.

With a jolt, we're on the move again and I shift my attention back to my current mission. Before I left Grandad's, I'd looked up the details from the news clippings, on my phone. A string of reports came up, all showing a pub in the background – The Hope and Anchor – with the photo of a girl's face in a circle at the side. Tracy Limehouse, aged eighteen.

The initial story gave the facts. There'd been a party at a house near The Hope and Anchor, in Southampton. It sounded like it'd been a rowdy affair and at around 10 p.m., a crowd had piled out onto the streets. An innocent passer-by, Tracy Limehouse, was hit by a flying object and fell into the path of a car. She was killed.

The driver, who was unnamed in the report, was never blamed. The girl was flung into the path of the car without any warning and there was no time to react.

In spite of the party crowd, it appeared that no one came forward to explain who threw the object. Everyone was drunk, messing about, not paying attention. Further reports, months, then years down the line, stated that no evidence ever came to light and no one was convicted.

Nevertheless, from that day on, the driver would have had to live with killing a young girl in a freak accident.

A reconstruction was staged in May 2002 to mark the tenth anniversary of Tracy's death, then it seems the crime was filed away as a cold case.

Why had Grandad kept the clippings in the loft?

As the train pulled into Southampton Central, I thought about the ten-year age difference between Grandad and Vera. They'd met at Southampton University, when she was working in the canteen and he turned up as an electrician to upgrade the wiring. Mum said he fell for Vera straight away, wooing her with soppy poetry and terrible songs on his guitar. We've always teased him about that. She got pregnant within weeks, with Mum, and they got married. Vera was nineteen and Grandad was twenty-nine.

It never seemed to matter to my grandparents. Did it matter to me, being twelve years younger than Peter? Along with a stack of other issues, we'd never really talked about it.

As I go through the ticket barrier, I return to the dates from the news clipping: May 1992 – before I was born. Did Mum know the girl? Was this somehow connected to our family?

The Hope and Anchor is in St Mary's, not far from the football ground, at the end of a densely populated row of terraced houses. It's often referred to as the roughest part of the city. I stride out, not sure what I'm expecting to find, but driven by the need to be doing something. I'm hoping that while my mind is preoccupied, I'll come to some clear-cut decision about Peter.

On the way, I mull over how I'm going to approach this and, having come up with a possible bright idea, I take a look inside my purse.

Good, I've still got it.

This might just work.

Chapter 37

Rachel

Beth is coming back with me if I have to drag her by the hair. I'm not taking no for an answer, this time. She needs to see that Peter deserves to be spoken to. He needs answers and I refuse to let her treat him like he's some kind of stalker she's trying to shake off.

The last bus to Abbots Worthy will have gone by now, so I punch in the number of a taxi.

On the way, I surreptitiously empty my purse out on the seat beside me and count how much cash I've got. It's enough for one leg of the journey, but I'll have to borrow from Adrian to get back.

Beth has taken over the box-room since she extended her stay with Adrian and, as the taxi pulls up to his cottage I notice that the curtains are drawn and the light is on. Good. She won't be able to slip through my fingers. No ifs or buts, she's coming back with me, this time. Peter is right. We can't have people totally wasting their time, travelling thousands of miles, for something that isn't going to happen. All because Beth's 'having a wobbly'.

I ask the driver to wait outside the cottage, but he insists I pay the fare I owe him so far. I dump the cluster of coins into his cupped hands.

'I might be five or ten minutes,' I warn him.

He shrugs, folds his arms and nods emphatically at the meter.

Adrian lets me in, his head bowed, his arms hanging loose by his side as though he's done something wrong.

'I need to speak to her,' I say, squeezing past him to get to the foot of the stairs. 'It's really important.'

I knock on the door to the box-room, but there's no reply. It doesn't surprise me, she's probably heard me arrive. Before I barge in, I need to take a breath and think about how I'm going to approach this. Calm, collected, definitely not angry – not at first anyway. I rehearse a few key phrases in my head as I take hold of the door handle.

People are about to come a long way, Beth.

It's not fair keeping Peter on tenterhooks like this.

I rap again, then open the door.

The room is empty.

I check the other rooms, then join Adrian in the sitting room. 'Where is she?' I ask, heading straight to the window, straining to see whether she might be outside in the back garden. There's no sign of her and no light on in the shed.

I turn to Adrian, wondering if the sheepish look he gave me when I got here means he's covering for her.

'Beth. Where has she gone?'

He wavers, rubs his head, moving his feet up and down as if he's climbing stairs.

'I…I don't know…'

'Has she popped out? Where would she go?' It's agricultural land around here with a handful of cottages. 'The pub in the next village?'

Adrian is starting to look distressed at the sharp tone of my voice. I lead him to a chair and turn the sound of the television down low.

I kneel on the floor at his feet and take hold of his hands.

'Beth's been staying here, Adrian,' I say, soothingly, stroking his knuckles with my thumbs. 'I'm here to see her. Where is she, now? Her room is empty.'

He's squeezing his knees together, a tight expression on his face, trying to remember.

'Shopping?' he throws out.

'It's late, Adrian.'

'Gone to bed,' he says in an exultant voice, as though he's cracked it.

'No. No. She's not upstairs.'

I know it's pointless to fire any more questions at him. I'm only going to upset him, so I go back upstairs to look for any clues as to where she might have gone.

In the bathroom, there's a second toothbrush by the sink and I recognise the old dressing gown hanging up behind the door. By the camp bed in her room, there's a hairbrush, a packet of painkillers, an unused brown envelope and tissues on an upturned laundry basket.

Has she taken off for a walk? Gone to see someone? I'm at the end of my tether with this girl. I ring her phone, but it goes straight to voicemail. I haven't seen it in the house, so she must have taken it with her.

'Where do you keep your torch?' I ask as I return to the sitting room.

'Under the stairs,' he says with confidence.

Sure enough, it's standing on a shelf next to a pile of batteries.

I pick it up and tell Adrian I'm just going outside.

The taxi is still there, so I lean in through the open window and tell the driver I won't be returning straightaway after all. I can't see the meter, but I'm sure he overcharges me. I hand over what he says I owe without a tip and watch him drive away.

Swinging the torch beam from side to side as I walk, I set out from the front gate, first one way, then the other, passing all the cottages.

There's no sign of her.

To the right there's a footpath leading towards arable land culminating in a farm and another path opposite disappears into the woods. Beth would have needed a torch to go further afield out here, as there's not one street light.

There's a yelp of a distant fox, followed by a gusty breeze that disturbs the trees and makes the tousled leaves sound like gushing water. The wind has picked up in the last hour and there's a storm brewing. In spite of being furious with her right now, I sincerely hope she isn't out somewhere in this.

I rub my arms and hurry back inside.

Chapter 38

Beth

Armed with my old pass from the TV company, I go straight to the bar and ask for the pub landlord. A woman, referred to by the barmaid as Lulu, heads purposefully towards me from behind a door marked 'Private'. Her sleeves are rolled up and some time ago, her hair must have been tied back into a style loosely described as an 'updo'. Since then, it has made a largely successful attempt to free itself from all the clips.

'Hi, I'm a production assistant.' I flash my pass, sounding bright and peppy. 'I don't know if you've had the letter yet, but we're filming a docudrama here. Have you been sent the details, yet?'

She looks blank. 'I don't remember any letter. What does it involve?'

'It's about a death that took place near here, nearly twenty-five years ago.' Her vacant expression doesn't shift. 'We're looking for the local angle. Anyone who remembers the incident.' I deliberately raise my voice. 'It was a young girl, Tracy Limehouse was her name, who was hit by a car near here, in 1992.'

The pub is humming with drinkers, men leaning on the bar and groups clustered around tables. A couple of guys have noticed me and there's a bit of nudging going on.

She pulls a face. 'That's a long time ago. I certainly can't help you, I was in Cardiff then.' She shakes her head and turns away.

I follow her to the end of the bar. 'I'm just looking for pointers. Anyone who might remember it and who'd like to be on prime-time telly...' I project the last part out towards the customers.

'Well, you can ask around, if you like, but I can't help you. What are you drinking?' She already has her hand on one of the pumps. She wants to make sure I don't get a free ride.

I order an orange and soda and join the nearest group, flinging my leg over a low stool and dragging it towards them as if they're my best buddies.

'What're ya sellin', love?' says a man with his glasses propped on his head and a beer belly spilling out from under his T-shirt. 'I've got nothin' for charity.'

I give them my patter, but all I get in return are shrugs and bewildered shakes of the head. I work my way around the room and it's thumbs down all the way until I reach an older couple near the fruit machine, who beckon me over.

'Is this about that girl that was knocked down?'

'That's right – in 1992…'

'That was the party of one of the Kirby sons, wasn't it?' She turns to the grumpy looking man beside her. 'Ben, that's it. Ben Kirby's eighteenth birthday. We weren't here that night,' she tells me, 'but I remember the story. My son might know something. He would have been about…what would he have been, John?' She plucks at the loose skin under her chin in an effort to remember.

'Around eighteen, nineteen, I'd say,' the man pipes up. 'Bernie used to drink in here all the time, back then. He might know something.'

'Does he live in Southampton?' I ask, half-expecting to hear he's halfway across the world somewhere.

'Oh, yeah. He's still here,' says the woman. 'It's just a bus ride away. Off Shirley High Street. Know the area?'

'Yeah. I know the high street.'

'I'll give him a call,' the woman says and taps her mobile phone. Before I leave, I slip back to the bar and buy them both another pint of Guinness.

Half an hour later, I'm pressing Bernie's doorbell.

'Mam says you're from the BBC,' he says, edging back from the door so I can go inside.

I don't correct him, flashing my pass at him instead, hoping he doesn't look too closely at it.

'Thanks so much,' I say, with a cheery grin, stepping onto the mat.

Bernie must be around forty-three, but looks older, not only because he's lost all but a few strands of his hair, but also because he's sporting a 'Goldeneye 007' T-shirt that's way too small for him.

He shows me into a sitting room with a sofa and chairs in stripy oranges and browns. It's made of that bobbly fabric that cats always get their claws caught up in. I remember Peter once telling me he can't stand it.

I perch on the edge of a seat and repeat the same pitch from earlier.

'Has this got anything to do with the police?' he says, folding his arms, looking dubious.

'Oh, no. We're just using the story as the basis for a TV docudrama. We'll use the same pub and have local people explaining what they saw, but it's not about re-opening the case. There's no new evidence.'

'So, it's not about giving statements or anything like that?'

I laugh. 'Oh, definitely not. Just a film. You know, like that drama about the landlord in Bristol who was hounded when his tenant was murdered…'

I wait for some signs of recognition. 'Oh, yeah…' he says. 'Something like that?' He rubs his chin, sounding interested.

'Absolutely. People love true-life crime, don't they?'

A small terrier trots into the room and as Bernie reaches out to make sure it doesn't bother me, I take a shifty look at the collection of DVDs stacked beside the television. Sure enough, with titles such as *Ted Bundy*, *Bonnie and Clyde* and a box set of *The Wire*, Bernie appears to be one of those very same viewers who get their kicks from real crime.

I pull a small notebook and biro out of my bag.

'Can you tell me what you remember of that night? Just some basics?'

'You're sure there won't be any police involved?' he says a second time.

Even though we're safely inside his house, his eyes keep dodging over my shoulder the whole time.

I shake my head. 'Not a police officer in sight, I promise,' I reiterate, trying to wipe all signs of irritation from my voice. 'Just the actors and the film crew.'

'Right, well, there was a party in St Mary's a few doors down from The Hope and Anchor. Some kid's birthday…and it got a bit out of hand. It was rammed, man, like *everyone* turned up… and the place was swarming with junkies and dealers and plenty who had form with the cops.' He clears his throat. 'Not me, mind, I've never broken the law.' He's not exactly convincing, but I don't care about his past.

'So, what happened?'

'Eventually, there were so many of us that it spilled out on to the street. We were having a good time, you know, yelling, drinking and arsing around. Next thing we knew, someone was yelling that the old bill was heading our way. A teenager, a girl, had been knocked down, just outside the pub.'

'Did you see it?' He watches me as I'm absently chewing the end of my pen. It probably doesn't look too professional, so I stop.

'No, not me, but one of the blokes near me said he saw a brick go flying through the air at her. She was walking past the entrance to the pub car-park and…bam!'

'A brick?'

That wasn't mentioned in the news reports. They stated she was hit by a 'flying object'. Maybe the police decided not to release that piece of information to the public.

'Yeah. This guy told me it smacked her right on the head and she staggered, then keeled over, right into the path of a car. He wouldn't have had a chance—'

'He?' I interrupt.

'Yeah, the driver was a bloke…middle-aged, not speeding or anything. It wasn't his fault…I mean, he stopped and was in a right state, but it was the scumbag who threw the brick who was to blame.'

'And no one saw who threw it?'

'I didn't see who it was…and no one came forward.'

'Do you know where it came from?'

'The bloke with me said it came from the car-park. There was an old outhouse at the back that we…that blokes used as a urinal. Plenty of loose bricks lying around. I do remember that.'

He's animated now. 'When we heard the sirens, it was chaos. Everyone scarpered. No one was in any hurry to give their names or to spill the identities of any of the others who were there, believe me. Those that stayed stonewalled the cops and said they didn't see a thing. No one wanted to be hauled off to the station to give a statement.'

'But you stayed?'

'Yeah, I didn't run, but I was no help. I'd gate-crashed, so I couldn't name names. I didn't even know whose party it was.'

I glance down at my notes. 'It was for a boy called Ben Kirby. He was turning eighteen.'

He shakes his head. 'I didn't know him.'

I tap the pen against my lip. 'So, everyone closed ranks?'

'Exactly…' he sniffs.

'What happened then?'

'That was it. The ambulance came and took the girl away. The driver had to get himself treated for shock, too. The police took a couple of statements and everyone cleared off.'

'Do you know the name of the driver?'

He shakes his head.

'What about the guy who saw the brick flying through the air?'

'No. Never saw him before or since.'

I jot down a few words, but by now I'm coming to the conclusion that my entire journey has been one ridiculous wild goose chase. I take his full name and phone number, but only to look legitimate.

'Thank you,' I say, getting up to go, deflated to say the least. The dog by his heels jumps up and starts yapping in little circles.

'Don't mind him,' he says. 'You think I'll be on the telly? Will they come to the house with cameras and all that?'

I tip my head on one side as I slide my notebook into my bag. 'It's early stages, yet. Sometimes these things never get off the ground. Often we don't get the funding or the producer goes for a different angle.'

'Oh…' He looks sorely disappointed. It seems like it could have been the highlight of his year.

He leads me to the front door. If I'm quick I should catch the next train back to Winchester.

'The car sticks in my mind, as it happens,' says Bernie, as he kicks a dog-chew out of the way. 'The driver who killed her.'

I stop out of courtesy.

'It was an old banger – a brown Ford Cortina.' He swings his weight to one hip. 'I remember, because my dad had one just the same and for one horrible moment, I thought it was him.'

He opens the door and grabs the dog's collar.

I clutch the edge of the doorframe as the meaning of his final words sink down into my gut.

Chapter 39

Rachel

'I think I know where she might have gone,' says Adrian. He's holding the brown envelope I saw beside Beth's camp bed. I'd thought it was empty.

He opens the flap and tips out the contents into my hand. 'She must have found these…'

I realise straight away what it is and stare into his face, then back down again to the news clippings. 'I didn't know you had these…' I say warily.

After all these years.

Adrian's wide eyes reflect my own sense of alarm.

'She was asking…I think it was Beth…yes…about Southampton.'

'Adrian, what did you tell her? What did you say?'

'Well, nothing…as far as I recall. I mean, I don't know exactly what happened, do I, so how could I have told her?'

'I can't believe she's gone rooting through your documents.'

'She hasn't. Not really. She's been tidying up for me, been such a help. She must have come across this in the loft with the photographs.' His voice is trembling. 'The secret Vera took to her grave.'

I shiver at those words.

'She's obviously curious and thinks she's found something here to follow up.' I flick my nail against the printed paper. 'She's been asking me about the past, too.'

'Perhaps that's where she's gone. To Southampton. To find out.'

I'm glad that at least I've caught Adrian at a time when all this lights are on, so to speak.

'What does she think she's going to find? It was nearly twenty-five years ago.'

He shrugs. 'The pub? The landlord? It might lead her somewhere.'

I can't believe Beth has taken off chasing some tattered fragment of our family history at a time like this. Little does she know that the timing for stirring up that period couldn't be worse.

'Oh, Adrian, why did you keep these?'

He shakes his head and squints, as though he hasn't quite grasped the question. I can see I'm losing him.

'Why don't you ask Vera,' he says merrily.

Has she seriously taken off for Southampton at this time of night? What is she hoping to find?

I write the words: *Call Way-Way when Beth comes back!* in large letters on a piece of cardboard and attach it with sticky tape to the inside of the front door. One of them will see it when she returns. Shamefacedly, I ask Adrian for money to tide me over and ring for another taxi home.

Before I leave, I give Beth's mobile phone a ring, on the off-chance that she might have left it behind, but as I do a little circuit of every room, I'm greeted only with silence.

It's raining as I clamber into the taxi and everywhere I look is obstructed by trails of water rolling down the windows. Even though I can barely make out a thing, I find myself shifting from one side in the back to the other, searching for her.

So much has been shattered in the last few weeks, I don't know what's real anymore.

My bond with Beth has been ripped apart at the seams. We've had little niggles over the years and fallen out now and again, but we've always been interwoven with each other like threads in a tapestry. Nothing like this has ever happened between us before.

Is it salvageable?

With the wedding due on Saturday, it's not my priority at this moment in time.

As the taxi draws to a brief halt at the next crossroads, there's not even a verge along the side of the road. I wind down my window and stare out into the darkness, but there's nothing out here other than overgrown hedgerows and trees, their spindly branches scratching the sky.

When I get back home, I race upstairs calling Beth's name, but I can sense straight away that the house is empty. I can't believe at a time like this, she's taken off on some Nancy Drew mystery expedition. Either that, or she's seeking refuge with one of her friends.

Going straight to her room, I track down Beth's address book – it's probably out of date, but it's all I've got. I ring two of her Southampton pals, but neither have seen her.

I sit on the bed and sigh. She can't have gone far – all her gear is still here and she only has a few clothes, a spare washbag and other bits and bobs she always leaves at Adrian's. I've just got to wait this out.

The next day, I'm punching the round hole into a box of cheese and onion crisps behind the bar, when Marvin appears beside me.

'The police are here,' he says. I jerk upright. He adds something else, but abject panic that something awful has happened to Beth blocks out his words. Only as we stride towards the officers do I realise he mentioned the word 'Skoda'. This isn't about Beth, they're asking about Marvin's car.

I recognise them both from before. PC Atkins, the pretty blonde one, addresses me first.

'We understand that Mr Henson left his Skoda with you while he was away…' She glances down at her notes, '…between February 19th and March 12th.'

It isn't exactly a question, but they're both looking at me, waiting for a response. Everything has to be done by the book.

'That's right,' I say.

'Can you tell us where the car was kept?'

'It was parked outside my house on Barnes Road,' I say, relaxing a little, 'either there, or in the next street.'

'Was the car ever left here in the car-park?' PC Atkins swings round to point to the rear exit. As she raises her arm, a surreal image of an air stewardess comes to mind.

'Here?' I shake my head. 'No, I always walked to the pub, if there was anything that needed doing – it's quicker on foot. In any case, with so many trucks coming and going for the refurbishments, it seemed best to keep it out of the way.'

'Was it parked here at any time during the period Mr Henson was on holiday?'

'There was just the once, a couple of days before he came back, when my daughter and I gave it a once-over with a hose. Parking outside my house is bumper to bumper, so it made sense to wash it here where there's more room. There were plenty of buckets and cleaning materials lying around.'

PC Atkins presses her point. This is clearly important. 'You never used the car to bring anything here or take it away?'

I shiver and rub my arms. Had someone spotted the car at the back, the night we took Carl's body away? The CCTV was down right through that period, but had someone been prowling around?

'No.' It comes out sounding scratchy and I clear my throat. Surely, they won't want to check inside Marvin's car, will they?

Marvin pipes up. I'd forgotten he was there. 'It's here now,' he says, taking a step towards the back exit, 'if you need to take a look.'

I've swung from feeling a chill to terribly hot all of a sudden. I reach out to hold onto a chair and swallow hard.

PC Dean responds. 'That won't be necessary at the moment.'

I take a deep breath in through my nose.

The two officers turn to each other. PC Atkins points to a line in her notes and PC Dean nods, but nothing else happens; no warrant is produced, no arms reach out towards me, there are no handcuffs. They're merely checking they've asked all the right questions. It's routine.

Once they've gone, Marvin turns to me as we head back to the bar.

'I was rather hoping I'd get to see a real CSI team in action, in their white bunny suits, crawling all over my motor.' He's laughing. 'They'd probably turn up something embarrassing dropped months ago behind the seats.'

I force a chuckle, but secretly I'm wracking my brains trying to figure out what they would find if they do decide to make a full forensic search. There was no blood, but did Carl leave a tiny piece of himself behind? And fragments from the rug? Even though Beth and I gave the interior a comprehensive going over with the vacuum cleaner, microscopic traces could have been left behind, linking the body to Marvin's car.

He's still rattling on as he wipes off yesterday's specials from the menu board: '…but forensics is expensive, so I don't suppose they're going to scour random vehicles without any concrete leads.'

'They're probably talking to everyone who had access to the rug,' I say conversationally, collecting up the damaged beermats that customers always seem to want to peel apart. 'Now that they've got a list of workmen, they'll be trying to match registration numbers with CCTV on the high street.'

I know for a fact that Marvin's car won't come up on any traffic footage; my meandering route through the city avoided all the official cameras.

Marvin adds a curly flourish in chalk at the bottom of the menu. 'They'll catch whoever did it eventually.' He rubs his hands together, as though the whole situation is rather exciting. I glance at my watch and flinch. Peter is going to be turning up in less than four hours. I try Beth's phone, but it goes straight to voicemail, just like before.

I've tried Beth hourly since then, but it's always the same result. There's no time left. I pull my last pint of real ale and rush out to meet Peter at the station.

As he comes through the ticket barrier his eyes spark into life for a second, clearly thinking it's Beth waiting for him on the other side. His expression wilts when he realises it's me.

'Hi,' he mutters listlessly, pulling me towards him in a cursory embrace. He's got the fatigued and harrowed body language of someone who has come a long way, expecting a funeral.

'How was your journey?' I ask superficially, unable to come up with anything better. He mutters a few words that include 'fine' and 'quiet'.

I'm feeling depleted, mortified. He's here to try to shake some sense into Beth. He's expecting to have a heart-to-heart with her. He doesn't know that she's nowhere to be found. I glance up to the skies as we turn to leave the station. I have no idea how I'm going to handle this.

We walk awkwardly to the house, making inelegant small-talk about the sandwich he had for lunch, the weather, the traffic. We don't mention Beth or the wedding.

As I open the gate, I wonder if it's kinder to tell him now that Beth's not here. That she could be in Southampton – but no one knows for sure. But it sounds so feeble when I say it in my head that I don't dare. It would make his visit a complete waste of time.

I genuinely thought she'd be back by now, but she's well and truly slipped through my fingers.

I take him into the kitchen and he clears his throat. He can see how tense I am and it's making him nervous. I offer to make some tea to soften the mood.

We sup in silence at the kitchen table like strangers.

'Shall I go up?' he says finally, 'or are you going to bring her down?'

'I'll go up,' I say, getting to my feet.

I get to the foot of the stairs and dither, out of sight. What am I going to do when I get upstairs? Come rushing down, putting on a big show of shock pretending she's gone?

I open Beth's bedroom door and step inside, locking the door. Instantly I'm swept up in the aroma of her floral perfume and see her before me in her belongings – the chiffon scarf she wore yesterday, the swimsuit from Friday dry, on the radiator.

That's when the idea comes to me.

I stand at the top of the stairs and call out: 'Peter, do you want to come up?'

There's an abrupt screech of the chair leg across the kitchen floor and he bounds up the stairs. I stop him on the landing.

'She's locked her door; she doesn't want to see anyone, but she says she'll speak to you. I'll leave you both and sit in my bedroom,' I point to the adjacent doorway, 'to give you some privacy.'

I back into my room and close the door.

Then I hurry through the connecting door into the bathroom and straight through into Beth's room.

There's a faint tap on the door as Peter knocks.

'It's Peter,' he says, keeping his voice low. 'Why don't you come out and speak to me, properly?'

I close my eyes and try to hear Beth's voice, her intonation, the tone she uses.

'I'm sorry, Peter. I'm in such a state. I can't face anyone right now.' My voice comes out shaky and uncertain.

'You don't sound right at all, why don't you open the door?'

I lift the pitch up a little. 'Please don't pressure me...I've been...I'm not...'

'What's going on, Beth? You've been so weird lately.'

'I know. Something hasn't been right in my head, Peter, for the last month or so...more than that...I feel sort of numb and mixed up. Mum wants me to go to the GP, but I'm scared...'

'What's wrong, sweetheart...are you depressed, anxious... what is it?'

'I'm not sure. I don't even know how it started. One day I woke up and I didn't feel right.'

'Why didn't you tell me?'

'I didn't want to bother you with all your important meetings and negotiations. I was shivery and lost my voice and felt all achy and then...I kind of got better. I thought it was just flu...you remember?'

'That was about three weeks ago, but I thought you'd got over that.'

'Yeah, but inside my head, I still felt all woolly and odd…'

'Odd…how?' There's a short gap. I hear him rap on the door. 'Let me in, Beth. I can't bear this…not being able to touch you, hold you.'

I can't believe how gracious he's being. He doesn't deserve this. I want so much to be able to make this right, to make everything heal and be harmonious again.

'I can't…not yet. If you come in, I'll just breakdown and cry and I won't stop. I want to try to explain it. You deserve that.'

'Okay…okay…I'll listen out here. Tell me more about how you feel. Is it the auditions? Has it been too stressful? Have I pushed you into doing too many?'

'I don't know.'

'Is it because of the wedding?' he asks.

The inevitable question.

I don't know what to say. Now I've got myself into this, I don't know where to take it.

He's speaking again, his voice raspy. 'I just want the truth, Beth. If you've changed your mind about marrying me, I need to know.'

What am I going to do?

If I say I'm not sure, then everything will be over and Peter will be catching the next train back to London. I'm certain of it. If I encourage him, then Beth *has* to be there in the church on Saturday.

I'm struck dumb. The silence goes on and on and I wonder if he might have already given up and gone downstairs.

'Peter…Peter are you still there?'

'Yes.' He sighs heavily. 'Listen. My parents are leaving New York tomorrow to get here for our wedding. They need to know if it's happening or not. *I* need to know. You have to make a decision one way or the other. Otherwise, I'm going to have to call it off.'

He's not being unfair, he really isn't. He's been incredibly patient with Beth all through this, but now it's crunch time and he's not the kind of man to hang around while people make up their minds. He's a straight-talker and a doer. I can see that. If he doesn't get a clear answer, he's going to walk right out of Beth's life.

He bangs on the door again. 'I'm not sure I can keep hanging on any longer, Beth. I've spent the last four weeks not knowing what's going on with you. If you're ill, you need to see a doctor. It might be something simple like glandular fever or it might be some kind of panic disorder, but you've got to do something. I'll support you, of course, I will. Are we getting married on Saturday or not, Beth? It's as simple as that.'

Somehow I find my voice again. 'But if I've got some sort of virus or disorder, shouldn't we wait until I'm better?'

'No. I'm not postponing it, Beth. That's just going to drag things on and on.'

'But, if I'm ill?'

'You've been well enough to get to auditions, to have a hen party. If you want to postpone it, I think what you're really saying is that your feelings for me have changed.' His voice starts to break. 'Is that what you're saying?'

'No…' It's out of my mouth before I know it. And I know why. I've fought for this, I want this marriage for my daughter and I want it for my own future, too.

'So…' he says, his voice softer. 'I need to get this clear. Are you going to be there on Saturday, or not? I need an answer. Now. You must see that. Is it yes or no? Which one?'

I can't go back now.

'Yes,' I tell him. 'Yes, I'll be there. I promise.'

'And you still love me?'

'Yes!' The tears come from nowhere, overwhelming me as I press my body flat against the closed door, my arms above my head, my palms reaching out to this man, my daughter's lover, on the other side.

I'm living this moment for Beth. It's about her. But it's also about me. And Russell. The wedding we never had. The one I missed out on. The one I hadn't realised I craved so much, until recently.

'Yes, absolutely, totally, utterly. I *do* love you, I do and I can't wait to be your wife!'

Chapter 40

Beth

I'm not sure when I fell asleep, but I must have dropped off because there's a jolt and in a flash I'm awake.

My eyes are open but I can't see a thing. I blink a few times. The curtains must be drawn.

I'm disoriented. Feeling woozy.

Wait…this isn't my bed.

Then I remember. Of course – I'm staying at Grandad's. I got back after 10 p.m. from Southampton. Grandad had already turned in, but I decided to have a mint tea, first. Mum had left a note on the front door asking one of us to call her, but it was late by then. It would only have been another plea for me to get my act together before the wedding, so I decided to ring first thing this morning, when I was feeling more resilient. I must have gone straight to bed after that.

Except the blanket doesn't feel right. It's prickly, made of wool and everyone knows I'm allergic to it. The pillow is different, too, smaller, like a cushion. And I feel hot in a cooped-up, stifling kind of way. As though I'm in a room that has no windows. As I sit up, a wave of panic hits me. This *isn't* the box-room at Grandad's. It's too dark – in fact, there's no room in his house that gets pitch black like this. He still has the thin pastel curtains Vera chose, at every window, because she was afraid of the dark.

The smell isn't right either. It's oily, greasy – like a shed or garage.

Then I realise I'm moving.

Where the hell am I?

Shapes, fragmented and broken up, begin to filter through the dense fog inside my head. Am I having some sort of crazy dream?

I need to backtrack, go over everything that happened in the right order. I scrunch up my eyes. If only I could think straight.

I was in Grandad's loft looking at photographs and came across the obscure newspaper clippings from over twenty years ago. With nothing better to do, I took off to the pub named in the news report and the trail led me to Bernie...

That's when things started getting surreal.

As I turn over in the pitch black, in a bid to get more comfortable on the mattress, I let out a yelp. My kneecaps ache, as though they've been hit with a hammer. Gingerly, I sit up and wrap my arms around them. My hip bones, my elbows and my chin hurts, too. I feel like I've got bruises all over me, on top of a throbbing headache.

I swallow hard.

What am I doing here?

I gently reach up and find a tender bump on the back of my head. At some point someone must have hit me. There's something gritty in my hair. Sand? A wave of dizziness catches me off guard. Someone must have given me something; drugged me.

I feel around with my hands. There's a wall to my right and one directly behind me. At the edge of the mattress, my probing fingers drop a few inches to the floor; wooden, no carpet. I slide my feet onto it and get up only as far as a crouching position, raising my hand cautiously into the space above me. I'm not sure how much room there is and I don't want to smash my head.

I reach up and up, gradually straightening until I'm upright. Then I put my hands forward, groping my way like a blind person. There's a wall to the side, another wall in front, all wooden judging by the texture of the grain. I reach a door. Locked.

I wrench at the handle anyway. It rattles against the bolt, but stays fast.

What's going on?

I go back in my head to the order of events as I last remember them. That's the only way I'm going to get close to fathoming out what's happened.

The pub in Southampton. Bernie's account of the night of the big party. A teenage girl was killed when a flying brick sent her into the path of a car. A brown Ford Cortina.

I hear my breath come out in shuddering bursts in the darkness. That's what Grandad used to drive in the nineties. I'd seen it in one of the photographs I'd found.

A clanging, grating sound breaks my train of thought. It reminds me of a clunky fairground ride and I get a weird sinking feeling like I'm going over big bumps in the road.

Was *that* the 'bad thing' that happened in Southampton? Was Grandad there? Was he the driver who accidentally killed a teenage girl? Had he been living with the trauma of it ever since? Why hadn't someone explained it to me? Why the big secret? It didn't make sense. I flap my hand in front of my face. It's so hot in here, I can hardly breathe.

Focus.

What happened after I got back to Abbots Worthy and made my mint tea? I was climbing the stairs to get ready for bed, that's right. Then what?

Ah, that's when I heard it. The beep of a car horn right outside the house, short toots, insistent. The cottages are spread out, so I'm not sure anyone else would have taken much notice.

I didn't want the racket to wake Grandad, so I stepped out into the front garden. It was dark and I was still in an old pair of slippers.

A Land Rover had pulled up in the middle of the road, with the engine running and the near door wide open, illuminating the front seats. I thought the driver must have hit a badger or a fox and had got out to check.

'Hello?' I called out into the sticky gloom. 'Are you okay? What's happened?' Rain was in the air and the wind was spoiling for a fight.

I heard nothing in response so I approached the open car door.

As I'm thinking back, the pictures in my head start jumping around like flash photography. An arm around my neck, a shove in my back, a clumpy boot stamping on my toes. I tried to call out, but a gloved hand was slapped over my nose and mouth, cutting off my air. I kicked out and punched with all my might, but I could hardly breathe. Scrabbling for air, I tried to keep my balance and fought back, but a sack was flung over my head and I was bundled forward. There was a metallic thud and acute pain shot through my knees as I landed. I curled into a foetal position to protect myself.

All I remember after that was a blue-black darkness. I didn't see or hear anyone – no faces, no voice. Just the smell of leather gloves, damp tweed and hessian.

It seems ages since I woke and I realise how thirsty I am. I feel around for a sink or bottle of water and my foot stumbles into a plastic bucket by the mattress. I reach down, but it's dry inside. A sting of bile reaches the back of my throat as the reason it's there dawns on me.

I pat my way around the walls until eventually I trip over something that sends splashes over my bare feet. I squat down and find a plastic jug. Cautiously, I sniff the contents, then dip my finger in and taste the tiniest drop. It seems to be plain water, but even though my tongue is crusty with dehydration, I take only a small sip and swallow, then wait a second or two. It's lukewarm, but otherwise there doesn't seem to be anything wrong with it, so I take down long gulps, coughing and choking as I tip up too much at once. A judder beneath me sends me lurching to one side, so I clutch the jug to my chest, desperate to stop the water from spilling. I need to think. Is this Mum's doing? Is this some half-baked idea to get me to come to my senses?

No. Surely, she'd never go to such despicable lengths.

Chapter 41

Rachel

I can't believe what I've done. I've dispelled all Peter's doubts and confirmed that the wedding is unquestionably *on*. Not only have I made him believe that Beth is here, but that she's one hundred per cent definitely going to be at St James's Church on Saturday.

After my final euphoric outburst as Beth, I went into the bathroom and wiped the tears from my face before joining him on the landing, as Rachel. He looks dazed when I creep up behind him.

'How is she?' I say, deliberately taking the register of my voice down, as far away from Beth's natural range as possible.

His hand is still holding the handle to the locked door. 'Well, I'm very worried about her,' he whispers, 'but she wants it to go ahead. She still wants us to get married.'

'Oh, that's fabulous news.' I press my hand over my heart and turn to him, no longer afraid to let him see my eyes are watery. 'Is she coming out?'

'She says she wants to rest.' He moves away from her door and heads for the stairs. 'I don't want to push it.'

I follow him down. When he gets to the bottom he stops. He labours over his next words, rubbing his chin. 'I'm worried she might be clinically depressed,' he says.

My eyes stretch wide. 'Really?' I look down. 'It's my fault. I've been preoccupied with the wedding and doing too many shifts at the pub…I hadn't realised she was so bad.' I chew the inside of my cheek. 'She's been moody and withdrawn, but I thought it was just a mother-daughter thing, you know? Wanting to spread her wings and all that.'

He stands back, leans against the edge of the sofa. 'I think we should get her to the GP as soon as possible, don't you?' He glances at his watch. 'Too late today, obviously.' He thinks for a moment. 'What about A&E, perhaps we should get her over there straight away?'

I can't believe this farce is still going on. I glance at the hairband dangling over the newel post, the asparagus fern splayed over the window ledge in the porch. Everything looks deceptively normal.

'Wait…' I swing round, my mind on overdrive. 'Let me give the surgery a call. The GP can sometimes do visits out of hours. My phone's upstairs – I'll be back in a tick.'

I re-join him minutes later.

'We just have to hang on until tomorrow,' I tell him, tossing my hair back with a flourish of fake relief. 'The GP is going to fit Beth in first thing.'

'And you'll keep a firm eye on her until then?'

'Of course. I won't go anywhere.'

He studies my face. 'You look a bit flushed, you okay?'

'Just relieved…'

He squeezes my arm and we drift back to the kitchen.

'What will you do, now?' I ask him. I need to get him away from the house at all costs, out of Winchester altogether until Saturday.

'I've got to get back to London.' He moves towards the lounge, looking for his briefcase and returns with it. 'Actually…' he pulls a haggard face, 'I could really do with a drink first.'

I want nothing more than to get him out of here, but what can I do?

Thankfully, due to our recent cutbacks, there's very little alcohol left in the house. I open the cupboard next to the oven and pull out the bottle with the least amount left in it.

'Brandy okay?'

He nods with a weary sigh and plonks himself down on a wooden chair.

He's understandably emotionally exhausted, but also reassured, believing Beth has declared she's definitely going to marry him on Saturday. When he empties his glass I feel obliged to refill it. Half an hour goes by, then forty-five minutes. He starts telling me anecdotes about famous people he's met and I'm trying to smile in all the right places, sticking to tap water, pretending that everything is hunky dory.

He's come a long way and thinks the woman who's just confirmed that all his dreams are shiny and intact is having a nap, only a few metres away. All the while, I'm dreading the sound of the front latch. Beth could slip in her key and finally come home at any time. I'm about to suggest we call it an evening, when Peter's phone rings. My mind leaps to the dire notion that in some ironic topsy-turvy reality it could be her finally getting in touch.

As he fumbles to find his phone, a raw charge of anguish flushes through my body when I realise that the countdown to Beth's wedding is also the countdown to her leaving me.

I've thrown myself into the wedding like it's my own, like it's going to take *me* to a brighter, better place, but once the initial joy has blown over, I'll be left behind. I'm not the least bit ready for losing her.

I hear the frantic jabbering of a woman's voice at the other end as soon as Peter answers the call. He gets up and mouths 'sorry', then sidles into the sitting room.

When he returns, his shoulders are hunched.

'That was Amelia,' he says.

My heart leapfrogs a beat. 'Amelia?' I swallow. 'How is she?'

'Not coping well at all. She's doing erratic, odd things by the sound of it.' He falters. 'How did you cope after Russell died. Is it okay to ask?

'It's fine. I think the situation is slightly different. Whilst Russell's death came sooner than we all expected, he was terminally ill. I can't imagine what Amelia's going through.'

He leans an arm on the back of his chair. 'Her friend isn't helping. Nancy. She's off her rocker – neurotic and dangerous. She's encouraging Amelia to go down all kinds of blind alleys.'

'Like what?'

'Nancy is making everything worse. She thinks she's helping, but…' He looks straight ahead. 'Because of her meddling, Amelia has got it into her head that Carl had a bit of a thing going with… with Beth.'

I let out a raucous laugh. 'How can either of them possibly think that?'

He takes his seat again, resting his elbows on the table. 'Well, there's the pendant I told you about, a photo someone took at a meet-and-greet party ages ago, the call she made to him…'

I can feel sweat prickling my forehead.

'Oh, yeah, Beth told me about that, but it was completely innocent. She rang him to ask for advice on getting her foot on the acting ladder. To be honest, she'd had a bit to drink and she should never have called him.'

'Exactly…and I think the call was only a couple of minutes,' he said.

'It's true that Beth also bumped into him at Winchester station one evening, but she didn't recognise him or speak to him. He was here for the theatre, I think, certainly nothing to do with Beth.'

'Anyway, now Amelia is saying she's found Beth's phone number in Carl's belongings.'

I throw myself back in my chair, almost tipping it backwards. 'Really?'

'Yeah, but it's all neurotic nonsense. She said it's written in a kind of obscure code.'

I stare at him with a perplexed frown. 'What kind of code?'

He lifts his shoulders into a shrug. 'Who knows? Sounds like some sort of private cypher Amelia and Carl shared for security passwords. Something so off the wall that no one else, and that includes the police, can make head nor tail of it – apart from Nancy, that is, who is saying it's obvious.' He lets out a heavy sigh. 'She's been goading Amelia to convince me to pull out of the wedding…'

I tut along with him as if the whole thing is outrageous.

'The crazy thing is, she's even harassing the police to arrest Beth. Honestly…' He rubs his eyes. 'It's not the first time Amelia has lost the plot. A few years ago her son, Alex, was ill and she was convinced the specialist he was seeing was trying to kill the boy. She wrote to the hospital and the local papers claiming the surgeon had suggested an operation when it wasn't necessary. Of course, the boy recovered, and it was all brushed under the carpet, but she gets these deranged notions, especially if Nancy is stoking the fire.'

He checks his watch. 'I need to think about getting back to London.'

I get to my feet and make a move towards the door, then change direction and turn towards the sink to rinse the glasses. I don't want to seem keen to get rid of him.

'Better check the trains,' he says, swiping the screen on his phone.

'The next one is five minutes past the hour,' I say, casually, resting his glass on the draining rack. 'You should have time to catch that.' I dry my hands and follow him to the foot of the stairs.

He stops and groans as he stares at the screen. 'There's been a fatality on the line near Eastleigh and no trains are getting through.' He checks his watch again. 'I'll stay in a hotel just for tonight and get going first thing in the morning.'

'Oh…'

That's all I need. Peter still hanging around.

'I'd suggest staying here, but…under the circumstances…'

We both look up towards Beth's room.

'No,' he puts his hand out, 'no need, honestly. I'll keep out of your hair for the final preparations.'

I suggest the Royal Winchester as a place to stay and give him instructions on how to get there. Finally, I close the front door behind him.

I go up to my room and slide the curtain aside an inch. Just enough to make sure he really is leaving the street, then I call Beth's phone. When there's no reply, I try Adrian. Beth still hasn't come back.

The next time I see Peter will be on Saturday at St James's Church. My hands go cold and clammy at the thought.

Chapter 42

Beth

I've completely lost track of time, lying here with a pounding headache. The perpetual darkness is unbearable. It could be morning, evening or the middle of the night, I've no way of knowing. I can't see a thing. I close my eyes and it makes no difference. My brain has started making up geometric patterns in different colours in the air, green and red mostly, to give it something to do.

I've already felt around for a light switch, but I try again. Maybe I missed it. Along with the dank, oily smell there's an undercurrent of something fishy, like burning rubber. It makes me want to retch, even though I'm also getting hungry.

If only I'd had my phone on me, even if I couldn't reach it, it would be trackable, but I know for a fact that I left it on Grandad's sofa. I'm still wearing what I had on when I stepped into the front garden; my jeans and a scruffy polo shirt. I had nothing else on me except for an old pair of slippers from the box-room. During my tentative explorations around this tiny space I haven't come across them.

As I feel my way to the jug again, I lurch heavily to one side as the floor tilts. It's then I realise why I'm feeling queasy – all the rolling and churning. We're not on the road – I'm on a boat.

What's going on?

Is this Peter's doing? Has he borrowed Carl's yacht again? A ridiculous abduction to make sure I'm where I'm meant to be on Saturday to say 'I do'?

I think back to the evening we shared on the luxury boat on the Thames and listen hard to the sound of the engine. There's a thrumming, purring quality that seems familiar. Is this the same one?

No, it can't be. Peter adores me. He'd never put me through something like this.

Where am I being taken? I could be half way to France for all I know. With a surge of rage I drop to all fours and scrabble around for the bucket, then ram it against the door time after time.

'What the hell is this?!' I yell. 'Help me, please. *Some-bo-dy!*'

There's no response. All that happens is the engine throbs and we seem to pick up speed. I flop back down on the mattress and stare into the darkness. I'm still woozy, drifting in and out of dozing. In spite of the uneven rocking to tell me otherwise, I feel like I'm underground, trapped deep within the bowels of the earth. The thought leads straight to the night we hacked at the soil to make a pit and buried Carl. We stuffed his body down and…

Stop!

I can't go there. Not here. Not now.

I try to bend my mind towards comforting memories and find myself drifting off into a story Mum told me when I was about two years old. We were in the kitchen and she was cooking and she left me briefly to answer the front door. When she came back, she couldn't find me anywhere. She screamed the house down, calling my name, checking every room, looking behind the sofa, the chairs, inside the cupboard under the stairs.

In the end, she found me in the cabinet under the sink, happily sitting amidst the bottles of washing-up liquid and fabric softener. I've got the photo to prove it. When she asked me what I was doing in there, apparently, I replied in a solemn tone with the words: 'I'm thinking.' I don't remember it, but I've laughed with her many times as we've relived that little scene together.

We were unfailingly in tune when I was growing up. Even when Russell came along, she always put me first. Mum never made a fuss when I dyed all my underwear black during my Goth stage and we all had stained fingertips for weeks afterwards. I remember I made a cake for a friend's birthday and decorated it to look like an ashtray, complete with cigarette butts made of icing.

It was gross, but Mum didn't bat an eyelid and told everyone it was 'very clever.' During my arty phase, I insisted that everything had to be homemade; clothes, birthday cards, jam, every meal – nothing could come out of a tin or packet. I brought home lopsided pots and vases I'd made at school, pinned drawings on the sitting room walls and had a fetish for painting stencils above every dado in the house. She put up with it all. We shared everything like best friends and she could almost read my mind. Things have changed radically.

The thought of her stings my eyes and I feel tears trickle down my face and into my mouth. She must be out of her mind with worry, wondering where I've got to.

Or is she?

What if she thinks I've done a runner just to get back at her? What if she's going to hang fire and wait for me to sort myself out, do nothing until I turn up again on the doorstep. That would be the worst possible thing she could do, because it would mean there's no one out there looking for me.

I shudder uncontrollably at the thought, my gut churning as I feel dizzy, shaky, seasick and helpless all in one. My hands shake as I touch my face to clear the tears. I cross my arms over my chest and hug myself in a desperate bid to feel safe. I curl up, burying myself in the blanket. The engine rumbles on, steady, unrelenting, filling up the lonely space around me.

Time passes. I've no idea for how long. If only someone would come to bring me something to eat. Then I'll have my chance. I'll tell them there's been a terrible mistake.

Almost immediately there's a click outside and bright lines of light appear around the door. Someone is coming. My heart is punching hard and fast inside my chest. There's a muffled thud, a sharp clunk, then at last the door swings open. My words come out in a mad garble, tumbling over themselves.

'Hey, what is this? Where am I? My name's Beth Kendall... don't you see? I don't know who you think I am, but...you've got it wrong...listen to me...what am I doing here...?'

Something spongy is flung across the floor – a sandwich wrapped in clingfilm – but I take my eyes back to the doorway. The light is so dazzling that I can't see who is standing there. I reach out, clawing at the blinding light, but the door snaps shut, the light goes off and everything is still again.

It's as though nothing ever happened. Except that the flash of white light has ignited the raging pain in my head again.

Finding myself abandoned in the darkness once more makes it seem twice as stifling as before. A new thought hits me. What if I run out of air, stashed away in this oppressive little storeroom? I snatch at each breath, sucking it in, panting, my lungs burning.

My inhaler…oh, God, where is it?

Chapter 43

Rachel

'Her asthma inhaler…I've found it, it's here.'

It's Adrian, ringing me the next morning.

'What?!'

'Her purse too,' he adds. 'I didn't notice. They were hanging in a bag behind her old jacket in the hall.'

I take a moment to process what he's saying. When I was last there, I'd looked for her jacket and it definitely wasn't hanging in the hall. Beth must have gone back to Adrian's cottage at some point and neither of them told me. Then she must have gone out again, only that time she'd taken virtually nothing. My heart rate charges off into a gallop. She's gone off without her asthma medication, her jacket and her purse.

'When did you last see Beth, Adrian?' I know it's hopeless as soon as the words are out of my mouth, but I have to ask.

There's a taut silence on the line.

'Adrian? Dad! It's important. I came over on Sunday, remember? We thought Beth might have gone to Southampton. To The Hope and Anchor.'

'Ginger cake,' he says emphatically, as though he's got the answer.

'Yes, she made a ginger cake, before I came over. What happened *after* that?'

There's a small keening sound and I know he's trying, but the rusty cogs inside his brain have got stuck.

'It's okay, Adrian. I'm coming over.'

Seconds later he's on the line again.

'Beth rang,' he says. 'Her phone.'

'She rang? She called you?'

226

He mutters something. 'Not quite…what I mean is, her phone kind of rattled. Buzzed. That's it. Someone was on her phone and it buzzed.'

'Beth's phone? It's in your cottage?'

'Yes. It was under the tea-cosy in the kitchen. I thought I heard a funny noise yesterday evening and there it was again, this morning. There was a call from a chap called Peter. Heard of him?'

I let out a loud huff of exasperation and grab my coat.

As soon as I arrive, I hurtle upstairs and check the box-room. Her few belongings are still there, but laid out slightly differently; a pair of socks is on the floor beside the camp bed and the sleeping bag is smoothed out. I can't tell whether she's slept in it since I was last there or not. I go into the bathroom. Her spare toothbrush is still there. A prickly shudder slips down the back of my neck.

My message on the back of the front door has been taken down, I notice, even though neither of them bothered to ring me. I find it squashed into the kitchen pedal-bin with the wrapper of a flapjack bar, Beth's favourite snack, on top. Beth certainly came back.

I look for further clues around the place, but there's not much to go on. A copy of the *Radio Times* is open on the kitchen table, still set to Sunday's programmes. Beth always ticks what day it is on the kitchen calendar when she's there, to help Adrian. The ticks stop on Sunday. It's now Tuesday. Did she go to Southampton, come back and go straight back out again? Without anything? It doesn't make sense.

I glance at the clock. We've lost so much time already. It feels like it's gone past the point where Beth is going to walk back in any minute.

Adrian hands me her mobile. She has twenty-five missed calls, including several from Peter prior to the time he thought he spoke to her at my place. I go back upstairs and sit on her camp bed, convinced there's something I'm missing.

Where would she have gone? My mind is charging off all over the place, my heart racing at twice the normal speed. I need to get a grip and think. That's when I spot them.

Her trendy sandals, behind the door. They were the only shoes she brought over with her, but she kept spare slippers and trainers at Adrian's, so where are they? I glance under the camp bed. Then check the bathroom. There they are, her trainers, hidden by a dropped towel.

So where are her slippers? Did she go out in those?

I hurtle downstairs, scouring the floor. I check everywhere. Where the hell would she go wearing her slippers?

I call 999 straight away. The first thing I tell them is that Beth hasn't got her asthma inhaler and she'd never go anywhere without it. I give the address of the cottage. Given the fact that Beth's been gone this long and left her medication behind, the emergency services tell me someone will be straight over.

An officer I don't recognise arrives. His name is PC Mallin. He has long fingernails and cheeks peppered with sandpaper stubble. He takes me through a list of questions about Beth's social media accounts, her access to funds and wants a recent photo. There's one in a frame on Adrian's mantelpiece. It was taken at a party shortly after Beth got engaged and she looks glowing and self-assured. PC Mallin takes more than a cursory glance at it, breathing in her image, before taking it out of the frame.

'Did she take her phone?' he asks.

'No. It's here. It was in the kitchen.' I hand it to him.

'Password?'

I write it down for him.

'And you said she left her purse behind? Is that the only place she would keep any money?'

'Yes.' I give him that too. He looks inside.

'These her only bank cards?'

'Yes. All in her purse.'

PC Mallin spreads his feet into a wider stance. 'Is there anything she might be upset about?'

Oh, Lord, where do we start?

I stick to the heavily-edited version. 'She's supposed to be getting married next Saturday and we had a bit of a row at her hen party.'

He nods knowingly and actually dares to chuckle. Given how nerve-wracking this is I'm stunned by his insensitivity. I have to lock my hands together behind my back, or else I might hit him.

'When did you last see your daughter?' he asks.

'Sunday afternoon, but she's been staying here with my father.' I lower my voice to a whisper. 'It's a bit complicated, because he's got memory problems and he can't actually remember when he last saw her.'

The PC looks up at Adrian, who's sitting immobile in front of the muted television.

'Right…' he says, pressing a pronounced full stop onto the page. I suddenly think of Peter. He could be on a train back to London by now, but the police will certainly want to speak to him. Then the waters are going to get well and truly muddied when he tells them he spoke to Beth on Monday evening in Winchester. His account of when he last saw Beth and the reality of the situation won't match up.

'Wait a minute…' I say, pressing my fingers into my forehead. 'I'm sorry, I'm so dizzy with what's happened, I've got myself all mixed up.' I let out a rush of air. 'Peter, her fiancé, spoke to her on Monday, late afternoon at my house. She was locked in her room and she wouldn't speak to me.

He glances at his notes. 'So, she was last seen on Monday, not Sunday?'

'According to Peter.'

'Did *you* see her on Monday?'

'No. I didn't. Not at all that day.'

'But she was there?'

'Well…she must have been.' I say vaguely.

He stares at me as though I'm mad, but I don't care. I just need him to find my daughter. Sunday, Monday – it doesn't matter. She's still missing.

'We'll be taking a look around both locations,' he says. 'Do you have a list of people and places she might have gone to?'

'Not here. At my house.'

'Okay, let's get over there. We usually suggest you try to get in touch with as many of her friends as you can.'

I turn to Adrian. 'Ring me straight away if Beth comes back, okay?' I say, before we head off.

'Yes. Of course.' He ends with a sing-song voice as though I'm five years old. 'Sleep tight, Way-way.'

It's not even 2 p.m.

PC Mallin gives me a sympathetic glance as he opens the passenger door for me.

'It's awful to see them go like that, isn't it?'

'I'll get the laptop and iPad from upstairs,' I tell him, as soon as we get to Barnes Road. 'Together with the contacts on her phone, it should cover everyone.' I grimace, knowing it will be a very long list.

I set the both devices down on the kitchen table and tell him the password is the same as her phone.

'We'll need to take these,' he says. 'If you don't manage to copy over all your daughter's contacts, we'll get them sent to you.'

PC Mallin tells me I'll need a USB cable, so once I've found that, I open her 'Christmas card' list and transfer it to my phone, together with other lists of college friends, drama contacts, old school mates. In the meantime, he's checking Beth's mobile.

'She hasn't used it since Sunday evening,' he says. He holds up the screen to show me the last page she looked at online. It doesn't surprise me – a press account of the manslaughter of Tracy Limehouse in Southampton.

'Do you know what this is?' he asks, scanning the report.

I explain that Beth seems to have found old newspaper clippings in Adrian's loft and could well have got it into her head to catch the train to Southampton.

'This was years ago.' He frowns, looking perplexed. 'Do you know what it's all about?'

'Not a clue,' I tell him.

I'm getting used to telling fibs, by now and it's best to keep everything simple. 'It seems she came back after her visit, so I don't think it's significant.'

'We'll check CCTV at the station,' he says.

While PC Mallin takes a look around, he suggests I punch out a private message to everyone on Beth's phone, so I get straight onto it.

Have you seen Beth? Very worried as she's missing since Sunday. Police involved. If you know anything, please let me know asap. Beth's Mum, Rachel.

Responses pop up immediately:
Have you tried Peter's flat in Chelsea?
Has she gone to see Tina's new puppy?
Try Maria…

As a result, I send more messages, but everything comes back negative.

Once PC Mallin has left with all Beth's electronic devices, my next call is to Kate, who insists on coming straight over. Before she's even made it over the threshold, I fling myself at her.

She grips my arms firmly. 'We'll look all day and night if we have to. What are the police doing?'

'They've got her photo. They're going to check CCTV footage at the station. She might have gone to Southampton, gone back to Adrian's, then taken off again.'

'Southampton?'

I throw up my eyes, shaking my head. 'I know!' I don't want to have to tell her about the newspaper cutting, about the pub, about what it means. 'Beth is just…doing her own thing at the moment.'

My phone rings. I glance at the screen and moan.

'It's Peter, I can't face him...I just can't.'

Kate snatches the phone from me.

'No, it's not...Rachel's friend, Kate,' she says. 'Yes...I know... she's going out of her mind. Everyone's looking for her.' She glances over at me. 'Er...not now...I'll tell her you called.'

'Thank you,' I say to her, dropping the phone back onto the table.

'He's in London,' she says. 'He has to do something first, then he's coming back.'

'Oh no, that's all we need.'

Kate is a true gem. She's always been one to roll up her sleeves and muck in and she doesn't ask awkward questions. We set about marking the locations of Beth's local friends on my A-Z. Kate has to get up at 5 a.m. to set up her market stall in Petersfield, yet she's prepared to get no sleep at all in order to help me.

Jogging at a brisk pace, my map under my arm, I start knocking on doors. Kate has gone to addresses further afield in her car. As I fly from one address to the next, I mull over the conversation I had with Kate, earlier.

'I've seen such a change in Beth recently...you must have, too,' she said. 'She's got no spark. She seems to drag herself around. Not the glamorous, upbeat Beth I know.' She looked up at me. 'She's still head over heels in love with Peter, then?'

Head over heels. I hear Kate's words and run them around inside my head.

After Carl's death, I was convinced Beth was feeling too guilty to bring herself to speak to Peter. She was riddled with remorse about the affair, aside from being hounded by images of the way in which we'd dealt with Carl's body. I thought she loved Peter *too much* to cope with the hurt it could cause. Then, when she continued to cut him off, I thought the reason she couldn't face him was because she'd be tempted to confide in him. But maybe that's not what's been going on after all.

Another front door is closed after a repeat of the same strained conversation and I jog on to the next one. As I stop for breath, my phone pings with a voicemail. It's Peter. He's spoken to the police in London and they've assured him that there's nothing to rush back here for. Thank goodness. He says he'll be tying up business interests, staying at the flat in case she turns up there, but he'll call soon.

As I break into a run again, snippets of my exchanges with Beth spanning the past few months drift into my mind. After she and Peter first met, she used to talk about him incessantly. Every conversation started or ended with a reference to him. Peter said this, Peter did that, Peter thinks, Peter likes… For months, he was embedded into our daily lives and our future. But since the fiasco in the cellar, I've been the one who's brought his name into our conversations.

Perhaps I'm the one who should come to my senses.

Chapter 44

Beth

My inhaler…I frantically pat the mattress, feel my way around every inch of the floor, but it's not here. Why would it be? I didn't have it on me when I stepped outside Grandad's front door. I thought I was only going to be out there for a minute or two.

Panic threatens to steal the air from my lungs. *Steady, stay calm, it's okay.* My chest hurts, I'm wheezing. How long can I last without my puffer? *In through your nose, out through your mouth. That's it. Purse your lips so you don't hyperventilate…* I cling on to the words I've taught myself and the moment passes.

Time has gone by, but my foggy head can't work out how many hours. I'm feeling wobbly, but it's not just because I haven't eaten much. I reckon there was something in the tuna sandwich. For a moment I wonder if we're on dry land, then I feel a gentle tugging sensation, a slight rocking, as though the vessel is moored.

If we're anchored in a marina we're likely to be close to people. I stand up and let out a deafening scream. I bang on the door, yell again making my throat burn. Nothing happens. Maybe everyone has left the boat. Maybe I'm drifting out at sea somewhere all on my own.

A drowsiness claims me soon after, then I'm shaken awake by a dazzling flash of light. Someone has opened and closed the door. I can smell food. A waft of spicy tomato. I kneel on the floor, sweeping my arms in front of me until I feel my way to a tin dish with a plastic fork. I greedily scoop up the first mouthful. It's baked beans. I never knew they could taste so good. I'm sure there's going to be a sedative sprinkled in it, but I have to eat.

When I've wiped the plate clean with my finger, I put it back on the floor, but it rests on something. I reach out and find a long tube. It's heavy and made of metal. There seems to be a switch at one end, so I press it and for the first time I have light. A torch – it's like the most blessed gift imaginable. I can see. There's a full jug of water standing behind the empty plate and a sheet of paper with a pen laying across it. I shine the beam on the sheet and find a block of text printed from a computer:

Are you ready to confess, yet? Were you having an affair with Carl Jacobson? Tell me the truth. I'll give you a little more time to think about it, but there won't be any more food. This is the last of the water, so you'd better make it last.

That's what this is about! This is no random or mistaken abduction. Is it Peter – did he find out? Or Amelia? Or someone else close to Carl?

I sit back on my heels and use the torch to illuminate the space around me. It's no more than a glorified cupboard, cleared of everything apart from the mattress and the other items I've already found. There is a pull-cord switch above head-height by the door, but there's no bulb in the ceiling. I sit on the mattress and turn off the torch. I need to save the battery for when I really need it. Once again, I sink into the black hole of obscurity.

Would Peter stoop so low as to act in such a cowardly way as this? It just doesn't seem possible to me. He's not that kind of guy. But then, how well do I really know him?

I reflect on the last few months. I fell headlong for Peter at the start. He made me feel important, special, significant. I was swept up into his world, full of magic and allure. Then I realised my feelings were more about how he made me feel, than how I actually felt about him, as a person. He's sparky and great fun to be with, but his views are often staid. He's sensible, down to earth and organised and I'm flighty, impulsive, looking for upside-down ways of doing things. If his colours are grey and brown, then mine are fluorescent orange and lime green.

In a phone conversation, shortly before my hen party, he took it for granted that I'd change my surname to his once we'd tied the knot. I flared up in outrage.

'I want to stay Beth Kendall. It's part of my identity, it's my history, it connects me to my family.'

'Come on, it's got to be Roper. It's not like you've built up any kind of following with your name as it stands.'

'Thanks for reminding me…'

'In any case, you've barely got any family. You don't even know who your father is!'

His remarks stung. All along he'd made it seem like my upbringing had never been an issue for him, but clearly it was. He even went as far as to say that it seemed disrespectful if I didn't take his name, that I wasn't considering his feelings.

'Changing my name is not a nice little favour I can do for you, like baking you a cake or giving you a foot massage,' I retorted. He ended the call in a huff and the issue was never properly resolved. More ruffled feathers I can't bring myself to tell Mum about.

Then there's the age difference. I didn't think it mattered, but it does. While he says he wants to help launch my career, he's apparently set his own private time-limit for it. His heart can't really be in it. What he actually wants is a family and I can't see that being on my agenda for at least ten years.

I draw my knees up to my chest and feel the rough familiarity of the denim fabric against my chin. Peter hates jeans. He thinks they make me look cheap. I love them, especially skinny ones with stilettos.

I need to face this. I haven't felt right about Peter for a long time, otherwise why would I have been tempted to go astray so easily? I flip the torch on again and re-read the note, then pick up the biro and anxiously chew the end of it while I think about how I'm going to respond. If I admit to the affair, won't that make everything worse? Won't it make my abductor more angry?

It could even put Mum in danger, because my confession would create the link between Carl and I.

Amelia has obviously become entirely unhinged with grief and rage. She might be capable of anything. This has to be her doing. She would have access to Carl's boat, just like Peter.

I pick up the pen and begin to write:

No, I did not have an affair with Carl. I met him at a party once and I barely know him. You've got this all wrong. You've got to let me out. I need my asthma inhaler – I could die locked away like this. Are you prepared to commit murder? Please don't leave me here. Beth

I slip it under the door and wait.

Chapter 45

Rachel

'You okay?' Kate asks me, stroking my face. She's packed up her market stall early this lunchtime and come straight over.

'Just…you know…fearing the worst,' I say. 'It happens.'

'I know,' she looks pensive for a second, 'but most people are somewhere unexpected, rather than missing or…you know… aren't they? Ninety-nine per cent of the time…that's what the police said, wasn't it?'

I sigh.

Now we've paid a visit to everyone we can think of, the police have advised me to stay at home. But I can't focus on anything.

'Peter's on his way back,' I tell her, betraying my unease. 'I don't want to have to go through it all again with him.'

Kate reaches into her bag and offers me a Snickers. I shake my head. 'It's another person who can help,' she says. 'Look at it like that.'

I grunt.

'The police confirmed that Beth *did* go to Southampton on Sunday night,' I tell her, as she munches her way through the chocolate bar, 'but that she returned to Adrian's and was dropped off at 10 p.m. in a taxi.'

'Then Peter spoke to her here, the following day?' She licks her fingers.

'Yeah.' I don't want to complicate things. I haven't got the energy. 'I'm sure she went back to Adrian's. I'm certain she went missing from there. Beth has never taken off like this before. It means she's regarded as "high risk" by the police.'

'What else are they doing?' she asks.

'They've checked local hospitals, gone house to house both here and at Adrian's and they've set up media coverage to appeal for sightings of her. Dogs have been through the woods near the cottage and the streets around here have been scoured.' I drop my face into my hand. 'We've contacted everyone we can – there's nowhere else to look.'

Kate cradles my head but doesn't offer empty platitudes.

Before she arrived, I'd been sitting at the kitchen table, staring at the packet of green tea Beth drinks, stuffed beside the toaster. I've had plenty of time in Beth's absence to re-run little conversations through my mind and I've come to the conclusion that I've missed something vital.

Beth's feelings for Peter changed a long time ago – even *before* 'the accident'.

Now I think about it, it was subtle at first and I probably didn't want to acknowledge it.

I ease myself out of Kate's embrace to look at her.

'I've been blind.'

'Why? What's happened?'

'I think Beth and Peter's relationship has been coming apart at the seams for weeks now.'

She stares at me in disbelief. 'Seriously?'

'It might have even been as far back as January. Peter wasn't featuring in Beth's chatty daily round-ups so much. She was more likely to be telling me about Maria or Tina, films or pop concerts she'd been to.'

The first splinters in the smooth veneer?

I shudder. 'Then, when she did mention him, it would usually be couched in a faintly disparaging tone: *Did you know Peter used to stammer until he was fifteen? Can you believe Peter has to wear a gum shield at night because he grinds his teeth? Peter never talks to me about his work.*' I swallow. 'She's been going off him all this time.'

'But Beth always speaks her mind,' Kate says with authority. 'She's the most outspoken person I know. Surely she would have told you if her feelings for Peter had changed.'

I stare at the back door. It's just dawning on me what has been going on.

'I wanted this for her, so much,' I prattle on. 'I threw myself into making their wedding a supreme celebration of their love. It's the one thing that's kept me going and Beth knows that. Yet as time has gone on, Beth's been getting smaller and smaller in the whole process. At some stage, she's practically become invisible. Marrying Peter stopped being about her. It's been about *me*.'

'You've only wanted the best for her. Peter's been wonderful, you said. Such a generous and warm man.'

'But I think her feelings for him have gone off the boil. I've not allowed myself to see it.' I drag my finger nails over my bottom teeth. 'I've been so stupid.'

'You mustn't worry about that now. Let's just get her back, safe and sound.'

Kate goes home to get some long-overdue sleep and shortly afterwards, Peter arrives.

I throw my arms around his neck and he pulls me hard against him for probably longer than is appropriate.

'No word?' he asks softly, resting his chin on the top of my head.

'No word.'

Now he's arrived, I'm glad of his company. I'd probably spiral into a frenzy, left on my own. He's brought a small overnight bag with him.

'Stay here, will you?' I say it more as a plea than an offer.

I lead him upstairs and invite him into the third bedroom, the one that used to be Beth's before she moved into Russell's. It's only once he's lifted his bag onto the bed that I realise I'll have to introduce him to the odd bathroom arrangement. He's only ever been here for around two hours at a time and has never asked to use the toilet before.

I show him how he'll need to enter from Beth's room and remind him to lock the door that connects to my room to avoid any embarrassments.

He seems to find the layout amusing. I only hope it doesn't prompt any suspicions about his conversation with Beth through the door on Monday.

Later, the sun climbs out unexpectedly from behind overlapping clouds, like a dog nudging open a closed door. After days of drizzle, we sit on the back patio with strong coffee. It doesn't seem right to drink wine, although we could both probably do with a glass. The only outdoor seats are the two old-fashioned deckchairs, and, to an outsider, we must look like we're putting our feet up, enjoying ourselves.

I'm feeling out of touch with reality. It was the same after Russell passed away. Moments would go by when the world seemed normal and how it should be, then my stomach would drop as the recognition of how things really were hit me afresh.

'I've had people asking about final arrangements for the wedding,' I say.

'What have you told them?'

'It's been on the news now that Beth is missing, so some of the local businesses seem to know. They're putting things on hold... but...'

He gives me a desperate look.

I suck my bottom lip. 'No matter what happens, I think we should postpone it,' I tell him. 'Don't you?'

He nods, looking defeated. 'Yes – I do.'

I'm silently grateful he's not putting up a fight.

'I've been putting together a list of everything we have to cancel; the big things like the church, the guests, the hotel, the catering and the smaller ones like the car, the music, the flowers...' I drop my eyes. I am on the verge of sobbing with every breath. 'My friend Kate said she'd help.'

'And I will, of course.' He flicks his cuff aside to look at his watch. 'I'll need to contact my parents,' he says. 'They've been holding off leaving New York until things were clearer.'

I take our empty mugs inside and wipe random surfaces down in the kitchen to give him privacy. When I re-join him outside, he's flushed and his hair is sticking out behind one ear.

'That bloody woman…' he growls, shaking his head.

'What's happened?'

'Sorry,' he says. 'It's Amelia again. She's hounding me. Throwing more accusations out about Beth. It's unbelievable.'

I stand with my arm shaking on the back of his deckchair, gouging out splinters with my thumb nail. 'Does she know Beth's missing?'

'No, but I'll set her straight.'

'Where does Amelia live?'

'Arundel.'

It's about an hour and a half from here, by car.

'What's she claiming now?'

'It's ridiculous. Honestly. You don't want to know.'

'No, go on.' I sit beside him once more. The deckchair forces me into a lounging position – ludicrous considering the grave matters we're discussing. 'Tell me…'

'She's saying not only that Beth had an affair with Carl, but that she killed him, too. I mean…' He shakes his head, his mouth gaping.

'How does she work that one out?'

'The police have identified the rug that…Carl was buried in. You know about that, right? It was one from your pub, I understand?'

I glance down. 'Yes, that's true. They think someone might have pinched it from the skip at the back…' I wave my arms around, '…you know, an opportunist thing. It was certainly open-house for a few weeks while the place was completely refitted.'

'Amelia…or most probably Nancy…is saying that you work in the "very same pub" and therefore it's another direct connection between Carl and Beth.'

I give a little huff. 'Is that all?'

'Plus, the fact that the killer buried Carl in the same graveyard where your partner is buried…again…the link.'

I feel a vicious kick inside my abdomen. Amelia has been a proper little Miss Marple.

'That's all true,' I say, trying not to let my cheeks turn pink. It's all purely circumstantial, but when you add everything together, you could make the assumption that it points Beth's way.

He laughs. 'I mean…I know Beth…it's just preposterous.'

'What do the police think?'

'Amelia has been pestering them on a daily basis and she says they've been rude to her. They've been checking the rug, obviously, looking for the most recent surface traces, but I'm sure if they'd found anything, she'd have heard something by now.' He runs his fingers through his thick hair. 'Amelia says the senior investigating officer has pared down that part of the forensic operation. It's all about costs. Amelia's not happy. She can't get it into her head that the police know what they're doing!'

I can't help thinking that as time goes on Carl's widow is becoming a loose cannon. And although the police appear to be treating her as a hysterical hindrance, she's still a cause for concern. What if she does eventually stumble on something that concretely links Beth and Carl together?

As the metallic clouds swallow up the sun again, I wonder whether I need to pay Amelia a visit.

On second thoughts, my chances of getting her to back off would be increased a hundredfold if Peter was by my side. As Carl's good friend, he has a vested interest in seeing the killer found, so he could persuade her to stop interfering better than anyone.

Chapter 46

Beth

When I next wake, we're on the move again. The put-put sound of the engine softens into a monotonous chunter. The torch I left by my side under the blanket is still there, so I flick it on to see what now awaits me by the door. The dish has gone, my bucket has been emptied and there's another sheet of paper on the floor:

I know what you were up to. Where were you on the evenings of Jan 4, Feb 19 and March 8? Write down exactly where you were and who you were with. Then sign the note and push it under the door. I'm going to wait for you to tell me the truth. I've got all the time in the world, but I'm not sure you have... No more food, water or asthma inhaler until you tell the truth. Pathetic little thing, aren't you? Can't work out what Carl saw in you.

I recognise the dates straight away. The first two were times when Carl and I secretly met at a hotel in London. The final date will always be a scar in my mind – the evening Carl and I went to the cellar.

What should I do? Even if I admit the truth, Amelia – it must be her – is obviously unstable and volatile. She's gone to these lengths already.

The jug of water is now only half full. My breathing is shallow, fast and short at the top of my chest, like an injured animal. I've got to get out. I switch off the torch to conserve the batteries and rattle the pen between my teeth. How should I respond? I'm not getting any more food or water. By the time I get another visit, I might be dead.

It's a hazardous gamble, but if I don't shake things up, I might never get out of here alive.

I flick the torch back on and write the names of the hotels we stayed at beside the dates, giving arrival and leaving times. For March 8, I write that Carl and I arranged to meet at Mum's house while she was out. At the end I put;

You're right. I, Beth Kendall, had a brief and meaningless affair with Carl Jacobson.

I fold the paper and slip it under the door before I can change my mind. Maybe my confession will force a confrontation. Now I've come clean about the affair, something has to shift, doesn't it? Anything would be better than rotting away in this airless pit.

Chapter 47

Rachel

The taxi crunches along the sweeping drive and leaves us at the foot of a double stone staircase. I take in a sharp breath. I feel like I'm on the film set of Downton Abbey.

Amelia's home looks like the kind of place where you'd pay at least ten quid for the privilege of setting foot inside the front door.

'It's a Georgian Grade two listed building,' Peter says, 'and Amelia is unlikely to set you straight if you make the assumption that she owns the whole place. In fact, she lives in the east wing; three bedrooms – the building is split into twenty apartments.'

'Ah-ha…'

I already know a great deal about this woman I've never met. She's neurotic, obsessed and now, it seems, has ideas above her station. Is she an abductor too? Has she taken Beth?

'Where do we go in?' I ask, hesitant about climbing the steps.

'It's round to the left,' he says.

We pass an old stable block and barn, both converted into living areas. 'Amelia keeps horses at a nearby farm,' he says. 'Riding is her passion.'

Amelia opens the front door before we reach it.

'I'm so glad you've come, Peter,' she says, throwing me a hostile stare. 'It's going from bad to worse.'

Without further explanation, she storms off across a hallway paved with flagstones. Her white-blonde hair has been scooped up into a beehive with stray ringlets at either side. It must have taken some time to construct.

To our left is an antiquated deep-set fireplace and, in the centre, a broad staircase leads to an oriel window.

We follow at a pace, as she brings us to what looks like the main room, with two L-shaped sofas, chandeliers and extensive views out across the lawns. Amelia sees me come to a standstill as I pause to take in the immaculate sweep of the grounds. I catch the self-righteous curl of her lip which fleetingly interrupts the consternation on her face.

'Tea?' she says, making the word long and sending it up in pitch at the end. She's looking at Peter, her chin held high, her arms out.

'This is Rachel, Beth's mother,' he says, ignoring the offer. Amelia gives me a cursory nod. Peter turns to me. 'Would you like something to drink, Rachel?'

I decide the brittle awkwardness might be alleviated by a central activity, so I accept. Amelia heads for a bell beside the fireplace and presses it. Wearing silk harem pants and a well-tailored ivory blouse, she's showing more than an inkling of cleavage. She's obviously someone who spends a lot of time and money on her appearance, but to me, the look says more 'celebrity interview' than 'grieving widow'.

'Darling, the most dreadful thing happened this morning,' she says dramatically, pointing to one of the peach-coloured sofas. Peter and I sit together silently, like a couple at their first appointment for marriage counselling. Amelia, however, seems reluctant to join us and paces around the room, wafting towards the window, the fireplace – where she takes a swift peek at herself in the mirror – then back to the centre. She flinches when a young woman dressed in a black tunic enters the room.

'Ah, Anna, there you are…tea for three, if you will. No biscuits…quick as you can. And tell Howard to cancel my massage at five o'clock, I've got to be somewhere…and make sure you get *fresh* mango for breakfast tomorrow, none of this packaged nonsense.'

Amelia's instructions come thick and fast in a wispy and affected aristocratic accent. As she turns away, I catch Anna's expression. Her jaw twists slightly to one side, betraying the slightest hint of animosity.

I'm here to persuade Amelia to call off her witch-hunt against Beth, but we're about to have polite afternoon tea and I have no idea where to start.

'Why is *she* here?' she asks Peter, staring at me.

Peter shifts to the front of his seat. 'Steady on, Mia.'

'As her mother, you should be ashamed of yourself.' She leers at me, shaking her finger, but keeping her distance as though I might bite.

I open my mouth, but Peter jumps in to defend me.

'Rachel and I just want to see how you are and—'

'Well, I've found something else,' she says. 'It's all adding up now. The graveyard, the pub, the rug…'

'You really have been jumping to conclusions,' Peter interjects. 'The police have no DNA from the rug and are still in the dark about exactly where Carl was—'

'The police…the police…what the hell have they been doing? Pussy-footing around, when it's obvious where everything leads…' In her anger, she's dropping consonants and her accent is slipping east towards Essex. 'And now I have this…' She turns to the mantelpiece and picks up a folded sheet of cream paper. She flaps it at the two of us.

'I've just found it amongst Carl's papers. Read it…go on… read it.'

Peter takes the sheet and I stare at a glass vase of white lilies on the coffee table in front of us, knowing it's not my place to join him. There's a delicate tick of a clock coming from somewhere in the room.

'It's not dated,' says Peter, looking up. 'Where was it?'

'Hidden away,' she snaps, 'this is the first I've seen of it.' She grips her forehead. 'He says it's all over between us…that he's really fallen for her…says he's going to leave me and the boys, this time…I can't…' Her voice splinters, then breaks off and she drops, finally, into the armchair beside the fireplace.

He hands me the sheet and I skim-read it. It's a handwritten letter, signed by Carl, declaring his love for an unnamed 'other' woman.

It's the sort of letter you might leave behind once you've secretly packed your bags, ready to leave.

'He never sent it to you…' Peter reminds her.

Amelia is in tears, snuffling and sniffing into her hands. She finds a tissue down the side of the chair and dabs at her eyes.

'Yes, but, he meant to. He was just waiting for the right time, wasn't he?' She narrows her eyes at me. 'It has to be your daughter.'

She swings her scowling glare over to Peter. 'And you? Did you know about this? He was your friend. Have you been keeping this from me?'

Peter is leaning forward, his elbows on his knees. He's too far away to reach out to her.

'Of course not. This doesn't make any sense to me. I mean…' He taps the sheet against the edge of the table. 'When did he write this? It could have been months, years ago.'

'No…this is recent. This is about that woman! That flighty young thing who seduced him when he was vulnerable.' She glowers at me. 'I'm in a total state, I'm not thinking straight, there are unpaid bills…'

'This isn't about Beth, Mia. Honestly,' Peter persists. 'You don't know her. She's not…' He clears his throat. 'Look, Beth has gone missing. No one has seen her. Haven't you seen the news?'

She looks momentarily taken aback, but holds herself in check, not wanting to betray any shred of concern.

She sniffs. 'When?'

Peter and I speak at the same time. He says Monday and I say Sunday. We look at each other. 'We're not sure,' I say, 'but, it's been at least two days.'

'Well…that shows you, then, doesn't it?' she says without elucidating.

There's a long weighty silence apart from the sound of the silver carriage clock. I've located it now, on the oval table by the window – reminding us of the passing of time.

'Carl never ever rang Beth's number or emailed her,' Peter says, pedantically. 'The police told you that. If anything was going on between them, don't you think he would have contacted her?'

'The police said he didn't call her from his personal phones or his office, but it doesn't mean he didn't ring her…from *the street*.' She says the words as if it's a disgusting concept.

Peter ploughs on. 'There was no evidence that the necklace was for Beth, you know that. And the photograph at the party – when Carl and Beth are supposed to be "sharing a moment"– well, that's completely open to interpretation. She probably trod on his foot, or something…'

Amelia gets up and snatches the letter. She raps it with her nails. 'This was *serious*. He was going to leave me…look it's here, in black and white…' She tosses it onto the carpet. 'Beth Kendall killed him, I know she did. Something must have gone wrong between them. She must have given him an ultimatum or threatened to confront me and it got out of hand.' She turns to the two of us. 'You see, this letter means there was a motive!'

At that moment, the door swings open and Anna shuffles in with a tray. She sets it down on the coffee table and stands back meekly, her head bowed.

'Shall I pour?' she whispers, sensing an atmosphere.

Amelia flaps her away. 'No, it's fine.'

'I tried my best,' says Peter, as we stride back to the front drive, shortly afterwards. A taxi is on its way.

'I don't think there was anything either of us could have said to change her mind,' I tell him.

In fact, I'd said virtually nothing the entire time. There didn't seem any point. If she wouldn't pay attention to Peter, why would she listen to me?

My phone buzzes. It's Adrian.

'Is she back?' I ask eagerly.

'No, but I remembered something. About the night Beth was last here. A sound outside the window. It was a diesel engine. I got out of bed and looked down. A Land Rover had stopped near the gate.'

'You're sure?'

'Yes. I'm not sure of the colour…grey, beige, green…I don't know, but definitely a Land Rover. One of the doors was open and the light was on. It was late.'

'Anything else? Did you see anyone?'

'No. That's all. Nothing else.'

'Okay, Adrian. That's really helpful.'

I end the call and turn to Peter. 'What does Amelia drive?'

'A mini. A red one,' he says, without hesitation.

'Oh…nothing else?'

Then as an afterthought, he adds, 'There are horses over at the farm. A few of Amelia's friends shift them around in horse boxes. To shows and events.'

'Amelia, too?'

'Yeah. Not using the mini, obviously.'

I wait for the words.

'She uses the Land Rover.'

Chapter 48

Beth

I'm looking up at the sky. A swirling fantasy in blue. It's like walking around inside someone's eye, surrounded by flecks of white and grey. I must be half-asleep, dreaming of wispy clouds on the move as they wait for no one. They slip away like whispers, like ghosts.

I blink and realise it *is* the sky.

I'm in the open air. A breeze kissing my hair. I can breathe at last. Am I dreaming? If so, I want to stay in this dream forever. To wake is to be locked away, incarcerated in the suffocating shadows.

The sun slides out from behind the next cloud and is blinding. It's then I realise this is no dream. I *am* awake. Alive. Outside. The realisation sends a shiver of bliss through my entire body. I wanted my confession to change everything and it has. Somehow. I am free. I lay back, let time stand still, mesmerised by the feathering clouds melting above me, like snowflakes. There's a gentle lulling movement beneath me. I am a baby in a cradle, a leaf bobbing along a winding brook. I let it go on and on.

A sound startles me, and I try to sit up. A cough. There's a blanket over my legs and I am not alone. Someone is sitting watching me. I struggle to get upright.

It's Amelia. I knew it!

When I come to my senses, I realise my hands and feet are tied. Surrounding us is an endless expanse of water.

'Where are we?' I croak. My lip splits as I speak and I taste the salty, metallic taste of blood. 'I need water,' I whisper.

'One thing at a time,' she says grumpily, as though I've been pestering her for hours.

She squats low beside me and tips water from a plastic bottle between my eager lips.

'Thank you,' I say.

We're in a small rubber dinghy and appear to be drifting in the middle of nowhere.

'This is one of Carl's favourite spots,' she says conversationally. 'We're in the English Channel, by the way. We used to regularly cruise to Alderney – did you know that?'

My eyes flick around the interior of the orange dinghy. It looks battered to me, with frayed seams and shiny patches of wear and tear, like it's been around for years. There's a bracket on the back for attaching an engine, but it's not there. Instead, two oars are clipped on the sides. Neither of us are wearing life-jackets. As if to warn me of how precarious we are, the kink of a wave suddenly kicks us up and my stomach lurches.

'It's probably the wake from a tanker somewhere…' she says, looking vaguely into the distance. We ride over the swell and bob up and down. The sun is low and bright and I can't see anything on the horizon, just open sea stretching for miles.

'Wind south-westerly,' she says, 'force three to four.'

She's completely mad, bringing me out in a tiny inflatable somewhere in the English Channel.

'We're safe,' she says, as if she's heard my thoughts. She reaches to the back of the boat and points to a thick rope attached to a plastic loop that trails into the water. 'We're attached with this rope to Carl's yacht. I can get us back on board any time I like.'

I whip around fully and spot a white shape in the distance. Carl's yacht. We are not alone.

'We used to see dolphins,' she says. 'Carl used to catch mackerel with a hand-line.'

A cloud the colour of pewter claims the sun and the temperature drops instantly. The breeze picks up. It's going to be dark before long. A blast of panic seizes my throat and I press my chest as my lungs fight to take in air.

'Asthma…my inhaler. I really need it…' I rasp at her.

She reaches into her pocket and as if by magic produces a blue inhaler. I'm starting to wonder if I'm hallucinating.

'My son, Alex, has asthma,' she says. 'This is his spare. It won't be the right dosage, but it'll tide you over.'

I take it tentatively and punch the spray into my mouth. The hit gives me instant relief, but it makes me cough.

'A stronger dose than you're used to, I expect,' she says lightly. 'He's got it far worse than you.'

I nod and splutter my thanks.

She carries on, 'I just wanted a little privacy to sort a few things out.' Her eyes are hard as pebbles. 'You confessed,' she says, her tone menacing.

Instinctively, my eyes dart over the side. I'm a hair's breadth away from going overboard. One little shove and it would all be over. My limbs are tied, I can't possibly swim. My body would never be found – not all the way out here. It's the perfect murder.

'So, you and my husband, eh? Sneaking around behind my back…'

I sit up tall and rigid, trying to figure out how I'm going to defend myself if she…when she…comes at me.

'People will be looking for me,' I tell her defiantly.

'Will they?' She examines her nails. 'Not doing a very good job of it.'

My heart rate is racing off the scale, thudding in my ears like bongo drums.

'Was it you?' she says.

'Me who what?'

'Was it you who killed him?'

I face her head on. 'No.'

'I need to know. You were screwing him, but what happened after that? Did you kill Carl?'

'No.' I make sure my eyes meet hers. 'I didn't.'

At least that part is true, but she's not going to stop there. I must be strong and keep my nerve. If Amelia knows the truth, no matter what happens here, no matter how things turn out for me, she'll go straight after Mum and hunt her down. I can't let her go through anything like this. I have to keep her out of it, I have to protect her.

'Are you lying to me?'

'No. I didn't do a thing to hurt him, honestly. I swear on the life of my mother, my grandad…I did not kill Carl.'

'He was going to tell Peter about the two of you, wasn't he? He was going to blow the whole thing out of the water.'

'No – that's not how it was. Why would Carl do that?' She hesitates, perhaps seeing the baffled look on my face. 'Peter and I were…getting married. *He* was the one I wanted.'

She laughs. 'Funny way of showing it.'

'I made a mistake. The whole thing with Carl should never have happened. It was just one of those "in the moment" things. Carl wasn't the least bit serious about me. There was nothing for him to gain by telling Peter, only everything to lose…'

It's her turn to look confused. 'Weren't you cooking up long-term plans together?'

'God, no!' I retort. 'It was just a silly fling. Mostly role-play. Ridiculous.'

'So, Carl wasn't going to leave me…the boys…for you?'

'No! Never,' I snort. 'It was stupid. Barely more than a game. It meant nothing. There was no way he was going to leave you. Not for *me*. Really, he wasn't.'

'You see – you're actually a better actress than everyone says, because I found the letter.'

'What letter?'

'The one Carl wrote. I found it amongst his personal papers. The one about having met someone special. It said you'd been seeing him for over a year.'

I shrink back. 'What? Me? No. That can't be about me. I only met him three months ago. At the party for the Hepworth Theatre. You were there, remember?'

She contemplates my response. 'Mmm. Three months. That's what Peter said…'

'You're looking in the wrong place, you really are.'

The tiniest glimmer in her scowl indicates she might believe me.

'Peter said that Carl made more than a few enemies over the years,' I say, seeing an opening. 'Apparently, Carl dropped out of contracts at the last minute. Various colleagues held grudges, he annoyed a lot of people.'

I'm not making it up. Peter had mentioned it once, during an awkward moment when Carl's name cropped up.

She twists her mouth to the side. 'That's true,' she says, 'he was fickle. He changed his mind about projects and people lost money.'

'So, what about these people who lost out? And the ones he fired? The actors whose careers he destroyed? Couldn't one of them be his killer?'

She stares at her feet. Her expression sours from one of snooty superiority to horror and for a split second I think I might have just planted the right seeds of doubt to make her reconsider.

But I'm wrong.

She's not paying attention to what I'm saying; she's fixated on something else. Water. The dinghy is leaking and we're sinking fast.

Chapter 49

Rachel

'I'm going back to Amelia's,' I tell Peter, grabbing his arm.

He comes to a standstill halfway along the drive. 'What? Why?'

'You go back home in the taxi – here's the key.' I pull out my key ring and unclip the front Yale. 'I'm going back to look for Beth. My father says a Land Rover stopped outside his cottage that night, the night she went missing.'

He laughs. 'You think Amelia's taken her?' He tosses out the words in a preposterous fashion.

'It would make sense. She's furious. She's convinced that Carl was seeing Beth and she's clearly off her trolley. You said she'd done crazy things before.'

He frowns, but doesn't contradict me. He wraps both my hands in his. 'I may not look it, but I'm going out of my mind, too. The police know what they're doing, though.' He glances down. 'I'm not sure your father is a reliable witness, from what Beth has said.'

'I know. He might have dreamt it and even if he didn't, it's probably pure coincidence that Amelia drives a Land Rover, but if I'm wrong, at least I tried. Searching for her is better than doing nothing.'

Beth went missing on Sunday and it's now late on Thursday.

'Sure,' he says, 'you're right.'

'I'm just going to take a look around, that's all. You go; it's better if you're not involved. Amelia trusts you, I don't want you to be the bad guy in this. Let it be me. Just in case I get caught.'

'Okay, but take this for the ride home.' He pulls a fifty pound note from his wallet. 'And be careful,' he says, as the taxi appears at the tall iron gates.

Amelia's windows have no view of the drive, so my hope is that she won't have seen the taxi move off without me. I hurry past the front of the house towards the west wing. There's an unobtrusive sign that says 'car-park', so I follow it round to the back.

I loiter by a large communal compost heap and consider the layout of the place. Amelia's property appears to start at the next gate, so I sidle over to see what's behind it. It's locked, but when I part the ivy on the trellis, I get a good view of the back courtyard.

Anna is there, bending down clipping herbs. After a second's thought, I take a risk. Tapping gently, I call her name. She looks up, startled, searching for the source of the voice.

'I'm at the gate. Sssh, please don't call out.'

She heads towards me.

'I was here earlier,' I say. 'I'm Rachel. I wanted to talk to you, but not when Amelia is around. Is she there?'

'She's in her bedroom, I think. Preening herself, probably.'

'You couldn't let me in, could you?'

She unlocks the latch and I step inside. The space is small with square beds of leggy rosemary, lavender and thyme laid out alongside a path of broken flagstones. It doesn't get much light. The walls are damp, and whilst there are a few amphora pots dotted around designed to add charm, the pervasive impression is of decay.

'I don't want to get into trouble,' she says, pulling back.

'I know. I don't want that, either.' I back into a spot out of sight of the back door and she comes with me. 'I'm looking for my daughter, Beth. She's tall, brunette, very pretty. Have you see her here anywhere?'

She looks disconcerted. 'No. What's happened?'

'She went missing on Sunday evening and the police are looking for her. It's a long story, but Amelia might have taken her. Hidden her somewhere, perhaps?'

Her eyebrows shoot up.

I go on. 'Have you been in all the rooms here in the last few days?'

'Yeah, I'm general dogsbody here, so I have to do pretty much everything. I'm sick of it, actually – I'm looking for another job.'

'You've been everywhere in her apartment and not seen anyone? No locked doors? No places you have no access to?'

'No…' She blinks a few times, in thought. 'I've been everywhere. Nothing unusual.'

A shout from inside the house cuts across us. 'Anna? Where are you?'

'It's her,' she whispers. 'Coming!' she calls out and rushes off. I hear a car door slam outside and soon after, Anna comes back. 'She's gone out,' she says.

'Any idea where?'

She shrugs. '"Something important came up" is what she said.'

I let my shoulders drop now we're alone.

'Are there any outhouses she uses? A garage, shed, basement?'

'There's the wine cellar,' she says, 'but it's locked.'

'Anything else?'

'No. Just the car-park,' she points towards the gate.

'Where are the keys to the cellar?'

'There's a bunch next to the range in the kitchen, but I can't give you them. I mean…I won't say I've seen you, but I can't—'

'I know…it's okay. Thank you so much.' I pat her on the arm and brush past her, making for the back door.

Two minutes later, I'm in the cellar, but Beth isn't here. I check for any hidden doorways or cupboards, but it's empty. As I cross back through the courtyard, Anna is filling a watering can. I try another tack.

'Do you ever see Amelia driving a Land Rover?'

'Yeah. She uses one from the farm.'

'Where's the farm?'

Anna describes the route, it's just over a mile from here.

'Does she own any other properties?'

She considers the question, but shakes her head. 'Not as far as I know.'

I turn to go.

'The main gate,' she says, 'you'll need the code to get out.'

She reels it off for me, then as I turn to leave, she grabs my arm. 'She has the boat. Did you know? It's moored at Littlehampton. It's called Spellbound.'

I race out across the gravel, before I lose any more time.

Chapter 50

Beth

'We're sinking!' I yell at her, holding up my bound arms and shaking them in her direction.

Amelia doesn't register. She's staring at her bare toes inside her sandals, as though she's watching her body turn to stone.

'Amelia, you've got to cut me loose. We can help each other.'

She frowns at me, apparently still not quite comprehending what's going on.

The water has completely covered the bottom of the dinghy and is creeping irrevocably higher.

Amelia suddenly springs into action as though sparked into life by the flick of a switch.

'There's nothing to scoop it out with,' she cries. She tries to stand, but the boat lurches to one side as she upsets the balance. She's manically glaring down at the water that's reaching for her ankles.

'The rope…' I call out. 'Pull the rope, so we can get back to the boat.'

She clambers over to the back and lifts the sodden line out of the water and gives it two hard tugs. Then stares at the shape in the distance.

I follow her line of sight. Since I last looked, the yacht has slid further away. A stab of dread shoots up my windpipe. A few moments ago, I could see the distinct arrow-like shape of the hull, now it's just a blob on the horizon. She sits on the rounded edge, gathers up a long stretch of rope and pulls hard, two more times.

'Something's not right,' she says.

'Untie me,' I beg her, holding up my wrists again. 'I can help.'

Reluctantly, she unpicks the knot and I wrench my hands free. They're zinging with pins and needles, so I shake them, rub them together, before releasing my submerged ankles.

'Right,' I say, reaching over for the rope. I can tell as soon as I gather it up in my arms that it's flaccid. It should be tight. Our one lifeline back to civilisation is useless.

'It's not attached to anything,' I tell her.

Amelia starts ranting, rocking backwards and forwards on the plastic seat in the middle.

'Not attached? What? No…that's not how it was supposed to work.' A grimace twists her features and she gets down on all fours in the pool of water and begins inspecting every inch of the interior.

'Here it is,' she says, triumphantly. 'There's a hole.'

I follow her long pearly nail to a small tear in the side that has been covered over with a piece of sticky fabric. She cries out, in despair. 'This looks like a patch you'd use to repair a bicycle puncture.' She flattens it down, rubs it in place with the heel of her hand, but it springs back up again. 'It's not even waterproof.' She looks around desperately for something to paste over it. Of course, there's nothing. She slaps her hand back over it, instead.

'Ah…' she says, 'I walked straight into this, didn't I?'

'What do you mean?'

'All this…business,' she wafts her hand about, vacantly. 'It wasn't my idea.'

She gazes out towards the small white dot in the distance that's shrinking with every breath.

'Come and cover the hole,' she says, 'we'll have to take turns. It's only fair.'

I can't believe she's uttered those last words after all she's put me through. I'm also about to point out that her 'turn' was bizarrely short, but think better of it. Self-preservation must come first.

I carefully slide over, while she sits on the bench, scraping her fingers through her hair. A few moments ago it was tied up into an elaborate bun, now it looks like a ruffled yellow feather boa has been plonked on top of her head.

'Listen, we won't go down,' I tell her. 'Peter told me that dinghies have more than one air chamber. If there's a leak in one side, the rest stays full of air.'

She blinks hard and looks at the side without the puncture, then she presses her fingers into it, like a child playing with Plasticine.

'Noooo,' she groans, 'this side is deflating too.'

'It can't be.' I'm watching from my static position pressing on the puncture as she pushes her thumb into the spongy fabric. It sags forming an indentation instead of bouncing back.

Amelia casts her eyes over that side in earnest, trying to find a hole.

'It could be tiny,' I say.

As I speak, I realise this isn't the dinghy that was attached to Carl's smart yacht the day we went along the Thames. This is an old one that probably hasn't been seaworthy for years.

She notices something and bends down, getting wet up to her knees. 'I've got it. It's here. It's the seal around the valve,' she says, 'it's all peeling away.'

Shit! Both sides are deflating. We're going down.

'I don't believe this,' she yelps, gulping noisy breaths that are rapidly speeding up until she's hyperventilating. 'The plan was supposed…to help me,' she whimpers in snatches.

'Sit down, Amelia, and slow your breathing. Make your out-breath longer than your in-breath.'

She gasps, holding her head in her hands.

'Slow it down,' I tell her.

'The plan was meant…to lead me to definitive proof that you were having an affair with Carl. This afternoon I got the email. With your confession note.'

An email?

So, Amelia wasn't the person who forced the truth out of me about the fling.

'The idea was for me to confront you privately – out here – and if I didn't like what I heard, I could cause a 'little accident' so you'd go overboard.'

I'm only half listening. Even with my palm pressed over the rip, the water is seeping in, dragging us down slowly but surely. It has soaked my jeans up to my calves already. We've probably got around five minutes before the dinghy fills to the brim.

'You're already missing,' she goes on. 'So no one would know. Quite clever, really.'

We can't afford to dwell on the reason we're here. We need to do something.

'What about your phone, Amelia…have you got it with you?'

She lets out a tired laugh. 'There's no connection out here. I left it on the yacht.'

She props her chin up with her hands.

'I didn't kidnap you, by the way, that wasn't me. We've both been set up, haven't we? With no rope and these holes in the side – it's sabotage. There was only ever going to be one outcome, wasn't there?'

She's right. All I can do is watch as the dinghy fills with water, disappearing into the sea.

Chapter 51

Rachel

'**A**melia has a boat,' I tell Peter as soon as he answers.

'Where are you?'

'Safely outside Amelia's front gates on the country lane. Beth wasn't there. But her housekeeper got me thinking about the farm. I take it you know where it is?'

'Yes, Shawley, just outside Arundel.'

'And the boat.'

'Spellbound,' he says. 'I've used it a couple of times on the Thames.'

'It's currently moored at Littlehampton,' I say. 'That's only four miles away. I'll get over there and you get to the farm and have a look around. We've got to try this.'

He puts up no resistance this time. 'Okay. I'm onto it.'

A swirling sickness fills my stomach as I wait for another taxi, clutching Peter's money. If the boat is a dead end, I don't know what I'll do next. I miss Russell so much. He would have grounded me, calmed my panic, soothed me. When I was upset, he had a way of playing with my hair that made me tingle all over. He'd slowly twirl tiny strands around his fingers then let them fall. When I tried it with Beth once, she hated it.

'Urgh – it feels like there's a spider in my hair!' she shrieked, pulling away.

A pang of loss twists my heart as I picture her defiant face. *Don't let her be harmed. Don't let her be suffering or frightened.* Could there be a simple explanation for her going off like this?

My mind leaps to the worst case scenario. All the young people who go missing every day and are never found. The ones you see on torn and faded posters, dated months…years earlier.

Don't let this be how things are from now on. Living a half-life, always waiting. Not knowing, always hoping the next sound will be my daughter coming home…

I think again of Russell, already on the 'other' side, and shiver. *Don't let Beth be with you. Please.*

The marina at Littlehampton lives up to its name and seems a compact affair, until I get down to the water's edge to see multiple clusters of boats on either side at intervals up and down the entire mouth of the River Arun.

I don't know where to start. There's a marine supply shop in the main car-park, so I ask at the desk inside how I'd track down a specific boat. I'm directed to the harbour master's office next to what looks like a converted grain store.

Inside, there's a man with his shirt sleeves rolled up sitting behind a computer.

'Sorry to bother you,' I say, waiting for him to look up. 'Do you have a list of which boats are moored here?'

'I might do,' he says in a way that suggests that even if he does, he's not going to let me see it.

I decide to switch into desperation mode.

'I need to get word to someone. Her father's just died and we can't reach her by phone. Amelia Jacobson on Spellbound, can you point me in the right direction?'

'Oh dear…'

He asks for my name and ID. 'I'm a friend,' I say, casually. He grunts, but gets up, reaching for a stack of sheets pinned to the cork board that fills most of the wall behind him. He runs his finger down the first page and stops.

'That boat came in this afternoon. Went back out again about…' he glances up at a large porthole shaped clock on the wall, 'half an hour ago.'

'It's gone? Do you know where? I…er…don't want to give her this sort of information over the radio.'

'Ah-ha…' he says, like a magician at a kids' birthday party. 'You can track the live position of all vessels in the English Channel using the AIS map…automatic identification system. Anyone can do it online.'

I must look flummoxed, but he appears to take pity on me and angles his screen towards me.

'The yachts are in purple,' he says, holding the curser over little boat shapes on the map. As he hovers over one of them, the name of the boat, speed and last recorded position pops up. At the top there's a search box and he types in Spellbound.

'Here we go…'

Ten records pop up, but only one says 'pleasure craft, GB'.

'That'll be it,' he says. He clicks a box on the right and there it is on the map. 'Heading west…about five miles off the coast.'

I thank him and call Peter straight away.

'Anything?' I ask.

'No. I've asked around, checked the barns, stables and empty horse boxes. No one has seen Beth.'

'While I was at Amelia's she suddenly took off in her car. Turns out Spellbound left the marina about half an hour ago.'

'Could be a coincidence,' he says.

'I know, but we should try. I've found out where the boat is on the map. We just have to get there.'

Chapter 52

Rachel

I've been sitting on a bench overlooking the water for what feels like an age. A vehicle screeches to a halt behind me and Peter charges on to the marina, out of breath.

'I'm sorry I took so long,' he says, 'couldn't find a taxi.'

He races off again towards one of the huts beside the sales showroom. Soon after, he's back with a smile on his face. With the help of his wallet, he's twisted a few arms and secured us the hire of a powerboat.

He takes me towards a man standing at the quayside.

'Shouldn't we call the police before we go?' I say as he signs a form and takes the keys.

'There's no proof Amelia has got Beth. Don't get your hopes up too high.'

The harbour lights came on five minutes ago and the sun is about to slip below the horizon.

'I take it you know how to handle one of these things in the dark?' I ask as we hurry across the tarmac.

He smiles as we step onto the jetty. 'Don't worry. Carl had one,' he tells me. My stomach shrivels at the sound of his name and I look away.

Peter hands me a lifejacket and while I clip the straps into place, he kneels down and spends a few moments inspecting the outboard motor and propeller.

'We can't waste time checking everything,' he says, straightening up. 'We'll just have to hope it's in good nick.'

He steps over to the controls and mimes various manoeuvres involving an array of dials, switches and levers, before putting the key in the ignition. I'm about to ask how long it's been since he last handled one, but I think better of it.

Peter switches on and asks me to stay put on a padded bench at the back, while he unties the boat. Soon, we're heading out along the river, passing a closed amusement park on our left, before we reach beaches and open water.

I consult the website I looked at earlier at the harbour master's office and call out the current co-ordinates of Spellbound.

It's 7.45 p.m. and the colours at sunset are a wash of pastel shades; dark pink, purple and petrol blue, rapidly draining to grey. With waves like white scratches across the surface of a canvas, it would be idyllic in different circumstances.

Once we get to speed, I feel like I'm in a wind tunnel. My hair's flying everywhere, the ferocious gusts clawing at my skin through my thin blouse. I didn't set out dressed for this, but I don't care. We're here to find Beth and even if I have to go without food, warmth and shelter for a week, it will be worth it. I only hope she's on Spellbound.

The low revving engine rises in pitch to a trembling racket and the wind whips past, roaring in my ears, as we charge across the waves. I wouldn't like to do too much of this on a full stomach.

'You can join me if you like,' he adds. I step up beside him and as I adjust my lifejacket, my neck-scarf breaks loose and is flung out onto the water. It serves to remind me how precarious we are, riding on this vast expanse of water where the only way is down.

'Damn…' I call out. I nip my lips together. Beth gave me that scarf last Christmas. I blink away the sting of tears, not wanting Peter to see how close I am to breaking down.

'We're close to a container tanker,' he says, urging me to go back to my seat. 'It might get a bit bumpy. Hold on.'

We seem a long way from the cluster of lights, but even so, all of a sudden the boat is tipped back, then we plunge forward in a big rush of water. It's like being on a big-dipper.

With the fading light, the sea has turned into an uninviting cauldron of onyx black, with a scattering of green, white and red lights in the far distance. I can't tell which are reflections and which are the real thing.

'There she is!' says Peter, pointing out on to the horizon. For a split second I think he means Beth, but of course, it's Spellbound he's referring to.

Peter reaches over to the radio. 'Spellbound, Spellbound, this is Peter Roper on Gloriana – channel 16, over.'

There's a long gap, then a voice crackles back. 'Gloriana, this is Spellbound. Switch to channel 68, over.'

'Gloriana switching to channel 68, over.'

He turns to me. 'Okay, I've got the boat on the radio. I'm just going to say we're pulling alongside and want to come aboard.'

He gets a response in acknowledgement and he turns the wheel. An odd rattling noise comes from behind me.

'Ooh, doesn't sound right,' he says. The sound amplifies and he cuts the engine. The quiet aftermath and gentle wash of the waves come as a relief.

'What's wrong?'

'Not sure,' he says. I get out of his way as he kneels down, staring into the water.

'Can you hold the torch?' he asks, handing it to me. I train the beam on the propeller and he feels around.

'There's something caught,' he says.

My hand goes straight to my throat. My scarf. Is this my fault? Will we fail to reach Beth in time because of a stupid loose knot around my neck?

I bend down beside him, but there's not much I can do to help.

'Get an oar,' he calls out.

I hand him the torch, then reach down to the clips at the side of the boat and hand him one. He leans out, almost topples overboard, grappling with the obstruction. Finally he turns around, red faced, holding up a large dripping object.

'Plastic bag…' he says, shaking his head. 'Bloody litter.'

It takes fifteen minutes before we're on our way again. I stamp from side to side, furious with the delay, precious minutes lost that could make all the difference.

When we reach Carl's boat, he manoeuvres alongside it. I expect to see Amelia at the helm, but instead, it's a woman with coiffured red hair.

'Oh, it's Nancy,' Peter whispers to me. 'Amelia's friend.' I recall the name.

A younger man beside her takes the wheel and she greets us at the side of the boat.

'Peter, how lovely to see you,' she says.

'We're looking for Amelia…and Beth…are they here?'

She gives an exaggerated jolt of surprise. 'Here? No. I saw Amelia earlier. She's on shore. And Beth? You mean your fiancée, Beth?'

'Yes. She's missing. Is she aboard?'

'Good grief, no! Why would she be here?'

As they speak I'm trying to get a good look at the rest of the boat, but it seems to have several decks and there's little to see from where I'm standing.

'Can we come aboard?' he asks.

'Be my guests…'

Nancy calls over the henchman and instructs him to tie our boat to theirs and help us step across. Peter waits to check he's done it properly.

As we join Nancy, there are no polite introductions.

'When did you last see Amelia?' Peter asks.

Nancy points to a decanter of brandy and raises her eyebrows in invitation.

He shakes his head for the two of us. 'Seriously, Nancy – this is no time for fun and games.'

Nancy is all multi-coloured chiffon scarves and bling. Her white wafty palazzo trousers and off the shoulder tunic suggest she's bound for somewhere like Monaco. She looks like she's spent considerable time trying to look chic and is just about getting away with it, although her hoity-toity accent sounds as fake as Amelia's.

'Like I said, I saw her earlier.' She tufts up the back of her backcombed French twist as though she's in front of a mirror. 'We came in at Littlehampton for supplies. She met us there, but she changed her mind about coming aboard.'

'Why?'

'I've no idea,' she says, as if it's none of her business. 'You know Mia, always flitting from one thing to the next. She must have had something better to do.'

'We'll take a look around, if you have no objection?' Peter says, already pushing past her.

'A little bit unusual, but go ahead,' she snorts. She turns away, leaving us to find our own way around.

Peter leads me to the back of the boat and once we've done a full circuit, we go inside, past a bar and into a salon area. The henchman, wearing a T-shirt that shows off an eagle tattoo pulled out of shape by overworked biceps, is close behind us watching our every move. Peter opens cupboards and storage spaces. He knows the boat, he'll spot any hiding places.

All the while I'm looking for something to indicate that Beth has been here, anything that might belong to her. Something she may have left behind.

We go through a door into the master cabin. A heady mix of spray deodorant, strong perfume and the biscuity aroma of fake tan greets us. The room is filled with bits and pieces I can only assume belong to Nancy; an open jewellery case containing green and amber coloured stones embedded in earrings and bracelets, copies of 'Vogue', 'Unique Homes' and 'Plane and Pilot' tossed on the bed, a silk dressing gown beside it. There are a pair of tickets to Ascot under an Omega watch on the dressing table. Everything smacks of a surplus of cash.

I crouch down to look under the bed where alongside boxes of shoes, I find a stack of wedding magazines.

'Who's getting married?' I ask Peter, straightening up.

He shrugs. 'Nothing to do with Beth and I,' he says pointedly.

He checks the ensuite, before asking our nameless escort if we can see the engine room. He obliges and we follow him down a flight to take a look. I check behind pipes and pumps while Peter asks for a metal cabinet to be opened. Apart from that, there's nowhere to conceal anyone down there.

There are smaller cabins with bunk beds and a storage cupboard, which is currently empty apart from stacks of towels, bed linen and toilet rolls on a mattress.

'What does Nancy do for a living?' I ask as we check out the kitchen.

'She's a lady of leisure. Her husband died five years ago, I think… he was a kind of Richard Branson figure – a super-entrepreneur.

'Had any stowaways?' Peter asks our escort.

'Nope,' he says, his arms folded, leaning against the sink.

'What about luggage hatches?' I ask him.

The hatches contain only empty suitcases and he shows us a couple of other places only big enough for a cat to hide away in. He seems very accommodating – in fact, they've both been far too obliging, which tells me one thing. They've got nothing to hide. Beth isn't here.

On the way back to Nancy on the main deck, Peter tells me we've covered everything. My heart sinks. We're going to head back without her and I don't have anywhere else to look.

'You'll stay for a drink?' she says, handing a clipboard to her right-hand man. As we hit the wake from a nearby tanker, he loses his balance temporarily and drops the pen he was holding. It rolls towards my foot, so I bend down to pick it up.

'No. We'll head off,' Peter replies. 'But you'll let me know if you hear anything about Beth, won't you? Anything at all?'

'Of course,' she says, formally.

I'm about to hand over the biro when the end of it catches the light. It has two tiny rows of indentations – one row at the end and another about a centimetre below it. A distinct pattern of teeth marks I've seen time and time again on the pens in my own home. It tells me all I need to know.

'Beth *has* been here!' I hold out the biro. 'This is her trademark. I'd swear to it. Where is she?'

Chapter 53

Beth

'I can't die like this,' Amelia whimpers, making a reckless attempt to stand. She loses her balance and splashes down into the sinking boat.

We both fight the inevitable, clawing at the dinghy trying to stay inside it, but it's futile. The sea is claiming us. It has covered our legs completely by now. Amelia cups her hands and is scooping up tiny pools of water, only she doesn't reach out far enough and the water ends up back where it came from.

'This was her idea to get rid of us both,' she hisses.

'Whose idea?'

'Nancy's, of course!'

'She was out to get both of us. You, for having a fling with my husband and me…because she must have got it into her stupid little head that I killed him.'

I'm trying to grasp what she's saying.

'She thinks you killed Carl…' I say, my voice juddering with the cold.

'She must do…to have gone to such lengths. She must be mad. She's the one who kidnapped you. She followed you and tracked you down at a cottage somewhere. She wanted you to confess to the affair.'

'It's true…Carl and I did meet up three of four times,' I tell her. 'But it was only a brief, silly fling. Carl certainly wasn't serious about me.'

'I believe you. I can see now that she did her utmost to point me in your direction.' She's frantically fighting the sea, her legs spread-eagled. 'And the letter he wrote about leaving me must have been about her. *She* was the one having an affair with Carl!'

I'm barely taking in what she's saying. My brain is already gridlocked with trying to figure out how we're going to survive this.

'Your name cropped up early on,' she says, 'and Nancy jumped on it, kept coming back to it, obviously twisting the facts to divert attention away from her own smutty affair with my husband.' Her mouth drops open. 'The emerald pendant was for her, not you, of course – with ginger hair, green is the obvious colour to wear.' She shakes her head. 'I don't know why I didn't twig that.'

The sun has set now, leaching away the remaining light in the sky.

'Ah…that's why this useless piece of junk was strapped to the back of the yacht,' she adds. 'It should have been the decent dinghy with the outboard motor…"in for repairs" she said…lying bitch.'

My mind latches on to an idea.

'Do you smoke?' I ask, noticing the slight bulge in the top pocket of her blouse.

'What. At a time like this?'

I reach down and grab the blanket I was wrapped in, dragging it away from the water.

'Do you!?' I say, raising my voice.

'I'm trying to give up…but with—'

'Do you have a lighter!?' I yell into her face, the blanket bundled against me.

She reaches into the pocket, looking mystified, but pulls out what I'm looking for. A surge of pure joy sweeps through my chest. Amelia is shaking so much that she almost drops the lighter. I snatch it away just in time.

The blanket is dripping, but one corner is still dry. I don't know if it will be enough. I don't know if this is going to work. I flick the spark wheel with my thumb and it makes a grinding sound, but no flame appears. Amelia is so caught up with unravelling the truth that she seems momentarily oblivious to our dire situation.

'I only found that letter this week, but Nancy must have thought I knew about it much earlier. She must have thought I killed Carl…because I couldn't bear the indignity of him running off with my best friend.' She snatches a breath. 'No wonder she was so keen to help me go through his documents.' She's staring blindly ahead, unaware of what I'm trying to do.

'I bet she found her own phone number in Carl's papers and destroyed it, putting the stupid coded one with your number there instead. She'd seen your number on the phone bill. She was obviously looking for anything she could find to incriminate you.'

'Amelia, Amelia!' I scream at her. 'Swim!'

She looks down and shrieks, as if she's been miles away. We're still sitting in the dinghy, but there's only the occasional glimpse of orange rubber. Before long we'll be on our own, floating without any support.

'Let yourself go into the water,' I tell her firmly, 'we can't stop this now. Just start treading water.'

Amelia is yelping like a dog, flapping about, trying to do the opposite and lever herself out of the sea. She's going to knock the lighter out of my hand if I'm not careful – then we'll have nothing.

'Let the dinghy go! Just imagine you're in an infinity pool somewhere. Kick with your legs and keep your head out of the water.' The sea is about to consume the last of the dinghy. 'You *can* swim, right?'

She nods her head slightly, her chin quivering.

The dinghy is too heavy with water and slides out of sight under the surface. 'Let it go,' I tell her. 'It's no use anymore.'

She looks horrified, watching as it's gobbled up by the sea. In seconds, it's gone. We're on our own, forced to kick harder. I hold the blanket up with one hand, the lighter with the other. I'm thankful for all those times I swam at the leisure centre and didn't give up when it got tough. I flick the flint again and this time there's a flame. I hold the two items together and wait.

'Please light, please light…' I hiss.

The blanket starts to smoke, but doesn't ignite. I try again. And again. With my arms full, unable to keep myself afloat, I duck under the surface getting water in my mouth. The churning swell snatches at my face and I'm gasping with the effort to hold the blanket up. The muscles in my arms are screaming.

Amelia is flailing around in little circles, gulping, splashing, not knowing which way to turn. 'Save me, save me,' she whines.

'Save your energy,' I yell at her, spitting out the salty spume. 'Go in slow-motion. You won't sink.' My voice comes out like a pneumatic drill, as my whole body spasms with the cold.

I try the lighter again and the flicker takes this time. As it meets the fabric, it starts to smoulder. I weave the edge of the blanket into the air to encourage the flame to grow, but I have little control as I flounder beneath it. Against all the odds, it flares up into a bright orange glow, but the rest of the blanket is too wet and within the space of three or four snatched breaths, the flame hisses and dissolves into smoke. I hold it aloft for as long as I can, then let it slide into the water. Amelia has at last stopped her blubbering, but she's clearly not a strong swimmer. The most she's probably ever swum is two lengths in a luxury spa.

I look up at the sky. It's overcast and the clouds have already eaten up most of the stars. Before long we're not going to be able to see a thing. To any boats out there we'll be completely invisible.

My hands are so cold they've solidified into useless claws. My mind keeps tugging me back to disaster movies I've seen. Ships going down at sea. It's hyperthermia that turns out to be the real threat at times like this. The real enemy that finally drags the victims under, their muscles succumbing to a frozen paralysis. Is this going to happen to us?

It doesn't take long before Amelia is in serious trouble. Her eyes flicker and she slides down under the surface.

'Amelia! Wake up! Keep treading water!'

She lets herself roll over face down, not fighting any more.

I can barely pick out her shape, but manage to get myself behind her and turn her over. Grabbing her hip, I tip her chin

Chapter 54

Rachel

Nancy takes a moment to react.

'That's not my pen. It's Amelia's,' she snaps. 'I know nothing about it.'

'But it's *here*,' I say.

'Well…Amelia has been here, hasn't she? It's not exactly damning evidence.'

Peter looks bemused and Nancy blinks through a lengthy pause. For the first time, her glib composure appears ruffled. Peter turns and takes several steps towards the back of the boat. 'Where's the dinghy?' he asks.

I follow his line of sight and notice a small empty platform at the rear, with loose ropes and clips.

'There should be a dinghy for getting sailors to and from the yacht at the marina,' he tells me, striding back.

'It's in for repair,' Nancy says, too quickly.

I stare out beyond the boat into the inky black malevolence.

'Peter, look…'

There's a thin plume of smoke, about 200 metres away, rapidly dissipating.

Nancy reaches down in a jerky movement, attempting to hide something in a cupboard under the control panel. I stick my foot out before she can close the door and snatch the strap of a pair of binoculars. I elbow her out of the way long enough to get the lenses up to my eyes.

'Someone's in trouble,' I call out, as I settle the focus on a commotion of splashes beside the trail of smoke. The boat revs with an injection of speed and we all lurch to the port side. Nancy is turning the boat the other way, but with our powerboat attached to one side, she's struggling to control it.

Without a word, Peter grabs my wrist and drags me back towards our boat. It's clattering against the side as we swing in a wide arc to face the way we came. I'm shaking with dread as the boat rolls and pitches all over the place. I lose my balance and bang into the side, catching my knee. The henchman comes after us, but Peter blocks his way. Having been a professional dancer, Peter's balance is extraordinarily good and while he's barely troubled by the turbulence, Muscleman is preoccupied with staying upright. I stumble, stagger upright, then take a running leap off the yacht, an audacious leap of faith into the darkness, hoping the boat will be there when I land. I hurtle down to the deck with a thud.

'Undo the ropes!' Peter calls out to me. 'Keep away,' he warns the guy behind him. 'Do you want to be charged with GBH? Is it really worth it, for her?'

Muscleman turns to Nancy at the wheel, waiting for instructions, but she's trying to control the boat and doesn't respond. Whatever scheme she's involved in, she hasn't thought it through to this point.

With the ropes loose, Peter leaps on board and activates the engine. There's an almighty surge as we power away in the opposite direction.

Chapter 55

Beth

Amelia is a dead weight and her moments of lucidity are over. She's been quiet for the last few minutes, leaving me only the lapping of the water for company. I'm not even sure if she's still alive.

I can't stop to check if she's breathing and I don't want to let go in case I'm wrong. I have to keep kicking and sculling or I'll drop down like a stone.

Nancy wanted rid of us both: me, for my affair with the man she wanted and Amelia for killing him.

The water slams into my ears multiplying the splosh and roar of the sea, turning them into vast echo chambers.

Nancy thinks Amelia killed Carl.

At least it means Mum is out of it, beyond suspicion. No one has dragged her name into any of this. Their misguided conclusions aren't going to be any use to me, though. The sea has me in a tight vice, crushing my limbs, squeezing the life out of every one of my muscles. There's no way I can possibly win this struggle without help. Eventually, this briny mass will snatch us from below and take us down. That much is certain and there's nothing I can do about it. Still, I kick.

I'm sure I'm blacking out in small bursts. The strain of staying afloat drops away for a few seconds, then it's savagely back again trying to rip apart every sinew in my body.

I've become one hard block of ice and I'm overwhelmingly exhausted. My kicking has become useless, tiny spasms. We're barely floating.

I want to stop. Every muscle in my body wants to stop.

I'm so sleepy…

I want nothing more than to let Amelia go. Her body is growing heavier, like a concrete statue, as I fight the ocean.

No one knows what we did, Mum. Even though I admitted to the affair, we're still safe. Well...you are...I didn't give you away.

There's a burning in my throat like I've swallowed flames. They're scorching my lungs with every breath. I almost hear my mother's voice in my head, calling my name. It's comforting, until I realise I'm moving away from her, drifting into a twilight place where she won't be able to follow me.

You didn't find me, but I know it's not your fault. I'm sure you tried. I'm so sorry about the way things ended between us...

My eyelids flutter and close for a few seconds. My thoughts slip in and out like a torch running out of batteries. I can hear a persistent roaring in my ears, the growling of a hungry ocean, below the regular rhythm of my rasping breath.

So sleepy...

Mum, I love you. I don't want to leave you, but...

I'm here, darling.

It's time to let go.

It's okay, sweetheart...let me take your hand...

I want to...but I can't stop, I've got to keep floating.

Give me your hand, Beth...

It feels so real...

No...don't take me...I have to keep kicking...I can't give up...

That's when I feel it. Two firm squeezes one after the other. Our special signal to each other.

'Beth! Wake up!'

There's a bright light shining in my eyes. A torch.

Another voice. 'Let me take hold of you, Beth...but don't relax, okay? Not until we get you on the boat.'

It's Peter.

Then the faint sounds come gushing at me in an ear-splitting explosion. It's as though I've just woken up on the central reservation of a busy motorway. I'm awake; trembling, gasping, aching, burning, all at once. But most of all, I'm being swallowed up, not by the sea, but by the thunderous roaring of a speedboat.

I glance down and Amelia has gone. I didn't even feel her float away.

'Mum…' I reach out and hook my numb fingers around her arm. My mother is real. She's flesh and blood and she's right here beside me.

'Beth. We're here, it's okay…it's okay…'

I no longer put up a fight, because I'm cradled in my mother's voice – and somehow it drowns out everything else.

Chapter 56

Rachel

Saturday, April 15 – Day of the wedding

I take a long early morning walk past Winchester College to St Catherine's Hill, with Beth by my side. We pass St James's Church on the way back, but there are no flowers outside, no ribbons inside tied to the pews. This is the place where they were supposed to be married, but there is no wedding.

It's one of those blank days when the sky looks empty – a bleached white, devoid of all colour. I am glad she's not getting married on a day like today. Beth deserves sunshine.

Since her return, I've barely let Beth out of my sight. That first night, she shared my bed. I kept a lantern lit on the landing, like I used to when she was little. After that, we left the connecting doors to the bathroom wide open so we could call out to each other. We've been more or less joined at the hip.

Over breakfast this morning, I kept reaching out to stroke her face, smell her hair and when she'd left the room, I sat on the bottom stair and listened out for every sound she made; the shushing noise as she cleaned her teeth, the flush of the toilet. All the while I'm on the brink of sobbing with gratitude. The tangle of anxiety in my throat has broken apart, the dried crust on my tongue has melted. My daughter is safe, she's back, she's here.

Amelia's survival was entirely down to Beth – and Amelia knew it. When we found them, Beth thought she'd let go of Amelia; feared she'd drowned, but we'd already dragged her unconscious body onto the boat. The press, too, were keen to make it clear she wouldn't be here if my daughter hadn't held her head out of the water with such diligence.

Nancy was arrested for abducting Beth and for the attempted murder of Beth and Amelia. Amelia's been charged with aiding and abetting the abduction, but was allowed to make a phone call to Peter. She told him how Nancy broke down in police custody and admitted that consumed by jealousy and grief, she'd dreamt up the scheme to kill both of them.

To distract herself from her secret heartache over Carl, Nancy had launched into a campaign to 'find the truth to help Amelia', when actually it was only for her own benefit. When she found out Beth had phoned Carl, she made it her mission to discover if they'd been seeing each other. Was it a one-night stand? Was it more serious? Were promises made? Nancy was frantic. She had to get the truth out of Beth. She'd loved Carl – she needed to know.

According to Amelia, the police were still in the dark about Carl's death. Nancy could give them no concrete evidence that Amelia was the guilty party and her own alibis meant that Nancy, too, was in the clear. Peter told us all this over coffee at the station the day he went back to London. He'd stayed around a few days to make sure Beth was recovering fully.

After we'd pulled Beth and Amelia out of the water they were taken to be checked out at A&E, but neither of them had any medical issues that a few hot-water bottles and days of rest at home wouldn't fix.

Throughout her ordeal, one thing became resoundingly clear: Beth hadn't given me away. She'd protected me, just like I thought I was protecting her. The doctor recommended an increase in Beth's asthma treatment for a while, but although her lungs were bruised, he assured us she'd bounce back. Psychologically, however, the lasting effects remain to be seen, but Beth is coping well. She's eating, has welcomed visitors and spent time sitting with me on the sofa watching television, instead of hiding away in her room.

Beth and I were on tenterhooks when Peter rang to suggest we meet before he caught his train. He'd dropped in to see her a few times, but they hadn't had a 'proper chat', as he put it. She was understandably nervous at the prospect.

He was grim-faced when he greeted us. We pulled up the noisy aluminium chairs and sat down with our paper cups. The café is alongside the ticket barriers, open and public, it was hardly the right place for a showdown. All the same, he didn't seem angry with Beth. I couldn't understand it. Surely, he must know by now that Beth confessed to having an affair with Carl.

I glance at the departures board. We still have twenty minutes to go.

'Nancy had been ready to pack her bags, poised to saunter off into the sunset with Carl a few months ago,' he says, continuing his revelation, 'but nothing happened. She thought it was because Amelia had found out about them. She thought Amelia had pressured him somehow or blackmailed him with the children, but then Nancy started to wonder if he might have been side-tracked by another fling.'

I glance at Beth, who's showing exactly the same expression of unease that I'm feeling.

'Amelia was adamant, though, that Beth was entirely innocent in this entire debacle,' he says. He turns to Beth, taking hold of her hand. 'Nancy claimed Beth signed some kind of confession, but Amelia said it was total rubbish. Nancy wasn't able to produce it.'

I feel the slightest nudge of Beth's foot against mine under the table. I don't look up, but I understand her signal. Amelia lied. Not only that, she must have ordered someone to get hold of Nancy's phone and delete the photo of Beth's confession that she'd emailed to Amelia. She must have been so grateful for the way Beth stepped in to save her life that she protected her, knowing by that stage that the real enemy was Nancy.

Peter carries on, patting Beth's hand in a fatherly way. 'She said it was all in Nancy's twisted little mind.'

It was a generous choice for Amelia to make.

Beth is off the hook. We are both safe.

Peter lets Beth's hand go and she slides it under the table and takes hold of mine.

According to Peter, Nancy thought Amelia had more of a motive for killing Carl than anyone. When Amelia became fixated on Beth as the 'other woman', Nancy decided to make the most of it. All she needed to do was get the two of them in a punctured dinghy in the middle of nowhere and wait for it to sink. Amelia agreed to it, because she thought the dinghy was tied to Spellbound, she thought Nancy was giving her the opportunity to send Beth to her death, if she didn't like what she had to say for herself.

Peter tells us this with a wry smile on his face. This is why he wanted us to meet. To give us both the facts. There's no awkward face-off about her affair – he's completely dismissed it.

With the wedding meant to be today, it still leaves Beth and Peter's position up in the air. He was understanding when she'd said she was too traumatised after the abduction to possibly think of getting married straight away, but it still leaves everything unresolved between them.

But I know what she's decided. She told me last night.

Chapter 57

Rachel

Peter checks his watch. His train is due any minute.

Now isn't the time to enlighten him, but last night Beth and I had a heart-to-heart. She'd spent a long time locked away on her own to reflect on what she truly wanted.

'It was weird being trapped in the dark like that for so long,' she told me. 'Part of me was terrified about what was going to happen to me, but having all that time to think...ironically, it kind of helped make up my mind.'

We'd been watching a programme about foxes and she'd finished off the crisps.

'You've made a decision about Peter?'

'Peter wants to give me a new life,' she'd said. 'He makes me feel safe, but he doesn't make me feel...alive. I want to be successful in my way, on my terms, not have someone else lay everything down for me like I'm a child. Peter doesn't really discuss things with me, he doesn't involve me, he decides things for me. If I marry him, I'll literally be "giving myself away".'

'Are you sure?'

All this time I'd never revealed the way I'd kept the relationship going with fake texts and calls. I thought I was helping.

'Peter is totally into me, I know that – but, I feel like he sees me as his "project" and not as his "partner". I don't want to be a product of his endeavours. I want to make my own path alongside someone, to be my own person. I want to have edges around me. To have someone else end and a space before I begin, next to them. Does that make sense?'

'Yes. Absolutely.'

'You don't seem that shocked,' she said, looking at me dubiously.

'I worked it out when you went missing. After everything I've said about how wonderful he is, I got it wrong. He isn't right for you, is he?'

Suddenly, I knew why it would never work. In Beth, Peter saw a glimpse of youth that would rub off on him, the promise of eternal gratitude, and a trophy wife, eye-candy who would turn heads and bestow a pride he couldn't achieve in any other way.

And in Peter, Beth saw her passport, a step closer to the fringes of that red carpet, perhaps even the father-figure she never had.

In that moment, I knew that for both of them it wasn't love and probably never had been.

'I've handled this entire episode very badly,' I told her.

She grabbed my wrist. 'No, it's my fault. I didn't want to let you down. I knew how much the wedding meant to you and I couldn't allow myself to have any doubts about him, at first. I thought it would destroy you if I changed my mind.'

I folded my hand over hers. 'I didn't see the signs. I assumed all your misgivings were about remorse, I hadn't thought to look deeper. Or look before that night in the cellar. I thought you were in shock and I ploughed on in denial, just wanting to get the two of you married. I thought it was just guilt. I didn't stop to think. I was too busy trying to get you over to the "other side", to money, success, security. I pushed. I didn't listen. I'm so sorry.'

She brought her feet onto the cushion and curled up against me. 'It's okay, Mum. It wasn't just you. I'm equally to blame. I've been swept along by how keen Peter is on me. I think that's the part I loved most. Feeling special, adored, his princess – I loved the feeling he gave me about myself, but I don't actually love *him*. The person he is. I don't really know him.'

She linked her arm through mine.

'To be honest, the sex wasn't great,' she added, with a giggle.

It was the first time I'd seen her smile for what felt like a lifetime.

'There's something missing for me. I think I fancied him, but it didn't go any deeper.'

Last night, everything seemed clear and at last we are both in agreement. The wedding is off for good. But as Peter gets up to board his train, he doesn't know any of this. Beth is going to have to be brave one more time and find a way to tell him.

Chapter 58

Beth

Mum's been to St Andrew's this morning to see Russell. I can tell, because she's got that sad-yet-serene look on her face. Summer is in the air, so I set out the deckchairs on the patio to catch the precious morning rays. I order Mum to sit and bring out a tray with coffee, toast and her favourite, scrambled eggs.

'What have I done to deserve this?' Mum asks.

'Just glad to be here,' I say.

My phone buzzes as I set down the breakfast spread.

'It's Peter,' I tell her with a grimace, answering the call. I point to the back door and disappear inside.

'We're meeting up,' I tell her once the call has ended. I slide into the deckchair beside her. 'For a chat about everything. In two weeks' time.'

'Can you wait until then?'

'He's busy with meetings, apparently. It's fine by me.'

I don't mention that I've been preoccupied with something else, now that it appears Mum and I are in the clear. For days, locked away on the boat, a jumble of unresolved questions about Southampton swirled around in my head. I need to know. I've waited long enough.

I dive straight in. 'I found a newspaper cutting at Grandad's… in the loft with old photographs.'

'Yes…I saw it by your bed at Adrian's,' she says, without batting an eyelid.

'About the girl who was killed…'

'Tracy Limehouse. She was a friend of mine. A good friend.'

'Really?'

I try to imagine the scene. That terrible moment when Mum realised that her dear friend had been run over by Grandad, her own father.

'He was the driver, wasn't he? Grandad was the one who hit Tracy, by accident, outside the pub in Southampton…'

Mum's face creases with confusion.

'No. That's not what happened.'

'That wasn't it? I don't understand.'

'It wasn't Adrian.'

We're interrupted by the phone – Kate calling for Mum – so the matter is left up in the air. After that, Mum has to rush off for her early shift at the pub.

Later, after she's taken a bath and is settled on the sofa with the newspaper, I ask a different question.

'There's one thing that has bugged me all along,' I say. 'I know you didn't mean to kill Carl. You didn't know all the facts, you didn't know I was in the cellar out of choice. But covering up the crime…it still seems so extreme. How come you were so fast to hide what we'd done?'

She leans back, her face set in an expression of resignation, but she doesn't say a word.

'You were so quick to plan everything. So quick to suggest we hide Carl's body and get rid of all the evidence. I can't believe it was just fear about Peter finding out about the affair… or about my reputation.' I slide towards her, force her to look at me. 'What was it really about?'

Mum folds the paper and sets it down on the arm.

I carry on. 'Amelia will have questions for the rest of her life about why and how. So will her boys. They'll never see anyone brought to justice. Why was it so imperative that we hid Carl's death?'

'Okay, listen.' She wraps my hand in hers, something she's done every day since the rescue. 'But, you might not like what you have to hear.'

'I'm ready,' I insist. 'I need to know.'

'When I was fifteen, I went to a party. Vera and Adrian knew there'd be alcohol and said I was too young to be there, but a friend of mine was going and she was eighteen. She said she'd look out for me, but she turned up late. Tracy Limehouse.'

I stay perfectly still.

'The party was held near The Hope and Anchor. We lived in Southampton then. The place was jam-packed with people – a boy called Ben Kirby—'

'Yeah, I know. It was his eighteenth,' I cut across her.

She sighs. 'He wasn't a nice boy. I didn't know it was his party and wouldn't have gone if I had. He was a horrible ring-leader with a gang who used to beat up kids at our school. He used to sell drugs and the rumour was he always carried a knife tucked inside his sock.'

She lowers a clenched hand.

'Well…I was on my own, feeling lost, waiting for Tracy and everyone was loud and drunk, passing out on the stairs. Ben was hyped up and strutting about the place. He started chatting me up. I walked away. He came after me, trying to touch me, being vulgar and sleazy, so I stormed out the front door. Groups were out on the streets by then, hanging around the pub car-park.

'Ben wouldn't leave me alone. A few of his friends were egging him on and three of them grabbed me and bundled me into a ramshackle outhouse in the corner of the car-park. They shut me in there with him. I screamed and tried to get out, but there was so much racket going on and so many people having a good time that no one came to….'

Her voice trails off. She closes her eyes. When she opens them, she can't bring herself to look at me.

'What happened? Can you tell me?' I ask.

She lifts my hand and rests it against her cheek. 'It will change everything, Beth – are you sure you want to know?'

'Yes. You've got to tell me…'

'He pushed me over an old barrel of beer and raped me.'

The words pierce my heart like pointed arrows. 'No…Mum…'

'When he'd finished, he turned to leave and I grabbed a chunk of brick from a pile by my feet. I was so angry and distraught that I hadn't been able to stop him. I swung it at his head, but he ducked away and ran outside. I dashed after him, still holding the lump of brick and I flung it with all my might at the back of his head. But he darted out of the way, near the edge of the pavement. And suddenly…there was Tracy…a big smile on her face, because she'd found me.'

Her chin quivers, her voice trembling.

'The brick hit the side of her head and she staggered backwards. It happened so fast. One minute she was smiling… the next there was a terrible thud. She was lifted up, her body tossed against the windscreen, then she slipped off and the car went straight over her.' Her face crumples and I pull her close, rock her gently. 'When I got to her she was lying all twisted in the road.'

'That's terrible…you must…' I can't find the words.

'I was raped. And my friend died, because of how I reacted… all in the space of ten minutes…it was just…'

'It wasn't your fault.'

'You thought your father was a cute boyfriend…well, it's not how things were at all. He was a rapist, a thug, a brute.' She spits the words out.

The truth is slowly dripping into my brain. My father. The sweet boy she knew at school. It was all a lie. I wasn't born of innocent young love, I was the result of a savage attack.

Tears flood into my eyes and career down my cheek.

My beginnings in this world were formed during a brutal assault.

She lets go of my hand and cups my face in hers. Resting her thumbs gently under my eyes, she smooths away my tears, but new ones take their place.

'What happened?' I mutter, snivelling.

'I've never seen a group of people disappear so fast,' she says. 'The ambulance came, and the police, but no one wanted to get involved. Lots of the boys had been in trouble with the law and didn't want to come forward with information. No one mentioned me. Ben ran with the rest.'

'And you? Did you go to her? Did you tell the police what happened?'

'No…' Shame crushes her features. 'I ran, just like the others.' She swallows and stares at her knees.

'I'd cut my hand on the edge of the brick. When I looked down after I'd thrown it, there was blood on my fingers. I knew enough about evidence to know my DNA would be all over it. If I'd gone to the police station, they'd have linked the brick to me and I would have had to tell them the rest. I just couldn't bear it. So I bolted.'

I stay quiet, trying to figure out whether I would have done things differently at such a young age.

'To be the one who caused the accident,' she continues. 'Can you imagine? I was totally traumatised. I didn't want anyone to know what he'd done to me, either. I was so ashamed and scared. The last thing I wanted was to sit down with the police and have to explain myself. I didn't want anyone to touch me, no examinations. I'd been interfered with enough. Can you understand? I was only fifteen.'

'Yes. Yes, of course, I understand.' I reach over and squeeze her knee. 'It must have been horrendous.'

'All that pain I caused Tracy's family.'

'You've carried that with you all these years,' I whisper.

'You were the only good thing to come out of it. Nine months later…'

'Did you tell Vera?'

'She was the only one who knew the truth. About Tracy and the rape. She kept my secrets. But, when I found out I was pregnant and insisted on an abortion, Vera wouldn't hear of it. Like I told you, she'd lost too many children herself to see another one die, even though the circumstances had been so repulsive. Thank God I didn't go against her.' She looks into my face with the glimmer of a smile. 'I was so blessed. You turned out to be an unexpected gift after so much hurt.'

I get to my feet, needing to move, to stretch my legs, to take a few moments to let this new configuration of my past sink in.

'And that leads us to you and Carl,' she says, vehemence in her voice. 'When I went down to the cellar that night, it was like a terrifying flashback, like I was reliving the nightmare. A stranger holding you down, the naked flesh, you crying out…it all came back and I didn't hesitate. I had to stop it.'

I snatch a breath. 'Of course…'

'That's not all. I knew as soon as Carl was dead that we couldn't report it. My DNA from the brick in 1992 would have been recorded as part of that crime scene, back then. The police didn't have a match at the time, but it would still be on the database. If we'd explained to the police what happened in the cellar and they took all the necessary swabs from us, there would be a match for me. One accidental death is unfortunate. Two starts to look very suspicious, especially when I hadn't come forward the first time. I was certain I'd go to prison. I couldn't take the risk. And it would have ruined everything for you.'

At last, it all makes sense.

She glances down. 'I didn't know Vera had kept the clippings.'

'Did Grandad know?'

'No. Adrian knew there was something about that night that had upset me and then you came along nine months later, so I'm sure he had his suspicions, but Vera never told him. No one else knew.'

'The secret she took to her grave,' I whisper. 'Grandad said just that.'

She nods with a sad smile.

'It would have destroyed him and he might even have killed Ben Kirby with his own hands, if he'd found out. We all wanted you to think your father was a lovely boy I'd fallen in love with at school. I never wanted you to know any of this.'

I feel like I've been inside a washing machine – been spun around, agitated and pummelled, then flung back out into the outside world again.

'Wow…it's a lot to take in…'

'That's an understatement. Are you okay? After everything…'

I stop her. 'Yes…I'll be fine.' I'm sure I will be, given a little time. 'Everything slots into place now.'

'No more secrets?' she says.

'No, thank you!' I say with a smile.

I've grown up fast in the past few weeks. It's going to take some adjusting to, but coping with this is the least of my worries. Now I can finally move on to the next stage of my life. It's not going to be easy, but perhaps now's the time to break it to her.

'I wanted to tell you something important, too,' I say.

She senses the gravity in my voice and jerks round to face me.

'I've been looking into the idea of going to a refugee camp. To help out. A few months, maybe, in Northern Greece. Somewhere I can make a difference.'

Her jaw drops and she doesn't speak for ages.

'That's very noble,' she finally manages, her voice trembling.

'Being stranded in the sea like that. It made me think. All those refugees who're desperate to escape. They start out in boats that are either too full or not seaworthy and end up in the ocean, fighting for their lives. It's just not right.'

She nods. 'I know.'

'If we're not going to turn ourselves in for what we did to Carl, then it only seems fair to do something…you know…good, in return.'

'That's my Beth,' she says, 'you're back all right!' She reaches over and clutches me to her chest.

'I'll put together my application,' I say, 'but I'll tell them it won't be for a few months.'

She nods, looking relieved. 'Good. Thank you. I don't think I could let you go anywhere, just yet. In a few months, I might have got used to the idea.'

Chapter 59

Beth

Two weeks later

We meet at Holland Park in Kensington, inside the walled garden. Wisteria tumbles over the brickwork and peacocks strut around nonchalantly. It's as though we've been lifted out of the metropolis and transported to the country. There are pockets all over London like this – little havens of tranquility, tucked away. It's one of the things I love about this great city.

I find him sitting on a bench scrutinising something ahead of him.

'That's Milos of Croton,' he says, as I sit down next to him. He's pointing to the Classical bronze statue in the centre. 'He split a tree with his bare hands to demonstrate his strength and it snapped shut, trapping him inside.'

'Let that be a lesson to us all,' I say, not fully understanding exactly what the lesson is, but simply relieved we're able to start on a light note.

He laughs and gives me a strained smile. 'How are you?'

'Oh. Getting there. Mum has been brilliant. Protective when I need it and backing off, when I don't. I'm going to have counselling... well, drama therapy, actually. One of my friends said it might help.'

'And the callback? Did you get the part?'

I smile. 'No. They said they wanted someone who was more consistent.'

He nods.

Even out here in the open, I pick up the resinous smell of his expensive shoe polish. He nods and stares out towards the intricate patchwork of pink, purple and orange tulips. He seems distracted.

'Let me take you to the Japanese Garden,' he says, getting up. 'It's serene and beautiful…there's a waterfall…'

I shake my head, vigorously. 'Sorry…I can't be near water… not just yet.'

'Oh…of course…bad idea…' He sits back down again.

He points out a peacock promenading along the far side, carrying its train of glistening feathers, jutting its head back and forth. I want to say something funny to break the brittle awkwardness that's now filling the air between us, but I can't think of anything.

I take his hand and place it, inside mine, on my lap. I can't bear to prolong this.

'I need to tell you—'

'I'm leaving London,' he says abruptly, slicing into my sentence.

'Oh…for how long?'

'I'm relocating to New York.'

I feel my chin snap inwards. 'Relocating? When?'

He withdraws his hand and taps my knee, stiffly. 'Next week.'

'What? You can't be serious.'

I wait for him to tell me I haven't understood correctly.

'A position has come up at the Broadway Dance Centre and I've accepted. That's what a lot of my recent trips have been about.'

I'm stunned. 'When? When did you accept?'

'Two weeks ago.'

I pull back so I can see his entire face. 'But…we were supposed to be getting married two weeks ago. You never said a word about it.'

'I did mention living in the US.' His voice is matter-of-fact.

'Only in passing. Only vaguely, once or twice.'

'Sometimes you have to act on opportunities when they come up. You'll need to learn that if you're going to get anywhere in show business.'

I'm taken aback. I get to my feet. 'Well…that kind of decides everything.'

'You're not coming?'

'You didn't ask me. You just decided without me.'

He gets up to walk alongside me. 'I thought you'd love it, once you got used to the idea. It's all happening too fast, I admit that. I'm sorry I didn't say anything more concrete, but you have been pretty difficult to pin down recently, you know?'

I ignore his chuckle. I refuse to accept this omission as my fault.

'What about Mum? I can't just take off again, so soon after what happened.'

'I see that. The timing isn't great. Perhaps you could join me later.'

I stop and face him. I need to deliver the final blow, so he knows there's no point in discussing our future any further, but my throat feels like it's clamped inside a giant nut-cracker.

'I don't think so.' The words come out more firmly than I was expecting.

'I see.'

He turns and walks on.

'You've had your big career and done it all,' I tell him, catching up with him.

'I've still got ambitions, still got plans,' he says in return.

'But they're not the same as mine. You're so far ahead of me.' My teeth are chattering, even though it's a mild spring day. 'I think I need to be with someone at the beginning of their career, like me, so we can share the same journey. Share the adventure and discoveries together.' I grit my teeth. 'The bottom line is, I feel like I'm your student, your protégé, not your equal.'

'I'm sorry I've made you feel like that. I hoped my experience would help you.'

'It would, I'm sure. But to be getting married? We decided too soon, don't you think? We don't know each other, not properly. We've never spent enough consecutive days together, to see how we are with each other. You're always leaving for your next business trip.'

He stops. 'That's my life. I'm busy. Successful. You knew that when I first met you.'

He has an annoying way of rolling forward onto the balls of his feet when he speaks to me – like he's a professor, giving me a lecture.

I carry on walking to stop him doing it. 'But I don't know who you are when you're doing simple mundane things…like going to the supermarket or getting stuck in traffic. I don't know who you are when you're grumpy, angry or tired. There is so much that is untested between us. We're like islands on an unchartered map. How will we be when we argue? How will you be when I'm upset? What will be the cruellest jibe you could throw at me? I don't know how we fit together.'

I can hear his breath coming and going loudly beside my ear and it's starting to annoy me.

'I'm not going to argue with you. We don't know each other that well, that's true. But I feel enough connection with you to trust we'll discover all those aspects of each other as we go along. It seems you're not interested in that, anymore. Instead, you want some kind of guarantee in advance that life is going to be utopian. A little naïve, don't you think?'

'It's not like that. I know even the best marriage isn't perfect. But, I've thought about our situation a lot. I think it's all been too much of a rush.'

'A rush or a risk?'

'Both, I suppose.'

'I thought you liked taking risks…'

Inwardly I'm bubbling with frustration. He's trying to trip me up.

'I've wanted to slow things down for some time,' I say, trying to get to the point, 'but Mum went charging ahead with arranging the wedding and it had a life of its own. I think part of me was doing it for her.'

I close my eyes for a split second. I know this is going to hurt him. 'Sometimes, I think you're really Mum's choice, not mine.'

'I see.' He sounds grim. 'You don't pull your punches, do you?'

In the sunlight, the blue in his eyes is pale, bleached out, with barely any colour at all – it makes him look like he's empty.

His phone buzzes and he reaches into his pocket. 'I need to get back. I'm renting out my apartment. I've got someone coming to view it.'

'Right.'

'But,' he says, 'I need to remind you I'm not a man who gives up easily. I hope at least you know that much about me.'

He laughs and I join in with nervous relief that this is nearly over. 'Once I'm settled, I might write to you,' he adds, his tone softer, lighter, 'if that's okay?'

'Yes. Of course. Tell me how you're doing, I'd like that.'

I'd prefer everything to end here, but it seems churlish not to agree. It's only a letter.

He takes my hand and kisses it.

'Goodbye, Beth. Take very good care of yourself, won't you?'

He's already pulling away.

I give him my best smile. 'I'll try.'

Chapter 60

Rachel

Two months later

I wake early and hear the letter box clatter as I come down the stairs. Waiting on the front doormat are the usual bills. Tucked underneath, there's a prepaid airmail envelope from the US. Beth told me Peter might write.

Beth has been up for at least a couple of hours. She's already been for a swim, bubbling over with energy with every day that passes. She looks amazing, ready for her audition later today. She's been asked to wear 'casual' to play the part of a homeless waif, and the ripped black jeans, green tie-dye T-shirt and denim jacket look perfect.

'Any post for me?' she says brightly, as she tips out a small portion of bran flakes into a bowl.

I wave the flimsy envelope in the air. 'Looks like there's something from Peter.'

Her mouth twists into a grimace. 'Ew…I don't want to read that now. I don't want anything to knock me off my stride before the audition. Can you open it when I've gone? You can tell me later if there's anything I need to know. Is that okay?'

'No worries,' I tell her.

I'm more than happy to read it for her. I want to be involved in her life in any way I can, although we've both agreed a new golden rule: no interfering from me – and honesty across the board. Since I got her back, it's almost been the way things used to be between us. Like sisters or best friends, being open with each other, speaking our minds, spending time together, sharing everything. I know it won't last, because it's my job to help her to fly the nest, but I want to hold on to it for as long as I can.

I get a text from Beth once she's on the train to London and it reminds me to read the letter from Peter. I take it to the sofa with a cup of coffee and break open the gummed edge. There are no return details on the back. Maybe he doesn't want a reply. The contents are typed, this time, not handwritten.

Dear Beth

I hope you're sitting comfortably. I wanted to fill you in on a few of my thoughts, as I've been looking back over our time together.

It started out well enough; you were beautiful, young, full of sparkle and star quality. I had big plans for you. In my hands, I thought you'd go far.

Then, just before Christmas, my world fell apart. It was after you came to London to audition for the Brian Lourdes' film and we spent the afternoon admiring the Pre-Raphaelites in the National Gallery. When we left, you said you needed to be on your own to go through your lines, but you're not a great liar, just like you'll never be a great actress.

I followed you after we left the gallery and saw the two of you together, walking up the steps to a hotel. Learning your lines – is that what they call it, these days?

I flop back on the sofa. He *knew*…Peter knew about Beth and Carl, all along. Yet he didn't say a thing, he didn't confront her… he carried on for four months as if nothing had happened. I don't understand.

Do you know how hard that hit me? After everything I promised you?! Let me explain something. The world of dance is vicious and I was treated badly. Roles were promised to me, only to be taken away at the last minute. My career never hit the heights it should have done, thanks to acts of treachery from those around me. Betrayal has always been my Achilles heel and when I knew you'd cheated on me behind my back, I was gutted.

So, why didn't I drop you like a hot brick? Why did I spend thousands of pounds on a beautiful wedding? More of that later.

My mouth falls open in utter dismay. Why would he go ahead with the wedding when he knew the truth? I feel a shivery sweat break out on my forehead, but my eyes dart back to the next paragraph:

You must have felt some semblance of guilt, eventually, because the time came when you couldn't bring yourself to speak to me. You were too ashamed to face me. A conscience, after all.

Your mother tried her utmost to smooth things over, but I saw through it straight away when she tried to impersonate you. Her phony reply to my letter to start with, then all the rest was totally off kilter: the emails, instant messages, the video call. I've got to hand it to her, she made a very good stab at it (she's a better actress than you'll ever be, by the way), but the tone, the language, the expressions just weren't you. When you understand body language like I do, you can tell. It was quite funny, really. I wanted to see how far your mother would go.

You should know, too, that from the moment you betrayed me, I never intended to show up for the wedding.

My cheeks burn with a mixture of humiliation and rage. He let me carry on pretending to be Beth, when he knew it was me all along. He was laughing at me. Everything was a lie. His charm, his good nature, it was all fake… Why? Why did he keep up the pretence?

We all know, including the police, that Nancy was the one taking the lead in the plot that nearly killed you, and Amelia wasn't far behind her. Nancy thought you'd stolen her lover and she'd goaded Amelia into almost doing the dirty work for her.

But, let me side-track a little. You remember the Rite of Spring? That performance you and your mother came to see? I helped to choreograph that production. I observed every step from the wings as the savage dancers built themselves up into a frenzy. I waited as they closed in on the pretty young girl, their sacrificial victim.

Their sacrificial victim? What's he talking about? Does he mean Beth? Did he *know* she was in danger?

I'd trained them so carefully, even though not once was I on stage myself, showing the world what I could do. The original concept belonged to someone else, but I gave precise instruction on the shaping, the speed, the timing – each beat of every bar was meticulously planned in advance. It was a pleasure to stand back and watch. All the dancers knew what to do, how to enact their precise part as the skittish young thing danced herself to death.

All the dancers…wait, does he mean Nancy and Amelia? The abduction. The confrontation on the dinghy. Was that all orchestrated by Peter? The perfect way to get rid of Beth for betraying him?

It took me ages to flag down a taxi the day you woke up in the middle of the English Channel; it caused a considerable delay to my arrival at the marina. And Amelia should never have set out in that old dinghy; a tiny hole had been slashed in the side and a faulty valve fitted, I understand.

Your mother and I would have reached you in our speedboat sooner, if there hadn't been problems with the propeller. She probably told you that a plastic bag was caught around it, even though I'd taken a good look at it before we left the marina. People will chuck their rubbish anywhere, won't they? It meant you had even longer to endure in the water with Amelia. It was sheer luck you didn't both drown.

Oh, my God. He didn't just know…he was *helping* them. Peter wanted Beth dead! From behind the scenes, he was guiding the whole thing, covering his tracks at every step so no one would suspect his involvement.

Did Amelia kill Carl in a fit of jealousy? If she did, she almost paid the price for it. To be honest, I've never been particularly fond of either Nancy or Amelia. Nancy tried to implicate me after she was arrested, but of course, you need proof to make accusations like that and she had nothing to back up her outlandish claims.

He doesn't know who killed Carl. He doesn't know it was me. This *isn't* a blackmail letter. Nor is it a confession. He's so cunningly put it together that he makes cryptic references, but doesn't actually incriminate himself. Clever.

So, has he written purely to gloat, or what?

In the end, my darling, you escaped remarkably lightly. You betrayed me and you hurt others, yet you're preparing to walk off into the sunset, no doubt, to live your perfect life by now. Your happy ending, just like in the movies.

My stomach clenches at his tone. I check the postmark of the letter. Definitely US. He's a million miles away. Isn't he?

Well, I'm pleased to say there's been a change of plan and I'll be returning from America. I shan't say when, exactly, because that would spoil the surprise. This month, next month – tomorrow? Who knows?

Be in no doubt, however, that I will watch and I will wait and one day, when I see fit, you'll open your eyes and there I'll be.

So, you see, for me it's by no means over.

Until then, my dear, take very good care of yourself.

I fling the letter to the floor and make a dash for the sink in the kitchen. I retch and retch, bringing up every last chunk of the scrambled egg I had for breakfast.

After my afternoon shift, Beth joins me in the kitchen with freshly showered hair. Her audition was, in her own words, 'tortuous'.

'Normally, it's just me, a camera and the casting director or whatever,' she says, 'but this time there was a guy with a handheld camera, another taking still photos and these other people, just kind of milling about.'

She lets out a burst of giggles.

'They kept asking me to sit on a chair and get up again, over and over, it was ridiculous…then they asked if I could ride a camel…'

She bends over double, unable to contain herself. 'I mean…
honestly, that wasn't mentioned anywhere in the prep notes!'

I laugh along with her, secure in the knowledge that her former
resilience is back, but my mood is far from cheery. Before she sits
down, she slides magazines, junk mail and old envelopes aside on
the worktop, searching for something.

'Perhaps I should read that letter from Peter, after all. Have
you got it?' she asks. 'I said he could write to me…to tell me how
things were going.'

I make a show of flicking through a pile of newspapers beside
the toaster. 'Mmm. I'm not sure where I put it, love,' I say, vaguely.
'It's around here somewhere, but honestly, Beth, there was nothing
to it. Just bits and pieces about his business affairs. All very boring
and nothing personal.'

'Really? Oh, well,' she tuts. 'Doesn't really matter.' She picks
up an apple from the bowl on the window ledge and takes a hearty
bite. 'Let me know if you come across it.'

'Of course.'

The truth is…I've burnt it.

Beth stares at the pepper pot in the centre of the table, her
mind still for a rare moment.

'You really liked him, didn't you?' she says.

I hesitate. 'Sort of.'

I get up and busy myself emptying the washing machine. I turn
and find her standing right behind me. I quickly change the subject.

'I've been thinking,' I say. 'Have you registered for the refugee
camp, yet?'

'Not yet. I wasn't sure…you know, about the timing.'

'Are you still keen to go?'

I need her safe. Away from here. As soon as possible.

'Oh, absolutely. I keep thinking about it.' She stalls. 'It's
just…I didn't want to go too soon…you know, leaving you after
what happened.'

'Listen!' I grab her firmly by the shoulders. 'You mustn't let me
hold you back.' Her eyes widen at the fierceness of my reaction. I

loosen my grip. 'You must never let me get in the way of the life you want to live, ever again, you hear me?'

She gives me a jaunty smile. 'Our new golden rule, right?'

'Exactly.' I think about the letter. I wonder how many days ago it was posted. 'I've been thinking. Why wait? It's such an important thing to do.'

I need to get her out of the country. To a place where he can't find her.

She nods. 'I've already had tons of pledges of support for the crowdfunding, so...'

'There you go. There's no reason to hold back any longer, is there?'

'You sure?'

'Yes. I am.'

More than you'll ever know.

'I'll get on with it, now, then.' She claps her hands together, gleefully. 'I'll fill in the profile and make sure I'm registered by the end of today.'

'Good. Just one thing.' I scrutinise her face, alert to the slightest shift in her expression. What I'm about to suggest is a huge step and a big risk – especially after our recent promises to each other. 'If I ask you something, will you answer honestly?'

Her eyes narrow, suddenly guarded. 'O-kaaay…'

'How would you feel…if…if you didn't go on your own… if I came to the camp with you?'

'Mum, that would be totally awesome!'

'You can think about it first, if you—?'

'No way. It's a fabulous idea. It would be incredible to do it together.'

'It would be a kind of new start,' I tell her, 'a new beginning. Who knows where it might lead us?'

She squeezes my finger. Once …twice … Our special signal.

Then flings her arms around me.

THE END

About the Author

A.J. Waines is a number one bestselling author, topping the UK and Australian Amazon Charts in two consecutive years, with *Girl on a Train*. The author was a psychotherapist for fifteen years, during which time she worked with ex-offenders from high-security institutions, gaining a rare insight into abnormal psychology. She is now a full-time novelist with publishing deals in UK, France, Germany, Norway, Hungary and USA (audiobooks).

Her fourth novel, ***No Longer Safe*** sold over 30,000 copies in the first month, in twelve countries worldwide. In 2016 and 2017, the author was ranked in the Top 10 UK Authors on Amazon KDP (Kindle Direct Publishing).

A.J. Waines lives in Hampshire, UK, with her husband.

Find out more at **www.ajwaines.co.uk** or follow her **Blog**. She's also on **Twitter** (@AJWaines), **Facebook** and you can sign up for her **Newsletter**.

Lightning Source UK Ltd.
Milton Keynes UK
UKHW011946301018
331482UK00001B/165/P

9 781912 604227